I Knew Him

I Knew Him

Erastes

Lethe Press • Maple Shade, New Jersey

Published August 2014 by Lethe Press, Inc.
118 Heritage Avenue • Maple Shade, NJ 08052-3018 USA
www.lethepressbooks.com • lethepress@aol.com

Print ISBN-13: 978-1-59021-275-2
ISBN-10: 1-59021-275-4
E-book ISBN: 978-1-59021-099-4

This novel is a work of fiction. Names, characters, places, and incidents are products of the author's imagination or are used fictitiously.

Edited by Chaz Brenchley

Set in Adobe Garamond and GatsbyFLF
Interior design: Alex Jeffers, Toby Johnson
Cover design: Ben Baldwin

Library of Congress Cataloging-in-Publication Data

Erastes.
  I knew him / Erastes.
    pages cm
  ISBN 978-1-59021-275-2 (pbk. : alk. paper)
  1. Gay men--England--Fiction. I. Title.
  PR6105.R37I33 2014
  823'.92--dc23
                                        2014016942

I Knew Him

Chapter One

He walked into my study-room, and threw himself on the bed as if he owned it. It was hard not to stare at him, so I didn't even try not to. His shirt had pulled itself loose from his flannels, displaying a delicious portion of his midriff, and the first few dark blond hairs which led downwards to some of his nicer points.

"It's a frightful bore," he said. "But I suppose there's no way around it. You'll come, though?

He had this habit, endearing and irritating by turns, of talking to me as if we'd been having a conversation, and I'd simply not been listening for half of it. How dare I be in a different room while he was having his portion of the discussion?

I put my pen down with deliberate effect as if to emphasise that I had actually been working, rare as that was. "If I had any idea of what you were talking about, I could say one way or the other."

"The summer vac, of course. I've been summoned home. It's loathsome. Mother knows all too well that I wanted to take you to Paris. What does Somerset have to interest us, when there are the hidden decadencies of Paris?" He stretched out like a cat, his arms well over his head, and more of his torso came into view. It was too much for one with as little willpower as I possess. I threw my pen down on the table and joined him, kneeling by the side of the bed and latching my mouth onto his skin.

"Mmmmm," he said. "That door's not locked, you know."

My tongue took a break from etching circles on his stomach. "The only chaps likely to barge in without knocking are Richardson and Gilbert. I can't see either of those two dropping dead from shock discovering a couple of queers in my study." I chuckled at my own puerile wit, my mouth reverberating on his skin, making him laugh too. It was good to hear him laugh, it was a rare enough sound and one I never tired of hearing. "And I'm not entirely sure that decadencies is even a word."

"Of course it is. It must be. Look it up."

"I'm busy. You look it up."

He leaned over and pulled my dictionary from the windowsill. There was silence for a minute or two, while pages rustled and I took outrageous—but not entirely indecent—advantage of his inattention. If I were a man more given to introspection, I might complain that he found it so easy to thumb through my copy of *The Concise Oxford* while I was taking such liberties with his person. But then, I was doing it mostly for my own gratification.

"If you do much more of that," he said, his voice dusky with want, proving me wrong as usual, "then I'm neither going to notice if the door does open, nor am I likely to care." He pushed himself up along the bed and propped himself up against the bedstead, removing the temptation of his skin, to my very great annoyance.

I reapplied my arse to my study chair, and turned to look at him. "Why does your mother want you at home? I thought she couldn't be happier when you wrote and told her you were buggering off—literally—until the autumn."

He frowned, delicate lines forming between his dark, straight brows, and he swung his legs back over the edge of the bed. His flannels were delightfully creased, and it couldn't have been just from our brief tumble.

Somehow he never managed to stay crisp for more than a few minutes, and had been the despair of our Head of House from his first day at our secondary school. "She doesn't say. Just how 'jolly' it would be if we all spent part of the holidays together. Her letter made me sound as if I were five. Really." He came and knelt by my chair and tangled his fingers in mine. "You'll come, though? I promise it won't be for the whole vac. I'll make sure we get time off for good behaviour."

I snorted. "Good behaviour? You? Your family must have an elevated impression of you, if they think you are well-behaved."

"Oh, they do. Mostly." He brought my hand to his lips, kissing each fingertip, his eyes closed as he seemed to be memorising each digit as he went. "A perfect little prince, that's me."

"You make me sick. And I'm supposed to play the part of your willing courtier, am I? God, what is there even to do in Somerset? Even when August comes you'll not get me holding a gun, and you are nowhere near the sea. It'll be deadly."

"Oh, there are things." Then after a silence-filled but passionate minute he said, in a husky tone, "What if I asked Gilbert and Richardson? If there's all four of us, it won't be so bad. If Gilbert takes his car at least we won't be trapped in the slough of despond. Say yes, Harry. Please, say yes. I can't bear the thought of being without you when we had so much planned together. Your mother is going to her family, isn't she? You won't be happy going to Scotland and having nothing but ghillies' knees to ogle."

"Perhaps I have more than ghillies' knees, and more than ogling." He was right, entirely right, damn him. Neither of us had planned to be with our families this summer. I sighed in mock annoyance, although I knew that he knew I'd already decided to give in, and it didn't need me to vocalise it, for his face broke into a sunny smile. "I'll write and tell her. If she wants me, she takes you."

"And Richardson and Gilbert. That's a bitter pill, two bitter pills, for any mother to swallow."

"Ouch." He pushed himself to his feet, kissed me briefly. "You are quite the bitch, Harry, when you want to be."

"And you love it."

He didn't answer that. He never did. I think he got a kick out of it, leaving me eternally uncertain.

Chapter Two

modicum of introduction is required, then. Let us pretend that these four study rooms on the long wall of the warm-stoned quadrangle are the social venue to which you have been invited—although with the all-pervading smell of academe which even the beeswax cannot subsume, I don't know why you'd accept—and I'll take you around and introduce you to the chaps. Those who are worth meeting, at least.

You've already met me, but I suppose I should share some of my credentials. Harry George Alexander Bircham. The Sussex Birchams, I'm afraid, not the Norfolk branch. According to family legend, or perhaps wishful thinking, we slipped above the Bircham blanket sometime in the 17th century: a liaison between a younger son and a visiting lady's maid. It's a nice story, and I'm sure it reassures my family that they are the higher beings in their little village circle, but it's just as likely that our ancestor simply came from Bircham and moved due to some entirely dull need or other.

I like to think he was, in actuality, some stern and intolerant schoolmaster—Isaac Birch'em who had to leave his village after flogging a boy to death for his declination of *Amo Amas Amat*. Life, I've found, is rarely as glamorous as history, and family wish-fulfilment, would have it be. If one were to believe every ghastly work of romance that people love so much (our scout is a devotee, and we are assailed with yearning middle-class women on the covers of her books on a regular basis when she leaves them behind in our rooms) then all heroes in historical times are really undiscovered heirs and are simply floundering around with the general populace until apprised of their true heritage.

Sadly I doubt that Lord Thingy of Bircham is going to spot me walking through London, see an exact facsimile of his great-great-grandfather and

Callooh! Callay! me back into the ermined fold. So I shall remain Harry Bircham Esq. and go into the law.

I'm average height for my year, that is to say there's only the freakishly tall or the freakishly small who stand out—my hair is on the sandy side of brown and I have brown eyes. I'm pretty unremarkable, or pretty but unremarkable. No title, middling fortune, no breeding. *C'est moi.*

You've also met *him*. Now he has breeding, or at least a family tree—rather than a legendary blanket—and the promise of a fair fortune. The Hollands once owned half of Cumbria. Or Tyneside. Or—well, wherever it was it was terribly earnest and hard-working, you know the kind of thing: honest and gloomy men you see in early photos. Grimy in striped shirts and those belted trousers with picks in hand and canaries in cages, hewing the coal from the subterranean with the sweat of their fetid brow—or some kind of brow, anyway. Well, that's his family for you. Filthy rich by the 19th century, then sold it all off (quite sensibly, seeing the mess the coal mines get into every so often) and invested it somewhere or the other and doing very nicely on it now thank you.

But for all that, you'd never know it to look at him. He's permanently creased, and I don't think—even when we've sat down to a formal hall dinner—I've ever seen him entirely groomed. He couldn't look less like a young man of Great Expectations. He told me that on his first day at our secondary school he was so untidy by the time he arrived the Head Boy mistook him for Rowlands, a boy in our same year who was Poor But Worthy and had a scholarship. The HB was quite put out to discover his real name and lineage and I'm afraid was rather set against him from day one, as if he'd had some prank played on him but wasn't sure what it was.

I didn't meet him properly for a term or two, and it took a long time for us to get where we are today. That in itself is a long, sordid, and at times uproariously funny story, the finer details of which are known only to two people in the world, myself and him, and I think I'd rather keep it that way if you don't mind. That story has no relevance to us—being where we are—wherever that is.

So, let me show you around. The entire wing is symmetrical and there are four studies on this floor. This is his study, opposite mine. I know what you are thinking; it's pretty tidy for someone I've just been slating as the untidiest man in college. But that's not his doing. That pile of detritus over by the bedside table; those layers of papers, books, banana skins and plates? That's what his entire room would look like if it wasn't for the scout, Crane. Crane is the unfortunate woman who does for the four of us up here, and she has strict instructions—upon pain of disrecommendation—not to touch anything within two feet of his bed. You can almost see the circle of dust, two feet in circumference around his bed, can't you? Almost. I have a suspicion that Crane pushes her broom into the hallowed area and scrapes out the worst of it, but I'll never voice my thoughts. Her secret is safe with me.

Further up the corridor here and nicely far apart—the doors being as far away from ours as could be—are Richardson and Gilbert. This is Richardson's study; as you can see he's rather a sportsman—as is Gilbert, to be honest. The Dean has complained several times about the gaudy display of cups and rosettes, because frankly too much display is showing off, however well-deserved it is—but Richardson treats the current Dean with the same level of contempt as do the rest of us.

I think it's down to the fact that we've never really forgiven Dean Winterbottom for taking the hallowed shoes of Dean Armitage, who where'er he walked, cool gales did fan the glade and all that. We all had a pash on Armitage, queer boys or otherwise. How could we not? A veritable Heathcliff in cap and gown, striding about the quad positively bristling with repressed sexuality. I say repressed because none of us ever heard of him having a woman—or anything else—but then I've never seen Richardson stepping out with anyone and he's hardly what one would call repressed or queer.

Anyway—back to the late lamented Dean Armitage, who is a far nicer subject to linger upon. Smouldering dark blue eyes (or at least we liked to consider they smouldered when looking at us) glossy black hair with that divine touch of grey at the temples, and a physique that had me weak at the knees. He reminded me hugely of Magnusson, the Head Boy in my last year at Druitt's Torture Academy for Young Gentlemen. He was another brooding Gothic Heathcliff, but as blond as the divine Icelander Hans Bjelke from *Journey to the Centre of the Earth*. Magnusson had thighs like tree-trunks and a posterior that positively wouldn't be disguised by an attempt at wearing the baggiest of trousers. The four of us (I had the misfortune to go to secondary school with all three of the miscreants on my current floor) became quite addicted to Le Sport during Magnusson's reign and we would actually be found on the touchlines at matches, cheering and causing some consternation, as our appalling disinterest in sport had long been a thorn in Druitt's collective side. But, ah well, he's dead and in his grave and oh the difference to me or however it goes.

When Armitage left and Winterbottom took the post of Dean, it was as if Paris had taken the mantle of Priam instead of Hector (had that ever been the case). Mrs Winterbottom would probably be scandalised to be compared to Helen, it has to be said. I don't think someone the shape of a cottage loaf launched so much as a punt, let alone ships. So *très* disappointing, and however good a job Winterbottom did, he simply wasn't going to get the slavish devotion of this study-wing who went so far into mourning at Armitage's departure that we posted black crêpe around our beds and would have painted red crosses in blood red paint on our doors had we not been caught at it and fined most unfairly.

Totally irrelevant really, other than to demonstrate how one man can't ever really step into the shoes of another. Back to the tour then. So if Richardson isn't in his own study, he'll be found here—in Gilbert's. And here they both are. On opposite sides of the room, too, each with a book, and as usual quite disappointingly not springing apart as the door opens unexpectedly. They share not the delights of Marlowe. Except they both smoke like chimneys.

"Dash it, Bircham," Gilbert scolded. "You could knock."

I smiled at him sweetly and blew him a kiss. "I could, but you know I never do." There was—and never would be—any need to do so, after all.

"He's not in here," Gilbert added, pointlessly. I could see that perfectly well. "He was earlier, complaining loudly about his spoiled summer. He invited us down to his mother's house. What's all that about?"

"I couldn't say," I replied in perfect truth. "Are you going to come?"

The two of them exchanged glances and I saw Richardson give the smallest of shrugs. "We haven't decided yet," Gilbert said.

"Well, don't do us any favours," I said with what I hoped was a scathing rise of my left eyebrow. It was something I'd been practising, and I thought it was devastating. "Abandon us to Somerset and the salt mines of deprivation. What were you planning to do instead?"

"Gilbert's people have a house rented in Torquay—" Richardson began.

"Torquay? Oh, for God's sake, that's worse than Bognor. If you truly wish to bury yourselves among the tweeded Boer War relics and the knitting widows, then by all means go to Torquay."

"You're such a snob, Bircham," Richardson said.

I paused for a moment in thought, leaning provocatively against the doorframe. "Guilty as charged. But then, Torquay isn't a million miles from Holland's people, we could move around to alleviate the dreary. Would your people have room for two more if necessary, Gilbert?"

"I thought you just eschewed the very thought of Torquay and its tweeded denizens," he said.

"I'm thinking ahead," I said. "Planning a campaign. If we are to be robbed of Europe and all her delights, we need to have some entertainments in hand. So? Would there be room, were we all to descend on your relatives?"

"I can't see why not," he replied. "The place is huge. We were there last year and it seemed to be full of bedrooms. You might have to share, depending on whom else the Olds have invited, but that wouldn't exactly be a burden, would it?"

"It would shocking beyond belief." I mock sighed. "Well, I'd better go and find him, or he'll be getting himself into trouble. Ta ta."

They ignored me, so I sauntered off. That's the neighbours for you, solid and dependable, and of course I've known them both since before the Ark was built. Granted they could be more exciting, but I find I have my hands full enough most of the time without pulling their collective chestnuts out of the fire. I have chestnuts enough of my own.

THE REMAINING FEW DAYS OF THE term passed, and there was the usual jumble sale scramble as every man in college attempted to find and retrieve everything he'd loaned, or had pinched, from everyone else. Trunks were dragged in from God knows where trunks were kept and despite there always being things that one couldn't retrieve—I lost five socks that term, and I know I started the year with a chess set I never saw again—there never seemed to be enough room in the trunk no matter how one folded and squashed. I wrote to my mother and told her that I'd be going to Somerset, and I imagine that she was wildly relieved that I wouldn't be gallivanting across Europe, although there was no time for her to reply, and I timed it exactly that way. She approved of his family, even though she hadn't met them—and the common bond that had originally made us friends, us both having no fathers, seemed to touch her sensitive mother heart. For reasons known only to her, she seemed to think we would be good for each other. She was right, of course, but not in any way that she would like to hear about, I am quite sure.

By the last evening, when our studies were tidier than they'd been for weeks, he slid into my room, locked the door, took my hand and escorted me to the bed. He was rarely so demonstrative; he usually liked things just to happen—spontaneity was something he lived for, it was something of an obsession with him, which was pretty ironic, to be honest. Other times he liked to be wooed, teased and explored, persuaded, as if the evil were mine alone and he was merely going along with it. It was a fantasy I was more than willing to encourage.

I thought I knew what he was trying to say that night, as he pulled me down and unbuttoned enough of my shirt to be able to invade my person and burrow around. Questing fingers pushed my vest aside and found skin, drawing my breath from my lungs and making me sink my lips against his neck. I imagined that he was making the most of the last privacy we might have for a week, maybe even weeks. Maybe his family would put us in rooms far, far away from each other, maybe they wouldn't like me—when they finally met me after all these years—maybe they would decide they didn't want a no one, a no name, hanging around their son with no clear motive. Whatever his reasons, I pushed them aside and let him mean whatever the hell he wanted to mean. After a minute or two I decided it really didn't matter after all.

Chapter Three

Personally I dislike houses with names. It's rather a thing of mine, and yes, it probably shores up Richardson's view that I'm a snob. But you can walk down any street in my home town and find the most revolting names on the gates of otherwise sensible Victorian red-brick houses. *Dunroamin* is the best of them, and that's no joke. *The Laurels* when there are no laurels; *Cozy Cottage* describing an end terrace two-up-two-down with outside lav; *Spencer's Lodge*—God, the hubris!—on a ghastly modernist monstrosity I noticed on my last sojourn home. I mentioned this to him pretty early on in our friendship, and he reminded me of course that his family home had a name. *Hellsingers*. I admit to having made a face. "That's worse than *The Laurels*, or *Dunroamin*."

"It's not something any of the family has called it. It's on the deeds from long before we bought the place. Some fanciful Georgian farmer, I suppose."

"Not some homesick Viking, then?"

He snorted. "That's probably the impression it's supposed to give. I am not sure that they ever got as far as Somerset, unless they were very lost. My father told me once that in Norfolk there are still villages named after Vikings. Filby, Ormesby, Scratby, Oby." He reeled the names off as if the conversation with his father had been yesterday, rather than years past. "The 'by' in the word means place."

"A Viking called O? His wife would have had fun with that." We found that hilarious, and we got a lot of mileage out of it over the years. So when it came to Hellsingers, I admit I was expecting something gauche rather than grand, and when it came down to it, it was a bit of a mix of both. The original house was Georgian, that much could be seen from the symmetrical core, and was probably grand enough in its day. Three large bay windows lay on each side of the door on the ground floor and were meant to impress in an age when glass was expensive, the upper windows being smaller, and the ones on the second floor, originally for servants were tinier still. But despite it being a largish Georgian house, it had not been large enough for the subsequent owners, and like many country houses with room to expand, expand it most certainly had. Wings had been built, rambling off to either side, with clearly no care for the perfection of the original building, and a carbuncle of a large brick porch, together with a glaringly white wooden conservatory, something every large country house must have—apparently—was stuck on the side.

The house's expression, I fancied, was gloomy as if to say, "Don't look round the side, please, remember me as I was."

"I know," he said, digging me with an elbow. "Frightful, isn't it?"

"I had rather expected ancestral towers, I have to say."

"There were ancestral towers, once," he said, striding towards the entrance. "But up north. Sold with the mine. I'll take you one day. You'll have to meet the family first. Then you'll see how ludicrous they'd seem in the shadow of Those Dark Satanic Mills." He jogged up the steps. "Leave your stuff there."

The door opened before we reached the top and a butler, who surprised me by being far more youthful than the ancient family retainer I had been expecting, stood aside for us.

"Hello, Stephens."

"Good afternoon, sir," Stephens said. "Well-timed, as usual."

"Tea on the lawn?"

"About five minutes ago, sir."

"Thank you, Stephens, we'll introduce ourselves."

He turned to me, took my arm and led me through the hall. Our footsteps sounded clear and intrusive on the polished parquet. "Stephens thinks that I must have been raised by jam-loving homing pigeons, because every time I come home it's exactly tea-time."

"Not taking into consideration that's the time of the only train," I said.

"My dearest Harry." He gave my elbow a small squeeze. "You will be truly frightening at the Bar. You will be able to look directly at the accused and see the truth without any cross-examination."

"So I should hope. Am I to be subjected to your family's scrutiny now, or can I hide somewhere and tidy myself up?" I couldn't add that I was rather untidied by the fact we had been alone in a private compartment for hours and had taken advantage of every solitary minute. We had still been tucking ourselves in as the train puffed into Minehead.

"You shall be—for once—shoulder to shoulder with my scruffiness," he said, pulling me forward. We entered a large, airy dining room which connected to the conservatory. "They shall see what we have in common and will not be so quick as to say that I'm a freak of nature."

"If only they knew," I murmured, *sotto voce*.

"Heaven forbid."

I stopped, and he was jolted to a standstill beside me. "What is it?"

"Just girding my loins," I said.

"Don't worry about your loins. Mother will love you, of course. Uncle Claude, well, he doesn't like anyone that's connected to me, you've known that for years, so no surprise there. Oh, don't worry, they are all ga-ga anyway. Nod away at them, Mr Bircham. That's what they like. Nod away at them if you please."

I hit him. "I hope I remember everyone's name."

"We aren't being swamped by *everyone* yet, thank the Lord." He opened the door to the garden. "Just Mother, Claude, and the hangers-on. And don't worry about it. No one expects you to. Knowing them, I'll be surprised if anyone cares. I'm completely stunned when anyone remembers my name, to be honest." He dropped my arm and waved at the group on the far side of a long, wide lawn. A group of people sat around tables beside two immaculate grass tennis courts. Several of the assembled wore tennis whites, and there were racquets propped against the tables, so I assumed play had been interrupted by tea.

I'm not a shy person. You may have grasped this. Wealth and privilege entice rather than cow me. My dear mother may not have a fortune gleaned from the sweat of the honest labourer but she's raised me to be confident enough in the company of those who do. And two years at Oxford will help one in that regard also, make no mistake. So it was with a friendly smile that I greeted the massed horde of his family.

All heads were turned our way; a slender woman rose from the nearest table. "Ah, here he is at last. Darling," she said, giving him a close hug and a kiss on the cheek. "I wasn't sure whether it was today or tomorrow you were coming." She turned and extended a hand to me, "And this must be Mr Bircham. Good Lord, darling," she said, turning back to him with a look of mock amazement, "he's just as you described him." She continued to hold on to him, but turned him around to greet the others.

"Well, what did you expect?" he said, and there was the touch of petulance in his tone. "Hello, Mother. Harry, my mother, Medea Holland. It was Medea who ate her young, wasn't it?"

"It jolly well wasn't," she said, "and that's quite naughty of you, darling. What if we'd had the Witherspoons for tea? It's Margaret, Mr Bircham, you must call me Margaret, not Mrs Holland. Mrs Holland makes me sound as if I should be wearing a lace cap like Mrs Abetheny in the village."

She pulled him close and kissed him again. "Darling, I'm so glad you could come. I thought you were bringing some more?"

"Oh, I dare say they'll be along in a day or so," he said.

"That'll be nice for the two of you," she said, and I had the feeling she was holding something in, the way she kept hugging him against her. "Mr Bircham had better meet the others."

"Poor Mr Bircham," said an elegant girl in a calf-length tennis dress at the furthest table. "I can't imagine how ghastly it must be to be subjected to us all en masse."

"What did you think I was going to do? Have him wait in the hall and have you brought in one by one?"

"Now, now, darling," his mother said, and I could see there was something making her on edge. I couldn't blame her, I felt much the same, standing there allowing them to squabble over me. "Mr Bircham, this is my family—well, in way, I suppose." She gave the most delightful laugh and for a moment she looked five years younger and entirely entrancing, if one was entranced in that manner. I could see flashes of him in her smile, veneered with the same brittle self-consciousness.

"Let me," he said. "Harry, this dark lady to whom I have written no sonnets is our Stevie. Stevie, meet Harry."

"Delighted," Stevie replied. She was indeed a dark lady. Black, fashionably bobbed hair, the darkest of brown eyes under eyebrows that I would have killed for. Dark lady indeed. I knew she wasn't his sister, but no explanation of Stevie's connection to the Hollands was forthcoming, it seemed.

"The brute beside her," he went on, "is her brother, Lawrence." A stocky, dark-haired young man with the face of Hadrian's beloved, Antinous, rose and shook my hand, then took his place and lit a cigarette as if I'd been no more than a fly he'd had to swat, and far less important.

He offered a cigarette to his sister which she almost reached for, which I thought was interesting.

I nodded and smiled, as ordered. I admit that I took little notice of the pretty Stevie but I lavished a long look on Lawrence because he was worth the effort. I prefer them dark and brooding. Or blond and brooding.

I like the impression that there is a great deal going on beneath the surface, although it's a terrible bore when one works hard merely to find out there isn't.

"This is my late husband's sister, Miss Clarissa Holland." The introductions moved to the second table, where a lady who—how should I put it without sounding ungallant?—looked liked she had swallowed a pygmy rhinoceros sat on a woefully small chair.

I didn't say I *wasn't* going to sound ungallant.

"And her brother, Claude."

I nodded at the country of Clarissa, and was surprised when Claude Holland stepped around the tables to give my hand a hearty shake. He was tall, with iron grey hair, the sort that seemed to crisp and curl naturally from his forehead, and his personality hit me like a hammer blow as his fingers crushed mine in a masculine grip, erasing all memories of the limp-wristed greeting Lawrence had given. "So this is Mr Bircham," he said, and the sentence seemed terrifyingly fraught with meaning. He glanced over to Margaret and her son, and I couldn't help but notice that their expressions rather emulated the theatre masks one saw—one smiling and one completely not. "We've heard much about you, haven't we, Margaret dear? It's wonderful you could come down and share in—"

"Let's go in, shall we?" Margaret said. "The clouds look threatening, and Stephens is lurking, he can bring tea back into the drawing room. We can all get to know each other better when the boys have settled in." She pulled him to her for a third time. "I'm so glad you came, darling." She took his arm and moved towards the house. "Mr Bircham has the room next to yours, of course. Come on, my dears."

I followed along, as Stevie and Lawrence paired up, picking up their racquets and meandering behind, and Uncle Claude began the process of excavating Miss Holland from her chair. Mrs Holland chattered away to her son as we walked.

"Where's Polonius?" I heard Stevie ask.

"He was at the back of the west court half an hour ago," her brother said. "Don't worry about him. It's not as if he could have gone far, after all."

"If it's going to rain."

"He'll take shelter, he's not entirely dim. Come on, do." His voice dropped, but with years of pretending not to hear things I could just make out his words. "I do hope you aren't going to be stupid again."

"Well, if I am," she said, and although I couldn't see her face I imagined her glaring at her brother in challenge, "I'll have you, dear knight, to protect me from my own destructive nature, won't I? And you've got a cheek, calling *me* stupid."

All of which had me wondering quite a lot of wondering by the time we'd settled down in the drawing room—entirely too much chintz for my liking—and tea had been transferred.

Claude took a position by the fireplace next to Mrs Holland. "So, I hear you hark from Scotland?"

Hark? Who says hark? I had a sudden vision of myself being pursued by kilt-clad lovelies across a purple-heathered landscape. Lucky me. "No, I'm afraid not, sir. My mother's family has a house there, where she goes during the summer. But we've never lived there. We hark from Sussex."

This unromantic aspect of my life obviously disappointed Claude for he concentrated on other things than myself, now I had rid myself of the heather in my hair.

I was handed, and about time too, a cup of tea. An occasional table piled high with cakes and sandwiches was placed by my side. This seemed suitable recompense for an interrogation, so I wetted my whistle and waited for more questions. I was not to be disappointed.

"How did your exams go?" Dear Uncle Claude asked, including both of us in the question, but looking at his nephew.

"Now, Claude," Mrs Holland said, "the boys have just escaped, and I'm sure we'll hear all about it, won't we?" She looked up as Stevie and Lawrence came in; they both looked out of sorts as if they'd been having a disagreement. I dare say siblings do that a lot. I wouldn't know, but I hear it's the case from those unfortunate enough to suffer them.

Mrs Holland sat on a long green and white settee beside her son. Seeing them both together I could appreciate why he was as beautiful as he was. His mother—although I'm only making an observation here, in the same way I know why a horse has presence, or why a Grecian urn can turn the heads of poets—was captivating. Her hair was the same bronze-gold as his, although slightly longer, worn to the chin. Her face was almost the same face, other than being obviously female, and with lips more rounded and full, and with far more macquillage than he'd ever worn (ask me another time). If you saw them in the street together, there would be no doubt he was her son. I looked from him to Claude Holland and tried to see any resemblance there. Claude was his father's brother, after all—so there should have been something. But if there was, I'm afraid I couldn't see it.

All the while they sat together, Mrs Holland attended to her son, passing him food—and he can put it away, believe me, despite that lean and slender frame—and touching him as if she didn't quite believe he was real. I knew that he hadn't been home for a year, and when he had popped back last summer it was only to grab his rucksack and some other essentials before we set off hitchhiking around France. Flying visits were all he'd done for years now, and so her behaviour seemed quite understandable.

She didn't want to let him go, and who could blame her? I felt the same. I was left to entertain Miss Holland, which wasn't difficult. She was one of those hugely, and I mean no disrespect by that, jovial people, with a joie-devivre (especially when it came to pastries, it appeared) that spilled over into everything else. She loved the summer, she adored travel, and she thought Scotland was exquisite and that Sussex came a close second. I was half tempted to ask her what she thought of the Kaiser, just to test a theory, but I reined my baser instincts in. I'd only just met these people, and they wouldn't understand the Bircham humour just yet. Comparing her to her brother was an interesting study; they were both full of personality, although hers was all on the surface, her brother's—as he stood, almost protectively next to his brother's wife, watching her wait on her son—seemed to be entirely internal. That force of personality I'd been buffeted with upon our introduction was veiled and his mood that afternoon over tea (going by his expression) was one of bland interest.

Whether he was really pleased to see his scruffy nephew (and his slightly less scruffy friend) was impossible to tell. I couldn't remember what it was he did—if anything. But I'd seen judges with more expression. If he'd gone into the law, or decided to take up poker, he'd have made a fortune. I wouldn't want to play cards against him. Luckily, most of the family—although I was still a little baffled as to what actual relation anyone was to each other apart from mother and son—had their attention focused on Mrs Holland and her pleasure at having her son back for a while and I was spared too much questioning.

Tea ended, as all teas sadly must, and we were released to "settle in" which expression has always unnerved me, I have to say. I feel I should plump my arse on the bed and wriggle, like a blackbird warming eggs or something.

I am sure that women have things that need doing upon arrival in a strange house—the bottles and potions they drag around with them have some place in that arcane art of primping and powdering, but once one has unpacked (or in this case, has one's things unpacked for one) there's little else to do.

And much of what I actually wanted to do was probably going to be *verboten* anyway for the duration, more's the pity.

After investigating where my belongings had been stored, I changed my shirt, had a quick wash, damped my hair down and sought out the adjoining bedroom. A connecting door ran between the two rooms, via a narrow passageway and a bathroom. I opened the door to his room. He hadn't noticed me, or heard me open the door, and my breath caught in my throat. There are times when I forget why I'm hopelessly, entirely in love with him—the times when he's casually callous or cruel, or when he showers me with indifference— but that afternoon, I was reminded of every single reason why. He was lying face down on one of the window seats; long, wide and built for comfort they were. His chin was in both his hands and his eyes were half closed, like a satiated and lazy cat, as he watched something down below in the garden. The afternoon sun caught his hair, turning the tips to gold, and my gaze moved from there down the width of his shoulders to the curve of his back and the ever-alluring wave of his arse. It's not just his body, although I sound like the worst of hedonists, but he can capture stillness whilst radiating more energy than most men can when running. Don't ask me to explain it. He glows. I don't think I made a sound, but he must have been aware of me eventually and he shoved a hand behind him without otherwise shifting in position and waggled his fingers in invitation. I moved to the window, sorry to have disturbed the candid moment—even if it meant proximity—and sat beside him. I looked out, following his gaze, which hadn't shifted even when I sat down, and saw his mother and Claude Holland walking out on the lawn, apparently deep in what seemed to be a serious discussion.

"Have you worked it out yet?" I asked. Charles had spent the last days of term and the entire train journey obsessed with why his mother had insisted he come home. "She hasn't said anything to you?"

He shook his head, still watching the now distant figures as they moved toward the bank of rhododendrons. "Uh-uh. Although it looks serious."

I couldn't disagree there. "And you really have no clue?"

"Oh, I have a clue." Despite my asking him to explain, he refused to be drawn further. "There's no point getting you all worked up," he said, "if I'm wrong." He took my hand and lay flat on the window seat after that, my hand tucked within both of his. There was nowhere else I wanted to be.

It probably shows my naïveté, or the arrogance I had back then, that I thought that the Hollands pushed the boat out that first night in honour of my visit.

Charles's mother stepped out of the drawing room, closed the doors behind her, almost furtively, making me wonder what she was being furtive about. "Oh, Lord," he said.

His mother turned and spotted us as we lurked at the base of the stairs. "There you are, you two. Darling, could I have a word before dinner?"

"I'd rather not," he said, taking a step backwards. "I know what you—and I feel the same. Stevie's like a sister, it's nothing to do with class."

"Stevie? Oh, darling, don't be silly. It's not about Stevie. Come into the library, I want to speak to you. Mr Bircham—if you will excuse us? We are eating in the Gallery, just go the end of the hall there."

"I'm not leaving him to find the Gallery by himself, you have no idea what chaos he can cause if left alone. Mother—I know what you want, and I'm not interested. Stevie, some girl from the village, just don't bother."

"If you'd—" she broke off as the drawing room doors opened again, and the entire company trooped out, led by Claude.

"Here she is," he said, "I told you she wouldn't be far. Shall we go in?"

Mrs Holland looked a little discomfited at being thwarted from her purpose but she put on her smile, took her son's arm and led the way down the hall. I walked behind them, as the other two ladies were already claimed.

"Good Lord," he said to me. "Eating in the Gallery? Who died?"

"Gallery?" I asked.

"It's the faux banqueting hall. It's ghastly and we almost never eat there. Must be a prodigal son thing, then?" He glanced at his mother but she didn't respond other than to give him another brittle smile. His face reverted to a gloomy expression and we entered the Gallery, the door held open by the butler.

It was indeed a banqueting hall, styled from an earlier time, although put in sometime in the Victorian era, I supposed. It had one enormous table, with the ability to seat at least twenty people and above us, lining the edges of the room was an honest-to-God minstrel's gallery. I gawped in an obliging fashion, as it was probably expected of me.

"Exactly," he said, drily. "And if you look carefully, the minstrel's gallery isn't even connected to any part of the house: no doors you see? The merciful few times we've had any musicians up there, the poor sods—souls have had to clamber up there via ladders, clutching their instruments and terrified that the floor would collapse mid-serenade. The room, *sans* table, is at least good for parties. But we haven't had one for…well, a while."

That made sense. Around the time his father disappeared, perhaps. I could imagine the parties held here; it was indeed a perfect space for that, if too large for a family of six or so to dine. Perhaps there had been one when the senior Charles Holland obtained his commission, back when the country was buoyant and just arrogant enough to consider that all the Kaiser needed was a bloody nose.

I was young enough to remember the elation of the country as it mobilised to go and "sort out the whole mess." People seriously did believe that they'd sort it out, and be back for Christmas. I did too—that's what all the adults were saying, even the boys at school who were off to fight, lucky beggars we thought them at the time. Of course we believed them. We were jealous. But then it wasn't over by Christmas; they never came back for Christmas; some never came back at all.

"God, don't you start looking glum," he said, breaking into my reverie. "You don't need to mourn the death of decent architecture for my sake, and anyway, you are here to raise morale. Where should we sit, mother?"

"You can sit beside me, Stevie on your other side, and Lawrence on the end. Mr Bircham if you'll sit opposite Lawrence?"

I sat as ordered, feeling rather below the salt. The food was good, and tempting as it is, I'm not going to allow this account to slip into a list of what we ate and when. I love good food, especially when it's free and he does too. We strap on the nosebag when and wherever we can, with the tenet firmly in mind that we never know where the next meal is coming from. This is entire rot, of course—we aren't exactly Napoleon's Army on retreat from Moscow, but we did once go a whole day in France with nothing but a loaf of increasingly stale bread so we know of what we speak when we talk of hunger, believe you me. Suffice it to say that the food at Hellsingers was better than college, and leave it at that.

I missed being close enough to him to be able to talk between ourselves, or to touch his foot with mine, but I soldiered on, finding Miss Holland once more an amiable conversationalist, as long as everything was positive, but discovering that Lawrence Whatever-his-damned-surname-was was a lot harder to draw out. I've had winkles that were more responsive, once encouraged with a pin. Did he travel? No, he did not. Did I play golf? No, I didn't. Did he visit the British Museum? He had been when he was a kid, but wouldn't be seen dead there now, and so on and so on. He was Sport, I was Intellect and our muses would never bond, it seemed, no matter how devilishly handsome he was. After twenty or so attempts from both sides to find a no-man's land where we could play allegorical football, we gave up and concentrated on the ladies beside us.

The dessert was cleared away (a strawberry meringue, if anyone is interested) and I half expected that the ladies would withdraw. Instead, Claude Holland rose to his feet and tinkled his coffee spoon against the rim of his glass. Stephens had reappeared with a magnum of champagne and was busy englassing—now I am fairly sure *that* isn't a word—as Mr Holland claimed our attention. I darted a look along the table; Mrs Holland smiled, but her son was looking as if some thundercloud had landed over his head and a miniature Thor was throwing thunderbolts straight towards his uncle.

"Thank you," Holland said. "I wanted to mark this occasion with just the immediate family, and so I'm more pleased than I can express that you all could be here tonight. Some news needs to be heard first hand—not via letters or telephone calls." He looked down at his nephew as he spoke. "As you all know, seven years ago—" One of the family made a sound like they'd dropped something on their toe, but it was impossible to tell which of them; each face was deliberately blank except for Mrs Holland, who looked happy but intensely nervous, her hands twisting her napkin on the table before her. "—the loss of my dear and only brother Charles," Holland went on, "made a hole in this family that caused pain to us all, pain that I wondered if we would ever come through." My *inamorato*'s hand slid from the tablecloth into his lap, where by the look of tension in his eyes I imagined it was clenching and unclenching at his father being described by Dear Uncle Claude. "With only one year between us, my brother and I were as close as any two brothers could be, and when we both went to war—" I saw my Charles give a deliberate intake of breath at that. "On the night before we left this very house, he asked me—if anything were to happen to him—to look after his family. 'They are your family too,' I remember him saying. And he was right. At the time I had known you only a short time, since returning from South Africa, but I felt I knew you all intimately from his many letters. It was the fact that he stopped writing that convinced me that he was never coming home, for he never missed a day unless for a good reason."

He turned his full attention to Mrs Holland. "I'm sure that my affection for Margaret is no secret. We both pursued her, and that tale has passed into family legend—the victor, Charles, received the honour of marrying Margaret and I went mining to ease my broken heart."

"Claude," Mrs Holland said. "Don't make a play of it."

"Sorry, my dear." I knew what he was about to say, I'm sure everyone around the table did, but I wasn't the only one who was finding it a surprise. Sitting bolt upright now, and staring at his glass of champagne as if it were full of cyanide, my friend sat, and his face was the colour of chalk.

"I'll cut it short with the news that probably is news to none of you—I have asked Margaret to marry me, and she has honoured me by saying—"

"No!" My ill-timed lover shot to his feet, still pale as milk, blinking as if he were entirely unable to process what he'd just heard. "No. You can't!" His voice was deeper than ever I'd heard it, and his face was contorted with absolute disgust.

"Darling—" his mother said at the exactly the same moment Claude Holland said "That's enough!"

He ignored Holland entirely and focussed his anger, almost a tangible lance of white-hot fury, at his mother. "That's…. Impossible! Mother? You can't! It's—it's bloody illegal for a start!"

"Darling, sit down, please." She looked up at both the men in her life who were by now squaring off at each other, like a couple of rather well-dressed boxers. "Please."

Mr Holland sat first, and finally, when she tugged at his jacket sleeve, she persuaded her son to sit too. The rest of the table were frozen in embarrassment, no one spoke. Lawrence and Stevie stared at the tablecloth, Miss Holland looked with some concern at her brother. No one had their glass of champagne in their hand now. Except me, of course. I took a healthy swig and concentrated my gaze on my *inamorato*, wishing at the very least I was near enough to be able to kick him under the table. "Perhaps Stevie, Clarissa and myself should move into the drawing room," Mrs Holland said, once a frigid order had been restored.

"Or perhaps Harry and I should be the ones to go."

"That's not going to help." Mrs Holland said.

"Your mother is right," Mr Holland said, glaring across the table. "I'm sorry if you were shocked at the news, I assumed that you'd realised what this gathering was about. You can't have been entirely blind to my feelings for your mother."

"Well, yes, obviously I was," he replied, his voice heavy with sarcasm.

"You know he hasn't been here, not properly, Claude," his mother said. "Darling. The law was changed. I thought you'd know that."

"Why you'd think that, I don't know. Harry?"

I nodded. "The Deceased Brother's Widow's Marriage Act, 1921"

Margaret gave me a grateful look, which somewhat countered his more poisonous one. "A woman can marry her dead husband's brother, perfectly legally—after all, it's been a thoroughly stupid law—Claude found out almost by accident."

"Oh, really," he said. "I bet he did. And since when is Father *dead?*"

"Oh, come on," Lawrence spoke then, his voice showing his contempt for the argument. "Your father was dead and buried a long time ago. You seem to be the only one who continues to reject the idea. After seven years it's almost automatic."

"I still think I had the right to be told," he said. "Not that it's any of your business, Lawrence, but my father was Missing." he said, and I could tell he was barely holding onto his temper. "Missing. Presumed. Dead. Not at all the same thing. He's buried nowhere."

Lawrence sneered. "Unless you count ten foot of mud."

"You shut up," he warned.

"Lawrence, dear, you aren't helping," Mrs Holland said. She turned to her son, and touched his hand. He drew away as if she'd burned him. "I was trying to speak to you alone before dinner, but there wasn't the time."

"It never occurred to you to make the time?" he said. "I saw you wandering in the garden, talking to…him. You could have come up…and warned me. And so, what happened? The anniversary passed, you ran hand-in-hand to the solicitors, and the moment the law changed he leapt into your bed?"

"Don't you dare speak to your mother like that!" Mr Holland snapped.

"Don't you dare order me about! You," he directed his attention at Claude Holland, "You I can understand, sniffing around here all these years after Father beat you fair and square, but you, Mother, how could you? After Father?"

"I said, that's enough, and by God I mean it." Claude Holland's voice rose, his urbane mask dropping away.

"You won't—"

"That's *enough*," Claude shouted, slamming his fist on the table. "God, boy, you've made your mother miserable enough these past few years, by staying away and never writing, ducking home only when you need money, or clean clothes, or to borrow something, but to spoil today for her, when she's looked forward to your return for weeks? We didn't have to do this. You are old enough and independent enough to stay away as long as you like—"

"Don't think I won't."

"Please!" Mrs Holland was on the verge of tears and I have to say, I felt for her. She'd obviously been looking forward to her son's return, and she'd saved this particular celebration up so the family could share in it together. I was, however, baffled. Did she not know her own son at all?

Did she seriously have no idea of how he would react to this news? I wasn't even in the family, and I could have scripted the way he'd behaved, almost word for word. I could see him gathering his control, and it was a close thing. He had a temper to match Claude Holland's, and it was a bitter, uncontrollable hawser when unleashed. He closed his eyes, breathed deep and pushed himself to his feet once more. "I'm sorry, Mother," he said, entirely ignoring Claude. "I find myself unable to see this as any kind of celebration. To me, we might as well go and find father's memorial stone and dance up and down in front of it. Harry." With a small bow to the other diners, sitting in stunned silence, he stalked out. The boy knows how to make an exit, I'll say that for him. Unfortunately it meant that my exit was rather hampered with having to decide whether I should obey his summons and insult him, or insult the family.

Of course I obeyed him. I'd only just met them, and they hadn't exactly won my affections. I nodded to all, and scurried out, trying not to look like the lapdog I very much felt myself to be. I heard an expression of disgust from either Lawrence or Claude just before I closed the door and I couldn't help but hear as a furious exchange broke out which I didn't linger to overhear, much as I wanted to.

Oh, God, I thought, as I trotted up the stairs to our rooms, how are we going to weather this one?

His door was locked, giving a clear message to the household, so I went into mine, and through the connecting passage which was not bolted, which spoke volumes to me.

He was lying face up on the bed, his dress jacket lying crumpled on the floor. He had a cigarette in his hand, and that hand draped over the side of the bed. The ash grew from the end of the cigarette and dropped onto the floor as he neglected to smoke the damn thing. Out of habit I picked up his jacket and hung it over a chair, took a cigarette from the packet beside him and lit it. It was a delicate moment; I had the feeling he didn't wish to be cajoled or sympathised with, but if I hazarded wrongly, I could end up on the milk train home, spending the summer alone and scheming how to win back his affection. His father loomed between us, as he always had, a spectre that I dared not speak of, or at least rarely, without being encouraged to by him.

It was his personal thorny subject—a shield he held between him and anyone else in the world who had a father—or who had lost one, like me. You see, he adored his father. Beyond and above the normal respect or adoration that any of us normally have for fathers. I lost mine around the same time, so many of us did in the war. I imagined that the sense of loss we had felt was on a par, but the difference between us is that I got over it. He never did.

Perhaps it was because my father—who died in the first few days of training camp before he ever got to France—is buried in the family plot at home.

But there's no Charles Holland Senior buried beneath that stone in France. Missing, presumed dead. It had the worst effect on his son, because he never stopped hoping, and never has stopped. I suppose the entire family was the same, stuck for years in some kind of ghastly limbo, hoping that every postman might bring news, whether good or bad. I know his mother did much to find out what happened, even to the point of going to visit his unit and talking to those that survived—few enough of them, I believe, too. She had even travelled to France with Claude Holland and questioned everyone they could, but there was no clue as to what could have possibly happened to him. One moment he was with his troop, and then he was gone, as swiftly and as effectively as if someone had reached down from the sky and taken him. He wasn't the only one to vanish like that, of course, but he was the only one of my friends' fathers who did.

And as I say, his son hero-worshipped him. I had known that from the first moment we'd met because his relationship with his father had been so far removed from my own experience it was if sometimes he was speaking another language. My own father was of the opinion that children raised themselves somewhere out of the adults' orbit and he didn't even allow me at the dining table until I was of an age to go away to school at ten. I rarely saw him alone, and when I did it was to suffer punishment, more often than not, so I have to say I didn't relish the times when we were together all that much.

I have often tried to put my father into the role that the senior Charles Holland had often been described to me, that of a man who loved to tell stories, who would romp on the floor with his son, had taught him to ride by putting his son on his back and cantering around the drawing room, but it was impossible to do. My father did not fit the mould. He was rigid and unbending, like an over-starched collar. The image of him on all fours was impossible to conceive, although the image of him dead had occurred to me a few times. I had never met the elder Charles Holland, although I dearly wish I had.

So I kept quiet, knowing he'd talk if he wanted to, and it wouldn't do to guess. He didn't. In the end I lay down beside him and together we smoked in silence, and I watched the swallows as they peppered the sky with flashes of blue and red. After an hour he turned towards me, buried his head in my shoulder. I curled my arm around him and listened to him breathe.

I woke with a dry mouth and a stiff neck. He was still curled around me, his hair damp against my cheek. Something had woken me and I lay there wondering what it was for a moment, until I heard a tapping sound coming from outside the room. I pushed him away with little ceremony, slipped off the bed and padded through to my own room. I had the sense to rumple the bed before opening the door, at least.

A maid was just walking away down the corridor and I glanced down to see a tray on the floor, and one outside his door. Perhaps she'd knocked there too, or maybe she hadn't. I scooped up my tray, dumped it on my bed and went back for his. There was an envelope on his tray with his name written clearly in a feminine hand, the elegant letters flowing across the paper. Hmm. His eyes were open as I rattled my way back in, full of smiles, breakfast in my hand. In my half evening dress I fancied I could get away with impersonating Alan, the terribly queer waiter at the Rose and Crown.

No one else seemed to have noticed his peccadilloes bar the few of us in college with perhaps an inside knowledge, but he's divine to watch. I waggled my hips as I walked (seriously, I don't know how he gets away with it, I'd be sent down if I ever walked like that), put the tray beside him and spoke in what I hoped was a fair interpretation of Alan's confiding tone. "Well, the sun's up before you, nothing new there. I think we've been spared some leftovers, so we won't be cast onto the roads to shake our sandals just yet, it seems. There's toast and," I lifted the lid "oh, kedgeree, that's a disappointment. I always feel kedgeree must have identification problems. What am I, exactly? Rice or fish? Neither fish nor fowl." I winked at him. "Know just how it feels, in that respect…"

"…If you catch my meaning, gentlemen, and I'm sure you do," he chorused along with me.

I beamed. He'd woken with a smile, and although his eyes had dark circles and the way he rubbed his temples denoted he probably had a headache, he was more chipper than I ever thought he'd be.

He drained his tea, buttered some toast and waved it at me. "After Paris where would you like to go? I fancy Berlin, myself, but if you still have a hankering for Morocco…"

There was no way around it. I knew I'd have to puncture his mood whether he liked it or not. "You mean leave? Today?"

His face darkened, perhaps recalling the argument of the night before. "I can't see one reason to stay."

"Look—"

He held up a hand. "Don't, Harry. You don't understand."

"Don't say that—after all this time!" I hated having to raise my voice to him, when I knew he was already feeling that the entire house was against him. "I do—really. I'd feel the same. If Mother wanted to," I screwed up my forehead as I spoke, as it wasn't an image one liked in one's head, one's mother marrying…doing all that other stuff. "But I'd want her to be happy. And it's not like either of us are living at home, or intend to do so."

He pushed himself off the bed, and started to peel off his clothes from the night before. I knew that was tantamount to an order to leave, but I sat stubbornly on the bed, finished my breakfast and we ignored each other while he had a swift wash and changed into flannels and a soft white shirt. I knew he was mulling over his next response, and frankly I was expecting a tirade.

"You're right," he said. See what I mean about him? He's like water down a window; you never know exactly which direction he'll run.

"I'm what?" I faked a heart attack and landed flat on the bed.

"Oh, shut up." A small smile formed on those lips. "Take your victory where you find it." He grabbed a jumper from a drawer and tied it around his neck. "I need to give mother that talk she was wanting, I think. Meet me by the gazebo in…" he glanced at his watch, "an hour?" He took a final sip of tea, spilling drops down that beautiful shirt, and all but ran out of the room.

I polished off both breakfasts with no sense of shame. I'm not a fan of kedgeree in general but when it comes to homemade bread, fresh salted butter and strawberry conserve—also homemade, I was perfectly sure, in the kitchens here—I can pack it away in neat layers and leave room for more. I changed, enjoyed exploring the ablutions and sampling all the pots and potions left out for guests, and was just changed—neatly brushed and ready—when a pebble knocked against the window. I opened the pane to find him down below, marching up and down and scuffing his feet in the gravel as if something had angered him hugely. Apparently the talk with his mother had not gone well. He glanced up. "Finally. I've been lobbing stones at the window for hours."

"Don't exaggerate," I said. "You said an hour, and it's nothing like that. Should I let down my hair for you to come up, or shall I join you down there?"

He ignored my wit and stomped off to slump beneath a tree. He was around the side of the house, still sitting beneath a tree when I found him.

I slowed as I approached, making as much noise as I could so he could stop scowling at the ground and take proper notice. I won't say he did much of either, but he pulled himself to his feet and marched off across the lawn.

I fell into step beside him. We walked past the tennis courts and into the copse. The dappled sunlight lit the path and undergrowth, camouflaging the ground so perfectly one had to be careful where one put one's feet. He glanced back toward the entrance to the wood and took my hand, evidently satisfied that we were unobserved. I was less sure; anyone could be sitting quietly somewhere in the half hidden recesses, but I was less particular than he ever was about anyone seeing our affection. As he took my hand, a cloud went over the sun, taking the golden patches from the woodland floor, just for a second.

He'd noticed it, I knew, because he made a move to pull away but I held him fast, refusing to believe in his superstition and talk of omens. "It's just a stupid cloud," I muttered, and the cloud moved away, putting the world back to rights. I could feel him relax, but he didn't reply. He said nothing, in fact, the whole time we walked, but he did seem rather alert; casting his eyes around him, as if seeking for something hidden—badgers perhaps? He'd never shown that much interest in wildlife. I let it pass, content enough with the warm weight of his hand in mine.

After half an hour or so of gentle rambling we came out onto a lane on the far side of the wood. "Let's go to the pub," he said, finally. "It's not far. I could do with a drink."

I nodded. Before we stepped through the gate he gave my hand a quick squeeze before dropping it. Then he gave me a mirthless smile. "Poor Harry," he said.

"Shut up." I pushed him through the gate.

It felt strange once we were in the village; it wasn't exactly Piccadilly Circus, but it bustled in its own small way, the way villages often do. One or two people were in their gardens, bent close to the earth, working away.

A woman stood by the front door of a thatched cottage, holding a bicycle while she chatted to another woman, dressed in black. The church, whose spire we could see from the house, came in sight as we turned the corner. Like so many village churches, it seemed far larger than necessary, given the size of the village. Set up on the top of the sloping graveyard, it seemed to tower imposingly over the whole area, which I suppose was the effect it meant to convey. While I was staring up at it, he ducked forward, plucked some purple flowers by the side of the road and moved into the churchyard without even a word to me.

I followed him, bemused. He moved confidently up the steep gravelled incline—I couldn't help but wonder how some of the older residents in the village managed to get to church, especially if icy, given the gradient—and I trotted after him. I found myself a little out of breath when I finally stopped around the far side of the church. Up here the perimeter wall hugged the church on one side, and almost hidden beneath the weighted arms of an ancient cypress, was a gate in the wall. Beyond the gate was a further, enclosed burial area, but here, there were no stones celebrating and commemorating their lives. The Church decided that these poor bodies did not merit them, and unconsecrated ground was all they deserved. On the floor, behind the rusted iron gate, several foxgloves lay abandoned on the mossy floor. He could have done no more than fling them there as he strode around, and I wondered at such attention, and yet such carelessness.

When I reached the lane once more, he was talking to the same lady with the bicycle I'd seen earlier. Close up, I realised she was older than I had assumed. I'd mistaken her youth, taking into consideration her bicycle and sporty clothes.

"And here is your friend," she said. "Mr Bircham, I presume. Do you like our church?"

"This is Mrs Witherspoon," he took up the introduction. "Wife to our vicar here." He nodded towards the wooden church plaque which proclaimed the name St Michaels, with a list of the service times and ended with "the Rev. H.S.G. Witherspoon."

Mrs Witherspoon, with her shingled hair, white tennis skirt and shoes, was not my imagining of a vicar's wife. Even if you took away her clothes—although that alone is as abhorrent a thought as I can bear—and replaced them with the attire more suited to a typical woman in her position, she still wouldn't come close. In my neck of the woods, vicars' wives are clad in grey or black, their clothes reminiscent of an earlier generation. They do not bicycle, and if they travel at all, beyond the brisk walking distance of their parish, then they have an almost unused black Austin and a gardener who doubles as a chauffeur. Mrs Witherspoon's hearty handshake and wide, welcoming grin was a breath of fresh and disturbing air.

"Imposing," I said. "I was just thinking that must have been rather the point."

"You are exactly right." Her laugh belied her years and status. "But sadly even with the summoning bell, the flock is not as cowed by the church as once it was. There's hardly a stampede on a Sunday."

"Perhaps the church should learn something from this," I said. "If the Church returned to some of its more…austere practices…"

I heard him choke beside me, but I was sure of Mrs Witherspoon's reaction. She beamed at me. "Don't think I haven't suggested something of the same to Hillyard."

"The vicar," he murmured beside me.

"But he's stuck with forgiveness and charity, sorry to say. He's not even open to suggestions of the threatening sermon. Fire, brimstone, promise of eternal damnation, that kind of thing."

"Wouldn't that put more people off?" he asked.

"Oh goodness, no," she said, blushing delightfully pink. "Mr Bircham has the truth of it. You'd be amazed how many people love to be bullied. If you give them the choice of coming to church or not, well then, often they'll find something else to do, but make it an order—well…" Her eyes went a little misty. "Daddy was old school, you see. Bible thumping and roaring from the pulpit."

"Ah," I said. "I bet he played to packed houses every week."

"He'd say your soul was at risk for simply suggesting a link between the Church and the theatre." She winked at me, which I found most discomfiting. "But you know?" She lowered her voice as if her father was likely to spring from the churchyard, Bible in hand. "I don't know if you aren't just a little bit right."

"Harry's going into the law," he said.

"There you go. More theatre." Her blue eyes twinkled. She put her hand on my gallant's arm. "Mr Holland. There's been some nasty talk in the village, but if you hear it, you're to take no notice. The law's changed now, and the genie's out of the bottle. Just because a thing has been wrong, it doesn't have to remain wrong forever."

"That's an odd attitude from a vicar's wife," he said, coolly. "Do you really believe that laws can change the natural order? A woman marrying her husband's brother has been illegal for hundreds of years, Mrs Witherspoon; perhaps there was a good reason for it to be so."

"Ah, but once it was not," she countered. "Kings and queens have been marrying their brothers-in-laws and sister-in-laws for years before the law changed. There's no blood reason for it, after all. And really. Your mother has had too many years alone. Take a leaf from dear Hillyard's book, perhaps. Try to be accepting, however hard it seems. It might be better all around, I feel."

"Did you hear they'd had him declared dead?"

"I did, yes." She put her hand on his arm again. I had a shiver, watching her, because she was so intense, like Clytemnestra, or whoever the sibyl was in Troy. You know, the one prophesying doom whom everyone ignored, the idiots. "The law gives us time to deal with the loss." She went upright and brisk and missed the flash of anger in his eyes, even if I didn't. "Well, I must be off," she said. "There's always more to do than time there is to do it in, don't you find? So nice to meet you, Mr Bircham." She stepped onto her bicycle and pedalled off, straight and spry, once more seeming like a much younger woman.

"Phew," I said in mock exhaustion. "Is she always like that?"

"That was mild," he said, moving forward again. "Sometimes she's got a personality to bend an iron bar."

"A handy trait. She strikes me as the type who chained herself to railings. So that skill might have come in useful."

To my relief, he did smile a little at that. "Oh yes, she votes, too. Because she can, and to the eternal shame of the entire village. She makes rather a thing of it."

"I can imagine." We walked toward the pub, an ivy-covered building set slightly off the main street, and I let him go first into the dark, wooden barroom. It was cool in there; the ivy was overgrown at the windows, giving the inside a muted, shadowed look, with a tinge of green. It felt a little like being underwater. "Who were the flowers for?" I said, as we paused at the door, letting our eyes adjust to the dark.

"Not now," he muttered. A man appeared from behind a green baize door at the back, and seeing us paused by the entrance, he nodded, and when he spoke it was with the slow country drawl that I presumed was the local accent. Not one I'd heard yet, and I'd only just realised it.

"Mr Holland, good to see you, sir." The 'you' was a drawn out version of 'yew' or perhaps 'ewe', and his 'sir' sounded like 'zorr', but I am not going to embarrass myself further by attempting to recreate what is a quite beautiful way of speaking. "You'll have a pint of best, and your friend too."

"I would—" I began but he adroitly stepped on my foot.

"That would be perfect, Coneybear." He pressed down hard with his foot, choking off my incipient giggle. "Thank you."

"You be down for the wedding?"

I found myself holding my breath, wondering what he would say, but he just took the pint glasses and nodded. "That's right."

"That'll be a shilling," the barman said. "I'll be in the cellar. You helps yourself if you needs anything else. Leave the money on the counter." He disappeared and we found ourselves a table in the deserted pub.

"No one usually comes in for an hour," he said. "Drink up. It'll put hairs on your chest."

"That," I said with as much dignity as I could muster, "is something I've been hoping to avoid." The dark brown stuff was surprisingly tasty: nutty with a tang of something sharp, and just cool enough to refresh the palate.

I found him smiling at me. "See? I'm always right."

"Don't I know it. Now, tell me. Flowers. I know you, you sought privacy for a reason."

He took a long draught of the beer and continued staring down at the glass. "Something I'd been meaning to tell you for years, I suppose. I had it all planned how and when I was going to tell you. All theatrical, me kneeling at an unmarked grave; you standing behind me so I couldn't see your face."

"In the rain, too, I would imagine. So, it was a friend, then."

"Yes."

"Ah. That kind of friend."

"Yes. The first one."

"Oh. Oh!"

I could see he was struggling, and I let him work it out. His big dramatic moment was gone, and I wondered why he'd not gone through with it. Perhaps the sun spoiled the moment for him; theatrics are always better with dark, malignant skies, I feel. Finally, he said, "Ian. His name was Ian." He looked up at me. "Don't go getting any ideas, Harry. It wasn't a great love affair that I never told you about, it was rather the opposite, in fact. It was—rather sordid, and put me off the whole idea for quite a while."

I said nothing, at first, but wheels clicked into place, and events that had happened, when I was trying to move our friendship on when it was clear that he liked kissing me but was reluctant to go further than that, made a little more sense.

When he was silent for a while, I said, as quietly as I could. "Did he live here?" This level of confidence was unprecedented, and even now I knew if I pushed him too far he'd startle like a hidden fawn, dash off, and I'd never hear the story I'd be waiting for years to hear, or even have it admitted that he'd begun it. The very fact that he'd felt it safe to discuss here, meant it was.

"No. Well, yes. He was from Newcastle originally. He had the most divine voice—I'd never heard anyone talk like it before, it was like singing. His singing voice was even better. He was a verger here, worked under Witherspoon who was, of course, dear man, entirely clueless as to what he was harbouring in his bosom."

"And the rather sharper Mrs Witherspoon?" I was a little concerned now, given the situation this Ian had been in. I had a feeling that there wasn't much that passed unnoticed under Mrs Witherspoon's bright blue eyes.

"No...no. I don't think. No, I'm sure of it. Her attitude toward me has never wavered in the slightest. And I don't really look...and Ian didn't."

"It's all right," I said, "you won't offend me."

He flashed me a quick, dazzling smile, the brightest he'd shown since the bombshell of the night before. "Harry. Dear Harry. Anyway. As you well know, I knew what I was, and apparently so did he, and to cut a long dull story of walks and hopes short he pounced on me in the vestry. And that really should have been that, but he got all serious and desperate about it. He started writing, and he was so bloody intense I had to write back just to stop him doing something even more stupid."

"Oh, Lord. Those letters you had. In our last year at Druitt's."

"I know you thought they were love letters, and I couldn't admit to what they really were. They were everything but love letters. He wanted us to confess."

The thought of him at confessional was enough to make me raise both eyebrows, something I rarely do, to preserve my forehead from unsightly wrinkling. "Really?"

He glared at me, obviously mildly offended that his big build up wasn't exactly driving me to sackcloth and ashes. "You immediately see the funny side, don't you?"

"It's hard not to. You in confession? It's a very funny image. Where would you start? God!" I began to giggle. "Where would you *stop*?"

He went on as if I hadn't spoken. "And not just to God, either. To Witherspoon, to begin with. To my parents, to the bloody police for God's sake. He got madder and madder, even came up to the school and met me outside the grounds. He wouldn't take no for an answer. He wouldn't be reasoned with. We'd sinned in every way possible, he said. The guilt was not to be borne. We needed absolution, punishment, treatment." His voice had dropped almost to a whisper, and he'd gone quite pale at the memory of it. "Can you imagine it? Can you imagine what they'd have done? After last time?"

The levity fell away from me, and I shook my head, not because of the fact that I couldn't imagine the scandal and the devastation it would cause to the family and community, but because I was angry at Ian and his utter incompetent idiocy. "He must have been mad."

"And that's the worst of it, isn't it?" He scalded me with his bitterness

"I didn't mean it like that. Listen, you did burn those letters—what the hell happened to your replies?"

"Of course I did. Your infernal nosiness would have prompted that, if nothing else. I was perfectly circumspect in my letters to him, believe me. If he'd kept them, which I doubt, there's nothing incriminating in them."

"Then what did you say to him?"

"Just that we must talk when I came home, and he was to wait until I did. But you see, he didn't. After he came up to school, I turned him away. I was so bloody angry, and scared in case someone saw him. He was half mad, trying to kiss me and attack me by turns." He broke off as I made a threatening noise. "Another reason I never told you. We weren't that far away, in Huntman's Copse, and there was bound to be someone other than me breaking curfew. I just wanted to get rid of him, so I said I didn't want to see him again, although I wasn't quite so…nice…about it."

I nodded, but said nothing. I could imagine. When he wanted to, he could flay the skin from your bones with his vicious tongue. He always knew just where to stick the proverbial knife, and he twisted it hard. "He just stared at me afterwards, and I knew I'd gone too far." Again, I knew exactly what he was on about. He always went too far. It was like someone else got into his head when he was like that.

"Do you want another drink?" he asked.

"Not really." I'm a terrible sissy. It doesn't seem right to be drinking and come out of a pub into the daylight.

"Good. Let's go then."

He was silent as we walked back down the high street. I wasn't surprised when he led the way back into the churchyard and up the hill, stopping at the iron gate where the foxgloves lay, wilting a little already in the warm sun, their grey-green leaves limp and uninteresting. He sat down against the perimeter wall and I sat beside him, our thighs touching just enough to bond us as I waited for the remainder of his story. Crows cawed in the elms above us, filling the warm silence until he finally spoke as if there'd been no interruption at all.

"He looked at me as if I was everything he accused me of."

"Hang on a moment," I said. "He accused you? Of what?"

"Oh, the usual claptrap. Temptation. Leading him astray. Making him act against his better nature, unleashing his baser desires."

"Oh, charming. After he'd been the one who—"

"Don't do that, Harry. Don't start. That's why I didn't tell you. I knew what you wanted, after the kissing. I…it was important for me not to have it be you."

Ouch. As I said. Knife. Right spot. Twist.

"He hanged himself."

"I assumed it was something like that." We sat for a good few minutes in the quiet churchyard staring at the poor wilting flowers. "Why is he buried here? Other than the obvious."

"No family, I gather. None that Witherspoon could find. The Parish paid for the funeral, and I heard nothing more about it, so I assumed that he hadn't left any incriminating suicide note or any half-finished letters to me."

"Thank God."

"I doubt He had much to do with it, at this point," he said dryly. "In fact the sheer lack of any note or reason for it prompted quite an investigation, damned busybodies even came in from London, but they found nothing. Well, almost nothing."

"Almost?"

"Oh, there was a nasty letter. One of these horrible anonymous things. I never saw it, and I don't know what it said. I heard it was done with letters cut out from a book, and quite vile. It gave him a reason, you see, and the suicide verdict was passed. I think the village hoped for something more, ghoulish lot."

Why? I wanted to ask him. Why, why, why? Why was it important that I wasn't his first? Instead I sat silently beside him and remembered that I was his second, and I was here with him now. I was grateful for that, although bitterly unforgiving to the first.

"Have you decided what you are going to do?"

He was silent a moment. "Will you stick by me, Harry?"

"Of course."

"Even if I tell you things that you know can't possibly be true?"

"What do you mean?"

"No, this is my turn. Will you stick by me—"

I started to feel nettled. "I just said I would, you arse."

"—Even if you think I'm wrong?"

"I said I would, and I meant it. You know me well enough, and I can see well enough you need the support, you are rather outnumbered. Of course I'll stick. You are stuck with me. I am the very burr of stickiness."

He looked away, and stared at the foxgloves for a moment. "I wonder."

"Well, I'm going to stay." I left the words drifting in the air.

"You are surprised."

"Can't deny that," I said, as quietly as if I were leaning over a bridge watching the most timid of creatures swimming, entirely unaware of the danger from above. "So, what did your mother say?"

"Mother?" He looked confused for a moment. "Oh. Well. She—she wasn't very happy."

"Really."

"I'll see her—again—when we go back."

"Do you really think she's making such a huge mistake?"

He turned on me then. "Has nothing I've ever told you about Claude Holland sunk in? Oh, what he said was true, that he'd been in competition with Father to marry Mother, and it has never been any surprise to me that he lost. But a real man would have just done the decent thing, gone away, and played at being the proper uncle. Sending cards and presents at suitable intervals. He never did that. He didn't mention that did he? He told the truth that Father had written to him, wrote to him constantly, all those years. But the bastard never wrote back. Not once. It was if by his silence, he was striking back at Father for winning."

"But your father never stopped?"

"No." His face was dark. "The part about the letters was true. Father—well, you know—loved his letters. And he knew Claude wasn't dead. It was Father's contacts that had got him a job out there, and they continued to report on his progress. He kept trying."

"And he turned up after ten years." I knew the story well.

"And Father welcomed him back as if nothing had ever been wrong between them."

He stood, and walked slowly back down the hill and I trailed after him, as always. Before his uncle's return, I'd not heard that much about Claude Holland. But when he did return, in the middle of 1910, that changed. The antipathy towards a long-lost uncle from a boy as young as he had been was probably unsurprising; and I'm sure his family thought he would get over it.

But then they didn't really know him as well as I did. There are crocodiles in the Nile who give things up easier than he does.

Chapter Four

"Mr Bircham?" The voice jolted me not a little. I think there are some places where a man should be able to be alone and prognosticate in private, and coming out of the lavatory is definitely one of those times. To be accosted, almost pounced upon, while the water is still damp on one's hands because it is one of the few times when holding one's treasured possession in one's hand for longer than a fleeting moment is allowed and encouraged and causes no earthly offence to anyone. Unsolicited pouncing should not be allowed, that's all I'm saying.

Dear Uncle Claude paced down the hall towards me, looking for all the world like a large, friendly owl with his ludicrously waved hair (I hope I have as much when I'm his age, I have to say) and a pair of half-lens glasses perched on his nose. I was quite sure he had staged this meeting—even down to the glasses and the book he carried. Did he really think I believed that people wandered around houses, lonely as clouds, with books in their hands? In this house, with its Ming and Spode on every surface, it would seem unlikely. There would be a lot less Ming and Spode around, and these things aren't infinite, you know.

The whole stagey effect unnerved me. If it had been Mrs Holland drifting around, her arms laden with peonies, I would have been more impressed, but Uncle Claude seemed far too prosaic. I could imagine him reading, even with those ridiculous glasses, but I had a vision of him behind one of those desks that Bob Cratchit was all but chained to, poring over household accounts.

"Mr Holland." I wanted to prove I wasn't unobservant. I resisted the natural impulse to rub my palms down the outside of my flannels, as that would indicate that I had not washed my hands.

"I wonder if I might have a word." He took off his glasses and slipped them into a pocket. He laid the book aside with such indifference that my suspicions of him being a big fat phony were pretty much proven. If you are so addicted to a book that you cannot put it down for the time it takes you to walk from one room to another, you hardly discard it at the first available conversation.

I resisted the theorisation as to whether he could, indeed, have a word, or if words could be had, bit my tongue and decidedly did not launch into the silly word play and the sort of rot myself and the divine Master Holland indulged in with ridiculous ease. Somehow I thought that the kindly owl might show its raptor side were I to do so. I had an Alice-like insight of how a small furry rodent might feel.

He led the way downstairs and into a rather nicely appointed library, the sort of library a man aspired to. I was jolted to awareness that he wasn't the man who had aspired to this particular library, and then I had a sudden crisis of conscience for being alone with Claude in the first place.

I knew just how well that would go down in certain circles. Calm, I said to myself. Tell him that you went along to see what the lay of the land was, a spy. Not some kind of double agent.

I took a seat on the pupil side of a very headmastery desk and crossed my legs a little ostentatiously, simply because I knew that would annoy him. The tiniest of movements in his eyes proved me right, and I scored one for the home team. "About what did you wish to have a word, Mr Holland?"

He didn't surprise me. "My nephew."

I raised an irritating eyebrow, and wondered if he could guess I'd plucked them, just a little, just enough to defer the Neanderthal one-browed look, and to give me a head start on the arch expression I so longed for. I hoped so, for I knew it would add to the list of "reasons why Mr Bircham is an excrescence."

"His mother is very upset."

I kept quiet. I was sure he had a lot more to tell me than something I could have already guessed for myself.

"I think, as his friend, you might have a steadying influence." I wondered how much that had cost him to say, for I couldn't believe that he truly thought that. Not now he'd seen me, at least. "A calming influence. It's very important to Margaret that her son approves and gives his blessing."

He paused, and I took the moment to say, "I can understand that," and was irritated when he said, "I knew you would," in what he must have considered a confiding tone. I went on: "But—and this is all I'll say about him out of his presence you understand—you did the worst possible thing by springing it on him like that. You've done a considerable amount of damage, and frankly whether it's salvageable is speculation."

"What has he said to you?" Holland asked.

"If he has discussed the matter," I said stiffly, "then I'm afraid I can't tell you one way or the other."

"Perhaps if you spoke to his mother…or asked him to speak to her?"

"They spoke this morning," I said. "It doesn't appear to have mended any bridges."

"Did they?" He frowned at me. "I didn't know that."

I brushed imaginary crumbs off the legs of my trousers before I stood, perhaps to indicate that a cup of tea and a cake or two might have been a better inducement for my betrayal. "I am sorry, Mr Holland. I know I am Mrs Holland's guest,"—you see? I can be subtle and barbed at the same time—"but I can't help you. I can tell you that he's decided to stay here, and I assume he means for the wedding itself, so perhaps that will be reassurance enough for you. Although of course that means I'll be staying here too." I gave him my most dazzling smile, which was returned with one with as much sincerity as I expected. "Please excuse me, won't you?"

I don't suppose I did myself any favours, but you see, I love him. No, of course not Claude; his nephew, obviously. I've never told him that in as many words, and he's certainly never said anything to me about it, but I live in hope.

There was no way I'd discuss anything of his private thoughts with the man he'd considered to be tantamount to an enemy for years. Claude Holland mattered to me not one jot. Whereas the divine Master Holland…

Sometimes I allowed myself to look into the future, after he'd inherited the capital of his father's legacy—currently held in trust—and we were both men of independent means. I'd have a flat somewhere in London; Chelsea perhaps, or Little Venice. It would need to be near the water, anyway. Two bedrooms of course, so no one (those who didn't know us as well as some, at least) would think anything impure of us. And he'd be there, every morning, over the boiled eggs. Rumpled in striped flannel pyjamas, his hair sticking up, dipping his soldiers salaciously into his soft-boiled and leaving heat rings and water marks and crumbs on my polished table. Call me an old romantic if you will, but it is images such as that which keep me hopeful. Don't get me wrong; he has a body to which I am drawn like the most helpless of iron filings to a powerful magnet. It's nothing special in the Olympic swimmer line, no hard, sculptured muscles, and certainly no one would compare him to anything carved out of

Italianate marble, but his body fits mine. And mine fits his. Whether we are standing up, lying down, squashed in a cupboard (again, don't ask), we fit (I could say slot, but the crudity of that image prevents me) together like two neighbouring pieces of a quality wooden jigsaw. It's nothing to do with sex.

Oh, well, all right, it's not *everything* to do with sex. It's about comfort in each other's company, and the ability to lie (or sit, sometimes even apart) in silence. And when we do move into each other's arms, it's about that surety of knowing that he's the other part of me, and that everything he does completes me in a way I could never put into words. Yes, I know. But that's how it seems with him. Does he feel like that? All I can hope is that he feels a fraction of it, because that would be enough for anyone. So here I go, travelling hopefully towards a rumpled vision in striped pyjamas. I could have worse ambitions.

I didn't see him again until lunch. He wasn't in our rooms, and I had made a pact with myself that I wasn't to go hunting for him in his own house every time I was alone; that smacked of far too much desperation. I was capable of amusing myself. I had books, and the library here I am sure would supply much in the way of education and entertainment; there were other people to spend time with if need be, and he was going to need some time to come to terms with events. If he needed me, he'd let me know. I settled myself in the morning room and was unbothered by anyone.

Neither Mrs Holland nor Dear Uncle Claude were present at lunch. However, the others were, and when I asked, Miss Holland told me they'd gone to Exeter and wouldn't be back until the next day. There was a discernible lightening of mood after this fact had been divulged. Whether it was that we were all aware the tension between mother, son and prospective stepfather had a reprieve, or whether it was the delightful champagne, chilled to perfection and dancing on the palate, that we had with the strawberries, I couldn't say.

I talked rather a lot, I'm ashamed to relate. It was for a good cause, I felt. I was the safe option, and I could talk about my background and experiences without lifting any stones which shouldn't be lifted. He knew most of my stories anyway, and it allowed him to chip in as he wanted, and by the time the coffee was taken away we were all terribly jolly.

"Do you play tennis at all, Mr Bircham?" Stevie asked. She—and her brother—had thawed during the meal, and if we weren't absolutely bosom friends, I felt we could all go out dancing without much bloodshed.

There was a snort from beside me, which I ignored. "I can generally hit the ball back across the net. But more than that, I can't promise."

"Stevie and Lawrence are good," he said, leaning towards me. "Very good. If they take us on we won't have a ghost of a chance. I don't think your ego could take that level of humiliation again. Harry once played the school champion entirely by accident. It was a bloodbath."

"Why on earth did you do that?" Miss Holland asked.

"It wasn't my choice, I can assure you," I said. "We had to sign up for something, and I was pretty sure I'd be knocked out in the first round and could sit around on the sidelines cheering whatever young idiot who moved through the tournament. It happened that the young idiot was me."

"In the first round he got Anderson, who's a complete duffer. A glasswristed oik who hardly knows one end of a racquet from the other, and couldn't hold onto it when hitting a backhand. Anyone could have beaten him," young Holland said helpfully.

"He's right, alas," I confirmed. "All I really needed to do was just get the damned ball over the net and I was assured of victory. The gods of tennis are probably still cringing. Then I had a bye in the second round—and there I was in the quarter finals. No problems, I thought, there's no way I'll get into the semis. By that point there's only the mean and the violent left in. I expected to leave the field bruised but with my honour intact."

"Instead of which," he chipped in again, laughing almost too hard to be understood, "Fraser Minor, who normally would have made mincemeat of Harry and left him gasping in the dust, had been out over the wall the night before and had the worst case of the...and I apologise for the reference, Miss Holland, Stevie, so soon after eating...collywobbles...on record that term—"

"—Thank you," I said. "I'm quite capable of describing my victories. Fraser was, to my entire horror, completely useless. I realised quite early on that if I didn't do something radical I was going to win, and seeing as how that meant the semis." Most people were smiling around the table by this point. "And believe me, I tried. One can't obviously throw a match, unfortunately, I had to keep up some kind of appearance, but if I'd been more feeble than Fraser—"

"—Particularly after the professional performance against Anderson of the glass wrist—"

I glared at him. "And my heroic performance in the bye. Well, as you have already ascertained, I won, much to my disgust and the general hilarity of just about everyone I knew. My mother was embarrassingly proud and even came up to school for the semi-final."

Stevie, to give her her due, wasn't laughing with tears streaming out of her eyes as was someone I could mention, but she obviously found my incompetence endearing and amusing. She smiled encouragingly at me. "Please, do go on, Mr Bircham."

"I think that once I've bared my soul like this for the amusement of all, you'll have to call me Harry. I can only cling to the shreds of dignity I have and know that when you meet Gilbert and Richardson you'll realize there are far worse horrors. Well, it's a short, sorry tale. The school were out in force. Most of them, sad to say, were supporting me. Word had got around, and I can't imagine where the false reports had come from"—I glanced at him who looked back at me with such wide-eyed innocence that only I would disbelieve him—"that I was a ringer, and that I'd simply been pretending to be rubbish to get the gamblers involved."

"Gambling, Harry?" Stevie pretended to look shocked.

"Oh, if the Old Man had found out there'd have been hell to pay, in fact there was, but that's another story. So there we were. The entire school, many parents and my mother all perched along the sidelines for what they assumed would be the greatest semi-final shock of the decade. And of course it was all a huge disappointment—"

"—for everyone except Harry and me."

"—Precisely. Twelve very very short games later."

"You lost every game?" Lawrence's scorn was obvious.

"Well yes, I hardly think I need to labour the point."

"Not that he won any," said my gallant with a jubilant tone.

"Yes, thank you. Anyway, in no time at all I was back where I belonged, in obscurity. However, my claim to fame, however fleeting, is that I faced Edmund Lakey—for fifteen minutes at least, anyway."

"Oh." I nearly jumped ten feet in the air as Lawrence came alive. "I know of him. He played at Wimbledon, didn't he?"

"He did. His glory makes me feel a little better."

"Were you there this year?" Stevie asked.

I shook my head.

"Tilden was magnificent." A gleam of hero worship came to her eyes. "He's rather topping, all legs and tan."

"I haven't seen him play," I said, "but I've seen the newspaper pictures, so I can't fault your taste." I was rewarded for my comment by a dark, scathing glance from Lawrence who made it more than clear what he thought about men admiring other men. I found it interesting that he followed up his dark look to me with an equally black one at Charles, who returned it with one of the most delightful of his smiles. I'm pleased to say that Miss Holland was at that moment rummaging in her handbag and had missed all the glowering and displays of manliness.

"I have a signed photograph," she said with a wide smile. "It was from Wimbledon two years ago. He didn't win then, of course, but he was terribly approachable." She passed the picture around, a shot I'd seen reproduced in the newspaper—which I assume is where Miss Holland purchased it. Tilden returning a shot with almost a bored expression, his hair rigidly in place and not a glimmer of masculine sweat anywhere upon his person, for all the sun shining down upon him. Perhaps American men were more used to the hot weather, and did not perspire as much. I wouldn't know, as I've not had the pleasure to know any American men on that level of intimacy. English men do not have this skill, let me tell you. Or at least the number—oh no, I'm not telling you how many—of men who I have become hot and sweaty with showed no talent in the keeping fresh department. Bill Tilden, it has to be said, looked as if he'd never produced one drop of sweat in his life. If I had been in a position to try—and were he of my persuasion (unlikely)—it would have been rather a delightful challenge.

The picture was duly handed around and appreciated by all at the table apart from Lawrence, who was in some danger of being tagged Stormcloud or some such nickname. Lawrence simply passed the photograph on without looking at it, his face in its usual scowl of disapproval. Someone should take the boy aside and explain that wrinkles are not at all attractive.

Stevie then turned to me with a smile and said "And so we are back at my original question, Mr Bircham. We have established that you can at least return a ball. So would you care for a game after lunch?"

"After all you've heard?"

"Well, perhaps it would be better if we split the teams. Perhaps yourself and I against Lawrence—"

Lawrence cut in, "I bags Bircham, if we are picking teams."

"For God's sake, Lawrence," his sister said. "There's no need to be so bloody schoolboy about it."

"When you and I play," he replied, "we are competitive. I don't see why things should be any different."

"Because Mr Bircham is a guest, Lawrence," young Holland cut in. I recognized his tone as being particularly vicious. "But you are excused. I don't expect you to appreciate the niceties that that involves."

Luckily no one threw anything. I had to remind myself that these people knew each other well, and they were used to him. Stevie laughed and was the first to raise herself from the table. "Come on, let's go and change before it decides it's going to rain on us or something. It's one thing playing tennis, but if it looks like I'm going to be forced to spend an afternoon with you three cavemen playing sardines I shall lock myself in my room until Margaret returns."

"Christ," I said to Holland as we trotted up the stairs to get changed. "Competitive tennis? I thought you said we were going to have an easy time of it."

"I know. I'm sorry, but it will shorten a dull afternoon. If Richardson and Gilbert come—"

"God willing," I murmured. The more people around, the more time we might be able to have alone together.

"—it will help," he said, echoing what I'd thought. "Perhaps it's about time I got a car."

"Oo," I said, easily distracted. "What colour?"

Chapter Five

The tennis was torture. Or purgatory. Whichever you'd consider the more unpleasant. I think I have established my own ineptitude at the game and although I am pretty good at being self-effacing and terribly modest and British I was not exaggerating. Our team lost quite resoundingly, and I was more than happy to leave it at one set, rather than going for best of three. I found Lawrence to be the most annoying of partners.

Having convinced himself that I was going to be hopeless, he proceeded to play the game almost entirely himself, throwing himself around the court like a man possessed and leaving me nothing to do. I noted that the other team's partnership was a lot more equable, and it was no wonder that we lost.

What interested me more and more was Lawrence's behaviour to Stevie and her partner. More particularly when they seemed united in their success. I noticed that every time Stevie received some praise from her partner for a good shot: "Well placed, partner," he'd say, or "That's the stuff to give 'em."

Lawrence would—and I would not have believed it possible—glower even more than his normal glower. I couldn't hear him but, from the look on his face at times, you'd think that he was grinding his teeth. I wish I'd known if he was. One reads about these things, but I've never actually seen or heard someone actually doing it. It's so deliciously melodramatic. Now I come to think of it, I could see Lawrence cast in the role of those wonderful screen villains. His eyes painted up with black stuff to make him look devilish, lashing young Master Holland to the railway tracks and twirling an elaborate moustache while laughing demoniacally. He was certainly better looking than any of the stock villains they generally cast in the roles. It annoyed me that screen villains had to be unattractive, and that only the hero was allowed to be handsome. One thing is certain though, Lawrence would look marvelous in moving pictures. Perhaps I'll get on his good side and tell him how good he'd look with a twirlable moustache. I have a suspicion that young Lawrence has more than a nodding acquaintance with his mirror and is quite aware of how handsome he is.

For years I'd heard Claude Holland being cast in the role of the Wicked Uncle, but never once had Lawrence even been mentioned. It intrigued me, and I was determined to find out why.

After the tennis, I flopped on the burned and crispy grass, refusing to be consoled by words or platitudes. "I warned you," I said. "I would say that we should swap partners next time, but I doubt I could stand the shame."

"Have some lemonade, and shut up," he said. "They've gone in, so your self-pity is entirely wasted on me."

"I dare say they couldn't keep the laughter in any longer." I accepted the glass with a deliberately shaky hand. "Look, I'm a wreck."

"You're an idiot." I paused for a moment or two, to give him the time to say anything, to save me having to ask him, but he said nothing. He gazed out across the lawn towards the woods, seemingly lost in some thoughts that I had no way of guessing.

"You've never mentioned them," I said at last.

"What?" He hardly seemed to hear me.

"Stevie. And Lawrence."

"Oh, don't talk bilge, of course I have."

I let a deliberate silence build up between us, to give the impression that I was checking his statement in my head, although this was not at all necessary. "No. You haven't. I have a fair idea of your strange and truncated family tree in my mind, and I can't see them in it."

"That's because they aren't, you arse." He threw a tennis ball at my head. It missed me and went bouncing off across the lawn only to halt on an oddly bare patch, the earth disturbed as if someone had interred a favourite rabbit, you know, a dead one. I'm not suggesting the Hollands went around burying live rabbits for fun. "They aren't family. We just—oh come on, I know I told you the story where we played pirates when I was twelve and they marooned me, and I was in bed for a week in the summer holidays?"

"But you told me that those were servants' childr—oh."

"Exactly." He threw another tennis ball at me, overarm and hard which hit me on the arm. "They are Stephens' children." When I still looked blank, he added, "Yes, our butler. Oh, don't look like an utter snob, Harry. We all grew up together. Mrs Stephens was a friend of Mother's. Married terribly beneath her and they came to live—and to work here. She died years ago, not exactly sure when. Stephens was planning to emigrate somewhere or other and Mother persuaded him to stay. The twins were schooled with me until I was sent off, and they've always been treated like the family."

"Isn't it odd for them, or for Stephens?"

"Never thought about it." He collapsed on the grass beside me. "Shouldn't think so. Should it be?"

"Well, yes, of course it would be, for some people." I gave up. Some concepts were beyond him. "So our Stevie is a Stevie Stephens?"

He groaned and rolled onto his back, chewing a long piece of grass. "Anyway, why the sudden interest?" He gave me a sharp look. "Don't tell me that Lawrence has caught your eye. He's not—"

"I'm not entirely dim." I tried not to notice that he still hadn't told me her name. "That's pretty obvious, and part of the reason, I am assuming, why he throws you such dark looks. What happened there?" The mood was so easy between us that I spoke without really thinking. "Did you touch his person during a rough game of sardines?"

As he rolled over and pushed himself to his feet, I regretted the words and cursed myself.

"You can be too crude sometimes, Harry." He marched off across the lawn and I knew better than to follow him. All I could do was watch him go, as I'd done too many times before.

"Done his stalking act, has he?"

I twisted round at the sound to find Stevie standing behind me. She'd changed out of her tennis clothes and looked quite fresh and much more fashionable than any butler's daughter had the right to look. I'm not an expert in ladies' hats but the large straw number with yellow and cream carnations around the brim that she sported today suited her admirably, even if it did slightly make her resemble a rather decorative mushroom. "He's rather good at that. Entrances and exits, I mean."

"Isn't he just?" I dragged myself to a sitting position, and leant against the empty chair. "Are we having tea out here?"

"Yes. In a while." She sat on one of the wicker chairs, and the fabric of her dressed billowed around her, coming to rest a full half hour after she did.

"It's very good to meet you at last, Mr Bircham."

"Haven't we already done that part? And I think after my performance today you should really call me Harry. I may have to insist."

She smiled, causing dimples to appear. I blinked in surprise, I had thought ladies had done away with such things when they threw away the whalebone and cut their hair. "Harry, then. It's odd to know about someone for years and years and yet never to meet them. He talks—or he did when he came home more regularly—of you more often than anything else. I dare say I can recount many of your adventures that you didn't regale us with at lunch."

"Adventures is probably pushing it. Don't believe everything he tells you," I said, with a vague attempt at modesty.

"Oh, I don't," she said. "He's never been terribly truthful, has he?"

I was rather stumped for what to say after that. I could hardly say, "I've heard next to nothing about you," or anything along that line, and to follow her last remark would be going into a conversation I'd rather not have. "He tells me you are twins." It was an inane remark, and I'm rarely lost for words, but there was something unsettling about her shrewd inspection of me, the way her dark brown eyes—eager and piercing like some inquisitive mouse—peered at me from under that huge hat.

"He's right." There was a suggestion of a laugh behind her words. "He's clever like that. Why has he stalked off, may I ask?"

I waved a hand to express everything or nothing. "Oh, you know. Something I did or said."

"Yes, it's generally something one does or says." She looked across the lawn in the direction he'd taken, although he was nowhere to be seen. "Why has it taken him so long to bring you here, do you suppose?"

Was I going to be pinned down and questioned by everyone in the house, one by one? I was more than a little nettled; however I interpreted her question, it was mildly insulting. "Perhaps he wanted to protect me from you all," I said as lightly as I could.

She gave what from a less feminine face and form might be taken as a snort. "Somehow I don't think you are in the slightest need of protection."

"Lawrence thinks the opposite."

"Ahh, perhaps you are here to protect *him*." She waved an elegant arm in the direction my dear friend had stalked.

I laughed. "I'm afraid I'd be as much a disappointment as a bodyguard as I am a tennis partner."

"I didn't say I agreed with him. However, if not a bodyguard. perhaps a distraction?"

"A distraction from what?" I asked.

"Oh, I don't know," she said. It didn't sound terribly convincing. Not that my experience of young ladies is vast—no one could ever accuse me of being any kind of womaniser—but she seemed quite knowing to me. "From whatever he finds is inconveniencing him."

I picked up some pebbles from the ground beside me and started to throw them towards the piece of bare earth. "And what would that be?"

"I'm not sure, yet. But he's a master of distraction. The question is, are you a distraction or a solver of problems?"

"If I were either," I said, aiming for a dark brown stone in the bare earth and missing it spectacularly, "then how would you know? Perhaps I'm here to stop you chasing after him into the woods."

"If you think I'd do that, Mr Bircham—"

"Harry. I would prefer to call you Stevie than Miss Stephens, after all."

"If you think I'd do that, chase him I mean, then you don't know me."

"Well, that's rather the point, isn't it?" I said. "I don't."

"No, but Charles does."

"Not that he'd said anything to me, but I rather got the feeling that… forgive me for being indelicate…the family rather hoped that you and he…"

"They did. Yes, I'm afraid that is still a bit of a sticking point. Parents can be so spectacularly dim, can't they?"

"I suppose so," I said.

"What I mean to say is that he waves you like a flag, and they see nothing but their son and heir with his good friend. You both must think you are terribly amusing, and oh so shocking. But really, you are like some kind of explosive buried in the ground."

It shook me. I'd reined myself in, I'd thought. One can be more oneself at college than one can ever be at home, both with attitude and language. I knew I was fairly outré, but so were a dozen other fellows I knew, all of whom were as red-blooded as they came and yet who rowed and scrummed and drank and chased the available and catchable women at Oxford. I suppose I thought my camouflage was pretty good. Or perhaps I was relying on the fact that people may think one thing, but actually believe another.

I opened my mouth to speak, but was instead frozen in place as her words seemed to come horribly true. The bare earth where my pebbles had been landing began to vibrate, then the very ground rumbled. My first thought was *earthquake* which was then slapped down by the more sensible part of my brain. Thank goodness I have this safety device in my head because otherwise I probably would have screamed like a nervous girl seeing a mouse. (I'm grateful for it, as this more sensible portion of my mind once saved me in a dark lane when I was drunkenly convinced that a patch of grass and a milestone was actually an angry ostrich preparing to kill me.) Although I had seen pictures, and had read descriptions of earthquakes, I was pretty sure that Somerset wasn't famous for them. However, something very odd was happening in front of me—the earth literally rose out of the lawn in a large rounded earth-covered shape, the dirt falling from around it, and from the terrible mound-shaped thing there came the most alarming noises, like an old man clearing his throat.

"Polonius," Stevie shouted, and raced past me to where this terrifying event was happening. "I thought you'd wandered off. Harry," she knelt on the lawn and began digging in the bare earth with hair hands, "run and tell my father that Polonius has buried himself again, stupid creature."

"What?"

"Just go!"

I fled. Things had become too odd for me to cope with, and I took the opportunity to get away from Stevie and her questions, grateful for whatever creature this Polonius was and the fact that he'd buried himself. I tore up the steps and into the house, relayed her message to the first maid I spotted who seemed not to be in the least perturbed by it, but simply bobbed and dashed through the green baize door, presumably to find Stephens and a spade perhaps. I was curious, but I didn't wish to be alone with Stevie until after I'd spoken with my friend alone, so I pottered about the house getting my bearings and opening doors until I had the geography straight in my head.

I found Clarissa Holland in the drawing room, writing letters at the desk. I started to apologise and close the door but she called me back. "It's all right, Mr Bircham. I've finished, just about. Do come in. Were you looking for someone?"

"No, not particularly," I said. "I was thinking about hiding under my bed, to be honest. Or at least until dinner. I've had an unsettling experience." I told her about the exploding lawn and she laughed.

"Oh dear. Yes, I can see how that would be if you hadn't been warned about it. Someone really should have said—he doesn't do it often, but when he does, he always picks his moment to surface."

"He's not some relative, is he?" I didn't think he could be, but Gothic novels sprang to mind of evil deformed creatures hidden away from the public's gaze. "Some malformed dwarf?"

Clarissa really laughed then, her wide cheeks shaking with mirth and her normal pinkness turning an alarming shade of puce. When she'd finally calmed down, she said: "You have a nasty turn of mind, Mr Bircham. No, of course he isn't. He's a tortoise. A giant tortoise."

She couldn't have said anything that was more likely to have stunned me. I wondered if I was still in the realm of the fanciful and whether grass and milestones could really turn into mad murderous ostriches. "I'm sorry," I said. "I know that certain eccentric families have the oddest pets. One man at college, his parents keep giant rodents from Peru or some such place. Disgusting creatures. But to be perfectly frank, in the main, I'd not label the Hollands as eccentrics. No offence meant, of course, I mean it to be strictly complimentary."

"I know you did. But Polonius came with the house, you see. Father bought the house from an actor. The place had quite the reputation when we first moved here. We had no idea about Polonius. I think perhaps the actor had lost him, or thought one of his guests had stolen, or eaten, him. Apparently Polonius had buried himself in the tennis court over the winter and the first spring we were here he came out of the ground like Beelzebub, nearly causing the groundsman to have a seizure. Father knew nothing about tortoises, so just let him get on with it, and he's been here ever since. He had his name painted on his shell. We thought that was rather unkind, so we let it wear off, and never replaced it."

I was still rather stunned from the exploding lawn. "That was my favourite play for many years. To be perfectly honest, when it comes to Shakespeare's Polonius, I have to say that I always considered that he got what he deserved. They say that eavesdroppers hear no good of themselves, and he was such a pompous ass." I giggled for a moment, the shock I daresay; I am not normally a giggler, truly. "Perhaps Polonius the Tortoise was emulating his namesake and hoping to catch Stevie and I in scandalous conversation."

"Just as well for him," Miss Holland replied, joining in with my infectious giggling, "that you were not armed."

We were still laughing when the door opened and Stephens entered. "Mr Bircham?"

"Yes?" The laughter left my lungs as if entirely sucked out. There was something about his face; it seemed the same as it ever had, but I'd seen that edge of almost invisible tension before, on the faces of other people. People sent to fetch me for a particular reason.

"I wonder if you might come out here for a moment?"

"There's nothing wrong, Stephens?" Miss Holland asked.

"Nothing to worry about, madam."

I stood. If Miss Holland hadn't noticed the deliberate evasion in Stephens' answer, I damned well had. "Lead on, Stephens. Thanks, Miss Holland."

"Ta ta, dear boy." She had already turned back to her correspondence.

"Where is he?" I said quietly to Stephens as soon as the door closed.

"I helped Master Holland to his room, sir."

I gave the man a curt nod of thanks and walked swiftly to the stairs. Then, there being no one around, I flew up them as quietly as I could and raced for our rooms. He was sitting—a good sign in itself—on the end of the bed, and he turned a pale, befuddled face towards me.

"How the hell did you get so plastered so fast?" He'd been gone about an hour, possibly less.

"He had a bottle of whisky," Holland said, reaching for me.

I sidestepped him. "You aren't half as bad as I thought you'd be. I—"

"You were thinking that you'd have to cover up again."

"Look, it's…. Wait a minute. Who he? Who had a bottle of whisky?"

Holland threw himself down on the bed and rolled over, propping himself up on his elbows and pretending minutely observe the pattern on the counterpane. "I suppose I'll have to tell someone, or I'll think I am going mad," his voice was almost too low to catch. "I want you to remember your promise to me, though, and not to start being all…Lawrence or something."

I stood by the desk and said nothing.

"It was my father," he said, without looking up. "And I swear if you say anything stupid now, I'll walk out of here and go to…Timbuktu or something."

I made sure that my face betrayed no emotion, and hoped he didn't see my hand, the one gripping the back of the chair, tighten around it until my fingers hurt and cramped. "Go on. When…where?

His face, which had been tense, looking up at me with an expression of something akin to fear, burst into a sunny smile as the tension flew from him like birds soaring from a newly opened basket. "You are the one person I know who wouldn't doubt me," he said breathlessly. He jumped up and grabbed me by my upper arms. "The first day, I saw someone in the distance, too far off to see his face, but there as…something…something. I felt he wasn't just a lost walker or a gardener."

"What was it?"

"I don't know, not really." He squeezed my arms and then threw himself back down on the bed, a broad smile on his face. "It could have been the way he was walking—you know how you can recognise someone even from the other side of the grounds. I can always tell when it's you, long before I see your face."

"Yes." I kept it as non-committal as I could. I had my reasons. I wasn't going to start skipping around the room in celebration. "Yes, of course. Same here."

"Well, it could have been that. It could, couldn't it? Oh I know—you're going to say that I couldn't know how he walks after all this time—and that's why I didn't say anything to anyone. I was sure I could. But I'd thought that before, and so I started to doubt myself. You know why."

I did. It was something that no one else knew at college, except possibly the Dean. After his father was reported missing, my brittle, beautiful friend snapped rather than bent under the news and he started telling people—that is, me, and his family—that his father was not dead. That he'd seen him. At first from a distance, and then glimpses of him wherever he went. He never spoke to him, but he was everywhere. We'd be walking in the town outside the school, for example, and he'd dash forward through the crowds without a word and I'd know without any doubt what he thought he'd seen, but every single time when he caught up to the man he was pursuing, it always turned out to be another man in uniform, or a man of the same height and colouring. This state of affairs was not allowed to continue, of course. He became more agitated the more time went on, angry that he felt his father was hiding from him, angry with me for obviously not believing what he'd seen, and angrier still with his family who insisted that his father was dead and that he should come to terms with it. I surmise—although I never really found out—that Druitt's had written to his family and matters escalated from there.

His mother (spurred on, he was more than convinced, by his uncle) was so frightened that her only son was suffering from some psychosis that he spent four weeks in a suitably discreet and expensive nursing home. It was put about at school that he had scarlet fever and I'd had the only correspondence from Mrs Holland I ever received, begging me for my silence. "For his sake." As if she needed to ask.

When he returned to school he was quiet and withdrawn, and that's when he became a little difficult to deal with. Certain subjects were taboo, and he'd fly into the most fearful temper if rules were breached. The trouble was, it was like playing a game where only Holland knew the rules—and until I learned them, and which subjects I had to keep away from, we had—to put it mildly—a pretty rocky time of it.

But we did come through it, and I think that our friendship was more solid because of it. He lets me rattle on, for the most part, and I stay away from topics that might trigger a problem, that is, unless he raises it first. He seemed to guess my thoughts, as he so often did. "It's all right, Harry. Really. I'm not going to start throwing things." He turned his head on the pillow and his fringe fell over one eye. "I can tell the difference now, you see?"

"The difference?"

"Back then, when I thought I saw him. That was just—oh, there's probably some fancy word for it. I was furious at everyone, I can still remember how I wanted to lash out at the world. I wanted proof, and until I had proof I couldn't see why the man in the street couldn't be him."

"I know." I sat on the desk chair. As much as I wanted to fall onto the bed and share in his happiness, I couldn't. There was an icy pit in my stomach that was scaring the hell out of me. "Go on."

"I even thought I'd seen him when we got off the train, and I got really rattled. All I could think was that the family were going to shove me away—in that place—or worse, and I'd never get out, not after what I'd said to Claude."

"Oh, come on."

"No," he said, and he was as calm as I'd ever seen him. "I'm serious. They couldn't wait to put me away last time, and there's no good trying to convince me that Mother wouldn't do it. I don't call her Medea for nothing."

"She adores you."

"Yes, it does come off that way, doesn't it? But I'm not what she wanted, we both know that. She's young enough to have his kids, you know. Father didn't leave the house to me."

I hadn't even considered that, and my jaw clamped tightly shut. "There was this man, at the end of the platform, as if he'd just got off the train with us—didn't you see him?"

"No," I said. "I'm sorry, I wish I had. Why the hell didn't you point him out? Wouldn't all this be a lot easier if you had?"

"God, Harry, you know why. All those looks you gave me—yes, you did— back then when I know damned well you didn't believe me but tried to be a good friend anyway. I didn't want to see that expression in your face ever again. Not ever, don't you understand? So I didn't say anything, and it took me by surprise, then I saw someone, as I said, someone in the grounds. So I went off."

"You told me you were going to speak to your mother."

"Did I? Oh. Perhaps I did. Well, I could hardly say what I was really planning, could I? And there he was. Walking near the gazebo as if he'd never gone away." He looked at me with his most penetrative look. "Oh God, Harry. You believe me."

"Of course I do, you arse. Didn't I say I would? Either you are telling the truth, or you've turned into a fruitcake. Personally, I can deal with anything." I was only partly telling him the truth, but he didn't need to know that. "Jesus. Although my father is very firmly in the ground, if he wasn't, I don't know how I'd cope with seeing him sitting in a gazebo like some demented Wilkie Collins character." God, wasn't that the truth. It was all a bit too Oedipal, although I really don't have any repressed feelings about my mother. If I were to see the shade of my father pointing at me, I'd go off my rocker, I'm sure. I shrugged the thought away. "What the hell did you say to him?"

"It was weird, in a hair raised on the back of the neck weird, because I'd been expecting to see him all my life, hoping against hope, and then—there he was."

"Pretty nifty timing on his part."

He refused to bite. "The worst timing. I know! We had no time to really talk. He did all the talking, really. He said that he knew I must have a hundred—more like a thousand!—questions but it would all have to wait."

"For what?"

"Until he can tell Mother he's here, I suppose. He said he couldn't show himself to her, not yet. Understandable."

"And his brother?"

"Oh, he's *particularly* angry with Claude," he said with glee.

"Where the hell's he been?"

"Harry—I didn't get a chance to ask everything I wanted. He's different. He used to be so talkative, so full of...life, I suppose. But he's changed. If I hadn't have recognised him, I'd not have know him, strange as that sounds. He's like a different man."

"And he didn't say where he'd been, what happened to him?"

"No. I tried to ask him but it was if I hadn't even spoken, as if he'd been rehearsing what he was going to say to me, and wouldn't be stopped. It was monologue, mainly of reassurance. To stop me being frightened out of my wits, I suppose. He must have thought I'd have thought he was a ghost or something. I didn't get the chance to tell him that I'd known, just known all this time that he wasn't dead."

"Oh, God," I muttered. This powder keg of a family reunion was going to explode into a million pieces of devastating shrapnel. I wanted to put my arms around Holland and pull him away with me. I didn't want him to vanish, not into his mother's schemes or this…man—his father's. I realised what a bloody lobster pot we'd walked into. We could neither of us leave now.

"What? No, Harry, that's good news, don't you see?"

"I do." I rubbed at my forehead "No, actually I don't." I got up slowly, went over to the bed and sat down next to him. "Take it slowly, and tell me everything he said."

I loved him, and I wanted to believe him. But I was having trouble taking him on faith, without having seen the senior Holland for myself. I don't know if I was more concerned that I couldn't believe my Holland, or whether he would discover that fact.

Faith is hard, and I have much respect for those who have it, and can stick to it without proof, without validation and throughout adversity. I wish I could be that way, I do. I watched my mother believe and I listened to her tell me of her conversations with God. When I was young, with eyes wide open to the world, I assumed that God would be along for me, just as soon as I was a little older and could understand it was Him, and not just some imaginary friend. But he never spoke to me, and I admit feeling rather put out.

I suppose the most I can say is that if I believed anything, I could believe in the fact that he thought he had seen his father, in the same way I believed that my mother heard the Lord. That's as much as I could do. But I know which one was easier to admit to. I was going to have to wait until I could stick my fingers into the nail holes, if you get my meaning.

It started out to be a quiet evening, and very nicely relaxed after dinner.

We all sprawled, in varying degrees, around the drawing room, either reading books and listening to Brahms on a Victrola. He was pent up, in that odd excited way he had; sitting almost sideways in an armchair, his legs kicking against the wood in a manner I'm sure his mother would have reproved him for. Every time I caught his eye he'd grin, and I knew he was being oh-so conspiratorial, hugging to himself the fact that he was holding this immense secret and wondering when he'd let it loose on the world. As I looked away, Stevie caught my eye and she looked away again without smiling. '*You're like an explosive buried in the ground.*' She didn't know how right she was—and it made no difference whether Charles Holland was alive or not, sooner or later the charge was going to explode, for the fuses were already lit.

Chapter Six

He was up and dressed and gone before I was even awake the next morning. The evening before, he'd kissed me at our connecting door, shook his head, then kissed me again, and I muttered something to flatter him, something about kicking me from his lintel, and I heard him laugh even as he closed the door on me and my needs. It took me a while to go to sleep, while I worried about him and why he hadn't at least invited me in for a few moments.

The idiotic boy had left a sweet pea on my spare pillow, and I carefully tucked it into the lining of my suitcase because that's the kind of romantic idiot I am. Then I forgot all about romance and set off in search of sustenance, because frankly, romance cannot travel without a full stomach and all those consumptive poetasters should take a lesson from this. Call me callous, but love seems a lot rosier when you've had your fill of devilled kidneys and scrambled eggs. Apart from the nagging worry of the missing-father-that-might-or-might-not-exist, I remained optimistic for now.

Even Lawrence's dear grumpy face over the marmalade did not dampen my spirits. Clarissa Holland was in fine form—she was the only female in attendance—and she regaled us with tales of her brothers as children I'm quite sure she would not have dared to repeat had Dear Claude been at the table. Sadly, she did not reveal anything too dark; Claude had shown no propensity for experiments on small animals, nor had he, it seems, done anything more unbrotherly than once tying his sister to the top of the banister rail and telling her that flesh-eating ants would come to eat her. I was quite disappointed.

Not that the ants didn't devour Miss Holland, for who would want that? It surprised me he'd done nothing more sinister. But it was diverting, all the same, and it took my mind off the fact my mercurial friend wasn't at breakfast and although no one had asked me where he was, the question was on people's minds.

I was almost relieved, then, when I heard a muffled bang. I had a suspicion as to what it was, but said nothing. Clarissa looked up at Stephens, who was carrying in some fresh coffee.

"No one's shooting, surely?"

"Certainly not, madam," he said. "They'd have to ask me for the key. I shall go and investigate."

"Thank you, Stephens." She turned to Lawrence. "Claude would not forgive me if anyone was poaching when he was away. I've always got the blame for anything that goes wrong when he's not here." This was even more mildly interesting to me than flesh-eating ants. The man struck me as the type to blame others, but it nettled me that he was taking responsibility in advance for a house that was not yet his responsibility to take. It was some information I could pass on, at least.

The noise was explained as a tumultuous din broke out in the house and newcomers made their way across the hall and burst open the door. As I had expected from the moment I heard the familiar bang outside (Gilbert's car, which backfired so regularly I had accused him of having a button on the dashboard to make it do so), Richardson and Gilbert burst into the room, all bonhomie, bland smiles and with that utter gloss of superiority that marked them as the sort of men who knew that they would be accepted wherever they arrived, purely because they were there. I rose hastily and made the requisite introductions.

It would have been so amusing to watch Claude Holland turn himself inside out to be polite as yet another two of that dratted boy's friends descended. I had no doubt that Mrs Holland would have no difficulty in being gracious, in the same brittle and all-encompassing way her son had, but Claude Holland would find it an intrusion, even though he had been warned.

And it had to be said, Gilbert and Richardson were, in every way, an intrusion. From their noisy car giving off smoke and foul-smelling fumes and (I had no doubt) dripping oil onto the driveway and marring the perfection of the weedless courtyard, to the piles of luggage they had in the hall, giving the impression they had come for a year, and not for a few days. From their loud exclamations of pleasure at the invitation to take a bit of breakfast before they settled in, to the way they took control of the conversation. Everything about them was intrusive. I had the feeling of a castle, slumbering for a hundred years and then woken, not by love's first kiss but by a couple of noisy clanking knights who'd got lost on the road.

I found them quite delightful. We like their bluff masculinity, and perhaps there's something in my slender wrists and blue-white veins, something they find as appealing in our rather more louche behaviour as we find in theirs.

What amused me was Lawrence. He perked up no end upon meeting them. I could almost see him wondering why two such masculine men could be friends with such a pansy as me. Sporting prowess, or the claims of such, are enough to merit masculinity in Lawrence's book. No wonder he had no time for me.

They went down well in both fronts as Clarissa obviously found them pleasant enough, although possibly a little verbose, as she had difficulty inserting herself into their enthusiastic conversation, but eventually she managed to say, "I don't know where my nephew can be, I'd have imagined he'd be here to greet you."

Stephens, bringing in a new plate of sausages, said, "He's just changing his shoes, Miss Holland. He'll be in shortly, he said." The conversation dimmed a little after this, as we waited, as we often did, for his arrival and when he eventually breezed in, his hair in delightful disarray where the wind had whipped it out of shape, he sighed a mock sigh. "Oh, Lord. So that dreadful noise was your jalopy. I thought Harry had got sick of Lawrence and had shot him."

"What a horrible thing to say," Clarissa Holland said.

"Oh, Harry knows I don't mean it," he said, plumping himself down next to Richardson and stealing some of his toast. "If he's likely to bump anyone off, I'd say the odds are on me, wouldn't you?" No one had anything to say about that, and I kept quiet, knowing he was acting up. "Hello, you two. Got sick of Torquay, did you?"

"Dreadful," Gilbert said. "You know you've quite ruined the place for me. I hadn't even noticed all the bally tweed until you went and mentioned it. Now I can't see anything else. And it's infectious too. I had to drag Richardson out of a tailor's where he was falling in love with some tweedy plus fours. Over my dead body, I told him, and I threw him in the car and we sped here for our very lives."

"Don't listen to him," Richardson said. "When we mentioned we were thinking of dropping over and invading you, Gilbert's father reminded us of Dunster Polo Ground. So of course that meant we had to up sticks and come over straight away. I remember you banging on about polo quite a lot at one point. Then you didn't. Do any of you play?"

There was a general shaking of heads, which surprised me in Lawrence's case as he seemed the type to say that he'd attempted any sport mentioned—whether he really had or not. Miss Holland excused herself, saying that if we were going to talk sports she had better things to do.

"Richardson's right, Holland," Gilbert said. "You were quite the polo fanatic for a term or two."

"I never played it," he said. "Oh, I rode a couple of chaps' ponies once or twice, and I attended all the games I could, but you need to have been born in the saddle or be quite, quite insane, and I am neither. You need to have pots of money too. Give me some of yours, Gilbert, and I might take it up. I rather like the boots."

"Who says you are sane?" I'd said the wrong thing without thinking and saw him close his eyes for a moment longer than blinking. All I could do was continue. "I wouldn't place money on that diagnosis. The truth of the matter, if you really want to know is that he had a tremendous crush on one of the players—I'm sorry, Lawrence, I know how distasteful it is for you to hear—and his hero-worship was entirely ignored."

Lawrence stood at this and walked out, leaving Richardson and Gilbert to exchange knowing glances.

"Brother? Cousin? No relation? I'd like to know before I'm rude about him," Richardson said.

"Oh," Holland waved a hand, as if it was too much effort to explain Lawrence, which it probably was. "He's just...around. Getting under one's feet. No relation. He'll tar you both with our brush, you realise."

"Doesn't everyone? Until they see us mashing the girls, that is."

"You'll be doing no mashing in this house, if you please. Lawrence has a sister who would spit you out and trample you underfoot. If he hadn't done it to you first."

They both perked up at this. I found it amusing, merely for the fact that Torquay was much more likely to be stuffed with women of all descriptions. If they wanted that kind of thing, they'd be better off there. Perhaps a captive audience was more their thing. I rather looked forward to seeing how Miss Stephens dealt with the two, rather useless Lotharios. I'd never seen them in action before, our female acquaintance being scant, to say the least.

They helped us finish off everything that was edible, and then we carried their bags upstairs. Stephens—give the man his due—offered to do this, but it seemed rather mean, and other than the occasional fag at school, and our scouts, we were pretty much used to coping for ourselves. Once ensconced, the two of them set off alone to "explore," which probably meant they were going to track down and find Stevie. I don't know which of them I felt more sorry for.

Alone together, Holland turned to me. "I wish you hadn't said that about Ari."

"They aren't dim. I'm sure they knew. It was hardly a secret at the time. You had photos of him all over the study." I hated to be on the defensive, but it wasn't something that I would normally have done, said that out loud, even to Richardson and Gilbert. I didn't like to probe my motivation too deeply. As much as I thought it had been an off-the-cuff remark, I wondered if it really was. If so, I deserved the rebuke. "Look, I'm sorry. I can't very well go and take it back, you know, it'll look too asinine, even for me. And what's the harm, it was only a crush. You've had them since I've known you, regular as clockwork."

"All the same. I'm having to think about things a bit more. It brings it home to me why I've kept you at arm's length from the family all this time."

I was sitting on the window seat with my back to him "Don't think I hadn't noticed."

A silence settled around us and it took real strength to stop myself from turning around and apologising for simply speaking my mind. I heard him sigh, and the bedsprings sounded; in a moment he was behind me, his breath against my neck. "For all your display, you'd be surprised how sang-froid you can be at times."

I had to struggle not to splutter at the slur. I clenched my teeth together in sheer manliness. I wondered if he was looking into a mirror, but I said nothing, therefore probably cementing my reputation as a man of ice. I wondered where the hell he'd got this idea from; I wouldn't be surprised if he was parroting something someone had said to him, for it was a sentiment never expressed before. It wouldn't be the first instance—he was like a magpie at times, repeating things heard, or told—I found it hard to believe it was original thought. It left me with a bad taste in my mouth, and a mystery to solve.

His hand felt warm, flat against my shoulder blade, and it was almost too tempting not to lean back against it, like a collie, starved of contact out there on the moor, that pushes his head into his master's hand any time it came close. "You make it all more complicated—as if it wasn't already complicated enough."

I nettled at this, bit back the first thought in my mind and took a more sensible tack. Believe me, it's hard to do that sometimes around him. Instead I concentrated on having a barrier around me. If he thought I was cold, I'd be cold. I can be spiteful, yes, when cornered. "I'm here because you asked me, and because I wanted to come." I turned around on the seat, away from the comfort of his hand.

He dragged that same hand through his hair. "I know, I know, and it would be a lot harder here without you, I'd have probably left the first night. But. Oh, I don't know. If Mother gets all peculiar about Stevie again, it could all get very awkward. You don't understand."

"Perhaps you should remind her which century we are in. And no, I don't understand the position, to be honest with you. If she was an heiress with adjoining land it would make more sense. But she's—"

"Don't say it," he said. "I don't expect you to understand. You've got"—he stood and started pacing, never a good sign—"this wall of class consciousness; and it's hard, when you've been raised like I have, to see the same barriers—the same lines that you do."

"I say, that's a bit unfair. I thought I was as accepting as the next man."

He gave a short laugh. "Well, yes, that's exactly it. You are exactly that. You are accepting. But it's something you can't help. A conscious decision. You'd go to Malaya or over to John Company and you'll be thought such a good chap and a good leader and everyone will admire how well you get on with the natives. Whereas I would probably make a real mess of things, getting too involved. Not knowing where to stop, the barriers of decency, all that kind of thing. '*That Holland chappie—loose cannon—he don't know the limits, you know, what, what?*'" His impression of a pukka sahib would have, under other circumstances, made me laugh.

"Just as well you'll have that solid Bircham chap to make you see sense. Or at least to cover up your indiscretions with devastatingly handsome maharajahs."

He exploded at last. This is him. Give him twenty reasons to lose his temper and he'll find the most inconsequential remark and blow it out of all proportion. "Oh, God, Harry! There was nothing between me and Ari— nothing! I don't understand why you think there was! This—this is why I never said anything about Ian, because I'd have got it thrown in my face every time I turned around, and it had nothing to do with you. You can't see that, can you?"

I got up, trying not to show anything, anything at all, to give him ammunition, and said, "Everything you do is something to do with me. That's how I see it. I'm sorry if you feel otherwise."

I walked towards the door and he shouted after me. "No, no you don't!"

"It's too complicated for me. Obviously. My snobbery offends you, my loyalty offends you, because heaven knows I'm not allowed to call it anything else. I'll see you later."

I heard him give a cry of sheer exasperation, and I knew how he felt. God alone knows I'd felt that way enough over him. As I walked out and downstairs, I tried to work out what we'd been squabbling over, and couldn't make any sense of it. It seemed to start and end with Ari, that much I could work out, just one of his many crushes. Ari was that clichéd thing, the devastatingly handsome maharajah. Son of one, at least, which meant, probably—I didn't know his history and background that well—that he'd be maharajah himself one day.

Ari Datta Wadiyar Kiri…something tum tum tum de Singh of Mayosore, or Bhuggati. Some principality tucked away on the subcontinent. Somewhere deliciously exotic. How could anyone compete with a prince? He'd been at Druitt's with us, a year ahead, but for the company he kept it might as well have been ten years. His set considered themselves to be entirely adult, and by the time they'd reached the upper sixth you'd have thought they were old and mature enough to rule the country. They certainly gave the impression that they could have done a better job of it than Asquith and his lot. They swaggered around in their coloured waistcoats and cravats and all others could do was worship from afar. No one who hadn't been in their set from day one could enter it, some had tried, and many had found it hard to live down the rebuff. To quote Pooh-Bah, Ari's set seemed to have been "born sneering."

I was surprised, therefore, when I discovered that he'd developed such a crush on Ari—he was pretty open minded in lots of ways, and bullying was one thing he couldn't stand. Ari, Matheson and the others—they didn't bully, exactly, but the sheer weight of their superiority made people want to be near them, like them, and those that tried were crumpled underfoot. Looking back at those turbulent years, when little things—like what your fellow school chums thought of you—mattered so very much, it seems ridiculous to me now, but then I never had that kind of ambition.

I don't think he wanted to be like them, exactly, but he wanted to be close to Ari, and despite knowing it was impossible, it didn't stop him wanting it.

He was adept, and perhaps he'll always be that way, at wishing on a star.

What hurt me most was not the fact that he wanted someone else—although I won't try and lie and say it didn't hurt like hell—but watching him dash himself against rocks that would never wear themselves into stairs was hard to bear. I'm sure that Ari was aware of this hero-worship, because to give him his due he was never deliberately or carelessly cruel to his feelings, but he never once seemed to notice the mere mortals we were. To do so, I suppose, would be to acknowledge the existence of the ground, and all the little ants that toiled upon it.

He got over it, as he always did, and we pottered along again. I won't say that I'm not a jealous person—I defy anyone to be his particular friend and not to worry about every new pair of bright eyes that comes along—I knew that one day I wouldn't be so lucky as I had with Ari. Someday, his crush might be reciprocated, and then I didn't know what I would do. Pushing unpleasant thoughts aside—so much easier than getting into a bloody internal soliloquy, I always find—I went for a stroll around the grounds. I revisited the scene of the Unearthing of the Tortoise. Now the immediate shock had passed I was a little curious; I had never seen a Giant Tortoise outside of scientific books. It seemed that it was to be my day for disappointments. There wasn't much to see: simply a patch of bare earth that was identical to the patch of earth there before. Someone had filled the hole in, or perhaps the behemoth had reburied himself beneath the soil once more. I scanned the horizon, thinking that an animal that size wouldn't have got that far, even in twenty-four hours, but there was no sign of him, and I was cheated of my scientific investigation. I made a mental note to ask Stevie where he was likely to be. In his hutch, perhaps. Richardson and Gilbert were strolling over by the rhododendrons. I joined them, as they sprawled on the grass.

"What time's lunch?" Gilbert asked.

"One," I said.

"Good, I'm starved." Gilbert patted his stomach which he was holding in, as if that would prove emaciation.

"Talking of one," Richardson whispered, "your solitary state is rather obvious, old thing. Had a spat?"

I forgave them for their informality. They'd lived next to us for enough years to know that all was not always smooth sailing on the HMS Holland-Bircham. "Hardly a ripple." I might forgive them, but it didn't mean I had to confide in them.

"Over young Mr Stephens?" Richardson asked.

Gilbert was inspecting the blades of grass around him, as if fascinated.

I felt a cold touch on the back of my neck, as if the wind had moved to the north, or a ghost had drawn ectoplasmic fingers up my spine. Fanciful, yes, I dare say. Some people say that it feels like a goose has walked on their grave, which I think is no more ridiculous an image. "Not at all," I said, giving no indication of the shock I felt at those words. "How moronic. We've always found something more important to argue about than that."

"Of course," Richardson said.

"Not that he's not attractive," I said.

"Oh, I'm sure."

"But he's not Holland's type."

"I believe you."

"And they are practically brothers," I added, nettled by the fact that I was sounding like I was having to explain myself, explain Holland. But I was angry.

"Oh?"

I detailed the circumstances, such as I knew, about Lawrence and Stevie's upbringing. It was rather a relief that both of them looked as baffled as I felt about the whole business.

"It's all a bit...odd," Gilbert said. "You've got to admit that. I can't imagine my mater doing anything quite so communist. Even if the woman had been her best friend."

"Perhaps it's a northern thing," Richardson supplied. "Bond of the common man, etcetera. I can see some crushed miner putting his hand into the pit-owner's glove and saying"—here Richardson slipped into the most egregious parody of a northern accent I'd ever heard—"Ey yup, maister, I'm for it an' no misstake. There's Florrie and t'kids—thay'll starve. Tha'll see them reet?" He collapsed, coughing up imaginary blood as the pitshaft that was crushing him did for him at last.

"Ass." But my mood was restored. Sometimes it takes idiots to remove it, and bigger idiots to bring it back. "It was nothing like that at all."

"I'm gratified you know so much about my family history." Lawrence's voice sounded from behind us. "So very typical of Holland to spread it far and wide. I'm sure he finds it hugely amusing that we live here on his family's charity."

Richardson and Gilbert shot to their feet, mumbled something about changing their shirts for lunch and strode off, charmingly leaving me with the Scowling Stephens. I myself had not done more than to turn my head, then turn it back, remaining sprawled out and comfortable on a small incline.

"Bugger off, Lawrence," I said. "It's such a lovely day, and your face is enough to send the sun packing."

"I have no intention of buggering off. Sorry to disappoint. I have just as much right to be here as you."

"Some might say a lot more." I put my hands behind my head.

"Would they? Who might that be? Your friends? Holland? You? I doubt it very much. Your pantomime made that very clear."

"Oh, don't be a dud, Lawrence, that wasn't meant to be your family. Richardson was merely expounding a theory. He was complimentary, in fact, if you'd heard it all."

"How very kind of him. I don't eavesdrop. I didn't go to Druitt' but some things don't have to be taught, even to *servants*. I didn't see you until I turned the corner. If I'd known you were there, I would have turned away."

Despite my casual pose, I was hammered by the number of chips on the young man's shoulders. I don't suppose—if I'd been in his position myself—I'd have thought much differently. If there's one thing you can say about me, it's that I have empathic bones. It's probably been honed through years of dealing with a certain someone and his mercurial moods. I put myself into Lawrence's shoes for a moment or two, imagined what it was like to be raised in this house, with every façade of gentility, but without the solid foundations of wealth and birth. Would I simply accept it, or would I feel constantly on edge? Being grateful all the time can do funny things to a person. If it were I, hmm—I'd worry constantly about my future, and what was more, my sister's future. Would she be introduced to eligible men of the Hollands' class? Or would she be expected to find men in Stephens' class? It would be a difficult situation in either case—and possibly only love and understanding families would resolve it. I had a pang of sympathy for him, and felt that I understood why he scowled quite so much. Having the heir to the house lurking around must be galling for him, in the light of Mrs Holland's hopes that Stevie would naturally gravitate towards the young man she'd grown up with. Having me around probably made it worse for both of them.

I empathised, but it didn't make me warm to him. Sulking does no one any good, and for goodness' sake, there were jobs. Or professions. I was quite sure Uncle Claude was under instruction to "see Lawrence right" when the time came.

"You went to a local school?"

"I did. And no, I'm not going to Oxford, since you ask."

"I don't recall asking."

The man was impossible. I rarely feel like taking a man by the shoulders and shaking him—in anger at least!—but two minutes in Lawrence's company had that effect on me. Heaven knows I'd had years of putting up with unreasonableness, but Lawrence took not only the biscuit, but the barrel and all the cheese.

"Sit down, at least," I said. "You are blocking my sun."

He hesitated, looked over towards the house, shuffled once or twice, which made me tempted to tell him not to bother. When he spoke, he still had an edge of defensiveness in his tone, but it was slightly metered, as if he'd finally realised how much of an arse he was being. "Not that I couldn't. I matriculated pretty damn well, and Margaret said she'd pay the fees if I didn't get a scholarship."

"But you decided against it."

For a moment the sulky look dropped away from his face and I wallowed in his beauty. His long face, the sweeping dark of his hair, this was not the face of a clerk or a draper. He pulled disconsolately at a patch of grass, uprooting it with a tearing sound. "Yes, well. It's not just the fees is it?"

"No. Look, I understand. I've seen scholarship men coming in—and I can tell you you've probably made the right decision."

"I don't know why I'm telling you this. You'll only go and pass it on. To Holland." The handsomeness melted from his features as they twisted into what, from what I knew of him, was his normal expression. I wondered just why he was so suspicious and unhappy. His problem was probably paranoia. I know nothing about the ailment, but I'm sure some eager professor with a thirst for knowledge would be grateful if I offered young Lawrence up as a case study.

"Do you think he doesn't know, then?"

"I don't know. *Master* Holand's never here, is he? I doubt he knows. I doubt he cares. As long as he's got enough money to throw around, or you to—"

"I'd prefer you didn't finish that sentence," I said. "Look, Stephens, I don't know you, and I certainly didn't invite you to blunder around, chase off my friends and then start throwing your reverse snobbery at me. You're Holland's family in one way or another." Lawrence made a disgusted noise. "That's how he thinks, believe me, and how he talks of you."

"He talks of me?"

I was tempted to say, "Never, actually," but it was probably crueler to say: "Not often, so don't puff yourself up about it. But when he does, it's like a brother."

Lawrence looked down and started pulling up grass again. "How kind of him."

"It's a damn sight more kind than the way you think of him, from what I've seen. You've been next to poisonous to him from the moment we arrived."

"You." His face went dark red in anger. "You have no idea—you don't know us, you were right about that."

"I generally am," I said in my most bored voice. "And now, if you please, I have no intention of storming off in high dudgeon, so either change the subject or shut up. This is a nice spot."

We sat in uncompanionable silence for a good few minutes, punctuated only by him tearing up grass. I closed my eyes and tried to pretend he wasn't there. "I'm sorry," Lawrence said finally.

"Good Lord. Where's Stephens gone?"

He threw a handful of grass at me and believe it or not, he actually smiled. It was like being hit by a warm wave of honey. The man is entirely wasted. But he shut up, and we lay together in the sunshine until the luncheon bell sounded.

MARGARET AND CLAUDE HAD RETURNED BY the time we got back to the house, and with their return, I couldn't help but notice the recurrence of a tension which seemed to affect everyone except the two new arrivals. If it hadn't been for Richardson and Gilbert, I have to say that luncheon would have been a hugely dismal affair. Desultory platitudes were exchanged between Margaret and her son as she offered to tell him how her trip had been and he politely declined to hear. Some small talk about hats ensued between Margaret and Stevie for which I wished I had been out of the room. Or the county. There's only one thing I need to know about a hat. Will it fit me? After that, I care little, and I certainly don't want to spend half an hour discussing shape and fabric and the type of band that goes around it. I *know* it's going to suit me, or I wouldn't be bothering with it.

Other than this stilted line of conversation, Margaret and her son hardly spoke, and he talked to no one else at all, even me, despite the fact that I sat at his elbow. I was still in the doghouse, then. Pardon me for caring. Holland was doing his very best glower, in fact. Concentrating fully on his plate, and other than when addressed directly—not by me, I hasten to add, for I know when an endeavour is hopeless—he didn't speak throughout the entire main course. When the dessert arrived, a concoction of apples and sponge, he brightened visibly, and although he still ignored his uncle in a pointed manner, he instigated a conversation born from an earlier meal.

"I haven't been to the polo for an age," Holland said, turning to Gilbert. "It might be jolly to get over for a match. When is the next one, anyway?"

"Tomorrow," Gilbert said. "First chukka at two o'clock according to Lance Bellingham. Some local teams first, then the main event just afterwards. He usually attends but he's squiring some girl around London, poor so—soul."

Holland gave the most brilliant of smiles. "Well I think we deserve an excursion. We could motor down to Minehead this afternoon. Have the hotel do us a basket, and go to the grounds tomorrow."

"Sounds topping to me," Richardson said. "Get us out of your hair, Mrs Holland, what?"

"You are no bother, believe me," she said. Even Dear Uncle Claude looked pleased, probably at the thought of being rid of us for at least twenty-four hours.

He turned the radiance of that brilliant smile around to Stevie. "Do you want to come?"

"*God* no. Don't get me involved in your excursions."

"Oh, Stevie," Margaret said. "You really should. You don't get out half enough. And someone needs to keep them in check or the next thing we'll hear of them is being thrown into some Italian jail or worse."

She rolled her eyes. "Oh, all right. But only if I'm promised dinner at The Metropole. And I don't have to go and look at any horses, or stamp sods back in place."

"Divots," I said with mock sternness. "The word is divots."

"I know what the word is," she said with a saccharine smile. Claude looked thunderous, but the exchange seemed to have passed Margaret by entirely.

Richardson looked elated. "Nothing would give me greater pleasure than to treat you to the best that the Metropole can provide. Perhaps we can lose this lot along the way. They aren't the sort of people with whom I'd wish to be seen dining in public."

Richardson turned to Lawrence. "Stephens? You'll come?"

"There won't be the room," Lawrence said.

Margaret appealed to Claude. "Why don't you lend them the shooting brake, Claude? There's more than enough room in that, and I'd feel happier if they were storming around the countryside with some walls around them. That way they can all go, including you, Lawrence, I'm not having you mooning around the place if everyone else has gone. And I don't wish to offend you, Mr Richardson, but that tin can you are driving looks like it will collapse if you put three people in it, let alone five or six."

Caught in the cross-fire as it were, Dear Uncle Claude's face was a picture. It was more than clear that the last thing he wanted to do was to lend any of his possessions to a group of miscreants and inverts, but with Margaret giving him her most winning smile—and I knew it well, because her son had exactly the same expression when he wanted to wheedle—he couldn't really be rude and say "Not on your Nellie" which was probably the gist of what was going through his mind. I think the smile on his face probably broke something inside, but after a stunned moment he nodded and said in almost an undertone that that wouldn't be a problem as long as we were sensible. He then went on, aiming his instructions purely at Richardson, as it appeared that out of all of us, he was the only one capable of remembering anything at all. The gearbox was sensitive, it appeared, when changing gear either up or down hill. We were to check the oil and water upon our arrival and halfway home at the garage at Cutcombe. We were under no circumstances to take the car (he called it "her," which I found disturbing) over thirty miles an hour as it was still running in. There was much more of this kind of thing, but I'd wandered away after a minute of it to scamper upstairs for a jacket and to change my shoes. Richardson was dispatched to the telephone to make a booking at the hotel, and there was a flurry of activity as bags were packed and taken out to the car.

"Are cars as complicated as he makes them sound?" I asked Holland. He'd picked some ghastly shapeless coat to wear which was far too short in the sleeves. I think when we are finally ensconced in a little flat somewhere I shall have to spend a good deal of my wages on a valet or something, because I can't spend every moment worrying about what he's going to go out in public in.

I was lucky enough to nab one of the maids and gave her instructions about evening clothes and shoes, or he would, I'm sure, have been happy to have dinner in what he was wearing.

"No idea," he said. "If I get one I just want to turn the handle and go." The prospect of an outing had cheered him up, or more likely the idea of getting away from the house for a while. I didn't blame him, but wondered a little that he wasn't fretting about matters more than he was. I was the one who could put on a front when needed, far more easily than he could.

"Richardson does take it rather seriously." He pulled the door open and waiting for me. "But he's always been the same, he likes to know how things work. Me, I couldn't care less. I don't get something just to learn how to take it apart."

"He might be handy if you do get one, then."

He beamed at me. "My thoughts exactly."

IT TOOK HALF AN HOUR TO get us all into the car, and then a further ten minutes as Claude Holland bombarded Richardson with further instructions. It might have taken longer, but luckily Margaret pulled him away and we were on the road, trundling at a beautifully sedate pace towards the gates. Gilbert was in the front next to Richardson; Lawrence was in the bucket seat opposite to Stevie and I was between Stevie and my glowering friend, next to the window.

As we reached the road, Richardson said, "Here we go!" and we scattered the gravel of the drive behind us, as he put his foot on the accelerator and let the car plunge forward down the road, taking no care at all to notice whether we were going under thirty, or whether some other vehicle might be careening towards us in the high-sided, single-track road. Luckily, we were saved disaster and a racy headline along the lines of "Bright Young Things drove car into tree" and we reached the A396 in relative safety. The sun was darting in and out from behind clouds, and with Richardson's constant barrage of abuse about Dear Uncle Claude's pride and joy—apparently she ran like she had her wheels in mud and only a steam train going downhill would get her to do any speed worth doing—we were a fairly jolly party.

Stevie managed her brother admirably. He was no happier out from under the feet of the older generation, sad to tell, and he stared gloomily out of the window like some consumptive poet without the skeletal frame. Stevie saved the day in this respect, which won me over to her more than anything else had done up to now. She obviously knew how to encourage and cajole her brother out of his blacker moods in much the same way that I could cajole the irritating bastard who was pressing his thigh against mine. Gilbert produced a magnum of champagne that he'd pilfered from his parents' house and the prevailing tension of people thrown together who didn't fit in many ways, began to lessen.

Gilbert began to sing that popular, annoying and all-pervading ditty about his Mammy, and soon Stevie and Richardson, and even Lawrence, during the chorus, were joining in. I took the opportunity to mutter sideways to my companion that it had surprised me that he'd suggested the outing. "I wanted to prove something to you, perhaps," he said, without looking around. "And Father said he had to go away for a few days, so there really wasn't any point hanging around at home. I'd end up dropping a statue on Claude's head before the wedding."

"When is it?"

"I'd rather not talk about the wedding." Holland turned to the others in the car, finishing our tête-à-tête. "What about 'My Man'? '*He's not much on looks, he's no hero out of books...*'"

I elbowed him in the ribs, and thankfully Gilbert snorted. "Ain't we got fun!" Thankfully we all knew that one quite well.

The jollity grew as the champagne level dropped in the bottle. We zipped past Dunster, noting the sign on the side of the road announcing the match of the day after and eventually wound our way down the cliffs towards Minehead. We found The Metropole fairly easily, looming over the seafront in substantial acreage of its own. By the time we all met for cocktails, you would have thought we were an entirely different set of people. We clung together in the midst of the respectability of the hotel and for all the world to see we were a group of tight-knit friends. How easy it is to fool others.

Chapter Seven

The next morning I woke with a muzzy head and lay there putting recent memories into order like a rather painful jigsaw puzzle. Firstly, I must have left his room at some point, that much was clear; this was my room and the bed had noticeably only one occupant: me. I really should consider detection, I really should. The evening had been a success— which is to say we spent a lot of money—mostly Richardson's—and drank a good deal of champagne, again, mostly Richardson's. We danced a lot, and as Stevie was the only girl in our party, she was never off the dance floor. There were other girls—the usual majority in most social situations these days—and we shared ourselves about, one doesn't like to be stingy about these things. If I couldn't dance with him—although there were places in London—and on the continent (which we'd looked forward to greatly) where one could—then watching him dance was a bearable substitute. One long-legged horse-faced girl swung me around in a really bumpy foxtrot and I imagined for a moment the looks on the Minehead populace, staring blankly from the edges of the dance floor, were they to see two men in each other's arms. I choked on a giggle and the horse-faced one gave me a look as if to say she knew I was mentally deficient and was now proved right.

On my dances with Stevie, who was a little more tipsy and more loose-tongued than I had yet seen her, I had used the Bircham charm, asked her about her brother and she had let slip to me that she was worried about him.

"He doesn't talk to me much any more," she said. "He's got some business deal or something, something—" She waved a hand, as if trying to recall a detail. "He's up too close, that's the trouble, and that's always a danger when one is in our situation. I've always had standards, and known about distance—

and Dad has always tried to maintain them—you know? But Lawrence really has this Great Expectation kick going, and he's going to be disappointed, I know it. Trouble is, his Miss Havisham doesn't even know they are in the frame."

I was as squiffy as she was, possibly more—sheets to the wind and all that, however many it is—and I recall I tried to get her to explain what she meant, but she clammed up, and seemed to notice me for the first time. I had a suspicion that in her cups, she had actually thought I was Holland and therefore knew what she was on about. Holland and I had blown along the corridor with the others, and Stevie had come into Holland's room for a moment—bless her—and then left quietly. We took advantage of the five minutes or so after she left but dared stay together no longer than that.

Breakfast was sombre, and several of the guests were decidedly coldshoulderish, which hinted that we had been rather too boisterous for such a staid and prestigious hotel. We all assembled, which surprised me; even Gilbert who had had to be half-carried to the lift the night before. Richardson and Gilbert were all for going to the polo grounds early, to be there for the first match, but they were generally squashed down by the rest of us. "It's bad enough I have to suffer this display of manliness as it is," Stevie said, sipping delicately at her China tea, "but I don't want to see a third rate exhibition."

"Oh, I say," Gilbert said, "that's bally unfair. You don't know they'll be rubbish."

"You said they were local teams, didn't you? Anything local is bound to be rubbish," she said.

"Well you bally well should be impressed by the Argentines and the Maharajah of Jaipur," Richardson said. "They are certainly not local, and exotic enough for anyone's taste."

"Terribly exotic," I murmured. I felt a kick on my ankle which I chose to ignore.

"I'll go and check with the front desk about lunch," Richardson said.

"And I'd better go and put on something more suitable if we are going to be outdoorsy." Stevie left us to mop up the remainder of breakfast, which I for one did with gusto, ignoring much of the conversation that lapped around me. I happen to have a passion for hotel food, especially breakfast. At a country house one has to serve oneself and one is always a little over cautious as to how much to take—one wouldn't want to deprive the family of their last rasher of bacon. However in a hotel one knows that there's lashings more of the stuff in the kitchens, just waiting to be cooked and lugged out for the next guest, so one doesn't need to hold back in at all the same way. Full to the brim of bacon, porridge, sausages and egg, I had to be rolled into the car, and forcibly wedged into the back seat. Suitably fortified, we barrelled back away from the coast and joined the small cavalcade entering the Dunster grounds. Richardson parked the car around the edge, and not too close to the next vehicle—a once magnificent but rather tatty pre-war Rolls-Royce. Once in place we piled rugs and cushions in front of the car and settled down, making a start on the champagne and delicious smoked salmon canapés provided by the hotel.

Ensconced, and scattered around Stevie like protective swans, we sipped our drinks and waited for the main event to begin. The last match had just ended and many of the crowd were walking the ground, stamping the divots back into the earth. Richardson and Gilbert grabbed Lawrence and took part, striding around the ground as if they knew what they were doing, but when invited, I merely yawned and leaned back against the car. Holland lay at right angles to me, almost at my feet. If we'd been alone together, no doubt his head would be in my lap, or mine in his—quite our most favourite position for lolling around in the sun—but despite our fooling no one in the immediate company, there were other citizens to remember and one didn't wish to scare the horses.

I should point out that one generally doesn't go to polo to watch the polo itself. It's a sport that doesn't lend itself to observation. If you haven't been to a match, then I can't say that I recommend it as a sport to follow, in the same way one would go and watch one's local cricket or rugby team play, as the scale is too vast, and sitting at ground level is not the best way to observe the action. The playing field is enormous—about ten times the size of a football pitch, or—as Gilbert carefully explained to Stevie—around ten acres. It is therefore, unless one glues one's eyes to a pair of field glasses, impossible to tell who anyone is, and unless they are thundering close by where you sit, pretty much impossible to tell what direction they are going. The pace is frantic, the action twisting, violent and unrelenting. A decent player can use up eight ponies in one game alone, so you can't even keep track of "Oh yes, that's Andrews on the light bay," as by the time you've worked that out, he's changed to a grey, and all his team-mates are also on different mounts. The only thing you can do is to keep score, or as we did, observe the scoreboard for information.

In the absence of her brother and the two others, Stevie pointed her conversation almost entirely at Holland, rather than the two of us together. I didn't mind much, as much of what she talked of was matters that only he and she would know—local people, local events—and I was perfectly happy to watch the world go by in all its jodhpured glory. Stevie seemed rather on edge, her hands flickering in front of her like moths as she described some gathering she'd been to the week before. "You were missed, of course," she said, her eyes never leaving Holland, although he hardly even opened his eyes to acknowledge her as she spoke. "We knew you couldn't come down early, but James Rutherford, you remember him, he was the one with the three older brothers who were all killed, well, he said there'll be a swimming gala at his place later this summer—perhaps we could all go? Harry, of course, and your friends too, if they are still here."

Holland wavered from attentive listener to bored young man. His flickering moods, like the frames of a moving picture, were disconcerting to more than just me. Stevie—as I'd noticed before—seemed particularly attuned to his state of mind. She seemed to relax when he was participating in the day, but became a trifle distracted when he sank back into silent reflection. She was worryingly like a mirror to me, which I suppose wasn't too surprising; she'd known Holland longer than I. It was merely interesting that, like me, she was more worried about his silences than his speech. I wondered if he had any idea of the effect he had on her. I knew damn well he knew how to play me like a violin—but for some reason I found it hard to forgive him if he was putting Stevie through the same torment he often inflicted deliberately on me.

"I don't know," he said finally. "I haven't decided what we'll be doing for the rest of the time."

"You've got to stay for the—"

"Please don't tell me I have to stay for the wedding, because I don't see why anyone should think that," he snapped, closing his eyes again.

"But your mother is depending on it."

Holland turned his head to face her then, and his face was as cold as I'd ever seen it. "Why? Why ever would my presence or otherwise make the slightest difference?"

"Well, because…because…" To my horror, I saw Stevie go bright red, and I felt bitterly sorry for her.

"Because she's not taken my opinion or presence into anything she's done or planned so far. Everyone—even people in the village—knew what she was up to, and yet she didn't bother to write and tell me until a few days before end of term, and even that didn't give any details. Just 'come home for the vac.' You could have written, you know. Instead of letting me walk right into it."

I saw the others returning and interrupted Holland and Stevie. "Perhaps we should postpone this."

"Oh yes, let's ignore the entire thing, that's much the best way to behave, isn't it?" He turned his anger on me, and I saw Stevie bristle with indignation on my behalf. He pushed himself to his feet. "Good old Harry—ever the mediator, ever the problem solver. Let's not discuss anything unpleasant in public, because we're English and that's not what we do."

"Don't be an idiot." I feigned an air of indifference. "Just lie down and shut up. Well, are all the divots plugged back in?" I said to the three returning heroes.

"Pretty much. Hey, what's the matter with you, Holland?" Richardson stepped aside to avoid being pushed aside as my touchy friend stalked off along the line of cars.

I caught Stevie's eye and she gave me the smallest of smiles before turning her attention to the others, deflecting the bad behaviour of some people. "Call of nature." We opened the hamper, despite him not returning.

Gilbert and Richardson professed themselves expert in the game, knew all the players, and—as luck would have it—came equipped with a pair of field glasses each, so they were able to keep some kind of track of what was going on, and they relayed the pertinent information to the rest of us.

I wish I could say I was interested enough to care. I had other things on my mind, understandably, and I fear that out of the five of us remaining, perhaps only two of us, perhaps two and a half, even listened to a fraction of what was being relayed. But the day was pleasant enough, the sun warm, and the company of a decent sort, and apart from irritating niggles I could think of worse ways of spending an afternoon. The only two flies in my ointment were that he was missing, when I'd liked to have had him where I could keep an eye on him, and that blasted Ari Singh's name was mentioned in the commentary on a regular basis. According to Gilbert he was "dashed good" at the sport, and seemed to score an inordinate amount of goals. Eventually I worked out which one was him and watched him for a while, half hoping that he'd fall off, but of course he never did, no matter how alarmingly he bent over the ball.

I may make it sound as if polo wasn't exciting and if so I've given the wrong impression. It was exciting, breathtaking at times; the pure power of man and beast as they gallop past you is positively thrilling. Even if one does get covered in mud and grass. To see a perfectly trained polo pony deliberately bump another pony in order to push it away from the shot its master is about to take is a heart stopping moment. I suppose it's the nearest thing we have to one of those medieval mêlées, where the knights would club each other to insensibility with blunted weapons until the last man was standing. It's just that with something like rugby, it's a hell of a lot easier to cheer your team on if they aren't specks on the horizon and aren't travelling at thirty miles an hour.

The match ended, and we were told with some reliability by Richardson that the Maharajah's team had won, which of course, going on his goal scoring rate, was Ari's team. We toasted the losers and the winners, as if they'd care that we were doing so, and finished off the soft fruit and the last of the champagne. It was then a case for waiting for our lost lamb to return. Other parties around us started their engines and packed up their rugs and baskets and soon we were one of the few cars left on our stretch of the perimeter.

"It's too bad of him," Lawrence said. "He only had to find a bloody bush or something."

"I hope nothing's happened to him," Gilbert said. "If anything's going to happen to anyone, it generally happens to him."

"Don't be wet," Lawrence said. "What could happen to him?"

Gilbert gave Lawrence an old-fashioned look. "You obviously don't know him as well as you think you do. That man could get into trouble in an empty room."

"Harry, go and look for him, will you?" Stevie asked me. "We can't leave without him."

"I'm tempted," I said. "Let the killjoy catch the train."

"Please, Harry."

"Oh, all right. Just don't go without me. He may deserve it, I don't."

"And hurry up," Richardson said. "I'd like to have a drink or two before we go back, and I'd rather not drive that bally car in the dark." At the mention of drinks Gilbert perked up, and they assisted Stevie with the repacking of the hamper.

With a sigh, I clambered up from my comfortable position and walked off in the direction he'd last been seen going in. More cars chugged past me towards the main road, and I could see the area, next to a small hut which I could only assume was the clubhouse such as it was, where the horses and riders were congregating. It was a goodish walk and I upped the pace, getting more and more annoyed as I marched along. It was one thing for him to storm off in a sulk at college, or at his own house, but out in public—it wasn't something he'd done before, and never in front of Gilbert and Richardson.

It took me a good five minutes to cover the distance and when I got there, the area, roped off away from the main arena, was a hive of activity. Polo ponies gathered in knots, and each pony seemed to have several attendants. It wasn't difficult to spot him, however, as he was the only one wearing that ghastly shapeless coat; and the only one (other than the very few women in attendance) who wasn't in jodhpurs of some description.

He was leaning against the bonnet of a gleaming grey-green sports car, one hand pressed against the metal of the bonnet and the other holding a glass of champagne. He was laughing, his fringe moving in that oh-so-seductive way back and forth across his forehead. It was a movement of his that I had never decided whether he did deliberately or not. Looking at him, relaxed and smiling, I chose to think that, in this case, it very probably was. I wish I could say that I was surprised that he was talking to Ari. Some part of me had hoped that Ari was just the same as he had always been, and that he'd got his own little clique here in his polo team as ever he had at school, and that no one would be able to get near him.

Oh, how I hoped that had been true.

In truth, from the moment Charles had stalked off from our party, I had run a dozen scenes through my mind, each one of them having him approach Ari, just the way he had at school, and each overture had been rebuffed by the ever cool and over-discriminating Indian gentleman. It seemed, then, from the way they were talking and laughing together, and the way that Ari was gesticulating with every sentence, that things had changed for our erstwhile schoolmate, and he was no longer as unapproachable as some frozen glacier.

However, if there's one thing I am, it's adaptable, and if Ari could change, then there was no reason why I couldn't bend with those changes. If Charles considered me to be a jealous bitch, then I could show him that I was nothing of the sort. I tried not to suspect him of finding the slightest little thing to become irritated about, just for an excuse to storm off and find Ari. Smothering my jealous bitch, I plastered a smile on my face, lifted the rope dividing me from the horsey set, and walked as casually as I could to join them.

Ari didn't see me until I appeared at his elbow, as his back was to me, but I know the opposite was true for Charles. He'd spotted me as soon as I'd lifted that rope, and although the pleasant smile directed at Ari didn't falter, his eyes were wary. Damned cheek of the man, being defensive instead of apologetic.

"Hello, Harry," Charles said. "Singh—you remember Bircham, don't you? He was in my year."

I'm not an expert at beauty from the subcontinent, Ari being the only one from that place at our school, but I had an opportunity, while Ari returned to flashing his deep brown eyes and perfect white teeth at the object of my affection, to glance around and survey the other Indian gentlemen in the vicinity. Ari was lighter in skin than some, though by no means the lightest, but his face was definitely the most delicate and handsome of those around. Slightly taller than me, he exuded sex appeal, although perhaps that was the effect of the boots, the white vest that clung sweatily to his nicely defined chest, and the rather kinky gloves. The jodhpured and turbaned denizens bustling around the horses were servants, that much was very clear, and not an attractive face was found among them, but several of Ari's team-mates were decent enough to look at. I wondered briefly at the correlation between class and handsomeness in the subcontinent and pushed it aside. I'm no mathematician, or indeed any expert in geography or anthropology.

"Of course." But Ari looked like he'd never seen me in his entire life, and I suppose it's possible he hadn't. That set the short hairs on the back of my neck on end, because he was behaving as if Charles were a long-lost friend, and the number of times he'd cut us both at school, neither of us qualified as anything like. He held out a hand for me to shake which, annoyingly, I had to do. One can't be as rude as he used to be, after all.

"Ari invited us all to the match next week, as his guests," Charles said, glancing between myself and Ari. "I told him there might be a gaggle of us, but that doesn't seem to faze him."

"How very jolly," I said, and I hardly need to express just how fake that sentiment was. "Isn't it a frightful fag coming all the way down here twice in two weeks?"

"Oh, next week it's at Roehampton." Ari looked down his aquiline nose at the woodlouse who had dared to interrupt his conversation. "Perhaps you might find the distance annoying?" He turned his smile on me and I smiled right back. All right, my teeth were not like dazzling slabs of marble but they aren't falling out of my head, either.

"Not at all," I said. "We'd love to. All of us."

"Splendid." I have to say that were I not feeling like I could kick him in the shins, his accent was still positively to die for. "Here's my card," he continued, handing it to me, as if I were some kind of valet. "You can all stay at our place in town. Pater won't be back until October, so we'll have the place to ourselves. Perhaps we can even have a party…or two, what?"

"Or three, what?" I ignored the daggers that were coming from our mutual friend's direction. "Why stop at two, when three will do, I always say."

"Do you?" asked Ari, smoothly, not at all fooled by my charm, I could tell. "I think two a much more perfect number, I'm afraid. Well, Holland, it's been marvellous to catch up, sorry you couldn't come on with us, but we'll see you next week? Both—or all of you. All welcome!"

I bet, I thought savagely to myself, but simply smiled my goodbyes and tried not to grind my teeth as Ari shook hands with him, holding his hand for a good two seconds too long in my estimation.

Ari moved away towards a cluster of ponies and pony-wallahs, and I was left with a scowling companion. "There was no need to be rude," Charles said.

"I was perfectly civil, and you know it."

"I know you well enough to know the exact opposite," he said. "Oh, forget it. This gives us an excuse to get away from the house, anyway." We started to walk back towards the car. "Damned women."

"What?" I said, caught out by his out-of-the-blueness.

"Don't you realise what a circus the house is going to become in a few day's time?"

I hadn't given it much thought, due to the fact that he didn't want the subject raised, but now I came to think on it, he was probably right. I'd had little experience of wedding preparations; my dear parent had been respectful to my blushes and had—so far at least—kept faithful to the memory of my father and hadn't cast her net back into the marriage pond.

But I'd heard third-hand from other fellows whose sisters and the like had got themselves hitched. It seemed an awful lot of preparation was needed to put on a wedding. A preponderance of flowers had to die, for a start, and their colour, shape and volume were all as vital as the bride's gown.

"Hmm. Yes, I suppose so," I said.

"Believe me," Charles said with vehemence. "When my mother organizes something, she doesn't miss out anything. We used to have parties, back— well, a while ago, and although I was too young to attend them, other than just to be paraded for the benefit of the friends and neighbours—I was well aware of the flurry they caused for days or weeks beforehand. I wonder why Mother hasn't started with the arrangements already, seeing when it is."

"Excuse me for belabouring the point, but when exactly is it?"

He stopped for a moment, and his fringe flopped endearingly into his eyes. "Oh. I've been an arse again, haven't I?"

I shrugged and started to walk on, letting him catch up. "Perhaps a bit. I'm used to it. But…"

"The others." Charles looked up to where the car waited.

"Exactly."

"I'll make it up to them," he said in a quiet tone. "I will. And you. And thanks. Thanks for not being an arse back there. You had every right to. About

Ari." He brushed my hand with his fingers, just a little, and smiled, just a little, before running ahead.

Sometimes just a little is enough.

Chapter Eight

As if Charles had had some kind of premonition, the circus, as he'd called it, began the very next day. I still hadn't had the date from him, of course. (See how easily he changes the subject and how easily he can deflect me?)

So I was forced to pin Stevie down after dinner when we got home, welcomed by Mrs Holland as if we were Odysseus and his crew crawling up the beach after twenty years, and found out that—due to circumstances— it was considered that a civil ceremony would be best all round and that the deed was due to happen in two weeks' time. "That doesn't really give us much time, so we'll all have to pitch in," she said.

I'm quite sure that entire wars have been planned and executed in less time, so I couldn't imagine what would take so blasted long and I said so. For my pains I was treated to a face which clearly said "Boys," and she left me to join the bridge players, leaving me to worry about what kind of pitching in I'd be expected to do. Richardson and Gilbert made a temporary escape that evening. Gilbert had a cousin in Minehead, and they went over to spend the night and the next day, threatening us all with their return. It was a sign that no one knew them that well that they were entreated to hurry back.

Shortly before luncheon I was reading in my room, although truth to tell it was more like dozing than actual reading. The connecting door opened and Charles barged in, his face full of some bright emotion. As I've indicated, sometimes I find it easier to let him express what mood he's in before I say anything at all.

"The vicar is here," Charles said, with as much dislike as if human-sized slugs had invaded. "He and Mrs Witherspoon walked through the woods to the garden. They nearly caught Father and me by the lily-ponds."

"That might have been painful," I drawled, not thinking for a moment he'd appreciate my wit, and I was right, as he threw a pillow at me. Luckily he throws like a girl.

"Why are they here?" We're all dragging off to London, I thought. I'd better get Mother to send me some more clothes. I looked out of my window but saw nothing except a gardener trimming something green in a desultory fashion.

"God knows," he said with feeling. "My guess is that Claude will be trying to strong arm Witherspoon into letting them get married at St Michael's. It would be just like him, he's got no idea. It's bad enough."

"Bad enough what?"

"Oh, nothing. Forget it." He paced up and down, running distracted hands through his hair. "You'd think they'd be ashamed, at their age."

"I'm sure I would."

"It's the look of the thing. Notwithstanding how it's going to look when it comes out about Father."

"Well, that's very much the point," I said. "Look, I'm sure you've discussed this with your father, but what's the position? With him, I mean?"

He stopped and slid down onto the floor beside me, and I took the advantage, dropping my hand to his shoulder and kneading it. "He's…. Well, he doesn't like to talk about it, to tell you the truth."

"Really," I said, with as much dryness as I dared. "You surprise me."

"I think he's keeping calmer than he wants to be, for my sake. I don't think he came back for her, you see. I think he came back just to see me. He could have seen her at any time, and he never did."

I kept quiet about the fact the elder Holland could have seen his son at any time too. "Am I going to get to meet him?" I asked.

There was a long silence, so I guessed the answer before it came. "No. Don't be cross. Not yet anyway."

"It's all right," I said, "I understand."

"You're not thinking stupid thoughts, are you?" Charles leaned back and hit me with the back of his head.

"Me? Never."

"I don't want you thinking I'm hiding you away, you see. I know it looked like that with the family. It's more I'm hiding him away, if you like."

"I said, I understand." I risked a quick kiss on top of his head. "You want to keep him to yourself, for now. For as long as you can."

He caught my hand, and pulled it around his neck, causing me nearly to fall off the window-seat. "That's exactly it. And…well, he's not…he was injured you see. Quite badly. He's horribly self-conscious about it. Skin grafts and the like. He spent a long time in hospital after the war. I've shown you pictures of before."

I nodded. He'd not been unlike his brother in looks, to tell the truth. I wanted to ask how it happened, but my imagination was providing that for me; it was impossible not to be aware of the injuries a man suffered during the war, it was everywhere around you. Men with missing parts, or with faces it was hard to look on.

"It's quite bloody, the hash they've made of it. I think perhaps leaving his face as it was might have been better, but who knows? No one would recognize his face the way he is. But his voice is unmistakable. So it put him off coming home, you see. And the longer it got, the more he thought to himself that he was better staying away."

"That's what he said?"

"No, of course not. He'd never say that kind of thing, not to me. Doesn't want to seem cowardly, does he? But it seems obvious, doesn't it? Coming home, looking like that, knowing that you might see fear, or worse, pity, on your wife's face, knowing you might terrify your son. I'd think it would give any man pause."

"But many men did come home, with terrible injuries," I said.

"I know," Charles said, "I know. And I don't know how I would have been, I don't. I would hope I would have been just pleased to have him home, alive, here. I'd hope I'd be that white about it. But you don't know, do you? What if I'd been ashamed of him, what if I'd started saying to him, 'Oh, don't come up for Sports Day this year, Father. Don't come to Prizegiving.'"

"You can't go around thinking that kind of thing," I said, "You'll drive yourself mad. I don't think for one moment you'd have done that."

"But it's what I do," he murmured. "I kept you away from here, and what did you infer from that? Because I didn't want the aggravation, or didn't want to subject you to the Hollands en masse, or I was ashamed of you, or what?"

"All of the above, at one point or another," I said.

He was quiet, for a moment but his fingers stroked the back of my hand. I wanted, more than anything, to draw him up on the seat beside me, but I was more cruel than that. I was going to let him whip himself, because God alone knows I had little enough opportunity. "Well, exactly."

"And your father doesn't know that you have these thoughts, so why are you kicking yourself? He's here, you are welcoming, there's no reason for this, you know that."

Charles made a noncommittal noise.

"So. What do you think he thinks about the whole thing? He's not going to leap up like Banquo and be the proverbial ghost at the feast, is he? I'll need a little warning if he's planning to do anything like that."

"No, I don't think he is."

"But you don't know."

He shook his head. "Would he? I mean, I think I might, if it were me. I'm pretty sure you would."

"Oh, I definitely would. I'll be the one declaring the impediment, if called upon to do so."

He snorted. "You know, I'd give good money to see that."

"You won't need to pay, dear boy, you certainly couldn't miss it. Because if I were to do anything so vulgar, it would only be at one ceremony, you know."

Charles smiled at me, quickly and as nervously as I'd ever seen him. I don't think he actually believed me, and that was a tad galling.

"Where does he stand, legally, I mean? I suppose I should know the basics, but what matrimonial law I have done doesn't really cover spouses coming back from the dead, particularly after they've been proclaimed officially dead."

He shrugged and for a moment he looked a little lost. It was an expression I adored, even though I rarely liked the situation that made him look that way. "I don't know. We...we just haven't spoken about it. We haven't talked about much, to be honest."

I could understand that. Charles wasn't the type to fire questions at anyone, and if he took after his father? Lord. What a jolly pair of conversationalists. I put my book down and slid down onto the floor beside him. We sat chastely side by side, only our hips touching, the warmth of our skins seeping through the material, a hidden and wicked secret. He'd drawn up his knees and was hugging them. The look in his eyes was one I wished I could wipe away with a kiss, but it was action, not kisses that solved matters in the long run; if my own father had taught me anything, it was that.

"Well, I think you'd better start talking to him about what he's planning to do, if anything. Claude, well, I won't care if he pitches head first into the wedding cake with shock, but your mother...perhaps forewarned is forearmed?

I know you are angry with her, but still. Your father. He does know what's going on, doesn't he?"

"Yes," he said. "That's what makes it so bloody. He heard about it from someone else, so I suppose he must have known even before I did, seeing as how I was almost the last to know, along with you."

"He's not harbouring any designs on Claude, then."

Charles gave a small smile. "No, nothing so theatrical. Claude was right about one thing, that Father and he were close. I don't doubt that Father would have wanted Claude to look after Mother. I just don't think he ever thought he'd be around to see it happen. But he's still pretty steamed."

And we were back to the unasked questions: where has he been? Why did he wait until after he was declared dead? Not questions I was going to ask. Softly softly, catchee monkey.

"I can't tell Mother. I can't. You've seen how happy she is."

I hadn't, to be frank. I'd seen her happy to have her son around, but I'd been spared any of her joy at future nuptials. She looked on edge and unhappy when Claude and her son were together in the same room, but perhaps she showed a different side to him. I'm sure she did, and why not? She didn't know there was a horribly burned man lurking around the grounds, talking in secret to her son. I was the only one who had that piece of information. I pushed aside the treachery that surfaced, the disloyalty I'd felt before: You only have his word for this. I had to believe him this time. I had to. And to do so I was going to have to do something he might never forgive me for.

"Oh well, let the games commence," I said. "It's not like we can run away now, is it?"

"More's the pity."

WHEN WE CAME DOWN FOR LUNCH, we discovered Stevie deep in conversation with Mrs Witherspoon at the foot of the stairs. Mrs Witherspoon turned to us with the cheeriest of smiles and hallooed at us as if we were errant foxes. "Well met!" she exclaimed. "I thought you young bloods had driven away and left us all to moulder." It was clear she missed little.

"Just to Dunster," he said. "No, we're here for the duration, just about."

"Oh, how lovely," she said, beaming, "I haven't been to Dunster in an age. Hillyard and I used to go from time to time. I don't think he would have taken me if he'd thought my mind wasn't entirely on the horses." She gave me the most wicked smile. Stevie took her by the arm looking mildly alarmed, and led her towards the dining room, with the two of us trailing behind.

"Mrs Witherspoon, you must help us with the invitations after luncheon. Margaret has left it in my hands and I can't keep it down to twenty, no matter what Margaret says. Someone is going to be mortally offended, no matter what I try to do."

"Oh my dear," Mrs Witherspoon said, "I'm afraid that's always been the case for every wedding that ever was or ever would be. One rather envies Adam and Eve in that respect. Margaret was most sensible to leave it to you." She lowered her voice, but was still very audible. "That way she will still be aware of the problems, but as she didn't cause them, she doesn't have to worry about them. Very good idea for a bride."

I saw Charles colour a dark red at the word "bride." I couldn't blame him. I suppose all young men find the word allied with their own mothers rather distasteful. It leads on to other such unpleasantness such as "wedding night" and "honeymoon." It hardly bears examination. In fact, what it bears is one sitting with one's fingers in one's ears and one's eyes firmly shut, singing *la la la la la la la*, that's what it bears.

That luncheon was the first time I had met the vicar, the Reverend Hillyard Witherspoon, and he was a pleasant surprise after his bone-jarring bluestocking of a wife. About the same height as Claude Holland, but with a lot more padding around the middle, he had a round, pleasant face, echoed by round, pleasant glasses. Almost entirely bald, except for a natural halo of hair which gave the impression it had slipped around his ears, his head was permanently shiny, which he dabbed at from time to time with a huge white handkerchief. In point of fact, he was the dampest man I had ever met; his palm was slick with moisture, his upper lip was constantly be-dewed and the sweat from his head trickled down his temples.

It didn't take long, over luncheon that day, to realise that he was as inoffensive as his wife was wicked, and the very thought of him thumping the pulpit and promising eternal damnation to anyone or anything—even the sun to which he seemed to be in constant torment—seemed impossible. For all that, though, he managed to hold his own against the virile force of Claude Holland, and although his voice was softer than I would imagine a vicar's needed to be, to reach over the footlights, as it were, it had a clarity to it, and an unstoppability, that undermined anything that tried to override it. It was, I mused as I devoured my crab salad, rather an impressive trick, and wondered if one had to endure theological school to learn it.

"Surely, Reverend," Claude was saying, "if the law is now being sensible, the church should follow suit."

"It rarely happens," Witherspoon said. "The Church isn't always in synch with the law. Of course you *can* insist on a church wedding—"

"In that case," Claude said, interrupting, but it was of no avail, because the irresistible force of Witherspoon's voice swept the immovable object of Claude Holland's away.

"—But I don't advise it, really and truly I don't. The law is far too new, and this village hasn't taken the news well. To them it still smacks of incest."

"Not only the village," came a low voice from my side.

Witherspoon blushed, which in a man of his profession and age surprised me a great deal, but it did look rather delightfully Dickensian. I'd hoped he'd not have heard the remark, but his ears, no doubt attuned to years of listening to choir boys muttering at the back of the chancel, had caught the words meant really only for me. "Yes, of course," Withspoon said, mildly flustered, but obviously determined to do his duty where he had been called. "But the talk will settle down in time." He looked straight towards us, as if he suspected me of muttering dissent as well, which was most unfair.

Margaret looked nervously over at her son and then back to the vicar. "I don't feel entirely comfortable with a Register ceremony, Reverend. God is not in the service, God is not in the building. Giving my vows to some clerk, well, it doesn't seem decent."

"And to be brutally honest," Claude Holland added, "I'd prefer to swear to a power who is going to care whether I keep those vows or not."

"You have a point, Mr Holland," Mrs Witherspoon said, "and Hillyard had the solution just this morning, didn't you, Hillyard?"

As the Reverend Witherspoon was sitting between Mrs Holland and Claude, they didn't catch the vicar's fleeting expression of panic but I did, and I think I fell more in love with the dreadful vicar's wife than ever at that point. "Yes—I think I do," he said, his features melting into gratitude as his wife took over. I wondered if he heard confession himself, and thinking about that for a moment, missed part of what she said. I had to mentally sprint to catch up.

"...have the ceremony at the Register Office as planned on the Tuesday," Mrs Witherspoon was saying. "Nothing wrong with that, and perfectly respectable. But don't drag everyone into London. Issue two invitations, one just for the immediate family for the Register ceremony. There's absolutely no point having everyone trawling into London, what with the crowds and the parking."

Hillyard Witherspoon nodded in agreement, drips of perspiration trickling down his temples. His face lent weight to the argument, and he looked positively horrified that anyone would travel to the fleshpots of London to do anything, let alone marry.

"What people expect these days," the redoubtable woman went on, "and I think they still use the deprivation of war as an excuse, but it's all getting a bit thin, don't you think?—is a smoked salmon canapé beanfeast and rather more champagne than is good for them. Now Hillyard disapproves of excess, and I know I should too, but the only way to do this, if you'll take my advice, is to do it in a way that the village expects."

"I don't know—" Margaret began, but she was no match for Mrs Witherspoon.

"To drive off and marry in London and to do nothing else," Mrs Witherspoon went on, "I'm sorry to be blunt, Mrs Holland, but it smacks of subterfuge; as if you are ashamed of what you are doing, and you aren't, are you?"

"Of course not," Margaret said, but she looked less than sure and she looked to Claude, as if for reassurance. I saw her in a way I hadn't done before, like a clear glass vase, made by expert hands, and created to be beautiful, holding the most sumptuous of roses for others' appreciation, but wafer thin, fragile and easily broken. "We aren't doing anything wrong," she said, and she looked, all of a sudden, like a young girl, a debutante before the war, holding on defiantly to the hand of the boy she loved and facing down disapproving parents.

I should write novels, you know. I really should.

Claude took her hand and beside me, a restless soul stirred in his chair. I felt on edge, as if I'd have to grab hold of him if he went for Claude's throat. Thank heavens for learned behaviour, that one doesn't tear the throat out of one's uncle in public. "I don't think that's what the vicar means," Claude said. Another shift on the chair beside me and I dropped my hand between us to brush against Charles's thigh.

"No one is saying that, Mrs Holland," the vicar said. "But the change in the law is very, very new and people are going to have to learn to adjust. I know it isn't incest and so do you, and so does the man in the street, but, well, we English don't adjust well to sudden change, do we? We have only just stopped reeling from a king being beheaded. At least the Church seems still be catching up."

"You're saying we should have waited," Claude said, his face darkening. "Don't you think we've waited enough?"

I had a very real feeling that he was saying "hadn't he waited enough?" and it gave me a rather uncomfortable. From the looks of the silent majority around the table, I don't think I was the only one. I was beginning to wish that they were having this discussion in private or *en famille,* and counting me as not one of the *famille* to be *en.*

"Hillyard isn't saying anything of the sort," Mrs Witherspoon said. "Are you, Hillyard?" She didn't wait to see her husband shake his head, but he did, all the same. "I think you are doing the right thing, if you ask me, and better that the village gossip about the wedding, and forgive me, but I'm going to be indelicate here, than that they gossip about the fact that you are living here without one." She blushed a little, but that didn't hold a candle to Hillyard's round cheeks, which flared crimson.

The chair beside me flew backward. "Is that what people think? The filthy minded—"

Lawrence cut in, "Steady, Holland."

Charles took no notice of Lawrence. "So you're saying that they should have to get married just to appease Mrs Gosling and the Misses Summerhaye and others of their ilk? You all know those vicious cats will say anything—imagine anything—so that's just about the worst excuse for marriage I can think of. Mother, please tell me it's not because of gossip?"

Everyone started to talk at once then, Stevie and Miss Holland reassuring Margaret, Margaret reassuring her son, Claude railing at the table in general. It went on for a good few seconds before he slumped back beside me, as if exhausted. He was pale, and I knew that just holding his secret to himself, and wanting to shout out the truth was weighing him down. It took Claude's intervention to silence them all, and they subsided. If I didn't feel myself vital to keep my friend from murder, I would have wished myself a mile away. If I had been a regular family visitor, I wouldn't have felt so uncomfortable, but what was odd was the fact that they treated me as one of them, and I wasn't sure I wanted to be.

Margaret Holland addressed the table in general. "Of course we aren't doing this to silence the gossip, darling, you know this family better than that. If we listened to every nasty rumour and took it seriously, well."

Someone turn the subject back to the wedding, I thought. The last thing he needed was anyone bringing up his past, his time "away" or perhaps even his history with the verger, not right now. I waded in, feeling like a naked swimmer in crocodile invested waters. "Mrs Witherspoon, you said that the Reverend had the answer, so what is it?"

She grinned, a grateful look in her eyes. "Nothing impossible. A civil ceremony in London, and then a church service here."

"But you said we couldn't have a church service," Claude said.

"I said there's nothing to say you can't," Hillyard explained. "But I don't think it's advisable, with the mood against this law the way it is. But you can have a Blessing, and that's much the same thing, you know. God in the Church, and a reaffirming of your promises to each other."

"And a big party," Lawrence said, which was probably the most sensible thing he'd said at the most sensible time. "Which will please the village."

"I think it will certainly help," the vicar said.

"You aren't going to silence everyone," Mrs Witherspoon said, "but then you wouldn't do that no matter what you did."

"I think having two ceremonies sounds wonderful," Clarissa Holland said. "Although, Margaret, that means an added dimension of organisation, but I'm sure we can do it."

"We'll all help, Margaret," Stevie said.

Mrs Holland turned to Hillyard Witherspoon. "And you can fit us in at the Church?"

"Of course," he said, and when he wiped his face again, I got the feeling that it was more than heartfelt. "The Saturday of the 18th is free. That gives you nearly three weeks. Esther Farthing's young man has got scarlet fever and they've had to cancel."

"Well then, Vicar," Claude said. "Come through to the library, and we'll sort it out there." He stood up and led the vicar out, leaving me feeling as if all the water had been drained from my vital organs. I had no idea, other than the fact that he loathed the idea of his mother marrying Claude, how he managed to create such a huge level of tension in the room. Perhaps it was normal, I mused. No one else seemed particularly exhausted and indeed Stevie, Margaret and Clarissa were chatting away as if nothing had happened at all. Perhaps it hadn't. Perhaps it was only me, too attuned to him, or perhaps I read more into it than was there, as now, once his uncle had left the room, he was making smart comments about whether they should have a circus theme. I had the feeling that if Claude Holland had been in the room this conversation would not have taken place, but Margaret was taking it in good heart, and laughing with him.

"And fire-eaters," Charles was saying, "perhaps in a line up to the church. That would mean that you couldn't have silk flowers in your hair, Mother, or anything too elaborate or you'd go up in a puff of smoke."

"Oh, really, darling."

"Does anyone know if we could get a freak show?" he went on.

"Now that's just revolting," Stevie said.

"I don't know," I said. "If it's good luck to have a sweep on hand, it might be even better luck to have a pair of Siamese twins, or a bearded lady."

"Or a horned man," Charles added. I had to stop myself from kicking him, or even looking at him sharply, because someone might have noticed. Stevie was sharp, especially over things he said. I might have guessed that the subject wasn't random.

"Or a dancing bear," Lawrence said, hopefully deflecting the barbed comment. "And Polonius fighting with the local cocks. No, it's a horrible idea, Holland. And you know it. Don't take any notice of him, Margaret. he has a macabre sense of humour, we all know that."

He bared his teeth at Lawrence; Lawrence probably thought it was a smile.

"Darling," Margaret said, still laughing. "Perhaps it was a rather bizarre idea, but your uncle would never permit it."

"Ah." He countered her with a charming smile. "You admit the idea has some merit then? You'd agree if Claude did?"

"Oh, I don't know. But he won't, so there's no point discussing it further. But I do like the idea of some kind of entertainment during the day, for the village."

"Perhaps a fair," Clarissa said, "rather than a freak show."

"That will take care of itself," Charles said.

Clarissa sensibly waded on as if he hadn't spoken. "I'm sure we could find a small private concern to run a few stalls."

Mrs Witherspoon, who had been watching but not participating, said, "Hillyard has several contacts there, of course. Saunders came in June, so I don't suppose he'll be willing to come back, as he goes from here around the coast of Cornwall. There's Rumbolts, who come for the Harvest Festival, and…oh, what's their name? No, I can't remember. The ones with the Morris. Probably just as well, Hillyard has a real theological dilemma matching pagan and Christian. Anyway, I have Mr Rumbolt's address, or where he can be contacted at least. Would you like me to get in touch and ask the question?

Perhaps he can spare a couple of stalls—we don't want the whole concern, do we? Not rides and traction engines and the like."

"No, I was thinking of a few stalls in the garden. Perhaps a pig roast and trestle tables."

"Hoop-la, that sort of thing," Stevie said.

"Win a goldfish," added Clarissa. "Oh, I had such a lovely goldfish as a child."

"Well, it sounds like you have everything in hand," Charles said, rising. I followed his example, of course, as did Lawrence to my surprise. "I'm sure you ladies will excuse us, or you'll have Harry and me wearing stripy shirts, bow ties and practising our 'roll-up, roll-up's. I'm sure we only wish to attend, and not make complete fools of ourselves."

"Darling, just a moment," his mother said. "Come out onto the terrace with me for a moment, will you?"

Charles hesitated, as if sensing a trap, and I couldn't see how it was anything but. I had no idea what Margaret wanted to tell him, but in his current state of mind, I doubted if it could be anything that he would consider to be good. Then he shrugged and followed his mother, leaving me free to depart with Lawrence—oh joy—and the other ladies to continue their nuptial discussion.

"What was that about, do you think?" Lawrence asked me as the door closed behind us.

"No idea, I'm afraid." Not that I would have shared my thoughts with him if I had.

"Stevie wants me to check on Polonius." His shy demeanour suggested fear I'd rebuff him. "Would you want to help me find him?"

"Is he lost again?"

"I doubt it. For a reptile he seems to have a surprisingly good homing instinct, but Stevie is fond of the monster, and likes someone to find him every day. Some girls get spaniels. I suppose she doesn't have to worry about exercise, at least."

That, from Lawrence was almost a joke, and I found myself giving him a small laugh as reward. We walked out of the front door and into the sunlight, crossing the gravel drive and making a wide sweep of the gardens. We passed the library, where Claude could be seen still closeted with the vicar, and at the far end of the house we saw Margaret sitting with her son on the terrace.

"Don't envy him," he said, "but she's the only one who could ever get through to him." As we stopped to watch them from a distance, Clarissa came out of the French doors and my friend stood and left. "My instinct tells me to stay out of the way for an hour or so."

"Suits me." I wasn't inclined to throw myself in front of the Holland juggernaut. It would seek me out soon enough. We continued in search of the giant tortoise. In a mad world, it seemed as unlikely as anything else going on.

Chapter Nine

Charles was missing at dinner. I was only half-surprised, because spotting him talking to Margaret that afternoon, there was something in his stance that I recognised even from the distance I was. His mother was as tall as he, but it looked to me as if he were looking up at her, like a child; and the set of his shoulders. I didn't know what was wrong, but saw that it was something. I kept it to myself, however.

We found Polonius under some rhododendrons on the far west side of the garden, almost obscured by foliage and the glare of the sun. Unsurprisingly, I know nothing about tortoises, particularly giant ones, so when he lumbered out from his shelter towards Lawrence I couldn't help but be amazed.

"Does he know you?"

"Of course he does," Lawrence said. "He's known me since I was born. No one has the faintest idea how old he is. But I don't think he greets me because he's missed me, or anything." He reached into a pocket and took out some neatly chopped apple. "Apple is a passion of his. He could probably smell it as we walked across the lawn. If he is missing, it's the easiest way to find him. He's not so often away from the house so much, I swear he picks up on an atmosphere."

We spent a few minutes with the tortoise, and I marvelled at the size of him, impressed for the first time by something at Hellsingers. I swear—and I feel stupid for this—that it was then, sitting in the sunshine watching a handsome man feed a giant tortoise, that I first began to see the whole Hamlet-ness of the entire situation. It took my breath away for a moment, that I could be so incredibly dense, and I was sure that everyone else had seen the coincidences and I'd been blundering around in the dark. I was so deep in thought that I hadn't noticed that Lawrence was standing, blotting out the sun and saying my name.

"I'm sorry," I said. There was a kind of mad jigsaw puzzle going on behind my eyes as each character seemed to step up on a stage, take a bow in medieval costume, and ally itself to a member of the household, but some of it didn't fit, it just didn't fit. I scrambled up glaring down at the tortoise as if it was all his fault, which in a way it was. "What were you saying?"

I never found out, because whatever it was, Lawrence obviously thought I should have been listening the first time, and he kept quiet all the way back to the house. I thought I had his part in the play, but then…I wasn't really sure. Freak show? No need to order one, Mrs Holland, it was already here.

I was sent to seek out another missing person later that evening, nothing quite as cold-blooded as Polonius, of course, but a hot-headed missing son and heir. No one had seen him since his talk with Margaret, and although she acted as if she had no idea why he might be missing, I was pretty sure she wasn't being entirely truthful, the smallest of clues being the way she kept exchanging glances with Claude. It seemed he was asking her a question she could not answer.

I searched half-heartedly around the house as directed, but I knew that wherever he was he wasn't going to let himself be found. If anyone could have found him, it would have been me, and as he was concealing himself thoroughly from my search, then he was nowhere that anyone else could find—unless he was in the attic and plummeted through the joists by accident, landing red-faced onto the floor below. Only an accident might reveal him.

Perhaps, I thought fancifully, if he had apples in his pocket, we could attach a leash onto Polonius and have the monstrous creature seek him out. As diverting as that might be, we didn't really have the time, and Polonius didn't have the nose of a gun-dog, even if he were seeking apples. At the speed Polonius moved, I would probably die of boredom or old age before we'd search half of the garden.

We dined without him, and his absence cast a pall over the proceedings so completely that the moment the dessert was cleared away the party broke up. Margaret excused herself saying she felt tired, and left us to do what we would with the evening. After she'd gone, we all drifted off to amuse ourselves. I braved the library, where Dear Uncle Claude was sitting at his desk writing something or other—probably a treatise along the line of *The Prince*—and picked myself out a book—*Moby-Dick*. Something long and dull, I was sure, although I'd heard it was improving, and one which I had always promised myself I would read one day. Gilbert had surprised me during the term having recommended it; the most surprise coming from the fact that Gilbert could read at all, but that was unkind of me, he got into Oxford somehow, and it wasn't via a tunnel. He'd offered to lend me the thing back at college, indicating that there were elements within it that someone of my inclinations would find "interesting." I think mainly it was his leer that put me off at the time and I refused his offer with dignity.

However, faced with a quiet evening, I pulled the book from the shelf and absconded with it, trusting that Claude hadn't noticed which one I'd taken, as it was unlikely he had an encyclopaedic knowledge and to my own personal chagrin I'd noticed that the books were jumbled around any old how, not a consideration for those of us who prefer order and alphabetical precision. This laissez-faire attitude to belongings was clearly a Holland trait. With my prize I sprawled in the drawing room, for the chairs there were supremely comfortable, so much so that with the warm evening sun pouring through the windows, and the leaden weight of Cook's treacle tart in my stomach, I found myself nodding over the book like some old gentleman in a London club.

When I awoke it was to find that the drawing room was almost dark; only the fire and a standard lamp on the far side of the mantelpiece pierced the gloom. Charles was sitting in the chair opposite, obviously deep in thought, his legs curled up on the chair and a look of such exquisite concentration on his face that I was loath to disturb him. He hadn't noticed I'd opened my eyes, but I was touched that he had crept in and sat quietly for some time, judging by the number of cigarettes in the ashtray beside him, without waking me. I found myself smiling fondly at the thought of us, like an old married couple, comfortable with each other, even when one of them was asleep, and wanting to be close for comfort's sake. I hoped that was the reason behind it—although I wondered if I veneered too many of my own longings and motivations upon him. I hoped not.

Of course I ruined this idyllic and rather erotic tableau in moments, as I had forgotten the white whale perched on my lap. Before I could stop it, it slid traitorously down my thighs and over my knees, crashing—or so it seemed in that quietude—onto the floor, causing that look of lost contemplation to be wiped off his face, and me to curse inwardly at my idiocy.

"Hello." The word was a caress; I could almost feel the touch of Charles's hand against mine, even though he didn't move, and neither did I, but the look he gave me brought him wafer-close.

"You were missed," I said, wishing that we were more alone—on a moor, or somewhere a dozen miles from the next human being.

"Only by you."

"Not true, of course. But yes, probably most."

He smiled and broke the eye contact, to my great regret. Looking into the fire he said, "Do you know what she wanted? She must have said at dinner, surely?" When I shook my head, his voice got hard, with a hard coating to it that he rarely showed, even to me. "She wants me to give her away, or rather, walk her down the aisle. I'm an idiot. I just…I just didn't see it—and you'd think I would, wouldn't you?" He turned around to me again and his eyes were shining this time. Not with tears—I've never seen him cry; not really—but with some kind of inner violence I could hardly bear.

"Don't. You do this to yourself, and it's always about other people."

He gave the shortest of laughs and curled up further in his chair. "Of course I should have, who else is there? Lawrence wouldn't dare, not without talking to me first, and her uncles are pretty much unable to travel further than a few miles. I don't know why I didn't see it coming."

"I think it's because you thought it would be a Register ceremony?"

He was silent, hugging his knees. "There you go, with your clarity. Why do I run away and labour over these things when time and time again you cut to the heart of it?"

"There you go, then. You'll learn eventually. Perhaps we could tattoo it to your arm, or something. When in Danger and in Gloom, seek Bircham out in every room." It was an appalling off -the-cuff rhyme, but it had the desired effect and he beamed at me and even looked like he might have recovered his humour enough to throw a cushion, had he had one to hand.

The hall clock began to chime; I counted silently. It was midnight. Seemed no one had missed me much, at least. But Charles had sought me out, even if it was after his gloomy period. "Everyone's gone to bed, I think," he said. "Come on."

I followed him, and we went to his room where he locked the door and made love to me in a way he hadn't done since our last vacation the Christmas before. He had a loathing of light when it came to sex, preferring to seek out everything by touch and taste. He drew the curtains against the moonlight, trapping us together in the soft half-real darkness.

His mouth traced words on my skin that I interpreted as I wished and when he'd pushed me as far as we both could stand, he clung to me while the contractions flowed away from us and our bodies cooled; his hands held me tight as ever I wished for, until at last he fell asleep.

THE WEEK ROLLED AROUND, AND IT was Friday before we knew it and we were on another train heading for London, and Ari. In the intervening days, the house had settled into a kind of cool *entente-cordiale*, concentrating on arranging two weddings with a kind of fervent zeal. When conversations had to be undertaken, they were polite. Professional and formal things. Advice about colours and vases, not about ethics and morality.

Which in a way, suited me just fine, but the strain had stretched my friend like putty. He lay almost comatose across the whole seat on the train, to the obvious disapproval of the only other occupant, a white-haired lady with a basket and very blue eyes. She didn't say anything about it, but she radiated distaste. He took no notice and to be frank, neither did I. At least he didn't have his shoes off, or his head in my lap, more's the pity.

Ari's father's house proved to be one of those lovely white Regency houses on the edge of Notting Hill. Several storeys high, whitewashed and just the sort of thing I could see myself in. The inside however had been quite marred by what was probably Ari's father's taste. To my mind the decoration should be left alone, letting the Regency speak for itself, but apparently the Indian taste called for dark wall hangings and native artwork on every surface. Ari had the bad taste to be out when we arrived and we were shown to our rooms by an Indian servant wearing a full length white cotton coat with white trousers beneath. It was rather glamorous, but I think I'd object to dressing like that in England—but perhaps he didn't have much of a say. Or maybe he was more comfortable, who can tell? I only know that if I was sent up to Notting Hill for a basket of foie gras and some quails' eggs, I'd rather not stand out quite so much.

The rooms we were given were on different floors and I had to restrain myself from commenting on it. Perhaps I would have done if Ari had been showing us around, so my restraint didn't deserve medals. I would dearly have liked to have known on which floor Ari's room was situated, but I had a horrible feeling that I already knew. I kept my face carefully blank throughout the small tour, because Charles looked at me suspiciously more than once.

We skulked in his room until just before four, that being the time when we had been promised tea—and I was starving, having missed lunch entirely—and the tea bell had just rung when Ari burst in room, all slab teeth and bonhomie.

I had to work hard on the blank face once again, because after all he hadn't gone to my room first, as far as I knew. "I'm dreadfully sorry," he said, clasping Charles's hand in his, then giving mine a less than perfunctory shake. "I really meant to be here, but Simeon, oh, you remember Goldstein, yes? He called me this morning and insisted I come and look at a couple of ponies with him, over at the barracks. I've only been there once before so it was hard to refuse."

"Surely people aren't selling off the King's horses?" he asked.

Ari linked his arm through Charles's. "Come for tea," he said. "No, of course not. It was merely somewhere handy to stable them while the man found a buyer. Totally against regs apparently, but as long as it's done quickly and the horses are out within the day people turn a blind eye. Nice pair of ponies too. If Simeon hadn't bought them, I might have made him an offer, but then it's not really cricket to poach."

"No, it really isn't." I followed on like a spare wheel and trying hard not to grit my teeth.

Sad to say the rest of the day—we dined in, which as it turned out was just as well—was one of the most frustrating, annoying and yet oddly boring times I have ever spent in Charles's company. I knew he was playing up, but whether that was because of my rash comments to Gilbert and Richardson or any relighting of the torch he'd carried for Ari for so long it was hard to tell.

I'd seen him have crush after crush and he'd never rubbed my face in it the way he did that day.

Oh, he was so bright, and *so* lively. He smiled, he leaned on the table with full attention listening to every boring detail of Ari's life since he'd left Druitt's. Believe me, it was not that exciting. Unless of course you are madly excited by a lot of show-off first-class sea travel interspersed with descriptions of every polo match. I think what was most galling was him attempting to bring me into the conversation at intervals, as if he had forgotten I was there, and then felt he needed to include me. I'd seen him do the same to Lawrence and my blood was boiling at the inattention, veiled as sociability. Oh, he had an anecdote for everything and he seemed to make Ari laugh on a fairly regular basis. I laughed right along with them, oh how I laughed. What a jolly threesome we made.

After dinner Charles sprawled on the floor with books of photographs whilst Ari sat on a chair behind him explaining each picture—who was in it, and which part of the globe it was taken on. Since they were mostly pictures of horses standing still with riders upon them, or of pony-wallahs holding horses or blurred or tiny horses, they could have been taken just about anywhere, and frankly anyone could have said "That was in Bangalore at my uncle's palace, the pony had to be shot after that match," or "That match was in Argentina, you really should go one day, Holland. So much space, it's terribly freeing." Whilst the man was obviously not the kind of poseur who *needed* to fake his photos, he came off as one. Secretly I determined to spice up my own photographs in much the same way, claiming Hong Kong for Edinburgh, Bangkok for Brighton, that kind of thing.

The evening ground inexorably to an end and my face positively ached with smiling as we said our goodnights. It was then—although I admit that he wasn't already my favourite person, you may have gathered this already—that Ari earned my bitter hatred. He shook my hand, saying "I'll see you in the morning. We'll need to leave quite early. I'll have Duleep wake you at eight, is that all right?" I began to turn away. As I did I caught him taking Charles's hand as he had mine but he brought that hand up to his mouth, looking Charles in the eyes. I toiled quietly up the stairs, but slowly. Charles did, to give him credit, pull his hand away, but not in any way which spoke of outrage or shock. Well, he could hardly pretend to be either. I pretended not to notice while my stomach stabbed my heart into pieces. I called down, "Oh, we'll sleep in, most likely. Don't be surprised if we are late. So difficult to get out of a warm bed, don't you know."

Without another word, Charles followed me up the stairs and followed me up the extra flight to my room. Then, to my surprise, he pushed the door aside and walked in, closed it behind him, and leant against it before commencing into an angry, if subdued attack. "What is the matter with you? You couldn't have been ruder, could you? Short of spitting in his face, that is. I'd apologise for you if I didn't think that completely infantile."

"Why did you ask me to come? It's bloody obvious I'm not wanted on voyage." I opened a cupboard and found a decanter of what looked like dark red wine. I pulled the heavy stopper out and sniffed it. Port in the bedroom? Interesting.

"Now you are being ridiculous." He watched me in silence as I poured out a glass of the stuff and drank it. "Oh, that's charming."

"That's me. Charmingly ridiculous. An excellent foil." The port travelled down my throat, rich and thick, and seemed to settle somewhere warm and elastic behind my knees. It appeared to like it there, and spread its warmth outward and upwards, loosening my tongue and mind. "I'm the foil, and you're the straight man." I giggled. "Except that's not right either. Why don't you just bugger off …and bugger off." I knew I was being ridiculous, and less than charming, but I hated what had happened downstairs, and I hated Ari and right then—just then—I hated both of us.

"I've given you no reason to make you so bloody jealous," he said.

"But he has. And you aren't some blushing innocent." Another full glass of port cupped in my hand. "You knew bloody well what he invited you down here for and you came, because…why, exactly? To get your own back? To strike out at who? Me? Him? Or do you really, really want his dick that much?"

"Oh, for God's sake, Harry. Don't be such a fucking bitch! You're behaving like the worst kind of—"

"Go on. Just go on. That's what you've always thought. And he's so bloody manly—it would make such a nice change. What? To be the woman for once?"

What colour Charles had in his face drained away and by now, if we weren't trying to be circumspect, we would have jolly well been shouting. "How dare you? I've never done…. And he's given you no reason to be like this."

"No reason? What do you call that little display, then?"

"I would imagine it was just to—Oh, God, Harry. If it's one thing I can't stand about you, it's this—"

"What? You know, that's it. Forget it. But it's not just one thing, is it? So that's not true. With you I can do nothing right. If I ask too much, that's something you can't stand; if I don't pay you enough bloody attention, then that's wrong too. God forbid I might want just a bit of you—just a bit, all for myself, instead of always being satisfied with what you deign to leave me."

"Oh, for God's sake." Charles was hissing at me, trying to keep the noise down, and his face was white with anger. "If you weren't always around to pick up the crumbs, perhaps I'd have more to give you. But you are always there, sweeping up—and being all fucking Uriah Heep about it!"

"You bastard." I bit my tongue and went to turn away.

"No, don't you dare," he said. "You face me and tell me—go on, tell me just what you want to—I'd like to hear it, just for once."

I snapped then. "For once! You never want to hear anything I have to say, not the truth. Never! God—I wish I'd been able to say half—" I stopped, fuming. Then carried on, regardless. "It's all about you—listening to you, falling in with your plans. Come to Somerset, Harry. Come to Munster, Harry. Come to fucking London, Harry and watch me fuck the Indian Prince, Harry—you'll like that! I'd like to see you manage—just once. Without someone there standing behind you, watching out for you. Stopping…Being…" I lost the thread in my fury. "*Applauding.*" I wanted to stop, something in me was saying *no no no no no* but I was loose now, and he'd set me loose. "I'd like to see how you'd be if just once, when you are suffering all your mind-numbing existential tripe, and all the live and die stuff, I just told you to fucking do what you bloody liked and leave me alone!"

I stalked to the door and flung it open, and held it open for him. I made sure I was the one who closed the door. I don't think I could have stood watching him slam the door on me.

THE NEXT MORNING WE WERE AS cool to each other as ever I could remember.

I think we were both grateful for Ari's presence, which after what we'd both said to each other was a little ironic. But the fact that we both had someone to speak to that wasn't each other helped us get through the morning with some semblance of dignity. We spoke when necessary, and didn't look each other in the face.

I'd finished the entire decanter after he'd left, and I am sure it showed in my eyes, which felt like I'd dripped acid into them all night, rather than resting. I have no idea what Charles's emotions were that morning—I never did learn—but my own were boiling in a ferment and if that sounds too melodramatic then there's nothing I can do about it. I was furious. Furious with him for what he'd said, with myself for not saying what I'd wanted to, with Ari for being in the way: large, looming immovable and a barrier to something I had considered to be a *fait accompli*. I didn't know where he spent the night, and I loathed myself for probably having been the instrument that created something that wouldn't have happened if I hadn't behaved like the jealous bitch he said I was.

I had not been to Roehampton before, but then I'd rarely been to any polo. When he was going through his polo phase I stayed out of it last time. This time he wasn't going to be able to scrape me off with a stick, no matter how much he tried. He'd have to tell me to go if that's what he wanted, he'd have to actually do it.

As far as I could tell from my limited experience, despite its prestige, Roehampton was much like any polo ground: informal and easy going. That is to say that anyone could pull up in their car, park along the edge and watch the action—there was no requirement of wealth or privilege, but if one didn't have a decent car, or a string of ponies, I would imagine that one would rather stand out. We, however, were especially privileged as we were with Ari, and Ari, it seemed, was the nearest thing to a movie star that we plebeians would come into association with. This is other people's reactions I'm referring to here, not my own opinions. If he were going to go into the movie business, I'd shove him into the same films as Lawrence and tie Ari to the railway tracks and not Mr Scowly, thereby killing—as it were—two birds with one stone. However this impression of Ari's popularity being on a par with some kind of film star was shored up by many as we walked across the paddocks to the pavilion, as he turned heads, It was an expression I knew, but I hadn't really seen it in action before.

Unlike Dunster, Roehampton had a rather nice pavilion, done in the Indian style with a deep veranda where one could sip one's gin sling, watch the ponies thundering past and imagine that, barring the weather, one was back in Rajasthan or wherever. Ari led the way over to the pavilion and found us chairs on the veranda. One of the doors was open and inside I could see a frenetic hive of activity as waiters and assorted staff laid tables, dusted and carried bottles from pillar to post. "One of the perks of having to get here early," he said, "is that you get the best seats. Don't get bullied into giving them up either." He pulled a third chair next to ours. "Save this one for me." A waiter materialised. "Ah, John, I know you aren't serving yet, but the moment you do keep these chaps filled up, whatever they want. Put it on my account."

"No problem, Mr Singh. Good luck, today. I've got five bob on you; don't let me down." The waiter waitered off, and we sat. I can't exactly say we were comfortable because the only person really talking had been Ari.

Ari put his jacket on the spare chair. "My team are over there, where that blue flag is," he pointed across the paddock. "If you fancy bolstering my ego at any point, particularly if we look like we are losing—quite likely, Tommy Hitchcock's team are on top form—then please feel free, Holland." He used the name like a whip, tacked on the end, and leaving me until that bitter end to realise that the invitation didn't extend to me.

We'll see about that, I thought.

He gave a jaunty salute and walked off. I'm quite sure he was aware how attractive he was from behind in those jodhpurs, and he didn't hurry away, or bear to the right which is what one would have thought he would do, seeing as that was the direction of his team. So we were forced to appreciate the view, and neither of us able to comment, however discreetly, about it.

I had made a pact that I damned well wouldn't be the one to break; time after time it was me who had spoken first, offered conciliation, etc etc but I swore that today would be different. If the worm couldn't turn when seriously confronted with a rival as dangerous as Ari, when the hell could it? So we sat in sullen silence as if in a dark dank dock and stared gloomily ahead, even when the distraction of Ari's behind had vanished into the distance.

Charles lit one cigarette after another; there was no ashtray on our table as yet, and soon there was a small pile of discarded dog-ends littered on the wooden slats beside his chair. The silence grew, and we both pretended to be interested in everything going on around us. Luckily for us both, there was plenty to see, but I know that for myself, I was only pretending. I stared at a young man with strawberry-blond hair who sat on a wooden horse, thrashing away at balls being thrown to him by an older man in tweed; his hit rate against miss seemed to me to be about half and half and the balls he did hit flew into the air to land in some middle distance. The man in tweed had a bucket of them, and there seemed to be no urgency in retrieving the ones let fly. Perhaps, I wondered idly, they were thought of as common property, and what you found, you kept. I was struck—as I had been so often before—by the pointlessness of sport in general. Running, kicking, dashing about, galloping in mad abandon, just to hit a ball into a specific area. Why? If you wanted people to pat you on the back and cheer at you, become an actor for goodness' sake. Or a fireman.

I caught sight of the unmistakable form of Ari, swinging onto a more than lively grey pony. Even from this distance I could see his pearly white smile and for a second I had a vision of my fist in his teeth, blood pouring from his mouth in a most satisfactory way. It lasted but a moment, because I don't think—despite having been to Druitt's, which encouraged all forms of violent sports—that since the age of eight, I'd ever attempted to strike anyone. I found other ways to achieve my ends, which by and large were far more successful.

I stood, and leant against the veranda's balustrade for a moment. Behind me the doors were being opened, and waiters brought trays of tablecloths and silverware out to set the tables. I moved down the stairs, hoping for just a hopeless moment that he'd call me back. Each step was a test and a firming of my resolve. I was out of earshot and halfway across the field before I gave up hoping. I don't think anything would have stopped me, though, at that point, not even Charles.

I followed the line of cars now parked along the perimeter, and sought out the paddocks where ponies and grooms stood in clumps. Most of the players were out on the pitch, warming themselves and their ponies up, and the grooms were fussing about the ponies in their owner's strings, readying them for the next chukka. I put on a face that was a good deal more interested than I felt and started to mingle. One or two fellows I recognised, and I joined their band with an open smile.

"Bircham," one of them said. I couldn't remember, frankly, whether his name was Rounder or Rivers or Robinson, so it was warming to me that he remembered my name after the gap of years since we'd met. "This isn't your normal bag, is it?"

"It really isn't," I said, accepting a canapé from Rivers' (or possibly Robinson's) man. "But one was dragged down. Holland's lording it over at the clubhouse and I got bored, spotted you chaps and knew you'd have provisions."

"You and Holland still rattling around together?" the chinless one asked.

While I couldn't remember his name either, I knew his nickname, but I wasn't going to shame him in the company of men who didn't go to Druitt's.

"That's us. Rattle rattle. We were supposed to be in Paris right now, in fact, rattling away, but his mother wanted him at home."

"How beastly. So you are escaping when you can, I take it."

"That's rather the idea. I say, talking of school, isn't that Ari Singh?" I said, as naively as I could.

Robertson or Robertson nodded. "Didn't you know he played?"

"I vaguely remember, but I'd have thought he'd have grown out of it. There are many things one did at school that one gets bored with. And I don't get the *Horse and Hound*, which I'm sure is no surprise to anyone here."

I was treated, at some length, to a history of Ari's polo career, which I gobbled up with wide eyes and many delightful shrimp-based nibbling things.

The match, which had started without me even being aware of it, paused briefly as the chukka ended, and players galloped their sweat-darkened ponies back to the lines. I watched, with running commentary from my new best friend, as Ari pulled up by a group of ponies and flung himself off. I couldn't help but be pleased that he looked anything but happy. He then blotted his copybook even further with me by bellowing at one of the pony-wallahs. Granted it was in his own language, but the inference was clear. One simply didn't treat servants like that in public.

Even pony-wallahs.

"Kicking himself for missing that goal," Robinson-Robertson said, grimly. "The pony didn't slow enough. He'll play like the very devil, until he makes it up."

"God help his servants and ponies if he doesn't," the chinless one said.

I checked my watch. "Good Lord, it's ten past one. I'm afraid lunch beckons. So nice to catch up." I pushed myself to my feet, leaving them sprawled on the rug. "I'll tell Holland you're here." More than that I couldn't promise, he was worse with names and faces than I was, and I didn't have much to go on, to describe them, even if we were speaking. Still, it was warming that they remembered me, at least. One doesn't like to fade into the background and be the one person in a school photograph that no one can name. Oh, you remember him? He hung around with Holland, I remember that much, but what the devil was his name?

I found Ari easily enough, but hung back until he'd cantered off, a fresh mount between those no doubt disgustingly hairy and muscled thighs. One of his pony-wallahs was scraping the sweat from the chestnut from the first chukka. I waited patiently, sure that he wasn't paying me the slightest attention before I walked quickly over to the remaining ponies, tethered in a line. I knew from my knowledgeable friend which pony would be used next, an oddly coloured roan, almost pink in hue, fully saddled and bridled with blinkers, ready to be used. I moved between the roan and a bay, which hid me effectively from Ari's servant, should he look up.

It took no time at all to achieve my aim. With a deftness that impressed even me—perhaps I should be a spy or something—I slit the girth on the offside, where, if I had any luck at all, it would not be spotted: just halfway. God bless my mother for that Swiss Army knife. I think she hoped it would spur me into outdoorsy pursuits or something. Well, look, Mother, here I am using it, and in the open air too.

I was careful not to cut the girth too deeply. I wanted to be fair; too much and I'd be entirely culpable, too little and I'd be watching for something that I knew would never happen. This way—just like my dear father and those dear, effective, Destroying Angels—what happened would be entirely in the lap of fate. I had a vague notion, although I wasn't sure how accurate I was, that Ari's people believed firmly in fate and all that, so it seemed rather satisfying.

I backed out of the horse-lines and made a wide circle via the back of the clubhouse so I would be seen coming back from the other direction, just in case anyone should wonder where I'd been.

Our table had been transformed from bare wood to a pristine lawn of white linen, lit up and sparkling with silver and crystal. This was more like it. I felt rewarded, somehow, and felt that fate could only be smiling down on me. A bottle of champagne rested in a bucket beside him, and he'd already filled his glass. Considering that Ari had promised to pay for everything, the sun came out in Harry Bircham's head and even the fag of making up a squabble couldn't dim the day. I sat beside him, a faint smile on my face and I waited for fate to decide: for me, or against.

The sun shone a little brighter as he reached into the bucket and pulled the bottle out, and without a word, poured the sparkling liquid into the glass by my hand. As a conciliatory gesture it was more than enough, and if no one around us knew what sweetness that small token meant to me, then the moment was all the more precious. I gave him the kind of smirk that I knew he was waiting for and he rolled his eyes at me.

"Arse," he said.

"Tart," I murmured, as loudly as I dared. There were people congregating around the steps, and soon the balcony would be filled with diners.

"What can I do?" He wrapped his voice wrapped in smiles. "I need something to make me less of an attraction. Perhaps you could give me lessons."

"There's nothing I can teach you, you only seem to appeal to the baser type."

The action on the field had started again, and a flurry of intense excitement flowed through me. It never dimmed, this feeling, and it's hard to describe for anyone who hasn't played with fate the way I have. It added a certain edge to everything, a piquant flavour to each and every experience.

The wind against my face, the feel of the crystal in my hand, the taste of the wine, the sting of the bubbles—all intense enough on their own, but with the added toss-of-a-coin decision yet to played out, it seemed like every touch, every taste, every sight was slowed, enhanced and given a breathless quality.

I think it must be like God feels, just before he places the final snowflake—will the avalanche wait another hour or will it sweep down now and engulf the party of skiers? Will the river flood with this raindrop? Or the next? It's beautiful, and terrifying—and oh so addictive.

We chatted, he and I, and I could almost hear myself saying out loud, "I'll remember this conversation forever. I'll replay this moment a hundred times." Of course I said nothing of the sort, and instead we dissected Robertson's personality (apparently I was wrong: Charles has a better memory for names than ever I do), recalled his huge failures on and off the playing field, and laughed at the times he was thrashed by the prefect he fagged for.

"Was there ever a term he didn't cry?" I asked, but I had no response because the snowflake had toppled the mountain and my heart leapt from my chest in triumph. The game had stopped and people were rushing to catch Ari's loose pink pony, while others ran to where Ari himself lay crumpled on the turf.

Chapter Ten

pressed the brandy into his hand. "I don't care if you hate the taste of it. I'm not denying it's vile, cheap stuff but you need something. You haven't stopped shaking."

He wrapped his fingers around the glass, and pushed himself back onto the wooden seat.

"Drink it," I ordered.

"How are we—"

"Don't start worrying again. Just drink it. Sit there and don't move other than to bring that glass to your face and back. I'll see if they have a phone here. Leave things to me. There's no rush, is there? We don't have to tear back to Somerset for anything. They aren't expecting us till Monday, anyway."

I watched, a stern expression on my face until he'd taken at least two sips of the brandy (it really was vile, people should be punished for charging the public for things like that. The most you can say about it was that it was restoring) before I went back to the bar to find out about telephones and taxis and the like.

"I'll telephone to Gregg's for one for you, sir," the publican said, doing his profession a great boost and going a good way to saving his bacon when the day came that selling revolting brandy became a crime. "How is the young man now, sir?"

"He's still a little shocked."

A woman came out from the back, carrying a tray full of tea-making equipment. "Nice and strong," she said, her voice grating in its gentility, but the sentiment made my heart warm to her common touch immediately. "Just what he needs." She slid past me and took the tray over to where he sat. I watched them for a moment as she poured him a large cup, sugared it liberally, and placed the cup in front of him. It took him a moment, but he responded, eventually taking up the cup and sipping at it, his hands curled around the blue and white china, probably for warmth, as they'd been icy when we'd arrived.

"Did he know the poor Indian gentleman?" the publican asked me.

"We both did, I'm afraid. We were all at school together."

"Terrible, ain't it?" the man said, sucking air in through his teeth. Unlike his wife, he had made no concessions to the gentility of the area, and his voice still reeked of London. "Makes you wonder why these people take such risks. We never bin to the polo, me and the wife, don't think we'd be quite the ticket, if you get my meaning, but we've seen newsreels and it looks proper dangerous. I suppose he must be used to that, being from where he's from, and such."

I rather doubted that Druitt's School for Young Gentlemen and the wilds of Chelsea posed the kind of dangers that the publican was imagining—cobras under the bed and tiger hunts mounted on panicking elephants—but I kept quiet. I let him imagine the danger, and get the pleasure from it.

His wife, as I assumed she was, for one likes to think well of such people, came back. "Your friend has a bit more colour in his face, at least. Must have been terrible to see. One minute hale and hearty, the next…" She shook her head. "That poor boy."

"He knew the risks," her husband said. "Gawd knows there's been enough injuries in the past few years over there. A death was only a matter of time." He lowered his voice, as if to spare his wife and the other occupant of the bar, but his voice was filled with a ghoulish glee and I knew I was right in recognizing a kindred soul, of sorts. "He weren't trampled to death, was he? I'd think that would be a terrible way to go."

"No," I said, as reassuringly as I could. "I understand that horses will do just about anything to avoid treading on a human. Seems the girth gave way, but not entirely." I tried to keep the mirth out of my voice. "He was dragged. The pony didn't realise that the others trying to stop him weren't trying to race, or that's how it looked from where I was sitting. It was quite unnerving. It took a good while before someone stopped it."

"Gaw," he said in a delightfully Alfred P. Doolittle way. "How horrible."

"I couldn't agree more," I said with feeling. I found myself liking this man more and more.

"Well, I'll let you drink your tea," he said, moving back behind the bar, "I'll telephone for that taxi. To the station, is it?"

"I think so." We didn't have our bags, but they would have to be sent on. I wasn't going back to Ari's house. Or to be more honest, I couldn't put him through that.

"Got far to go?" he asked me.

"Oh yes," I said, with what I hoped was a mournful smile. "Quite a long way to go."

We travelled as far as Minehead, but missed the connecting train. I suggested that we telephone to the house, to get Stephens or Lawrence, or even Gilbert and Richardson to come and collect us had they returned, but Charles wouldn't hear of it.

"I'm not in any great hurry," he said. He had been terribly quiet, sunk into a corner of our carriage and staring out of the window for hours on end, but it was a good change from how he'd been at the polo field.

When Ari had toppled from the saddle, reaching, it seemed, for a hard swipe towards his goal, a collective gasp had arisen from the field, a gasp that seemed to echo around the perimeter as it was clear he hadn't fallen cleanly and was being dragged alongside his horse. Shouts rose from the spectators, and beside me, Charles had risen to his feet, the colour draining from his face.

"God," he'd whispered. "Oh, God."

"Why doesn't someone stop the horse?" I shouted.

"They are trying," a man on the next table said, binoculars to his eyes.

"Oh, God." His female companion gave a moan of distress and he stopped atching to attend to her. All we could do was to stand in stunned silence, and although I couldn't see much of Ari, bouncing around the hooves of his pony, I for one could imagine it. I think we both could.

"Come on," he said. "We'd better go down there."

By the time we'd made the edge of the field, the pony had been stopped and a crowd of players stood in a circle, a fair way away from the ropes. Two men in St John Ambulance uniforms were attempting to move everyone back. The spectators were as hushed now as they had been noisy earlier.

Someone pushed through the crowd and stood beside me. I looked up to find Robertson and his chinless friend close by. Robertson took one look at us, or rather looked sharply at Charles, who was clutching my arm so hard it hurt, and nodded curtly at me, before ducking under the rope and running toward the knot of concerned players and steaming horses.

"Come back to the pavilion," I said. "Robertson's going out there. You don't need to." For a moment he resisted me, then turned, still holding on to my arm and let me lead him away. Then began a wait, twenty minutes or so of rumours, false hope and intermittent bulletins from runners off the field.

Robertson made his way up to where we sat and I could see from his face that the news was bad. "Broke his neck. Damned horrible." He sat down and leaned back in his chair. "Dragged…and at that pace. If he'd fallen clear, he might have had a chance, but they will drive their feet so far into the stirrups. If the girth had broken completely—"

"He wouldn't have been dragged," I finished. "That's pretty beastly."

"It was. Seems the saddle just slipped to one side. He didn't have a chance, really, not at that speed. Just as well you two didn't go over," he said, "there were too many people as it was, they weren't letting—"

"I'm sorry, I'm sorry." We both turned to find him paler than ever and with a gloss of perspiration on his brow, almost rocking back and forth.

"I'm so sorry, Harry. God."

"What is he on about?"

"I don't know. What is it?" I said to him.

"I didn't mean—" His eyes were huge in his face, and he was beginning to sound hysterical. "I'm so sorry."

Robertson muttered to me, "For God's sake keep him quiet, Bircham, people are beginning to stare."

He was beginning to shake. I turned to Robertson. "He's not good with… this kind of thing. I think I need to get him away from here."

"Dashed good idea," Robertson agreed.

"We came down with Singh, we don't have transport back. Can you take us back to Roehampton? We can get the train from there."

Robertson looked like it was the last thing he wanted to do, and he looked over at my quivering friend as if he was looking at something diseased, his face a study in revulsion at a chap who would drop the stiff upper mask in public.

I could see the thoughts running through his head, and the names he was calling him. Grateful that the object of his derision was too upset to be aware of the scathing expression on Robertson's face, I simply made a mental note to pay Robertson out one day if I ever had the opportunity. However, now we needed him, and if that meant Bircham pretending to be his best friend in the entire world, then so be it.

Getting away from here was paramount, for more reasons than just one. "People have already seen you speaking to us," I said, letting the implication of "mud sticks" hang in the air. "You can say what you like to your friends, just help us get out."

Robertson went into action at last, nodded grimly. "My car is over there," he said, pointing vaguely. "It's a blue ABC, it will be a bit of a squash. I'll have to go and make some excuse as to where I've disappeared. I'll meet you there in five minutes."

He ran down the steps, the relief of leaving us behind coming off him in waves. Robertson was almost entirely silent during the drive, his face set grimly in a frown as he negotiated the crowds. The match—and the following ones—had been cancelled and shorn of their entertainment, the bright young things were moving on, starlings all, to find the next entertainment, the next diversion.

Death was outside their ken, and no one wanted to be inconvenienced by it. Robertson's silence didn't bother me, it was decent enough of him to transport us, and in any case I was more concerned with my companion's state of mind then what he thought of him, or me.

There was no reason why we'd ever meet again.

Charles threatened to start his apology again in the car, once he was in and comfortable, but I shut him up. "Not now," I murmured, rubbing his chilled hands between mine. "Later, if you must. Not now." It was moving, and almost tragic, the way his eyes never left mine as if looking aside would show him things that were too terrible to see. It was just as well he did, for we drove past two men carrying a stretcher, and one arm dangled from beneath a grey wool horse blanket. He didn't see it, and that was a good thing.

It took twenty minutes or so to get back to the town, and Robertson drove off without a word, not that I cared. We stepped out of the sunlight into the bar of The Angel public house, and I found him a seat in the snug before ordering brandy for us both. The landlord looked a little shocked himself, so I had to explain matters—I was quite sure, being a publican, he'd seen young gentlemen who wanted any amount of alcohol at any time—but I would rather not be taken as the type of man who hits the brandy early in the afternoon, not if I can possibly avoid it. "No station here," he announced with a worried expression, as if somehow it was his fault, "but Barnes is not much more than a mile."

Charles drank his tea. He'd calmed a great deal, and some of the colour had started to return to his face, which was a relief. The landlord's wife took the tray away with a reassuring "You look much better," and I turned to him.

"What did you mean, you were sorry?"

He looked a little glazed, still but seemed to be gathering his faculties around himself once more. "It sounds idiotic."

"You aren't wrong, you sounded like…" I paused.

"A lunatic?"

I gave a small smile, caught out in the thought.

"I dare say," he said. "But, and I know it sounds mad. But I wished for something to happen. Just…not. Not this. Not this."

"Look," I said, "you'll have to stop thinking like that. You wouldn't hurt a fly."

He looked at me for a long moment. "You really believe that, don't you?"

"Of course I do—do you think I'd…well, you know." I kept my voice low, even though the publican was at the other end of the bar, serving. It wasn't a large bar. "If I thought that? And you know it's mad. Thoughts don't cause girths to break, feet to get stuck in stirrups. Anyway," I said, "I thought you liked him. It was rather one of the reasons we had words."

"Not really. I was pleased, I suppose, that he remembered me, and flattered at the attention. He is—oh, God—*was*—a Prince. Then I saw the way he spoke to you, heard what he said about all the people he used to be friends with, and I realised I had enough poisonous people in my life. The look he threw at you just before the match, that was the end, and I sat there wishing to hell he'd fall off and land on his pompous, arrogant—"

"The fact he did had nothing—nothing, you hear me?—nothing to do with you."

"I know." Further introspection was spared at this point as the door opened and an elderly man with a cloth cap said, "Two gentlemen for Barnes?" which amused us both, and Charles smiled for the first time since God knows when.

"Sounds like an Edwardian play," he said.

"Two men in a carriage," I said, getting up and leading the way out.

"Better than Three Men Up the Bummell," he snorted, his equilibrium restored.

"I always wondered about that title myself," I said.

"It's 'on', not 'up', and you know it."

The further we travelled away from the tragedy, the more he returned to his normal self. This I was grateful for, as I didn't want him going doolally once

I got him back to Somerset. I couldn't see that Claude would take "I killed him with my thoughts" as a sign that his nephew's mind was altogether normal, and the stupid boy would blurt it out, if not to Claude, then to his mother, or to Lawrence. I didn't trust any of them, not even Mrs Holland. She'd been complicit in his institutionalisation, after all.

It would be a useful skill, though, wouldn't it?

We stayed at Claude's club overnight, which meant he had to telephone to his family and explain matters. He managed it well, without getting emotional again, although he said that it really sounded as if Claude didn't believe a word of it, and that we'd made the whole thing up just to stay at the Club. Nonsense, of course. Claude's club was indicative of the man, and having stayed in more liberal places in my life, it wasn't at all the kind of place I would queue for if tickets went on sale for membership. Dour and staid as a tweeded ghillie and just as much fun. From the rotund and sour-faced concierge to the wizened bell-hop who looked askance at our luggage consisting of one small knapsack—hardly the accoutrements of gentlemen's sons, I could hear him thinking—it was clear that the place let us in on sufferance alone, and that we were connected to that stuffed shirt, Claude Holland. We were shown to rooms that frankly I would be ashamed to put servants into, so small were they, and advised that dinner was at six, but one needed to change. I bristled at this, for the implication was that we wouldn't know what was correct. But it was true that neither of us had evening clothes with us, as they languished in Ari's guest rooms, so we said we'd dine out.

I was also more than certain that there would be absolutely no chance of grabbing a moment or two to make overtures. He needed it, badly, and so did I if truth be told. There was something about death that made me want to celebrate life in the best, and the very worst way. The Club, however, although of course men only (except Tuesday afternoons when one could bring a female blood relative by appointment only and only in the tea-rooms) bristled with aggressive masculinity. I found myself adopting a more manly pose than ever I'd bothered to for years, just in self-defence.

It strikes me as odd, though, that a society of men who have negotiated their way through the maze and moral morass of the English boarding school (where sexual contact with one's peers is condoned, or at least ignored entirely) pretend that it was "just one of those things" once they mature and would flog you out of the reading room if you ever reminded them how you discovered them in flagrante with Hobbs of the Upper Sixth.

And they call *me* a queer fish.

We arranged to meet in the bar; we were allowed in there without dinner jackets at least. After a swift scotch taken in silence, I asked: "All right?" One doesn't really ask one's companion how he is feeling, not in a club like the Roland.

Holland shrugged, which was enough, and choosing not to have another drink, we walked into the West End looking for somewhere to eat. The odd thing now is that I can't remember anything much about that evening. It's strange. I remember the Club so clearly, with its dark panelled walls and the warring scents of hair oil, beeswax and a certain tang—probably purely imagined, given the preponderance of tweed—of urine. I haven't asked him to remind me, because perhaps he thinks it's something I should recall, perhaps he has it all stored away. Perhaps not. I remember the scotch we had in the bar, even the cool feel of the cut crystal in my hand. I remember the way he'd brushed his hair; as smooth as it ever went, causing it to make natural waves that Marcel would die for.

I remember even walking out of the club, past the sweating and odorous gatekeeper, down the steps and into Charing Cross Road, but after that, I can't remember much at all, and I really wish I did. If I'd only known how much things were going to change once we returned to Somerset I would have bottled that evening up, moment by moment, and buried it deep in the floorboards of my mind, so I could bring it out and treasure it when things got dark.

"Shall we stay here?" I asked as we clambered from the train at Minehead.

"No," he said, "although I would, for two pins. I don't have a sou left, and I know you don't. I saw you scrabbling around in your pockets to buy me the newspaper." I opened my mouth to make a suggestion but he seemed to read my mind. "No. I'm not going to ask them to send the bill home. They—or rather Claude—would raise an inquisition about extravagance when we could have just come straight home."

"Please don't make me get on a bus," I whined. "For the love of everything I hold dear, don't subject me to a rural bus full of women carrying pigs and men with smelly extremities."

Charles gave the loudest laugh I'd heard for days. "Oh, Harry." The "I do love you" was implied and I took it gratefully. "I'm tempted to do so, just to see you react. This is Somerset, not Bangalore."

I was saved from the horrors of a bus, as a "halloo" sounded so loudly and convincingly across the tracks that you would have thought the Devon and Somerset Staghounds were galloping towards the ticket office. We both looked around to find the dear, idiotic and beaming faces of Gilbert and Richardson.

Once we'd scurried across the bridge, Gilbert led us out to their car. "We arrived back yesterday. I said we should check whether you were in situ, but Richardson seemed to think you had nothing better to do than hang about and wait for our return."

"Mrs Holland rang the Club," Richardson said, obviously considering that we couldn't have worked this out for ourselves. "And they said you'd most likely be on this train."

"So very bright of you to piece it all together," I said. "Academia should realise they cannot hold you, that you are clearly destined for Scotland Yard."

We were racketing our way south, me in the front with Gilbert, when he turned to me and said, "Is it true what young Stephens said? About Singh? He's dead?"

I nodded, then sat as Gilbert went through the litany of surprise, shock and regret on behalf of the deceased. I find this a curious emotion, that others can regret what someone did—or usually didn't—manage to do in their lives. It seems rather intrusive, and what's it got to do with anyone anyway?

"I'd rather not tell the whole story more times than I can avoid. It was pretty dire—"

"I can imagine. God," Gilbert said.

"—so, if you don't mind, I'll just tell everyone about it once when we get him home."

"Of course. Perfectly understandable. No one would want to relive that over and over, not if they didn't have to." He knitted his manly eyebrows together and stared furiously at the road as if it had annoyed him. If I hadn't been playing the delicate card, I would have laughed, right there beside him.

It struck me as hugely funny that no one could see how much I loved to relive moments like that. Over and over. If I closed my eyes, and I did now, knowing that should Gilbert notice—unlikely, he was as empathic as a toadstool—he would think that I was shutting out the horror of watching someone die, when it couldn't be further from the truth. But when I closed them, forcing the sound of the wheels from my mind and replacing them with the gentle chit-chat of the upper-middle classes at play and the chink of glass against bottle, I could see the polo match again, the sheer animal brutality of it. The way the ponies—half a ton of death—collided with each other, trained to put the other rider off balance. The way the polo sticks whipped from front to back, so fast sometimes they blurred in the eye. As for the ball, the only way you knew where that was was to watch which way most players were galloping.

Polo, I'm told, was invented by the tribes of Asia, donkey's years ago, and someone told me, although I don't know how true it actually is, the original ball was actually some poor soul's head. That the English would gentrify such a violent game, and place it in a circle of champagne and crumpets, says a lot about them. I wondered if I wasn't alone in my anticipation of tragedy. I wondered if that's why some people went to see such games with such high risk—in case there was some dreadful accident.

Was this need—this red, acidic, primal need that I succumbed to, let loose and wallowed in—was it something that all men had, but didn't pander to? There were hints that this might be the case. Many high risk sports such as car racing had a huge following, and the publican in Roehampton seemed just as ghoulishly delighted at the idea of Ari's brains wiped all over the green grass of the polo field as I was. But I suppose I would never know the real answer to that, it wasn't something I could ask. If so, I felt sorry for them, for they didn't know how rich the vein of pleasure was they missed out on. But then, I felt sorry for them a lot of the time, particularly well-meaning idiots like Richardson and Gilbert.

Mrs Holland must have been watching from one of the windows, because she was out on the gravel at the front to meet us when we pulled in. "Oh, thank goodness, they were on that train. I sent the boys to get you, darling, you don't mind, do you?" She positively enveloped her son in a hug as he clambered out of the car and then she led him away.

Richardson echoed my own thoughts as the door closed behind them, leaving us alone. "Just as well you are made of sterner stuff, eh, Bircham?"

I threw him a glare and grabbed the knapsack. "Just as well."

Chapter Eleven

We found the rest of the family gathered in the drawing room and I was fussed over just a little, which placated me, although nowhere near as much as him. The conversation was slow and stilted and it was obvious that no one wanted to be the one to broach the subject but there was an odd strained quality too, as if they were all leaning on their leashes, like coursers who have scented a hare. It shored up my thoughts of earlier, that people were naturally ghoulish—it was just the tea and crumpets that diluted it, perhaps.

As the afternoon went on, the conversation moved from subject to subject, artificial and butterfly-like. We spoke of the vegetable show which was due to take place on the green the weekend after the wedding, and what Mrs Antringham had said at the last Women's Institute meeting. But each subject wore away at the atmosphere of gentility and each subject not pertaining to Ari and his sudden death seemed to press even heavier upon the room. The veritable ghost at the feast, if you will. Or dead man among the crumpets, which would be a ripping title for a murder mystery, were I ever to write one.

I watched Charles when I could; he is like a barometer to an atmosphere; I don't know if his family can read him, and I doubt they can, or they would have got the whole macabre subject out of the way as early as possible, but as I observed him, I saw him retreat inch by inch into his own mind until finally he was hardly speaking at all, even when directly addressed. It did not surprise me one bit when he excused himself, leaving an untouched cup of tea beside him.

"If you don't mind," he said, when his mother asked him to stay. "I didn't sleep well last night."

His mother clutched at his hand. "All right. Probably for the best, darling. You'll be down for dinner?"

"I don't know," he said.

She blinked at him, an odd gesture; a slow closing of the eyes, and a deep breath in—which was strangely and disturbingly erotic. "You'll try, won't you? I'll send Stephens up at seven," she said. He leant down and kissed her, nodded perfunctorily to Claude and left the room.

I was even less surprised when everyone else except Margaret, who was watching the closed door, a small frown on her face, turned to me with expectant faces. Yes, definitely ghoulish. The afterglow for me was gone, the breathless anticipation lost, but I told them what they wanted to hear, and thereby gained just a fraction of it back for a while. There are always ways, you see, to relive such moments.

AFTER TEA, AND AFTER MY LENGTHY and—I don't mind admitting it—erudite and rather embellished account of Ari's demise, I stayed in the drawing room at the request of Claude Holland. Mrs Holland had not taken the story well, more concerned by the effect that it had on her son than anything else, and I was rather put out that no one—not even Clarissa, who I had always considered to be more on my side than anyone else in the house—seemed to be concerned for my well-being. I suppose I managed the whole thing too well, and I don't mean the accident itself, I mean the mopping up and getting the son and heir back home in one piece. I had the feeling that they—or at least Margaret and Claude—felt that I'd taken my time about it, and we should have come straight back, no matter what.

I suspected that Margaret's concern was for the well-being of her son, and that Claude's was more centred on the fact that we had soiled his club by attending it. They would not have wanted to see him at his worst, I knew that much.

And I suspected that my interview with Claude Holland was going to touch on that touchy subject, and I wasn't wrong. "Mr Bircham," he began.

"Harry, please," I said.

He took a seat opposite mine, but didn't bend to my informality. "I, if you remember, expressed a disinclination to allow my nephew to go on this jaunt, so close to the wedding."

I forbore from pointing out that he was hardly in a position to do anything regarding allowing anyone to do anything, and that talking like a prig was the easiest way to get his nephew to bolt. But I was quiet, kept my face from making expressions that I knew Claude would dislike and listened patiently.

"The fact that this…unpleasantness has happened is unfortunate, and it has unsettled the entire household. It could have all been prevented if the boy had listened to me in the first place. I therefore would be grateful if you would tell him that I'd rather he not go away again."

"May I ask," I said, raising one hand from my knee and letting him have the full beauty of my long fingers. Really, I know that I'm accused of being an effeminate queer at times, and perhaps I am a little more noticeable than some, but I'm not really as bad as all that. There's just something about Claude Holland that brings it out in me. Six months in his oh-so-masculine company and I'd be wearing berets, chiffon scarves, and beads, and then there would be no hope for me at all. "May I ask how I'm expected to do that? I think you rather overestimate my influence. And you may not have noticed it, but he has a mind of his own. Quite a decided one, at times."

"I really must insist," Claude said.

"Dear man," I said. (You see? There I go again, I just can't resist it.) "You can insist until you are blue in the face, I neither have that kind of control over him, nor do I wish to have. He's my friend, and should he decide to do something, it's not for me to say one way or the other what he does." I know I was burning my boats as far as Claude was concerned, that it would have been all so easy to just say that I'd do my best, and he'd never have known one way or the other, but he rubbed me up the wrong way—demanding this and that without a care in the world how anyone else felt about it.

"So you won't accede to my wishes?"

"It's not a case of acceding," I said. "You may have forgotten that I'm planning to be a barrister, sir, and one thing a barrister cannot, can *never* promise is something that's beyond his control, that is, anything that has to be done by a third party."

"This is hardly relevant. This is not a question of law."

"Oh, but it is," I said. "Not law, but relevant. I could promise you that I could try to do what you wish, but I can't promise that he will do or not do something."

"Will you at least promise to convince him to stay put until after the wedding?"

"No, sir. I can't promise that. I've just explained."

"May I remind you that you are a guest in my house, Mr Bircham?" His face, once set in an amiable friendly fashion, dropped into darkness so quickly that I'm surprised I didn't hear something break.

I stood. "I hardly need reminding. Although if this is the way you speak to guests, I'd be surprised if anyone came twice. And this is not your house, may I remind you of that? If you had approached him in a reasonable fashion, he might have done as you wished—I know of no plans to the contrary—but it seems that your natural inclination is not for any straightforwardness at all. The fact that he went on this 'jaunt' is something you can very probably put at your own door. If you tell him not to do something, you should know…. But you don't know, do you? No, each time you've pulled me aside, asked me to spy for you, and each time you've gone behind his back, and that, let me tell you, is the worst possible course you could have taken."

"You…" He rose from the chair, his lips trembling. Claude Holland had obviously not had anyone stand up to him for a long time, and he was almost incoherent with annoyance. "How dare you accuse me of spying on my nephew?"

"What would you call it? Does Mrs Holland know what you've been asking me? To report on his actions, to control his movements? I would bet good money she doesn't. I know she longs for him to be here for her wedding, but I will say this with some assurance, that if he went to her and said that he did not want to be here, and was going elsewhere, she wouldn't stand in his way."

"I'm trying to prevent that," he said, some of the wind taken out of his sails.

"Obviously." I sat down again, which seemed to throw him somewhat, and after a moment, a little flustered, he sat too, but this time, as was my aim, I had his attention and he was no longer talking at me, he was listening. "Now, you are obviously aware that he has…some problems coping with the fact that you are going to marry his mother."

He nodded. It seemed he was a little stunned at the role reversal. Silly man.

I was beginning to really enjoy myself. "We have just over a week, and I think it would be to everyone's benefit—guests included—if there were a little more *entente cordiale* about here. Don't get me wrong, if you were to start to be nice to him, he'd smell a rat, he's cagey and he's not at all stupid. But if you both stopped behaving like rams in a contest..."

He was silent for a moment, his eyes on mine. Then he spoke so grudgingly that I could almost hear gears breaking in his head. "I suppose I could, if—"

I didn't let him finish. "Of course you can. Not nice, not sycophantic, just... less you if you catch my meaning. I'm not suggesting you ask him to go for a Turkish Bath and a deep discourse, after all. Just—perhaps small concessions? Perhaps give him some freedom, or at least don't start laying down the law about where he can go and when. Then you can be silently pleased when he doesn't go anywhere?" I smiled winningly at him, and he returned it with, if not quite a smile, a lessening of the tightness of his mouth and a handshake. I noted before how attractive he was, and his handshake was firm and warm. Oh God, I thought. This wedding cannot come fast enough, because getting a crush on another older man in authority was simply not something I wanted. And the thought of anything with Claude Holland, however attractive, made my skin crawl, even if he did more interesting things to other parts of my anatomy.

I fled, and walked around the house once before going up to my room. He was not in his, which came as no surprise to me. I had a feeling he was shamming his tiredness, and felt that he would probably try and see if his father was about.

He came in a little later and plonked himself down on the bed next to me.

"Do you mind?" I said. "Bouncing is very disconcerting when one is reading about rolling ships."

He pulled the volume towards him so he could read the spine. "*Moby-Dick*? The deathless love and sweet domesticity of Queequeg and Ishmael?"

"It is rather obvious, isn't it? It makes me wonder how he got away with it, to be honest."

"People were more innocent?"

I snorted. "Not people who knew, I'm certain of it. All the bodily fluids are a bit much, even for me." I put the book down. "Did you find him? Your father?"

"I was looking for him, but no go. I rather doubted he'd be around. He comes to see me, after all, he's not lurking around to see Mother."

"That's reassuring," I said.

"He didn't know we'd be back so early."

"All the same, it's days yet to the wedding, and you can't keep disappearing off like some wandering cloud. People are going to think you are up to something, even if they can't work out what it is. Your father will turn up when he wants to, and until he wants to let us all know where he's staying and whether he's alive or not, it's up to him. Are you really sure you want to stay around?"

"Of course. I wouldn't leave him now."

"I didn't mean that. If he's capable of finding you when he wants, he can track you down at college or you could leave him a *Poste Restante* address. I—I just don't think it's going to be much fun for you—or anyone, here. And we *were* planning on having fun this summer."

"Leave before the wedding?" He looked slightly surprised, then frowned. "No, I can't. Despite everything I've said, I can't do that to her. She's making a huge mistake, and perhaps she'll realise it, but if she's determined to marry that man, then I've got to be here."

There. That was easy, wasn't it? Really, I should have charged Claude for doing as he asked.

"You've decided to give her away, then?"

He made a face. "I know. But someone has to do it, and rather me than Lawrence. I can glare at Claude in a menacing fashion and make it clear he's got to look after Mother."

"Much the best idea. You have the knack of doing 'if looks could kill,' I've always found. Lawrence hasn't got glaring down to the fine art you have. He'd just scowl, which, as he does that ninety-nine percent of the time anyway, no one would take seriously, or probably even notice."

He was silent for a few minutes, and I made a show of reading, then he laughed and said, "You know, if I could wish anyone away with my thoughts, it would be much more prudent to get rid of Claude, wouldn't it? Oh don't look like that, I'm not going to have the vapours again. But I can wish for it anyway, can't I?"

It took me some control not to look thoroughly delighted with the turn of the conversation and instead I attempted to change the subject, knowing well he wouldn't be derailed. "Look, I'm sorry about Ari," I said, and I almost meant it. He'd made me see that it had been pointless, and darn right dangerous. And all for what? Over nothing. I was like a child again, lashing out at that kitten who had scratched me. I should have had more faith in the bond between us, had more faith in him. I knew in my heart that he wouldn't just chuck up years of solid friendship and—whatever else it was—to clamber aboard something that could vanish overnight, or because of some ancient crush.

"I suppose one should say the right thing," he said. "That he died doing something he loved, but that's just tosh, isn't it? If I were to go I don't think it would matter to me how it was, or what I was doing. The most I can hope is that it's quick. Painless."

"I'm sure it would be," I said with as much heartfelt emotion as I could give him. It was something I could promise, I suppose.

"I wish I knew for certain that it had been that way for him. Oh, people say that, don't they? 'It was quick, he wouldn't have known about it, wouldn't have felt a thing,' but they haven't a clue." His voice rose a little. "That's what they said yesterday."

"I shouldn't have mentioned it." I reached over and touched his arm. For years it had been our signal to each other in crowded places. A calming effect. It did that now, and he took a deep breath in before leaning back against the bedstead.

"Anyway," he said, as predicted. "Back to the dispatching of Claude."

"All right, if you insist. If you could do it, with the power of your oh-so-deadly mind"—he hit me playfully—"how would you go about it? I'm thinking that you can't just get his heart to stop in his chest, so it would have to be something physical."

"I don't know," he said. "I don't know if I should, really…"

"Oh come on. It's only a game."

"I don't know if I'd start with him, anyway," he said. "I'm sure there would be far more worthy candidates. If one had that kind of power, shouldn't one use it for the public good, and not just for one's own selfish reasons? Also," he added, very reasonably I thought, and it amused me how he'd gone from not really wanting to discuss it to embracing the concept, "if one did, and it was someone one had a reason to do away with, it would be more suspicious. Better to put away someone no one could connect you to personally."

"You really are no fun," I said. "How absolutely common-sense of you. All right. Say you could do away with…the Kaiser, for example. You can't deny that the world would be a better place without him in it. You don't know him, you have no personal beef with him. No one would suspect you, a thoroughly English chap, of having any truck with the Germans. So how would you do it?"

"We are still talking about the power of the mind, yes? I'm not going to start stabbing or shooting anyone."

"Yes. And no."

"Hmmm." He frowned and went quiet for a moment. "I'd want to be sure that it would work, really wouldn't risk it twice. Would I have to be…you know, there?"

I gave it some thought. "Well, I'd say so. Perhaps it works by line of sight like radio waves or something. I doubt you could do it from here, for example."

"Well, considering that I'd be unlikely to get close to him, it would have to be some kind of public ceremony then, wouldn't it? Like a parade."

"That would be perfect." I added a smile. "Well done."

Before dinner, I caught Dear Uncle Claude alone in the drawing room and I tried not to be too irritatingly smug—although it was hardly my fault if he thought that I was—when I told him I'd managed to achieve what he had not, and that his nephew would not be planning any more excursions between now and the wedding. At dinner the discussion was, as ever, all about the wedding. I applied myself to my food, glowing in the new rapport between myself and Claude as he at least spoke to me, and topped my wine glass up when needed. I didn't pay much attention to the main bulk of the conversation until it turned around to the giving away of the bride. Margaret was of course thrilled, and clasped her son's hand in gratitude. He laughed off the affection and said, "Well, I could hardly leave it to Lawrence, after all, could I?" He raised his glass in Lawrence's direction. "Could I, old chap? You might get confused as to which way you were going and change course halfway up the aisle."

This remark caused some laughter, in fact I remember a lot of laughter over those next few days, but Lawrence coloured and refused to pick up his glass in response to the toast. If he had done nothing, it would not have piqued my interest.

Chapter Twelve

I spent some time that night, in between wading through interminable dead whales, scrolling back some of the conversations I had with Lawrence and about Lawrence. It didn't take me long, as I sifted the warp and weft of the clues I had been given over the past week, to realise that I had been very stupid, it seemed. Words played around in my head like fog in the dark, drifting in and out of memory; but however confusing they had started out to be, in the end, when the first light of dawn started colouring the sky, I could not help but see how things were. Lawrence—I was quite sure of it—had had some deeper relationship with Charles; and I should have seen it straight away. Stevie's attitude, things that had been said here and there. All nothing when in separate boxes, but when all tipped into a pile together and joined up, they made a lot more sense.

Was this then the truth about why I'd been kept at arm's length for so many years? I knew that I had to know, and resolved to get it from Lawrence once way or another before another day was out. If true, it was rather serendipitous, and that was a shame, really, because I rather liked him, in a "gaze upon but don't dwell on how dim I am" way.

Still. One can't be too sentimental about these things, can one? Needs must and all that.

I leant heavily on the fact that Lawrence and I had come to a mutual understanding over the past week. I knew he knew who and what I was, and I appreciated that he'd gone from a sullen revulsion to almost confiding in that time. I put this down to my ineffable charm, of course, and not that he must already know about Holland and was a trusting fool, but who knows? Was I supposed to feel grateful that he could stand being in the same room as my good self?

Breakfast was a sullen, quiet meal, as dinner had been the night before. The weather had decided to change, punishing us for thinking that summer was settled in and we could relax. A thin drizzle sank from the sky, more cloud than actual rain, but just as dampening to body and spirit. From time to time the gardener would pass the window, his salt-and-pepper hair and his hat coated with beads of moisture which dripped onto his jacket as he moved. I had wanted to take a walk out with Lawrence but was frustrated in that plan of attack, and of course there was no further chance that day of him further humiliating me at tennis, which would have been a good way to get him to open up, so I was obliged to think again.

Margaret had claimed her son, Stevie, Clarissa, and Claude and they'd all gone off somewhere no doubt to discuss frills, furbelows and feathers or whatever it is that has to be discussed prior to a wedding.

"You are very quiet," Richardson said with that razor observation that made him such a candidate for the Metropolitan Police force.

"That's right," Gilbert added. "And I was just wondering what it was that was different. You put the nail in place, Richardson, it's th soupçon e lack of the patented Bircham's Banal Banter. What's up, Bircham? Tragedy struck you dumb? If so, it's a bonus for us chaps. Never could abide your endless prattle before eleven."

Lawrence looked revolted at this, and Richardson turned on him, quite rightly, I thought. "Oh, come on, Stephens" he said. "You aren't the *chevalier sans peur et sans reproche* you like to make out. We were told what you said about Holland's father."

Lawrence looked daggers at me and I held up my hands. "Don't blame me," I said with what I hoped was a winning smile. "I didn't say anything. Blame Holland, or your sister. And I'm thinking how I can get free from you two boils if you must know."

"Well, that's charming." Gilbert said. "We are all too useful when we can drive you somewhere, but a bit of rain makes us redundant."

"You said it, dearie." I turned to Lawrence. "Is there somewhere we can get away from these two? Somewhere we aren't going to be forced to deciding on chrysanthemums or roses."

He was quiet for a moment, and I could almost see *between the devil and the deep blue sea flitting* through his mind. He hardly sounded grateful when he did speak, the brute. "We could go into the gallery. I could do with some practice."

Intrigued, I trailed after him, with a saccharine smile at the two hangers-on, down the hall and he stopped in front of the vaulted and horribly anachronistic gallery door. "Give me a bunk up," he said. "The key's kept on the top of the door. I can't be bothered to get the ladder."

It wasn't until I'd hefted him by the hips as high as I could lift him that I realised it would have been a lot easier if he'd lifted *me*. He was quite solid, and I might add, not an ounce of softness—not in any of the places I got to handle, anyway. I was panting when I put him down, and leant against the wall for a moment while he opened the door.

"Why is it kept locked? Is this where they keep the guns?" I asked brightly as we entered and he flipped on the lights. It was dim and grey outside and the high gothic mullioned windows didn't let much light in. Not necessary, really, as the room was generally meant to be used at night.

"No. Margaret keeps my cups in here. She thinks the silver and stuff adds a medieval touch. The guns are downstairs with Dad…Father." I found it a little pathetic, the automatic way he corrected himself, like a grammar-school boy constantly under scrutiny by boys better than himself.

"Fencing?" I asked.

"No," he said, his tone dismissive. "Trust a college man to think fencing. Far more low-brow than that." He opened a cupboard and took out a leather punchbag which with some effort he hung on a cunning hook under the minstrels' gallery.

I was seriously surprised, although it explained the asymmetric handsomeness of his features. That nose had indeed been broken, it seemed.

"Oh, *boxing*!" He winced at that. "I've never tried it."

"Really."

"I know, amazing, isn't it," I smirked at him. "With this physique?" I bent an arm in demonstration of my prowess.

"Stop that. And turn around."

"What?"

"I'm going to change and…"

"You don't want me to watch? How about if I just close my eyes?"

"All right, I'll go and change in my room."

"Oh, do stop being a prig, Lawrence. If it's so important to you." I turned around and hoped my back radiated my disapproval. Honestly, such pathetic modesty spoke volumes about his schooling.

I stared at the wall for a few moments, whilst getting delicious images attached to the noises I could hear from behind me. The unmistakable sounds of disrobing. Really, Lawrence was a child; he obviously had no idea just how alluring sounds can be. The vision I was conjuring up was probably much more erotic than watching the real thing. My undergarments became a little tighter and I thought frantically of Gilbert until the feeling went away.

When he finally allowed me to turn around I was still a little tumescent, and glad that my trousers were nicely roomy and unlikely to show it. He was dressed, quite modestly I thought, in a vest and very baggy shorts. I doubted he would have removed his underpants—unless he was wearing combinations, and the thought of that made me snigger internally—so I really couldn't understand the obsession for secrecy. I doubt he had anything to boast about, or could compare with Holland.

I leered appreciatively, all the same, because he deserved it for being a prude, and heavens alone knows he expected it of me, and he went brick-red in response to my compliment. He had some kind of frame with a sack attached to it over in a corner, for punching I assumed. I was grateful he wasn't intending to practice on me. "Give me a hand with this, will you?" he said. "We have to lift it, not drag it, Father would kill me if I so much as scratched the varnish."

Together we moved the piece into place onto some matting, although I'm certain he gave me the heavy end, then I had to help him on with his boxing gloves, during which he kept himself as far from me as he could, given the process. Honestly, one could get offended. Then I sat down on one of the chairs dotted around the edge and let him get on with it. It was fearfully dull, as I knew it would be. There's only so much skipping, punching and grunting that I can stand before I start to get bored, however masculine it is, so after a while I drifted over to the shelves which held an array of cups. It seemed that our Lawrence was modest about more than his person because if the silverware and shields were anything to go by, he wasn't at all bad at this sport. Was a cup worth the risk of having the teeth—or the brains—knocked out of your head? Lawrence was more than capable of defending himself if necessary. Useful to know. I sat back down and simply watched him afterwards, making no comment on his trophies, and after some endless time he stopped, took a towel from a chair and started to wipe his face and body. He was glistening all over with sweat which gave him a bronzed god look, and his hair had come loose from the Brylcreem and hung in black spikes around his face. Dewdrops of sweat clung to the end of each spike making him quite, quite beautiful and far more appreciable to my eyes than when he was posturing and punching. However, I suppose he had to posture and punch to get to the sweaty and disheveled stage.

I gave him some applause. "Thank you," I said.

"What?" He was out of breath, and it suited his voice admirably. Goodness, what with a nascent crush on Claude Holland, and this Greek god wandering around the place, I simply wasn't safe to be trusted. Except that I was, of course. In that way.

"That was lovely."

"Shut up. I don't want to hear that from you. I should have known you'd make into something—queer."

"Don't be horrid," I said, touching him lightly on the arm. "I mean it, I do think it's lovely. To watch."

"Yes. But—" He put the towel down slowly, then turned around so suddenly that the sweat flew from his hair in a cascade. The words burst from him as if he'd been waiting to explode for days. "That's it, isn't it? You—*all* you queers. You can't just watch chaps doing well at sports. You are looking at the men themselves."

I raised my eyebrows. "Oh, really. Isn't that what everyone does who watches sport? I mean, one can hardly just watch the ball. Or the net. That would be fearfully dull. And there's nothing else *to* watch in boxing after all, is there? And anyway," I looked directly at him, "you thought like this, and yet you still brought me in here to watch you. Isn't that—to put it in your terms—a little bit queer?"

"Shut up."

"Well, you did. We could have just gone into the library and talked, or somewhere, anywhere. You could have said you didn't want to spend the time with me, but knowing that 'us queers' as you so sweetly put it, salivate and leer at sportsmen—even sportsmen we know can't possibly be interested in us and our queer ways—you invited me here, stripped off and—"

"I said, shut up, Bircham."

"Positively *displayed* yourself for my salivation. I say, is that w—"

He threw himself at me then, and pushed me back against the wall, pinning me quite effectively, although I could have fought him, kneed him in the genitals (funny how men forget about how vulnerable they are there). I had him just where I wanted him, and a lot faster than I had expected to. Now for the kill, as it were.

"Was this how it was with Holland?" I simpered, egging him on. I wish I felt worse about it, but then do I? "Did he push you a step too far? Did he proposition you? Come into your room? Was there a moment when you were skinny-dipping that his hands ended up places where they shouldn't be? How was it, Lawrence?"

"You bastard. I wouldn't let you touch me, it would make me sick if you must know. And *if* you must know—and you must, because either he's already told you, or you'll ask him anyway. It was me. All right? It was *me*."

I dislike the expression "my jaw dropped" but that's exactly how I felt, and his confession was quite the last thing I expected to hear him say. I wasn't going to let him see that, however. If he thought I already knew, then that's how it would stay. I laughed, and he tightened his hold on me, pulling me forward and then back so my head banged sharply against the wooden panelling. That stopped me laughing, at least, but I wasn't going to lose my advantage, and I knew he was close to losing his control.

I think the sound of my head crashing against the wood brought him to his senses, because he dropped me, but his face remained a mask of disgust. Both with me and himself, I was quite sure. Oh, I knew him now. I knew— had known—a few men like him. Men who knew who they were but would never ever admit it to themselves. Men who would tolerate a bit of slap and tickle but it was all just boys together, wasn't it? Then they'd go and get married and have ghastly children and talk about "Jolly old Hoggy at school, he was such a good chum." But they'll never tell their wives *how* good a chum old Hoggy was, will they? They bury the past, however enjoyable. Lawrence would be exactly like this, fighting what he probably called his baser nature. In a way he was better than that verger Ian, because he could just deny it, not treat it as something to be cut out of him with the scalpel of government and justice.

Again, I blame Lawrence's education. If he'd gone to a decent school he'd have had more chance of working it out for himself. Got it out of his system, or found out what he wanted one way or another.

"Sorry," he said, grinding the words out as if they hurt him. "You are right, and…I didn't think."

"I was pretty unbearable myself," I said, smoothly. "I'm sorry too. Seriously. You are safe with me, Lawrence. You might look all you want at girls, but it's not like you are going to start goosing them, is it?"

"Of course not." He took up the towel again and started to dry his hair.

"Then why on earth would you think it's different for me? For us queers?"

I could see him thinking this over. He didn't like it; he didn't want to be reasonable. But eventually he nodded. "All right. Just don't...don't..."

"I know. I know what you mean. I won't do it anymore."

"Just stop doing...what you do."

"Cross my heart," I said. "Oh, don't make a face. It's a last hurrah. I shall be the model of manliness around you from now on."

"I doubt if you're capable," he said.

"Lawrence Stephens, I'm shocked," I said. "Oh, all right. I'll stop. Now. Do you want to tell me what happened or not?"

"Not really, but you'll get it from him anyway, won't you?"

"I probably could. But I won't. I find it interesting enough that he hasn't already told me."

"I don't know if I even believe you."

"You'll have to take that chance, won't you? I can't think of any reason why I would want to hear it again, though, if I had—can you?"

"I suppose not. But who knows what you think?" He sat down on the chair next to me, and glanced at the door. It was closed, although not locked, but he lowered his voice anyway. It was rather delightful being his confidante. He leaned a little closer to me, and the scent of the sweat of his exertion mixed with the a manly bay rum he wore was alluring. I wore my best listening face and kept my mannerisms under control.

"It wasn't much, I suppose. I...we grew up together, I mean, when he wasn't at school. It was just after that verger died, I don't know if he told you about it, some overstrung God-obsessed freak. And—well, you know him as well—better, I suppose." He gave a small smile. "He doesn't react well to bad news."

"No, he really doesn't."

"Well, he knew this guy a bit—nothing between them though," he added hurriedly. It amused me that he had gone from trying to knock my brains out to caring about whether I was jealous or not. I could only blame it on the winning Bircham ways.

"And he came home that holiday, just for a few days and he sat and told me about..." He broke off and went silent.

When he showed no sign of continuing, I had to prompt him. "About what?"

"About death." He shook his head. "I shouldn't be telling you this. He has this theory about death—quite unChristian—look, ask him. But he got himself all worked up the way he does and—well, I put my arm around him. Really I didn't mean more than that, but he turned to me in surprise and I..."

The self-disgust was rising in his voice so I put him out of his misery. It was the kindest thing to do, under the circumstances. Plus, really—these schoolboy confessions bore me entirely, and it seems so huge to the person telling the story.

"You kissed him."

There must have been something in my voice, although I would have sworn I kept it as banal as I could, because Lawrence reacted. "Yes—and I... it...I would never. I don't feel like that—never have, never!"

I patted his shoulder. Really, I know I should have felt sorry for him, but it was so laughable. The man was wracked with horror about an action that meant nothing. "He's very kissable," I said.

"I might have guessed you'd make a joke of it," he snarled. "What was I thinking when I thought you'd be any kind of person to tell?"

"Oh, my dear Lawrence, calm down," I said. "I'm not making a joke of it. I'm making *light* of it, which is an entirely different thing. He's your friend, yes? You won't deny that, no matter what your...differences in attraction happen to be?"

"Of course."

"Then think of it as a brotherly affectation," I said. "Like the French, who kiss each other for the slightest excuse. Celebration, welcome, goodbye. All you were doing was sympathising."

"Yes. I was."

"It's not as if you pushed him down onto the floor and started—"

"Please," he said, looking dark again. "Shut up. No," and he pulled away from me as if I'd slapped him or something. "I didn't really *know* he was queer, you see. Not for sure. Not until he turned up with you in tow."

"Oh." That made a little more sense.

"He could have bloody told me, you know."

He could have at that, but that wasn't the way he played things, was it? He'd find it far more rewarding to let Lawrence stew in his own guilt. I'd have done the same, and it was why we were such a perfect fit.

He stood, and started picking up his clothes. "There you go. Tell him, or not. It's all the same to me."

"That," I said, touching him lightly on the arm, "I doubt."

Before he left he gave me a peculiar look then, half-scowl, half-smile, and I wondered if I'd made a friend. I hoped not, to be honest. I had enough friends.

WHEN ONE COOKS, ONE HAS TO get the ingredients together before one starts. I had most of them for the dish I was planning, but not all of them and it was the final piece, the essential centre of the dish which was eluding me. What would I use? With Ari it had been all opportunity and luck, but I knew that wouldn't work here. Unless some external event prevailed to aid me, like a man-eating lion invading the gardens, I was going to have to be careful and put events into motion in a way that did not lead all the way back to me. I didn't share Lawrence's confession with anyone. There was little point, and frankly, the less people who knew that we were anything more than guest and servant's son the better. If anyone got wind of our disagreement in the Gallery it might go badly for me, and "badly for me" was not a phrase I liked.

So I kept quiet and when anyone asked me about Lawrence's training session I merely looked impressed (or bored, depending on who was asking) but said that I was glad it was him and not me, as it was all too exhausting for words. So, over the next few days, as we got over the shock of Ari's terrible accident and the lumbering wedding came ever nearer, I watched the players around me play their parts and I became the perfect guest and I puzzled over what to do.

My dilemma was resolved quite unexpectedly, as it turned out. The Saturday before the wedding week was warm and sultry, but large clouds overhung the sky, grey and portentous. That is, portentous for anyone who might have the gift of knowing what was likely to happen. We had lunched in the house, it being far too hot to eat in the garden, but afterwards we escaped outside, where it had a soupçon of breeze, unlike the house, which was positively stifling. I lay in the shade of a bank of laurels, *Moby Dick* still unfinished and lying abandoned by my right hand as ants crawled over it, showing more interest in it than I. I felt like Alice, wishing for pictures and conversation instead of interminable description of all the disgusting things you can do to a whale carcass. The rest of the family were dotted around equally between house and garden. Claude and Margaret sat in English perfection under a huge white sunshade: Claude with his newspaper, and Margaret embroidering something dainty, probably for the wedding. The Stephenses were in the house as far as I knew, as they couldn't be seen from my vantage point.

A large gathering was planned for that evening. Friends and relatives who had already begun to congregate in the vicinity were invited for dinner. I was rather looking forward to it, but Charles, lying with his head on my stomach, leaning rather uncomfortably on the double portion of fruit salad I had consumed, was most certainly not.

"For two pins I'd feign a sickness," he said. "But Mother was always too ruddy perceptive about that sort of thing. She'd have Nanny advance upon me like Blind Justice armed with a knowing look and a thermometer and I'd admit the deception immediately."

"You have no nanny now, at least," I said.

Charles snorted. "That wouldn't stop her."

The image was too revolting for me to dwell on.

"Isn't there something I could take?" he asked, turning his head hopefully to face me. "Plants are poisonous, aren't they? Isn't there something I could eat to give me a genuine reason to be sick?"

"My dear boy," I said. "I would think that most plants would do more than that. As far as my limited knowledge goes, the garden is full of things that can kill you. It's hair-raising to think that in every garden in the land, little old ladies and dahlia fanatics are pottering about amongst fields of death."

"Not worth the risk, then?" He dropped his head back onto my fruit salad.

"Most certainly not. Women have been poisoning their husbands for millennia with homemade concoctions. However, I've never really understood why people take the risk of signing the poison book and purchasing quantities of cyanide or strychnine, when a perfectly good laurel in the stew instead of bay leaves, or a few crushed laburnum seeds will do just as well. So please don't eat anything," I said, ruffling his hair with affection, "I'd rather miss you."

He shrugged my hand away, and I pulled back, obedient. "Are you meeting your father today?"

"Yes," he said. "At two."

"Where?"

"Oh…you know…"

"May I come with you?"

He rolled sideways onto his front and began pulling at the grass. As the silence lengthened between us I had a hundred things I wanted to say; the frustration and bile of being constantly tethered in some field far from his life was beginning to pick at the threads of my patience, but I said nothing. That of course was as bad as speaking, and I can do no right for doing wrong, at times. "Harry," he said, his eyes still on the grass he was pulling up. "Don't." "I wasn't aware that I *was*."

"Oh, you were. All injured pride but a steely determination not to show it. Save it for the Bar. You'll have entire juries bursting with a zeal to hang anyone you point your finger at."

"I may defend."

Charles snorted with laughter. "You? Don't make me laugh." He pushed himself up with a lithe movement, entirely failing to brush off the grass and dirt from his clothes before striding off.

"Will you—" I started.

"I don't know." And he was gone around the corner of the laurels.

I was tempted to follow him, but instead I told myself it was too hot and I was too comfortable. I had other things on my mind, anyway, things that were more important than the constant back-and-forth of control that our friendship had. In the shade of the speckled laurels, in the most tranquil of English country gardens, I was totally absorbed with death—or rather the process of bringing it about.

Book forgotten, even the bittersweet disagreement pushed to the back of my mind, I bent all of my thoughts on Claude and how to—and you'll note just how self-sacrificing I am, for the good of my lover and his peace of mind—dispose of him from this world and usher him into another. I stared up at the leaves above me, waxy and laden with toxins, and realised that I had been given the answer when I needed it, as I had so often in the past. Really, when something like that happens how can one not believe in Fate?

Chapter Thirteen

As I said to my dear, irritating, and often impulsive friend, you cannot just blindly go stuffing plant material into your face without knowing what you are doing, and the object of my desire, that is death for Claude, was not going to be achieved by simply asking him politely to "eat this."

Claude was not Alice, who, incidentally, even when I was a child I found most amazingly stupid for obeying the labels on food and drink she found just lying around. If it were as simple as to tie a label on a bottle, or leave a mushroom lying around with instructions to ingest, life would be a lot easier, and certainly a lot more colourful. What person in their right mind (other than Alice, of course, the idiotic child) is going to eat suspicious looking foodstuffs just found lying around untended?

So, somehow I had to arrange for a similar kind of accident as befell Ari or my father, something where fate would decide. I lay in the dappled warmth thinking this over with a kind of indolent pleasure, and came up with a rather elegant solution—if you'll excuse the pun. I would have to be careful though, I didn't want *mi amore* or myself gagging it, after all.

I got up, strolled about a bit, and then, when out of sight of Margaret and Claude I walked briskly around to the gardener's shed. I have a fair bit of experience in sheds, one tends to find them useful when a passionate moment needs to be addressed but one can't do it on the lawn for fear of startling the peacocks. The Hollands' shed was more like a small cabin and as I pushed the door open, tutting at the laxity of it not being locked, I noted that this one was even better equipped for passionate encounters than most, having a neat camp-bed along one wall.

Gardeners tend to have methodical minds. This is something of which I highly approve and this son of the soil was no exception. All his seeds were neatly stacked in boxes and paper bags along a wall and several shelves. Everything was beautifully labelled in a neat, round hand. It's odd, but you rarely find an illiterate gardener. I suppose they need to know how to read labels too. Wouldn't do to go scoffing things marked "poison," would it?

I restrained myself from sniggering at this. Solitary sniggering is a dangerous habit to acquire.

The poisonous plants were, quite rightly, placed on the top shelf. And were in a little tin trunk handily marked not only with *Poisons* but even with a skull and crossbones that the gardener must have taken from a proprietary container. I had looked around for a bottle of something or other, actually, but even though there was a bottle of cyanide spray, I decided not to take it. Its loss would be noticed, and I had nothing to decant it into. And cyanide.

Really. It's so *de trop*.

My heart nearly stopped when I heard footsteps outside, and I froze, unable to place the tin back without being heard, and frantically coming up with an excuse why I was doing what I was doing. Luckily the fact that my startled mind didn't rescue me didn't matter as the footsteps went past, and a moment later the gardener plodded past the window in the direction of the house. I found I could breathe again after a minute or so, and did, gratefully.

Within there were dozens of packets—surprising me at quite how many plants were dangerous, more than even I had thought. I grabbed one without bothering to select it. *Datura*, the label informed me. I couldn't for the life of me remember what they were, and I tipped a large handful of the black seeds into my handkerchief and fled, after putting everything back where I'd found it, and very carefully wiping the tin; one didn't want to leave fingerprints and one has read *some* crime fiction even if it was when no one was looking. Then I sauntered as casually as I could back to my place in the laurels where, warm and comfortable in the dappled sunlight, I promptly nodded off.

I woke with a start at someone calling my name. The sun had moved appreciably from where it had been and my little bower was now entirely in shade as the shadows lengthened over the lawn. Stevie stood on the lawn before me, and she'd obviously called me more than once, judging by the impatient expression on her face.

"Good Lord," she said, "I've never known anyone sleep as deeply as you—apart from Lawrence. With him, however, I can get away with throwing a shoe or a book."

"I'm glad you restrained yourself."

"If it hadn't been for the snoring, I would have thought you were dead."

She stood to one side as I retrieved my book and scrambled to my feet, brushing off the detritus of my lazy afternoon.

"I do not snore," I said, with as much dignity as a man can have who suspects he may have twigs in his hair. "I have it on the best authority." We started to walk towards the house. "Then…whosoever that might be"—she led the way with a burst of sudden speed—"is lying to you. And you a single man, for shame. I was sent to round everyone up. The party guests are due to arrive in half an hour and Margaret wants the bathrooms and such-like cleared in case anyone needs to use them."

"Cripes." I broke into a trot and passed her. "You expect miracles if you think I can be ready in a mere half hour. It takes time for perfection, you know."

"I am sure we can muddle along without it," she laughed as I sped up and fairly sprinted through the French doors and up to my room.

Charles was just coming down the hall as I hurried up it and I had to stop and give a whistle of appreciation. He looked mouth-wateringly beautiful. His suit, courtesy of Stephens, was immaculately pressed, and his hair had just the right amount of control for my preference. After a dance or two, after he'd messed it up thoroughly with a nervous hand it, would be unruly again. His shoes shone like the glossiest Chinese lacquer, but the entire effect was spoiled by his tie being missing. He held it in his hand, and proffered it up to me as I approached.

"Thank God," Charles said. "Where the devil have you been? I sent Stevie to find you. You know I can't manage this bloody thing."

"I was exactly where you left me, of course," I said, leading the way into my room. "If you had bothered to look."

"*Unter den laurels*? Oh. No, I didn't think you'd be still there."

"Hold still."

"I can wait if you want to wash."

"No, no. Not with you looking like that," I said, finding him too irresistible to keep at arm's length, so once the tie was done I pulled him into my arms. His hands skimmed my torso and worked their way down. Too late I realised the danger. "What's this?" he asked, feeling the bulge of my hanky.

"Nothing." I pulled his hands back up around my waist. "Boys who pry don't get presents."

"It wasn't *that* in your pocket I was curious about. But I am now."

I kissed him, while I had him still and compliant. His lips were cool, his breath sweet with peppermint and his back curved under the guiding mastery of my hand. By sheer willpower I broke away, leaving less than an inch between our mouths. "If I don't go and have a rather cool bath right now, you and I may never get to the party and thereby scandalise the entire county. Unless you think that's a good idea."

"I do, and I don't," he murmured, briefly catching my lower lip with his teeth. "Staying here would be heaven, but the ensuing row would be hell."

Something tingled between us, the air like static electricity. God alone knew we'd been so circumspect for so long, and if he hadn't moved backwards, leaving me cool and empty with a teasing touch on the front of my trousers I don't think I would have cared whom I offended.

"I'll have to hold you to a promise deferred." The want sounded husky in my voice.

"It's here when you want it," Holland said.

"Don't tempt me," I said. "And bugger off."

CHARLES WENT AND I STUCK MY head around the door to watch him go, to make sure he'd actually gone, then I nipped into the bathroom. It wasn't going to be ideal, but it would have to do. I lit the little burner which was left for me to make tea at any time I wished and boiled water while I dressed and changed. Then over the sink, I poured hot water over the seeds into my shaving mug, hoping for some kind of noxious infusion. I didn't really see any other way of getting them into my target. It's not as though I'd studied poisons in between my tutorials, although it would have been jolly useful, it has to be said. I was woefully unprepared for this sort of thing. No utensils, no sieve. No wonder poisoners tended to be women. They were used to getting things all lined up before they started cooking, weren't they? I had to fish out all of the seeds with a pencil. Then, allowing myself a satisfied grin—this is more acceptable than solitary sniggering—I poured the liquid, which had gone a dark amber-brown, into my hipflask. It looked not unlike a strong tea, or, if it had been a little clearer, a whisky.

Thus armed, I trotted back down the family stairs. Stephens was hovering in the hall. I heard the sound of tyres on gravel and fled into the drawing room where the family was gathered. How resplendent everyone looked. It's odd but that's the strongest memory of that night—because frankly much of it was tedium—the memory of finding them standing around, drinks and cigarettes in hand. If I'd had a camera in my belongings, I would have liked to have captured them like that, so perfectly beautiful, so seemingly at ease, the upper-middle classes at their peak—if you didn't know where to look for the hairline cracks. It was, after all, the last moment they had together. What a shame that they didn't know it, they might have made better use of it.

"A car's arrived," I said.

"That will be Abigail and Ian," said Margaret. "My cousins from Scotland, they have the terrible vice of punctuality. No one from around here would dare to be so on time." As she said this, the clock on the mantelpiece began to chime prettily, followed a second or so later by the great booming grandfather clock from the landing.

I went to stand next to Charles.

"What do you wager cousin Ian will be wearing the kilt?" he said, in an atrocious Scottish accent.

"I'm not falling for that one," I said. "You know him and I don't."

Charles grinned. "You're no fun."

"Talking of which," I said, "where are the ghastlies?"

"I think Mother gave them a small hint about it being a family gathering. Richardson had a fit of memory and recalled his people asked him to be back for tomorrow."

This made me rather happier than I already was. One didn't like to run the risk of poisoning one's college-mates, it seemed a little incestuous.

Margaret walked forward as an elderly woman of about fifty and a grey haired man sporting full ceremonial kilt complete with sporran and skean dhu entered. Greetings, introductions, drinks, polite talk. All this broke out and it set the tone for the next hour.

I'm good at mingling. I dislike it a great deal, holding much loathing for the human race in general—with one or two notable exceptions—but I am good at it. I treat it as a skill like any other. If one can be good at cricket, or violin, or whittling—and I'm not exactly sure what whittling is but give me a whittle and I'll learn it—then one can develop the skills needed for social niceties. If it wasn't for my dream of that shared accommodation and a tousled face over my morning paper, I would have excelled in the Foreign Office, ingratiating foreign visitors at an Embassy in some far-flung potentate. All the while my hipflask seemed heavy in my breast pocket and just the sensation of it there, the metal moving as I moved, bumping against me, reminding me of its hopefully deadly payload was enough to excite me so well that I breezed through the chit-chat and greetings with something approaching pleasure. All my senses seemed alert, the way they had when I was cutting the girth on Ari's saddle. It was far more intoxicating than the rather mediocre champagne Claude had provided, and it raced around my mind like cocaine, fizzing away and making me breathless.

All the while I looked around me for a chance to effect my plan. I soon realised that it was going to be unviable in the drawing room, for every minute that passed, another couple or a family group entered, and soon there were chattering groups in every corner of the room, and it became impossible to see who was noticing what.

I located Charles, and went to stand beside him where he stood alone. He looked hard at me and his voice was full of concern. "Are you all right? You're shaking like a leaf!" He grabbed my elbow and brought my free hand up between us. True enough my hand was shivering like a palsied grandmother, my excitement showing far too clearly.

I fell back on the fact that I appeared more delicate than I was, after all, I could hardly tell him the truth. "It's all a little overwhelming, I suppose," I said. "So many people, so many names."

"Hollands *en masse*," he said with a wry curl to his lip. "Yes. They can be a bit much. It'll be easier when we are seated. Have another drink. Relax for a change. It won't kill you to relax."

Charles turned away to stare out at the room and I was glad of that because I gawped at him, and he'd have wanted to know why. The clarity of what he'd said hit me like a mallet. I looked down at my drink. Could I? It was simple and beautiful. "Hold this for a moment," I said, handing him my glass. He took it and I dropped to a crouch for a moment as if adjusting my suspender, then stood and took the glass from him again with a quick smile.

I touched his arm as if to say "It's all right," and drifted through the room, then out into the hall and quickly into the downstairs W.C. Then I decanted the mixture into my own glass. It mixed easily into the sherry. So far so good.

After all, I wasn't sure what I had in my glass, didn't know what effect it would have. I might do the deed and nothing more than give Claude a headache or a dicky stomach. That wouldn't do. If it had to be done, then it had to be effective. A dress rehearsal was called for, then. Just to make sure of the outcome.

Back I went into the room, Margaret was counting heads and consulting with Claude; it seemed everyone had arrived. I slipped over to the other side of the room where Stevie stood with her brother. "Quite a turn-out," I said. I looked carefully around the room, noting who was drinking what and where their glasses were.

"It's not everyone," Stevie said. She looked over at Margaret.

"People didn't come?" I put my glass down on the table and adjusted my tie in the small mirror behind Lawrence. Lawrence glared at me. I grinned at Lawrence. Lawrence scowled. All was right with the world.

"No, I meant there are more Hollands. Smaller satellites who didn't merit the family feast. They'll be coming to the wedding and the bunfight afterwards."

"God," I said with feeling. "I had no idea families came in swarms. I don't know this many people, let alone being related to them." I took the drink from the table, raised it to my lips in mock toast. "Here's to the Hollands. Well, it looks like we are going in. Stevie? May I take you in?"

She raised an eyebrow at me, but collected her own drink and without another word took my arm and we queued up, ready to move into the Gallery. It was hard, so hard not to show more attention to my guinea pig than I would normally give. I was placed between two relatives, and a good way down the table from the family, or from Stevie and Lawrence. I kept calm, keeping an inane stream of gossip and speculation going as soup came around. I noticed that the mixture was drunk, and that's all I could do at that time. The rest was in the lap of the gods.

Chapter Fourteen

Once I'd seen Stevie to her seat, I watched her as carefully as I could, given the circumstances. She finished the wine she had brought with her, then she had another, and yet another. She was sitting quite close to Charles and was engaged in lively conversation with him and a few younger members of the family. It was good to see him smiling, but I couldn't help but wish I was included in their fun. I was a little too far down the table to be so.

Time wore on; ten minutes passed. The soup was cleared and sorbet served before the fish, but still she showed no sign of ill-effects. The sense of elation and excitement which had me buoyed up like a Zeppelin plummeted within me like a rock going over the edge of a waterfall. What had I done wrong?

Perhaps an infusion was the wrong thing to use? Perhaps I should have left it longer? If the damned seeds weren't poisonous, then what was the point of putting them in a box labelled "Poisons"? Idiot gardener. I slumped back in my seat, feeling an utter failure and more than aware of the wedding racing toward me, hating that I was letting Charles down. The conversations washed over me as I sunk myself in gloom.

"I said, have you been to Cannes, Mr Bircham?" my left-hand companion asked me, for what was obviously the second, or perhaps even third time. "You should, you know, if you get the chance."

"Yes, yes. Once," I muttered, uncaring, staring gloomily at my melting sorbet. "But I was only ten. Hardly old enough to enjoy its delights."

"Absolutely," she fluttered at me. I wasn't aware women still did that. I felt like hitting her with a fan and telling her to desist. "It's a very wicked place, very wicked." A murmur of consternation rippled around the table and my heart leapt in hope. "Oh, dear me," she said, craning her neck around. "What is the matter with the Stephens child?"

I looked up the table at Stevie, but she was no different, except now she was raising herself to her feet, her forehead wrinkled in concern. "Lawrence?" she said.

My head snapped around. Lawrence. Finding him a few seats down on the same side as myself, I saw—as others got to their feet—that he had slumped sideways in his chair, but his eyes were wide open. His sorbet had been knocked out onto the table, caused no doubt by his arm which was twitching violently.

"He's having a fit!" someone said. "Get him on the floor, give him room."

"Don't be ridiculous," Stevie's voice cut through the general hubbub. "He's never had a fit in his life." She reached Lawrence's chair and knelt beside him. Lawrence's face was pale, with pin-pricks of pink on each cheek. His eyes were open and staring; one hand picked at his clothing as if pulling something away from his jacket. "Lawrence. Lawrence!" She patted his face, then slapped it a little harder, calling his name over and over. It was quite disconcerting, watching her desperation and his complete indifference to her well-meant violence.

Claude strode around the table. "No doctors in the entire party," he muttered. "That's typical." He sounded as if Lawrence's incapacity were personally aimed at disrupting his evening, the way you'd callously hear train travellers complaining that their journey had been delayed by a suicide further up the line. "Loosen his collar," he ordered.

Stevie pulled at Lawrence's tie with shaking fingers and it undid in her hand. "He's choking," she said, her voice on the edge of hysteria. "Get Father, Margaret, please—get Father."

"I'll go," I said. I dashed out of the door and pulled open the green baize door to find Stephens just climbing the stairs, ice bucket and champagne in his arms. "Stephens. You'd best come—"

"I'm coming as fast as can, Mr Bircham," he said, with a small edge to his tone. No doubt he was a little put out at having to do the work for the party with no extra staff, and who could blame him?

"No, just put…all that…down. Or give it to me." My voice must have sounded urgent enough, for he looked sharply at me. "It's Lawrence. He's choking. Or a fit. Or something. I don't know. Just come." I prided myself on my sense of urgency and bafflement.

It took a second or two for Stephens to process the information, but when he did he put his burdens down carefully on the stairwell and fairly sprinted up the stairs past me and into the hall. I followed and stood at the edge of the crowd around the stricken young man and watched them flail around like beached fish. My eye moved around the room, sucking in the various reactions, finding them quite fascinating. Some simply stood, hands to their mouths—mostly the women—while others—mostly the men—spoke encouragement to Stevie and Stephens as they attempted to resuscitate Lawrence. "He's still breathing," one said. "That's good. Can you see any blockage?" "Try sitting him up and slapping his back," said another. "Put his head between his knees," yet another advised. "Oh, for God's sake," Stevie cried, "there's nothing in his throat. Someone telephone for the doctor!"

It wasn't until this moment, when the crowd broke apart and Claude went out to the telephone, that I thought to look for Charles to see how he was taking it. He was standing with his mother, his face as white as her own, and his hand clutching hers. He caught my glance across the room and I poured everything of my love into one short look. I wished I could hold him as tightly as his mother was, but all I could do was to share one look—he must have known how I felt at that moment, how I felt about him, anyway.

Charles called out then, "I think it would be better if most of us moved into the drawing room. I'm sorry about dinner, but in the circumstances..." I gave him a brief nod of encouragement.

People muttered their agreement and most of the onlookers moved away, filing out into the hall. People began to make their excuses and to say their goodbyes to Margaret on the spot, expressing their concern: "You'll be better off without us crowding round," and "I'm so sorry, you will come to us next month, won't you?" their platitudes ranging from solicitous to callous.

Most of their solicitations were for Margaret, though, I noticed, and not for the young man in distress upon the floor. I made myself useful, dragging myself away from the tragic little tableau in the dining room, and finding coats and hats and shawls, matching guest to attire. I wasn't terribly good at it, and really I wanted to go back in and watch what was happening. I needed to know, needed to observe.

When the final guest had taken the hint and gone, Holland touched me briefly on the shoulder. "Thank you, Harry. You are a rock, sometimes."

Then the front door bell went again, and he answered it. The doctor fairly sprinted through the door and into the dining room, under Holland's direction, and I followed.

They had Lawrence sitting up, but he was not conscious. Or at least, he didn't appear to be so, not fully. His eyes closed and opened, but slowly, as if he kept slipping into a dream and then out of it, never fully managing to make it back to normality and alertness. His tongue licked again and again at his lips, as though they were dry.

"Have you given him anything to drink?" the doctor said as he took Lawrence's pulse, and looked in his eyes and mouth.

"We tried to get him to drink some water."

"Good," the doctor said. "That may have helped. There's no blockage to the airway and his breathing, although fast, doesn't seem to be restricted. His heart rate is slow, enough to worry me." He paused and looked around. "I'll need to get my other bag from the car."

"I'll get it," Charles said.

"No, it's quicker if I do. You don't know what you're looking for."

"What's wrong with him?" Margaret whispered. "It's—"

"I think Mother would be better out of here," Charles said. Claude gave him a curt nod, clearly resenting losing the upper hand to his nephew—as if he had ever had it. I experienced a sweet twist of triumph that Claude had been so entirely perplexed in an emergency. The doctor hurried out while Stephens looked around him. It was clear Lawrence had vomited on the parquet. "I'm so sorry, Mrs Holland, I'll clear it up immediately," Stephens said, getting to his feet.

"Of course you won't do any such thing," Margaret said. "Claude, ring for the kitchen maid. They need to know to stop preparing any more food anyway. Oh, Lord, we'll have to manage somehow." Claude took Margaret and Clarissa out, who had at least not collapsed or panicked.

Minutes past, punctuated only by the maid receiving instructions from Claude at the dining room door, and then the doctor said, "He hasn't deteriorated any further. I think we can risk moving him. Is there anywhere on the ground floor he can lie down?"

"The morning room," Charles said. "Harry and I can take him. Harry?"

"Of course," I said. Together we lifted Lawrence as carefully as we could. As we did Lawrence seemed to revive slightly. He mumbled something, and that damn arm started to wave again, like he was dementedly pushing something away, or pulling something towards him. With no reaction in his face it was extremely creepy. God alone knows what he was dreaming about. I was intrigued with it all, if a little disappointed.

"What's he saying?" said Stevie? "Lawrence? Lawrence? Please speak to me."

"Miss Stephens," the doctor said. I had no idea of his name, funny how this doesn't seem to matter with doctors. They can breeze into the house and take over and hold such respect, and frankly they could be anyone. I was on a train once and someone called for a doctor and this chap on the seat along from me said he was—and everyone just believed him. One could do anything with power like that. "I think you would better off with Mrs Holland."

"No," she said, but I saw her bite her lower lip as if utterly conflicted. "He might need me."

"I can assure you that he is not in the slightest aware of you, me, or his surroundings. And I will need to examine him…thoroughly."

"I'm his sister…surely—"

"*You* may be comfortable with that, dear," Stephens said gently. It was the first time that I'd heard him speak outside his role as servant. He had his arm around his daughter and a good job too, for she looked as if a stiff breeze would have knocked her over. "But the doctor might not be."

She paused, and I saw her face tightening up as she gained control of herself. "Stevie," Charles said, as gently as I'd ever heard him speak. "We'll look after him. I promise. But Mother needs you and you can do more good. Being the level head. Rather than Claude."

She looked up at him, her eyes bright with unshed tears, and her face was sheer defiance. "All right. All right! But you'll come…and tell me if…you'll tell me. If, if anything…"

He nodded and we continued to carry the dead weight through into the morning room and placed him on the chaise at the doctor's direction. The doctor proceeded to inject Lawrence with some clear liquid, checking his pulse before and after, then with Stephen's help, he stripped Lawrence down to his underthings and went over him meticulously, looking for God knows what. It's probably rather wrong of me to find looking at his half-naked form as attractive as it was when he was boxing, but there you go. Ogling cannot sustain the soul for long. I was rather bored by this point, and rather than show it, I made noises about placating the rest of the family. The doctor nodded and continued to work. Charles gripped my arm, the length of the grip showing his appreciation of my efforts. And I should think so too.

Once in the drawing room the family turned to me en masse as they would do more than once in the days to come. I assured them that Lawrence was still with us and no, the doctor hadn't said anything at all, let alone hinted at what the malady might be. It was a sad, silent little group that waited through the next half hour. All dressed up in our finery, and no doubt as hungry as I was, but caught in a moment of time until news came through. To give her her due, Stevie did suggest we order sandwiches but everyone seemed against the idea, so I could hardly give my approval and be the odd one out. I had to blend in, and I was taking my cues from Margaret as to how to behave.

Eventually, muted voices were heard in the hall, and the doctor came in alone. "There's no change," he said, before anyone could speak. "But he's breathing a little easier, and I've given him some adrenaline to buck up his heart." He looked grave. "I have to ask you the same question as I asked your father, Miss Stephens, has your brother a habit of taking barbiturates of any kind? Does he take morphine? Cocaine?"

Stevie stared at him for a long second or two. "Lawrence? N-no. I don't think so. I'm certain he's never—"

"But you aren't entirely sure?"

"I'm only as certain as I know my brother," she said. "He's particular. He runs for exercise. He plays tennis. He boxes. I…" I could see the doubt invading her mind. "He'd tell me. I'd notice. Someone would notice?" She looked around at the group of them, and they all looked sympathetic, aside from Claude who looked alarmed. I found that interesting. "Don't dopers have tiny pupils or something? Behave like maniacs? He's not…"

"His eyes are very dark," Claude said, surprising me. "Would we notice, Doctor?"

"*Possibly* not," the doctor said. "It is easier to tell the size of the pupils with lighter eyes, but the pupils don't always contract. It depends on the drug used. Best we start there."

Clarissa came forward and sat Stevie back down, patting her hand. "The doctor's not certain," she said. "Are you, Doctor?"

"No. I think he would be better off in the hospital—at least until he regains consciousness."

"He will, then?" I said. "Oh, jolly good," I added quickly.

"I will be honest with you, I won't stick my neck out and say anything either way. He's healthy, he's young, but these things are tricky. I've seen overdoses in a dozen cases and none of them could be thought of as really similar."

"Overdose?" Stevie's voice had shrunk to near nothing. "You don't mean he'd tried to…that it was deliberate? No…no…he was looking forward to the party. He was! And he'd never—*never* do that kind of thing in public—if he were ever to do it, which he absolutely would not. He had everything to live for."

It was hardly true, but I appreciated her sentiment.

"I didn't say anything of the sort, Miss Stephens. But if he had misjudged the dose, or it was a new batch, stronger than he has been used to…or had been tampered with—"

"Deliberately?" Charles asked.

"Used to?" raged Stevie. "You are making it sound like he's an old hand. I won't believe it."

"All I will say is—and I should go back to him soon—that it looks like a case of overdose. Does anyone here take Veronal? He doesn't?" Everyone shook their heads. "He's drifting in and out of a conscious state, but even when he's awake, he's not aware of where he is. He's constantly fighting something, or someone away—I think, which is what he seems to be doing with his arm."

"Hallucinations? Is he safe?" said Claude, now looking more alarmed than ever. It was as if someone had unmasked Lawrence as Jack the Ripper.

"I am sure he's seeing things, or people who aren't there, while having no idea of what is actually in front of his eyes. There's no scalp injury, so all I can rule out is brain damage caused in that way. I cannot rule out that he ingested—or, I'm afraid to say—injected something that he shouldn't. There are small marks on his arms which indicate he's used a syringe at some point recently."

"No," Stevie said, as surprised as myself. "Why would he—"

"If it's any consolation to you all," the doctor said, "it doesn't look like he's been doing this for any length of time. The signs on a man's arm who is used to the drug for a long while are unmistakable. This might only be his second or third time. I doubt that's any comfort, but it means that—should he recover—it will be easier to wean him away from whatever substance it is."

"You seriously think he may not recover?" Claude said.

"As I said, it's very hard to predict these things. People can die with their first use of a drug. Some can use a drug for years, working—having a normal life—and no one suspects them of anything at all. Then suddenly—they might die after creating what you'd think would be a tolerance. There simply isn't enough research, and no set pattern to these things."

Clarissa put her arm around Stevie who was trembling as if with cold. "None of us know people as well as we think we do," she said. "I was once very much in love with a young man—a friend of Claude's, in fact. He, Bill, seemed to me to be like the bubbles in champagne. The centre of every party, making me the absolute envy of all my friends, or so I thought. He died at a party—I hadn't been able to go—and when they found him he had a needle still in his arm."

"Oh, God," Stevie said.

"That's not very reassuring, Clarissa," her brother said. "Stevie doesn't need to hear about Bill Pentlow."

"Oh, I didn't mean…" Clarissa flushed deep scarlet. "I'm simply saying this might be a blessing in disguise. It might dissuade him from being foolish again. You know, you have to be optimistic. For him—and for your father."

I was sorely tempted to say that no one in their right mind could compare scowling Lawrence with bubbles or lives and souls but I kept up my mask of concern and empathy.

The doctor spoke again, and there was an impatience in his voice as if he was surprised at the tangent the conversation was taking. "I'll call for an ambulance."

"Hospital is quite out of the question," Claude said. "The boy can have every care here, surely?"

Margaret nodded. "We can't let just anyone see him like this. He deserves better. We can hire whatever help you think he needs."

"I advise against it, but if you can get both day and night nurses, then I'll not force the matter. I can see to him here, of course, and I know his history. Now I must go back and monitor him. I suggest you get some help as soon as possible. If someone can telephone to my wife and let her know that I will need to stay overnight?"

A galvanised Clarissa said, "Of course. I'll ring the exchange regarding nurses." It was like one of those weather dolls, as Stevie retreated into her shell, Clarissa came out of hers and started being organised. She bustled out to start making calls.

Stevie looked up at the doctor, wide-eyed and tragic. "May I see him?"

The doctor paused at the door, then nodded. "Quickly and quietly, though." Stevie hurried out after him and a silence filled the room as we processed everything that had been said, and I especially had much to think about. Once again fate had stepped in and helped me out. How very jolly decent of it.

Claude went to Margaret's side and put his hand on her shoulder, and she gave him a brittle smile. Then he left the room, muttering something about speaking to the doctor. Charles moved away from his mother then, and walked over to the bar, pouring himself a drink and one for me. Then he joined me, sitting on the arm of my chair. The group of us sat in silence for what seemed like hours but was probably only five or so minutes.

"This is bloody," Charles said, at last, making us all look around at him. "I'd never have taken Lawrence for a doper. I mean—why on earth? And how? He's hardly rolling in money."

I'd been wondering that myself. Still water ran very deep, it seems. It was absolutely perfect that Lawrence had been taking the drug. I suspected it would make things a little easier all round. But who would have thought it?

"Who knows anyone, really?" I said. "But then, he did have the most alarming mood swings."

"I don't believe it, not Lawrence," Margaret said.

"Well, what else? This isn't a murder mystery, mother. No one's got any gripe against Lawrence,for goodness sake. He's an inoffensive as a tulip. If anyone wanted to kill anyone it would be…" He waved an arm. "Me. Claude. Harry."

I raised my eyebrows at that, thinking myself pretty inoffensive too.

"You know what I mean," he went on. "It's fantastic. And impossible."

I rather felt that way myself. Lawrence was the last one I'd have thought to be shooting anything into his veins. I couldn't see him allowing anything hard into his body, and I had to smother a childish smirk at that. But fate, luck, or whatever you call it—that devilish luck that had seen me through so much, was working for me again.

Claude came back in. "It seems the doctor was right," he said. He was holding a small leather case. "The man knows what he's talking about."

"Did you search Lawrence's room?" Charles exploded in anger. "How bloody dare you! What right did you have?"

"As the boy is my guest—"

"Your guest? Yours? Not bloody yet, he isn't."

"Darling," his mother tried, but he didn't stop for her.

"He's Mother's guest, as this is still Mother's house. And will remain Mother's house even after you've jumped into my father's bed!"

"Darling, please."

"Well, won't it?"

"No, of course not, but this is hardly the time and place—"

"You had no right—no right at all, without her permission—to go poking around in anyone's rooms. Certainly not Lawrence who's been here for a damn sight longer than you! God, you disgust me, both of you."

"Darling—"

"Excuse me, Mother. I'd better see about getting a bed ready for the doctor."

Charles had shut his temper down, as though he'd slammed a steel door on the raging inferno and was outwardly calm again. I knew better. He left swiftly without even a glance at me to ask him to accompany him.

Claude continued into the room as if the argument had not happened. He placed the case on the table and we gathered around. Opening it up, he revealed two steel and glass syringes, sitting snugly on indented silk, together with and two vials of dark-coloured glass. Neither vial was labelled.

"I don't know what it is, but—" He shook his head. "Stupid boy."

"Surely the doctor will have to report it?" Margaret asked.

"It depends," Claude said. "Actually, Margaret, I don't know, to be honest."

"Does he even have to know about this?" she said. "He hasn't seen it yet, has he?" Claude shook his head. "Then it's just you, me and Harry. Harry won't say anything, will you, Harry?"

I shook my head too. "And your son," I said. "And he's only seen the case, not the contents. But you can trust him." Claude made a noise, "I'll speak to him, anyway. Oh, and Lawrence of course…but…"

"When Lawrence comes round he'll have the sense to keep quiet, or I'll know the reason why," Claude said. He was braver without his nephew facing him down. "It's important that this case is not found, then. Are we agreed?"

Margaret and I nodded.

"So you will speak to the doctor, Claude?" Claude kissed her cheek in assent. "Good," she said, more briskly. "There's been enough talk about the marriage. We can't have the idea going around the village that we have a house full of dopers, especially with half the family already having seen Lawrence collapse. He can simply recover and we'll tell them all…something. That it was a fit. Or a stroke, or something. No one has to know about this."

"If he dies, dear, I don't know how much good that will do."

"Of course he won't die!" Margaret said. "Things like that don't happen here. He'll have every care. Every care. He'll wake up tomorrow. You'll see. You'll see." Her voice had gone from hysterical to determined in one small speech as if she dared the world to defy her. I was very impressed and had it not been such an inopportune moment, I would have offered my congratulations, or given a rousing hand of applause.

Chapter Fifteen

went and found Charles after my mulling. It was tempting to do so earlier, but it would do my pride and our relationship no good at all.

He was in his room, staring out at the dark garden, and every muscle seemed to vibrate with his suppressed rage. I loved him when he was angry, even when it was directed at me. I loved the way he sometimes took the world on single-handed. It was for this bravery that I loved him, that and for a hundred other reasons. The way he never really hid what we were, except by dint of his own personality. If homosexuality were legal and men could love openly, I doubted he'd change his outward behaviour towards me—or any lover—in the slightest. There was something natural about his actions, not natural in that "everyone acts this way" but natural to him. He had a knack of keeping me eternally in love with him, while still keeping himself behind a shield. Perhaps it was that very shield, and the few moments when it melted, that kept the spark alive in me for him. The innate unavailability of him. And that shield. What was it for? Perhaps it was a safeguard—against himself, his own nature. Perhaps it was a way of keeping himself in check around his family. I wondered if, without the shield of self-control, Charles would have announced his proclivity, explained it all to them. Although he was sure they knew, and they knew he knew they knew. What would happen? Would everything change? Decidedly yes. I am certain of it.

Even the most abnormal of families would find that kind of announcement impossible—and as much as the Hollands occasionally played the upperclass eccentrics, they were not *that* abnormal. Would he shrug it off, take it on the chin (although that mixed metaphor would make him some kind of contortionist at the very least) and continue on in his life with or without them?

Therefore there was just one small conversation between the way things were and the possibility of so much change. One sentence spoken out loud to his mother and to watch walls crumble and the English veneer crack with disbelief and incomprehension.

That was what the shield was for, I surmised. To *stop* himself from dragging something into the light, like a carcass everyone had been ignoring. Looking at Charles, his face tight with anger, I wondered if that's how he really wanted it. Would he change the world if he could? I would, certainly. But would he? Perhaps it would be for nothing. Perhaps he knew his mother would stop him before he reached the end of that first sentence, and there was no danger after all. I hoped that wasn't the case. Because why else did he extend that shield— even to me?

He tipped his head towards me in acknowledgment of my presence.

"*Bloody*—"

"Come on," I took his arm. "Let's go out. Take the car. Walk into the village. Get drunk. I can get some food sent up here if you want."

"No. " His voice was grim. "It won't be fair to Stephens. We'll go and get something to eat from the kitchen, then I need to check on Lawrence. I'm not going anywhere."

"But—"

"I said no, Harry." I don't think I'd ever seen him look quite so grim. He led the way out into the hall and didn't even mute his voice, even though Stephens was in the hall, placing a vase of rosebay and rhododendron on a hall table, rather unnecessarily so, considering the circumstances. "I'm seeing this thing through. I'm not letting Claude get away with this. If it means a showdown, then he's welcome to it. It's me or him."

"That's…" I stopped, choosing my words as carefully as I could. "Not to state the obvious or anything, but he *is* marrying your mother in a few days."

"We'll see about that" Charles said and trotted downstairs. I saw Stephens cast a startled look in our direction before he reapplied himself to picking up ⌐ ⌐   's from the table.

BREAKFAST ON SUNDAY WAS A FAIRLY dismal affair. I was stuck with Claude and Clarissa, a Holland sandwich, if you like, due to my innate greediness and inability to ignore my stomach over current events. Mrs Holland had not come down, Stevie was probably with her brother, and as for my mercurial friend, I had not seen him since he left me disappointed at his door the night before.

It depressed me that I obviously didn't have the sensitive soul and stomach of a Holland and was not delicate enough to be put off my food at the slightest thing. However, I got over it, with liberal application of kedgeree and kidney. I asked Clarissa about the state of Lawrence and I showed restrained happiness at the fact that he had made it through the night. "I only knocked and spoke briefly to Stevie," Clarissa said. "She looks awful, poor girl. The doctor was up with him half the night, and she's taken over while he takes a few hour's rest. It seems he's not much better. Still not quite here, if you know what I mean."

"Been better if he'd died," Claude rumbled from behind his newspaper. I think that people who read at the table deserve a particular spot in hell. One with spikes. "Tried to talk to Margaret about it last night—what we are going to say to people—she wouldn't even open her door." Clarissa shot him a look as if to say that bedroom doors should not be discussed at breakfast in front of non-family—although it could have just been shock or loathing. I'd have done the same had I cared enough about his opinion. Clarissa was a good egg, and the difference between her and Claude was an abyss wide. She obviously took more after her other brother.

"And Margaret's boy is causing more problems than he needs to," Claude continued. "Worrying Margaret when he's not here just as much as when he is. Floating around, disappearing—speak of the devil." He was glaring at the French windows where, as if on cue, or as though he were eavesdropping, Charles drifted into sight. His hands were in his pockets and he was walking slowly, deep in thought, kicking at the gravel as he went. "There, see?"

Claude said, dropping the paper on the table, quite ruining his breakfast. "The boy's not right. I've told Margaret this, more than once. Wandering around in the rain—not even a hat on, let alone a jacket and coat."

"I hardly think a disregard for the elements counts as a mental deficiency," Clarissa said, making me want to hug her.

"It's all a part of this larger thing—this staged effetism—"

"Perhaps I'll pop upstairs," Clarissa said, standing up with as much noise as she could make, her chair scraping against the parquet, "and see if I can offer any assistance to Margaret. There's still much to finalise." She stopped for a moment. "Are you going to go ahead?"

"Of course," Claude continued to stare out at the rain, even though the object of his disgust had meandered off. "I think, in the circumstances, it would be better if only the household—those who can travel—attend the London ceremony."

"People will understand," Clarissa said. "Do you want—"

"If you have time," Claude said.

She gave a wistful smile which Claude didn't see, as he wasn't paying any attention to her, and with a brief nod to me she bustled out. Claude became aware of me, in a rather slow and alarming manner, like a pterosaur who, sitting on a high cliff nest, looking in the valley for prey, is alerted to the presence of warm furry mammal right inside the nest itself. Claude's head turned toward me. "Ah, Bircham," he said, rather unnecessarily. After the crack about staged effetism, I wondered that he had the gall even to speak to me, but I swear the man had a hide like a rhinoceros.

"Mr Holland."

"I wonder if you might track down my nephew. I know we are at odds on this matter and appreciate your loyalty, but I would prefer that he was at least close to hand at this time of crisis. Rumours abound in this place, and—"

"If you mean that he might be talking to people in the village of the events of last night, I can assure you that you don't know him very well. The boy is like a mollusc in that respect. It would take more than a knife and boiling water to get him to open up. I will find him. But not for you."

I left after that, not without a strong wish to exit dramatically. But I resisted. Heavens above, that I might be accused of effetism! I looked this up later and it is not even a word, so Dear Uncle Claude is not as clever as he likes to think he is, which bodes well.

I didn't hurry to do Claude's bidding, for it would have looked far too much like I was rushing to do it, and eager to please him. I still felt that small frisson of his manly dominance, despite my absolute loathing for him, and the best way—I'd found in my experience—to avoid getting overcomplicated crushes, was to simply baulk the demands of such a person as often as possible.

They'll get peeved with one soon enough and the crush dissolves. Rather moot in this case as I was planning to dissolve the crush pretty thoroughly myself in a day or so. So it wasn't until after lunch that I set out, having determined that my wandering friend and lover had not reappeared. I could feel Claude glaring at me across the table. Entirely wasted for I didn't meet his gaze, annoying soul that I am. Then, assured that Claude was even more irritated than he had been at breakfast, and dressing more sensibly than Charles had, I donned a sturdy overcoat, a hat, although I hated to wear one unless the formality of the occasion demanded it, and Stephens found me an umbrella. Thus protected against some of the elements, I ventured out. It wasn't cold, just very wet, and the lack of any appreciable wind meant that at least the rain came down in stair rods, and the umbrella then was of some use. Nothing better than a mixture of rain, a high wind and a large umbrella for teaching one the meaning of futility.

I was passing by the vicarage, just thinking I had escaped, when a "Cooee!" sounded and I turned to see the redoubtable Mrs Witherspoon waving a duster from an opened window. I gestured, as if to say that I was heading for the village, but she gestured in response, and having run out of gestures, or at least polite ones, I had no recourse but to hurry over her lawn and stand beneath her dripping thatch to speak to her through the window.

"Looking for young Holland?" she asked.

"Not particularly," I lied. "Mrs Holland has sent me to check on the order for beer and such." It was an inspired lie, if I say so myself. "Why, have you seen him?"

"Not for a few hours. I think you'll find him in the King's Arms."

Considering that she couldn't possibly see the pub from her window, I wondered how she knew this. "That's handy," I said with a smile.

"I hope the stress isn't getting him down," she said with enough leaden meaning in her words to have me imagining him dead drunk in a ditch by now. "How is everything up at the house?" she asked. "Hillyard has been wondering whether he should go up."

"I don't think Lawrence is any immediate danger," I said.

"Oh, heavens, that's not what I meant at all!" she said, looking a little flustered. "Hillyard isn't that kind of ghoul." *What kind of ghoul was he, then?* "Just to offer succour and the like. Mr Bircham, you have a wicked eyebrow."

"I'm sure it can be saved. Perhaps Hillyard will take it on as a project." I waved my goodbyes.

If he wasn't in the pub, I didn't know where to look for him. It's not as if I could go knocking on every door in the village, and he must know a good few people here, although he'd mentioned almost none to me. It was with a sense of relief then that, as I approached the pub door, I saw him barrelling out. He spun me around and marched back down the high street with me.

"I saw you coming," Charles said, as if that explained everything. "Thank God for large umbrellas and pouring rain. I'll have to take your arm. How awful."

"Have you been in the pub all morning, you reprobate? God, you are wet."

"No, it wasn't open. So I walked about. I couldn't find my toothbrush, and I thought Dewar's might open up for me, but I think they are away. I'll have to use yours."

"My germs are your germs."

"Did Mother send you?"

"No."

Charles was silent for a moment. "Well, then I came along here for a quick pint to try and warm up, and when Coneybear was down in his mysterious cellar, Father appeared."

"Really? What did he want?"

"Nothing much. I told him—well, about what's been going on, and he rather calmed me down. Told me to think of Mother. He's not happy about the whole thing, obviously, but—"

"None of us want you to make a scene. I don't think it would particularly wise for him to do so, either."

"He says he'll be leaving on Saturday. After the wedding. Abroad. He's promised to send me his address—can't do it now, as he's not sure where he's going. But we can go and visit him next vac. If…you want to."

"Why is he waiting until afterwards? Is he hoping that it won't go through?"

"I don't know," Charles said, pushing his wet fringe away from his face. "Perhaps he just wants…an end. But Mother won't get an end."

"I rather think she's said her goodbyes already." I sensed Charles tense up at that, and I regretted saying anything. We hadn't talked about his father being declared dead, but I knew how it was affecting him. "Where's he planning to go?" I asked.

"I don't think he knows yet. Somewhere where he doesn't have to see anyone much. He says he'll let me know when he's settled. He's already got me to promise that I'll visit. You'll come too, won't you?" For a moment he sounded lost and I dared not turn my face to his, for fear of showing too much. I gave his arm another squeeze.

"Wither thou goest," I said with emphasis and things were all right between us. "Of course we'll go. Lord," I said, as dramatically as I dared. "Now you've distracted me again. There was something I had to do."

"So you *didn't* come looking for me? I'm crushed."

"I had to check on the alcohol for the party." I was finding it a convenient lie. "Bear with me. I'll be there and back in two shakes. Take this." I thrust him the umbrella.

"I'm not getting waylaid at the vicarage," Charles said. "I'll meet you in the wood."

I ran all the way back along the damp high street, and entered the pub puffing slightly.

I tracked Coneybear down by bellowing from the bar. He smiled when he saw me. "Mr Bircham, isn't it?"

I nodded. "Mrs Holland has just sent to me double-check everything is in place for Saturday. No problems with orders, marquees, that kind of thing."

"Triple-checking, more like," he said with a smile. "Although what with young Stephens being taken bad, I wouldn't be surprised if things were at sixes and sevens. You tell her…. No, if you'd be so kind as to wait, I'll write it down this time. Just tell her that if she wants anything else to let me know by tonight, please, or else I can't be certain it will be delivered on time."

I waited while he painstakingly wrote the order down. "Her son—he just came out of here."

"That's right," his brow furrowed as he wrote, no doubt trying to work out how to spell "beer."

"I didn't see who he was with, who was it?"

He paused for a second, and then wrote on. "Can't rightly say that I saw he was with anyone. Came in on his own, and I didn't see anyone, and there was only one glass when I came up just now."

I felt a slight coldness flood through me, a fear that I had been hoping would stay away. Please, I thought, please don't let him be going through that again. I had suspected it, but he had been so, so convincing. But then, he had been so convincing after his father had been reported missing too. But no one had seen the senior Charles Holland, not that time, and not this. Not Mrs Holland, not Claude, not even Coneybear or Mrs Witherspoon, and if anyone would have been likely to see this wandering—phantom, almost—it would be those two.

I was a little heavier-footed and heavier-hearted as I made my way back up the village, but I managed to plaster a smile on when I found him in the wood, sitting on a log like a rather wet pixie.

If Charles noticed my reticence as we made our way back to the house, he didn't say anything. I think the weather was affecting him too, and he probably thought the same of me.

As Stephens was helping me out of my coat, and peeling an absolutely drenched jumper from my companion, Margaret came down the stairs and fussed over us as if we were four. We were ordered to change and then come down into the small family lounge. "I have to see Lawrence," he told her.

"I've been up to see him. I don't think you going in will do either of you any good." She caught my eye over his shoulder as if asking for my support. "It's quite distressing, and the doctor still thinks he should be moved to a nursing home."

"I must see him," he insisted.

"Change first, please, darling."

"All right." He dashed off, taking the stairs two at a time.

"I feel particularly useless," I said to her.

"You should change, too."

"I'm pretty dry, actually. My trouser cuffs will dry in front of the fire. I wish there was something…. Oh—I was in the village and Coneybear gave me the list of the drinks for Saturday. He said that if you needed anything changing…to let him know by today."

She took it, with hardly a glance. "Thank you, that was thoughtful." She didn't clarify who was being thoughtful, but I took the credit. "I wonder if we should…one doesn't really know what to do for the best. I must speak to Clarissa…" but she had already started to wander off, leaving me in the hall.

I followed his trail upstairs. Clarissa had said that morning that Lawrence had been moved to his own room, but where that was I wasn't sure. I spent an interesting time knocking on doors and opening them to no avail on the first floor before climbing the final flight of stairs and doing the same in what was, I assumed, part of the servants' quarters. I found Lawrence's room by dint of the doctor coming out of it. He looked tired and a little mussed.

"How is the patient?" I asked.

"No worse," the doctor said.

"Oh, that's good."

"Is it?" The doctor pushed open a door at the end of a corridor to a black and white tiled bathroom and began to wash his hands. "He's not changed much at all. He's a little more lucid, and he's eating by himself, with a spoon, at least. He's talking but making little sense. I wouldn't say he knows where he is, or even who he is." Wiping his hands on a towel, he grimaced. "These drugs. It's a bloody business. I have a good friend in a ward in London that deals with withdrawal cases and overdoses. That's where Stephens should be, if I'm honest, but Mr Holland won't hear of it. You can't anticipate these things. Some men—and women—can take the damnedest concoctions for years with little more than a blinding headache afterwards, although they have idea what damage they are doing to themselves; and then some people take one dose of something and it can kill them stone dead. Or blind them, drive them mad, give them the heebie-jeebies for the rest of their lives. There's just no predicting what can happen, a lot of the time. That's not even getting into the unholy mess caused when drugs are so-called "adulterated" with God knows what—just to make them go further."

This was all news to me, and of great interest. "And I suppose," I said, "that the trouble is, if you go around preaching 'this will happen to you if you take…cocaine for example'—and then that someone does, and nothing horrible happens, it really undermines your advice."

The doctor wasn't as stupid as some people I could mention and looked at me extremely sharply. "What do you mean?"

"Oh, I mean nothing by it," I lied, sowing the seeds of chaos as far and wide as I could, hoping they'd bear fruit later, "it's just that it must be a bit galling. Were that to happen."

"Is there something about Lawrence Stephens you think you should tell me?"

"No," I said, looking him straight in the eyes. "No, nothing at all."

I could see the doctor had labelled me a bad hat, probably influenced by others, and he turned on his heel and stalked off down the corridor. People tend to do that to me a lot, I really must address it.

Stevie was sitting by Lawrence's bed as I entered, and it was clear, from her wan face and her normally immaculate hair being distinctly out of place, that she had slept not at all. She glanced at me as the door opened but hardly registered my presence at all other than a flicker of light in her eyes.

I sat on a chair opposite and regarded Lawrence with interest. He looked much the same as he had the night before, although paler, but then most of us were that. He stared at the ceiling as if he saw something there that concerned him greatly, and plucked at his sheet with one hand while the other was clutched across his chest.

"He slept," Stevie said. "It was a relief. Because…while he was asleep he stopped. Stopped doing that. The moment he woke again, he started up again…" Her voice trailed off and she let her head sink onto her arms resting on the bed. "Why does he keep doing that? Why can't he hear me?" Her voice teetered on the hysterical. "Why won't the doctor give me any answers?"

"He's waiting and seeing," I said. "Does your father think that it's best if he stays here?"

She nodded, looking up. "He agrees with Claude. Notwithstanding that we couldn't..." She swallowed and stopped, turning her face away for a moment.

No, I thought, they couldn't afford a decent nursing home. And Stephens would baulk at accepting that amount of charity, so it seemed easier to agree with Claude. Still, if he was going to stay like this, it had been an interesting experiment, but not what I needed.

The door opened after a few minutes and Charles slipped in, went round and kissed Stevie on the head. "No change?"

"Not much. He did sleep a little."

"And you haven't," he said. "Harry and I will sit with him. I promise we won't leave him on his own for a moment. I promise," he repeated, as Stevie made signs as to disagree with him. "We'll be here until the doctor or the first nurse arrives. Go and rest, go and eat—because when he comes round he's going to need you firing on all cylinders and not being a damp handkerchief." She hesitated a moment, staring ardently at Lawrence's face, perhaps wondering if that would be the last time she would see him breathing, then jumped to her feet, gave Charles a swift kiss on the cheek and left us alone. "That was kind of you," I said.

"What do you mean?" He was staring at Lawrence in the same way Stevie had and my heart got a little bruised.

"Giving her a 'when'."

"I'm a kind person," Charles said with a quick, brittle smile. "Hadn't you heard?"

Chapter Sixteen

We sat with Lawrence for the rest of the morning, through lunch, with trays sent up. Stephens optimistically sent three trays. Lawrence couldn't be persuaded to eat anything, although he drank some beef tea, seemingly on reflex. It was past two o'clock before a nurse arrived with the doctor and we were bustled out, our duty done for the present.

Charles had been quiet during our time with Lawrence, and when I casually asked him if he was all right, he snarled at me with typical unpredictability. "Of course I'm not all right. What do you expect? God, Lawrence drove me mad—and we've not been anything like friends for a long time—but why the hell did it have to be him? If anyone deserves—"

He pulled his arm away where I had attempted to hold it. "He didn't deserve it."

This was it. I sat down on the bed, and pitched my voice as low as I could. "No...and I don't think he took the stuff—or at least..."

"What?" Charles turned towards me, a frown creasing the skin between his eyes. "He must have taken something. Harry? What do you know? Are you saying someone did this to him?"

"No," I said. I didn't want him barking up *that* particular tree. "But..." I quickly explained how Claude had been so quick to "find" the leather case with the syringes. "The case itself was something, calfskin, crushed velvet. I can't see Lawrence forking out for anything so expensive. If he was doping himself—which I don't see at all, he's so *mens sana in corpore sano*—I could see him keeping the stuff in a cardboard box, or hidden under the bed in a pair of socks."

Charles was quiet for a moment, but the frown didn't leave his face. "So you're saying you think Claude—"

"My dear, I'm not *saying* I think anything. Only what happened. You can't go leaping off into suspicions like that, for heaven's sake. Not with the wedding in two days."

"But if it's true I *can't* let Mother marry him, don't you see?"

"I see perfectly. But box clever my dear. Why don't you speak to your mother?"

"Yes. But you've been pulling me back from doing that."

"She might think differently if she thinks he's a doper. And even more if he's been encouraging others to do so. After all—" I almost felt guilty for pushing him in the direction I was, almost. "If you had been down here, he might have offered it to you. I can't see your mother being altogether happy about that. We don't know if that's what got Lawrence, but it seems a little coincidental, doesn't it?

WE LEFT IT AT THAT, AND I assumed he'd speak to his mother at some point the next day. However we had not kept ourselves in the loop, for in the morning Margaret had disappeared before he and I came down for breakfast. Stevie was either with Lawrence—who was awake and eating, but still not aware of his surroundings—or she was rushing about speaking to tradesmen and dealing with deliveries. I tracked down Clarissa who was in Mrs Holland's study with quantities of lists.

"She's gone to stay with Claude's cousins in London and the first we'll see of her now is at the Register office. Tradition, you see. The groom shouldn't see the bride, and really shouldn't stay under the same roof."

"Bit of a moot point," I said dryly, "after all this time."

"Mr Bircham!" Clarissa looked genuinely shocked and I realised that there was a bit of a gap in our generations. Perhaps Margaret and Claude hadn't been "*doin' it, doin' it*" like everybody and it was just my grubby imagination.

"I apologise. Her son was looking for her."

"Well, he'll have to wait, I'm afraid. Now clear off, there's a dear. I need to try and get hold of Rumboult. About the carnival stalls, you know, for Saturday. I just know he's not going to be pleased. He'll not want to cancel at this short notice, and I can't blame him, really. He's bound to demand at least a fair proportion of his fee."

"Yes, it would be rather tasteless to have a circus atmosphere," I said, still going for the arid theme, but Clarissa had forgotten all about me and I had to leave without being recognised for my genius.

"It's all right," I said to Holland later. "You can nobble her tomorrow morning."

He was sunk in deep, deep gloom. "Don't be mad," he said. "So I meet her at the door, hopefully bypassing Claude—it's not like church, where at least I'd be sure he was waiting at the altar. And I casually say, 'Oh, Mother, by the way you can't marry Claude because he might have given Lawrence the dope.' No, it's no good. I've made my feelings clear enough on the subject of Claude. I shall simply give her the option to change her mind. She's a little stubborn. But if she's set on him, despite my feelings…"

Stubborn. No surprise. I was, I have to admit, rather glad that he had said that he wouldn't do more. And I was sure, quite sure, that Margaret was not the type of woman who would do a Jane Eyre and rush sobbing from the church. Or sordid Register Office. In fact even if he had told her in advance I doubted it would make much difference.

The rest of the morning was spent "getting ready" and if the organization before gave me a headache, the bustle that Clarissa put into that morning was enough to drive me to drink, and did at least once when I tiptoed into the study to steal a snifter and to my disgust found Claude there, morosely looking into an empty glass. Hardly the mien of a man about to gain his fondest dream. By two o'clock all was prepared as far as we were concerned, and Charles and I were packed off to the station to catch the London train. The rest of the family would be driving up in Claude's motor later and would meet us at the Dorchester.

How different that train journey was to the one we had taken down, the first time, only a short time before. Charles was edgy and distracted, oh, polite enough on the surface but as soon as I stopped talking—and I can, believe you me, given the opportunity—he would slump into his seat again and glare at the passing countryside as though he could stab it to feel better.

I knew him better than to jolly him along. The one unprovoked sentence he uttered was one that stirred that ember of jealousy that always waited deep in my soul.

"It's bloody, doing all this and Lawrence not being here. Just…bloody."

I had guessed right about Margaret. Charles told me afterwards that he had simply managed to slip an "Are you sure, Mother?" in private before Claude claimed them, and she had simply smiled and said, "Of course, darling, don't fuss." The bride looked a picture of summer in a blue creation which appeared to be slightly Russian influenced, with gorgeous embroidery on the cuffs and a wrap around collar. The ceremony went ahead and I had to stand beside my friend and feel every radiating tremor of fury and frustration that emanated from him. Thank God that he was placed behind the bride and groom because the sheer dark expression in his eyes would have put more than a dampener on their obvious happiness—despite the already soggy effect of Lawrence's misfortune.

It was the first Register wedding I had attended, and I found it a little soulless. I think you know *me* well enough by now to know that the Almighty and I aren't exactly on a standing of mutual belief, but there is something more effective about a church wedding, all full of brute beasts and the reasons for copulation, and the threat that only God (or in this case, a war, unless you believe that God is responsible for bombs) can put people asunder. It puts the willies up me—if you'll forgive me—and I'm not the one being threatened. Then, outrageously quickly, with no stops for songs, or readings, the deed was done and the bride and groom were man and wife. For better, for worse.... But *not* till death us do part.

We had a small wedding breakfast at the Dorchester. Margaret said she would rather go straight home afterwards, rather than stay overnight as originally planned. It was then, in the midst of tense smiles and truncated toasts, that I realised that my plan, that is to finish with Claude what I had rehearsed with Lawrence, was scuppered. Despite me having risen early, made a much stronger concoction of the datura mixture and secreted it successfully without a wrinkle in my suit, it wasn't going to work. We were seated in a table in the dining room, causing some smiles from the other diners, and the drink of choice was champagne, and nothing else. As gorgeous as the drink is, it wasn't any use at all for disguising the deep amber colour of the mixture which now seemed to be burning within the metal of the flask. I waited on tenterhooks for quite a while before giving up completely, hoping that Claude would call for a claret—particularly to go with the grouse—but it didn't happen. The oaf.

"Despite the sad circumstance that overclouds our happiness," he said, using every ounce of his sledgehammer charm, and with every crisp grey curl perfectly in place, "this champagne will symbolise the fresh start and the bubbling joy I feel in the fact that Margaret said she would be mine. She is like the drink itself—"

"Oh, God," Charles said *sotto voce*. "Spare me"

"—sparkling, fresh, heady and refined."

"And gives you the most god-awful headache," Holland muttered.

If anyone overheard him, it wasn't obvious. Even I took little notice, as his constant criticism of Claude and Margaret was beginning to grate on my nerves a touch, especially as I was doing all the hard work and planning regarding solving his problem, and he was doing nothing. When I refused to rise to his bait and showed no signs of joining in, he slumped down in his seat, glass in hand, glaring at the happy couple.

God, that day was unbearable. To be pulled towards it by the lure of that brain-lightening excitement: the promise of death only to be shoved backwards towards the sludge of disappointment—it was just too much. The atmosphere was bloody. Holland was sulky and caustic by turns; Clarissa watched the brewing situation between Claude and his new stepson with such attention she looked as though she were at a tennis match. It was as though she thought they were likely to launch at each other's throats at any minutes. Stevie sat drooped, distracted and glum. The only people who seemed not to care were—oddly— Margaret and Claude. They were clearly happy, and that, of course, did not improve the atmosphere for the rest of us in the slightest.

Coming back from the unmentionables after the dessert had been served, I passed Clarissa going the other way. "I hope," she said, obviously assuming that I was worried about it in some way, "that Saturday will be more celebratory all round. Perhaps I shouldn't have cancelled the sideshows. Well, it's too late now. I shall keep the rest of the arrangements, the hog roast and dancing. Perhaps the village celebrating in unison can help to alleviate matters. Such a shame," she finished, bustling off. "Such a shame."

I slid back into my seat. Nothing much had changed, other than one empty chair. Two would have been better. "Do you want to stay up tonight?" I asked Charles.

He turned to me, as if drugged, his jowls seeming heavy, perhaps giving a hint of what he'd look like in middle age. Slowly his expression lightened, as if someone were drawing each expression on a card and replacing it with another. I realised that I was offering him a lifeline, so I tugged on it very gently, as though I had a trout just opening his mouth to the fly on my line.

"We could take it easy tomorrow, perhaps. Tonight, have a drink, have a stroll about. Perhaps see a show."

Charles smiled, and it seemed like the first time for months. His breath sounding my name like a prayer. "You…you're always there. And I'm beastly to you."

"Well, I won't argue with you on either point," I said with as much mock-archness as I could muster. "What do you think?"

"I'm in your hands, entirely. It's a wonderful idea. Mother's going back tonight, and I really didn't want…ah, but you knew that, didn't you? You always do."

I smirked, and looked as modest as I could. It was the very least I could do.

Chapter Seventeen

'm afraid I'm going to have to be quite horrible here, because I'm not going to share much of that evening with anyone. Suffice to say that, without the gloom-inducing family and the woes of Lawrence at a distance of a hundred miles or more, we regained something of our old *amicitia*, although it felt slightly strained at the seams. Neither of us mentioned the wedding, nor the upcoming Saturday, nor Lawrence. Although it was easy to let the subjects drift to more impersonal matters such as sports and the upcoming Michaelmas term and the inevitable Collection to be endured—although I don't think either of us were worried we would fail—the ghosts of all the things we would not say stood at our shoulders, and we may as well have brought them into the light.

But it was warm and good to be with him alone in the anonymity of London. I knew it better than he, and we walked arm in arm down the broad swath of Shaftesbury Avenue. Not trusting the Dorchester entirely—always sensible to assume that a staff that would be discreet and silent for a duke and an actress might not be quite so forgiving for two undergraduates—we spent little time in each other's rooms, and were circumspect while we were. I left the door open, just in case, and it was probably just as well, for more than one employee passed by, and one at least looked in. All he saw—sadly enough—was two friends sitting in opposite chairs sharing a bottle of burgundy. The burgundy would have made things so much easier if it had been present at the wedding breakfast, but never mind. I am nothing if not patient.

Which leads us neatly onwards to Saturday. There's really no point filling in the gap from Tuesday to Friday. We longed to linger in London—and as tempted as I am to add "louchely" to that sentence, I will refrain—but we were good boys and returned to Somerset in good time on the Wednesday afternoon. I noticed a marked difference to our first arrival, though.

Despite us arriving at tea-time, there was no tea on the lawn to greet us. The house seemed empty, although everyone—we found out—was present. But it appeared filled with a gloomy brooding. Or perhaps that's just me being fanciful because I didn't get my own way.

Lawrence, to my initial pleasure, was up on his feet. Look, just because I poisoned the man, doesn't mean I can't be pleased he was making some kind of recovery. It wasn't *personal*, and I hope I made that quite clear. It was rehearsal. Some things are necessary—broken eggs, omelettes, that kind of thing. On Wednesday, after dinner, he was led into the drawing room by Stevie. But any exclamations of pleasure that might have sprung from my lips were silenced by his appearance. He had turned, in a week, from a fit and energetic young man to a shambling, lumpen thing. More Lon Chaney than Bill Tilden, I'm sad to say. Stevie placed him gently on the sofa, and sat beside him, her hand holding one of his—the one that he was previously flailing around. I wondered if she held it to disguise that he was still doing this. Lawrence was—or seemed to be—aware of his surroundings, but couldn't take part in any conversation. He would listen intently, moving his head to focus on the one who spoke, but didn't comment, even when addressed directly. The worst of it was when he did speak; his voice was exactly the same as it was—and one would expect a infantile slur by the way he looked—but he made no sense, his sentences as random as cutting the words out of a page, putting them into a hat and pulling them out one sentence at a time.

When we discussed the show we'd seen in London, he took a deep breath. "It's outside the curtains, you see. Never inside. You'd think that it would know better, but it doesn't. And it won't listen to me."

Honestly, if I hadn't had a tight rein on myself already, I think I would have laughed. Not at Lawrence, poor soul, but at the English middle-class family dealing with something so terrible that they have no name for it, no real way of dealing with it. And too ashamed to put him away, which is probably what he needed. We all looked at Lawrence for slightly too long, then most of them nodded enthusiastically and Margaret even went so far as to say, "They never do, do they?" A piece of improvised brilliance, in my opinion.

"What makes it worse," Stevie said to me later, "is that I swear *he* thinks he's being perfectly rational. I am sure that there is complete lucidity in his eyes at times. I'm *sure* of it, but the doctor says that he's not, that he's entirely disconnected from everything. But that can't be true, it can't—can it? He wouldn't know me, or Father, or the house—and he seems to know his way about."

I made suitable noises, as one does, but I was actually thinking that Polonius knew his way around the place, but it didn't make him mentally on a par with me. Stevie was like a beautiful piece of porcelain those last few days, her clay seemingly becoming thinner with each passing day. They say that porcelain is stronger than general pottery, but I'm told that porcelain shatters into a thousand pieces, whereas ironware simply cracks.

The doctor attended every day, and each time he visited he suggested that Lawrence would be better off in a "facility" but the family wouldn't hear of it. I think I wouldn't be so kind—purely for the fact that I could now see that Stevie's life was effectively ruined; her loyalty and love for her brother was going to mean that she could never leave him—and with a shortage of young men already in the county, her prospects looked bleak. I have to say it was something I hadn't anticipated. It was interesting to watch the ripples.

THEN IT WAS SATURDAY, THE DAY of the blessing; Claude's last day on earth. I was determined nothing should go wrong. Confident in my rehearsal I had made an even stronger batch of the potion and had carefully poured Tuesday's mixture out onto the grass whilst out walking.

As I dressed, I felt the rising of the relentless excitement, the rush of heady exhilaration I had felt before. With luck I could ride this wave of elation for most of the day. But this time I could not be random. I had to have luck on my side this time, not fate—I couldn't place a glass just any old where in the hope that Claude would pick it up. Whatever I did, and I had no idea what I was going to do—it had to be sure.

However, I like to travel hopefully, so I was whistling with some exuberance when Charles blew into my room and flung himself on the bed. It seemed so much like his old self I felt parts of me melting and parts of me positively not. I may have already said, he looks particularly fetching in pyjamas; if the choice lay with me he'd wear nothing else.

"I thought we'd leave this evening," he said. "I think I've done more than my duty. The deed is well and truly done and today is only a show for the village."

"But my dear," I said. "There won't be a train any later than seven, and we can hardly leave that early. How about we leave first thing in the morning, before anyone's awake?"

His eyes hooded for a moment as he thought it through.

"We can't exactly stay in the village," I added.

"You are right, damn you. I suppose one more night won't kill me."

"No, dear thing," I said, giving him a brief kiss on the head. "It certainly won't. Think of it as leaving home. You knew you would eventually—for good, I mean. You can still pop down—"

"I won't."

"—if you *feel* like it. Get some distance between them and us. And think about it. Hmm? I know I won't be in any great hurry to come back, but leave doors open." I pulled the pillow from his face, ducked down and kissed him as hard as I dared, but made it seem perfunctory, casual. I took a deep breath. If I succeeded in killing Claude, I didn't think any of us would be going anywhere for a while yet, but there were certain things I could never share with him.

I wouldn't have a chance if Claude—once again—decided to drink nothing but champagne. The likelihood of that, I reasoned, was pretty remote. There was more wine on order than champagne, and by the end of the day, I was sure that he would have moved on to his favoured wine, a rather nerve-jangling Beaujolais, or perhaps even the deep-brown malt whisky he favoured—and the mixture would do well in either, being the same colour as the whisky itself. I had considered buying a bottle of something eminently drinkable for the occasion but on reflection realised the stupidity of the idea. Either I was going to be in luck or I wasn't.

The day bored me, weddings always do, particularly weddings that aren't weddings, if you see what I mean. This had all the paraphernalia of a wedding: interminable waiting around while women fiddled with their hair and apparel, strangers dashing around carrying vases, and a gradually growing throng as guests arrived. By the time we were finally outside the church I was almost catatonic with ennui. Charles gave me a bright, glassy smile, squeezed my arm and I went into the church to join the family at the front. Just that sheer fragile expression would have been enough to spur me to putting Claude out of the world, if I hadn't seen all the other emotions he'd suffered.

Hymns were sung, the blessing made and the bride and groom—or blessed pair, not really sure of the correct nomenclature—moved serenely to the front of the church where a local newsperson took some photos.

Holland tried to get me into the group shot but I ducked away under the yews and into the unconsecrated section of the graveyard. There were no wilting blooms lying on the grass this time, and the world seemed strangely muffled, as though the yews formed some kind of natural sound-proofing. I caught a movement at the far end, where the woods met the graveyard and walked towards it, without thinking—as if fate had actually led me away from the wedding party and into the dark gloom of a neglected churchyard. The woods were cool and shaded after the warmth of the day, and I stepped along the path for a moment or two, with thoughts as fanciful as how long I might be away were I to step into faerie right now. You could easily—were you eight years old and full of hope—mistake the toadstool rings for entrances to forbidden places, and just to be certain, I didn't step into them.

Laughing inwardly at my idiocy, I turned back towards the entrance to the wood. If he hadn't have put a hand up to his face to remove his hat and wipe his forehead, I probably wouldn't have spotted him. In between two of the large yews stood a man, camouflaged by his dark clothing in the dappled shade. He was staring intently up the hill in the direction of the church and it did not require the detection skills of a Richardson to work out who he was. The curiosity almost tore at me. It always had, but I had been cautious with it up to now. If he'd ever caught me trying to find his father—even merely to convince myself he existed—I don't think even I could predict his reaction. I had to force myself not to step forward, to demand who he was—to *know*. To know for certain that my friend wasn't losing his mind.

As if he had been reading mine, suddenly he was behind me—somehow I knew before he spoke. "Well, then, Harry. Not mad after all, am I? Curiosity killed the cat, you know. Wouldn't you like to meet him?" The question was so loaded—and for that you would have to have been in love with him for as many years as I had—that I couldn't speak for a moment.

Of course I'd like to meet him, but whether I should admit to it, or sound as eager as I felt was another matter entirely. So I turned, schooling my expression into what I fancied was a veritable Percy Blakeney of boredom and said, "Oh, only if you think it's a good idea."

He paused as he turned towards the yews, then glanced back, and his expression told me that I was not fooling him. Smug wouldn't have described him at that moment.

We made very little noise on the bare floor of the wood, but the man heard us all the same, perhaps attuned—my Boy's Own brain imagined—by standing sentry during the war, ears pricked for the very sound of Fritz sneaking close.

Whatever sense it was, he heard us and turned around. My first reaction was one of surprise and shock. I had expected a man with a half-covered face, a mass of scars that melted together, but he wasn't scarred at all, and I gave my friend a swift accusing glare for telling such lies. There was no doubt who he was. Not only had I seen photographs of him, but he was an older version of my friend, taller and clearly thinner even under the loose-fitting coat he wore. His resemblance to both his son and his much more heavy-set brother was remarkable. What struck me was the complete lack of a melted-wax face. What my Charles's motives had been for that little lie, God alone knew. Or didn't. "Oh, Lord," I said, unable to stop myself.

He ran forward and grasped his father's hand. "You shouldn't have come," he said to him.

"We've discussed it," his father said lightly, but there was tension around the man's eyes and mouth, again so like my friend that it was as if I knew what he was thinking. *Not in front of this person.* "And this can only be Harry Bircham."

"Delighted to meet you at last, sir," I said, shaking him by the hand.

"I won't stay long," he said, in answer to something no one had said. "I wanted to meet you, and hoped I would. Thanks to Mr Bircham—"

"Harry," I said.

"Harry." He gave a smile, but it was sadder than one merited. "And now I shall go."

"Father. Will I see you—later? We are leaving in the morning. We were, that is. If you…"

"I'll pack up too," he said. "There's no reason for me to hang around. Not now."

"You aren't going to—"

"No, Charles," he said. "Nothing's going to change. I've said that enough." His tone of voice indicated that that should be the end of it and although I could feel the frustration and anger radiating from my dear idiot, he obviously knew his father well enough, despite the long separation. "There's nothing to be done."

"But—"

"Nothing, Charles. And that's the end of it. Promise me."

A sullen silence followed.

"Charles."

"Yes, sir. I promise."

"Good boy. You don't have to like it. I don't blame you. But your mother… don't blame her. Go tomorrow. Get drunk and have fun tonight. I'll meet you by the lych gate. At nine. Don't be late, because I won't hang around."

"Yes, sir."

"Now clear off, I want to have a word with Mr Bircham." He looked mildly startled but he obeyed his father and slipped back through the trees. The elder Holland was silent until we both saw Charles emerge near the church and join the party who were just beginning to move towards the road and the car. Then he turned to me.

"I don't approve," he said. "I don't suppose any father would. We all want a dynasty—not something you chaps would appreciate, I suppose. It's taken me a while to have this conversation with you, and I didn't want to have it with Charles around. He would get…excited about it."

"Whereas I'm all calm veneer?" I said. It had shaken me more than I wanted to show that the elder Holland had brought up the unmentionable subject, and I felt like the unsuitable suitor twisting his cloth cap in his hands and about to be paid off by the aristocratic father-in-law to be.

I'd irritated him, which didn't surprise me. I did seem to have that effect on people. "I don't know what you are like," the man snapped. "I only know the nature of your relationship by piecing together the jigsaw pieces that Charles admits. He hasn't said anything. I tried to pretend to myself that I must be wrong. But it seems I am not."

I had to stop my eyebrows rising at this. "This is…rather an unusual conversation to be having, sir," I said.

"I'm aware of it." The man's voice was terse, to say the least. I did hope he wasn't going to be awkward, not now. He went silent then, and looked towards the church, which was now entirely bereft of anyone. A few pigeons had fluttered down in front of the door, pecking at the rice thrown.

"But I've travelled a good deal."

"If you going to tell me to leave off, sir," I said. "I'm afraid I can't do that."

The silence continued. I could hear Charles straining his ears from some thicket or other to try and hear what we were saying. Then his father said, without turning, "I know. I know that it's not your fault. You didn't corrupt him."

I bridled at the very notion, doubly so that our friendship, our love affair— call it what you will—was openly considered corrupt in the first place, and that he didn't think twice about stating the fact, not caring whether he off ended or not. But ignorant souls cannot understand what they cannot experience.

"I don't think anyone *corrupted* him," I said, choking back everything else I wanted to say. If the man was choosing to think he was being white about it, then I would be mad to argue with him.

"You're wrong," he said. "But there's no point in this. This is not what I wanted to say, and God alone knows I've been turning this around in my head for long enough. If you continue to be friends with my son—then may I please request that you look after him?"

I went to say something but he cut me off: "I've done a rotten job, and I don't think that will change. I can't stay. I've been here too long as it is. You know him—and from what little I've seen of him he hasn't changed that much from a boy. He's nervous and I think I've been the cause of a great deal of that. What they did…" He glared at the hedge as if he wanted to kill it, an expression his son had in common, then started again in calmer tones. "He'll need looking after, and protecting from himself. And what…what he is. Society. You know."

Anger fluttered through me again but I forced it down. The man thought he was being a good father. Let him continue to think it. For the sake that he was, once.

"You don't need to ask."

He didn't reply and we stood in awkward silence for a minute or two. You might not think a minute is a long time but when you aren't sure whether a conversation is over—while hoping to God that it was—it's excruciating and endless. Just try it. I wondered if he thought I'd gone. I trod on a twig and said. "Well, it's good to meet you, sir. Perhaps we'll see you. On the Continent. He'd like that."

"Perhaps," he said, still with his back to me. Obviously he couldn't bear to say the things he'd said while looking at the unnaturalness of me. "Goodbye, Mr Bircham."

I scarpered. With dignity. To my surprise Charles wasn't lurking behind a tree-trunk but was sitting on the gate to the entrance to Hellsingers. He was lit up, practically bursting to ask what had been said, but I simply linked my arm with his and walked him across the lawn. "I like him," I said. It wasn't true, but it was worth it, to see the smile on his face.

Chapter Eighteen

The house was buzzing with people. Laughter and congratulations echoed through the rooms as we nipped in. I saw Margaret trying to catch our attention but we slipped upstairs to change before we could be ambushed.

I determined, with the dull anger of Mr Holland's reluctant acceptance and veiled insults to fuel me, to see to Claude sooner rather than later. The euphoria I had felt simply getting the datura potion ready had worn off, but as I tucked the flask back into my jacket and trotted back downstairs, I felt something nudging at my spirits, as if an internal imp was handing me champagne and telling me "buck up." He was entirely right, that sprite, too.

I had only a little way to go now, so I bucked up accordingly. A buffet lunch was laid out in the dining room, and Claude and Margaret were holding court there, in front of the bay windows, meeting and greeting. I stayed close to Claude, never leaving the dining room and attaching myself to any guest that came within my immediate horizon. I was quite the card, cracking jokes and telling perfectly untrue tales about Charles at college.

From time to time I would find that the people I spoke to would drift towards Claude and Margaret and when they did, I went too, taking any opportunity I could to top up glasses, and being oh-so-useful, Stephens being busy enough, even with the extra staff hired to help. As I mingled and smiled and helped I managed to cobble together some semblance of a plan.

It seemed—if not foolproof—difficult to disprove, seeing as how the main witness would (hopefully) be too dead to contradict anything I said. But a lot depended on innocent witnesses, and of course fate. I had more faith in fate than I had in witnesses, innocent or otherwise.

I sploshed Claude's wine around like it was New Year's Eve, whilst keeping my own head the best I could. Sad to say this entailed pouring a good deal into the house aspidistras or down the water closet upon occasion, which was a crying shame. But needs must, and the devil was driving. By the time the dancing had begun most of the guests were squiffy, those in the house, at least. The village occupants were, in the main, celebrating in the garden with a local musical ensemble and a lot more fun they seemed to be having of it too.

I refrained from dancing, kept circulating, kept filling glasses where needed. By nine o'clock it had become a positive bacchanalia, with the Holland celebration turning to country dancing in the Gallery accompanied by loud whoops and cat calls. Charles, who had at first stayed by my side, drifted away the more alcohol he had and was soon threshing willows, crossover heying or braiding the ribbons or whatever peculiarity each country dance seemed to need. He knew them all, it appeared, something I had never known.

As for poor Lawrence, he was in attendance but whether he was even aware of the celebration it was hard to tell. Sometimes he would sway to a well known tune—I saw him move in rhythm to the Dashing White Sergeant. Stevie hovered around him, until Margaret gestured to me and I trotted over, bottle in hand.

"My dear," she said. Her eyes were mildly unfocused and her breath smelled of currants. "You seem—aside from Stephens, and I couldn't put any more on his head this evening—to be one of the few people still left with any sense of the per…perpendicular. Have you seen Charles?"

Yes, I thought. *Junior and Senior. What would you say if I told you that?*

"Dancing. Another glass?"

"Just a little, then. You've been so very useful, Harry, my dear, and it seems wrong to ask it of you, but would you please take Lawrence to bed soon? I found Stevie fast asleep in the cloakroom, and I didn't have the heart to wake her. She's worked so hard."

I gently touched her on the hand. "Of course. Only too pleased to do it.

"I'll grab Charles and we'll see to him straight away." It was a step in the right direction, getting out of the public eye.

As I left the room to find Charles, Claude passed along the hall in the throng. I followed him noting that he went into the study, then hared off to the Gallery, grabbed Charles, pulling him out of his set, to the annoyance of the other dancers.

How he'd managed to do any dancing more complicated than a two-step, I really don't know, for he was absolutely disgracefully drunk. He has a talent for being as drunk as most people comatose on the floor and still managing to give a performance and remaining upright. I doubt anyone in his dancing set knew how many sheets to the wind he actually was, but then I've known him a long time. Very soon now he would pass out, but not before throwing up at least once. Ah, my boy, such a creature of habits. And such very nasty habits, too, but for the most part I'm happy for them.

I held him up while I led him along the corridor. "We've got to put Lawrence to bed. But I think you'll be first."

"Oh, *do* take me to bed," he said in irrepressible tones of glee. "I promise I'll come quietly. Law'rns could come. But you wouldn't lettim."

"Shut up, you." I hit him. We passed the back door, and I pulled him outside, hoping some night air would cool him off in several ways. The side of the house was quiet; most of the guests were in the Gallery or the drawing room and that was how I wanted it. If he was going to be shockingly familiar, it was best no one except a few shocked owls spotted us.

"Sit there." I plonked him down on a bench and waited. It didn't usually take him long once fresh air hit him.

He sang quietly for a few moments, and I don't know where he learned such a filthy song because I hadn't heard it before, but it only took a short while for the fresh air to do its work. His suit was well and truly spoiled (again) as he vomited violently in a stream between his legs, getting quite a lot on his trousers and jacket.

I rubbed his back while he continued to retch and inwardly cursed him for the time—and the opportunity—I was wasting. I could probably have got Claude on his own, and now he was bound to have gone back to the party. A footstep sounded behind us in the darkness and the senior Charles stepped out from behind the laurels.

"I thought you'd gone," I said. He was dressed for travel, as though he had a motorcar beyond the nearest bush. Perhaps he had. Where he went and how he got there was a mystery.

"I decided to stay, just in case he was going to make a fool of himself."

"He's been pretty well-behaved so far, the drink makes him happy, until it doesn't. He can be a troublesome drunk unless someone..." I had a thought. "Look sir, I need to deal with Lawrence, I promised Margaret I would take him upstairs." This of course was perfectly true. "And Charles's state sort of caught me off-guard. Could you look after him for a while? I shouldn't be too long, and I can't exactly hand him over to his mother, or Stephens. Not like this—and I don't trust what he might say. You could keep him with you—for half an hour?"

Charles—the one of my heart—looked up and murmured something which sounded like "I could fash 'em. You jus' let me. Nebberam." I glared at him, but all he did was grin.

"Thank you, sir. I won't be long." I dashed away, back into the quiet around the side of the house and in through the door.

I had one chance—if Claude were still in the study. So I waited until no one was around (which took longer than I liked), before sprinting along the now deserted corridor and into the study. Claude was there, sitting at the desk and looking a lot more miserable than a man who had just achieved a lifetime's ambition had any right to look.

I grabbed fate by the throat and squeezed. "Oh, I'm sorry, sir. I just wanted to get out of the noise for a while. I'll go—"

"No, no, Bircham. No need."

"Thank you, sir. The party's going swimmingly." I locked the door. "That'll stop anyone blundering in looking for brandy."

"I should have thought of that two minutes ago," he said with ice in his voice. How very rude.

"I say, sir, are you all right?"

He glared at me without answering.

"It's just that you look a little unwell. Hmm. Not...unwell. Tired. Not surprising, of course, it's been a long day, a long week—"

"You don't have to patronise me," he snapped. Just when we were getting along so well, too.

"Hardly, sir. I'm feeling a little strung out myself. Just had to pour Charles into bed, and now I have to return and do the same for Lawrence. Thought I'd need something a little stiffer than punch before I re-entered the breach. May I pour you a drink too?" I began to pull out a couple of glasses, poured one for me and then hesitated, the bottle over the second empty glass. *Now*, I thought. *Now.*

"I don't.... Oh, damn it. Yes, thank you, Bircham. I damned well will."

"Good for you, sir," I said with a smile. I covered his gaze with my back, blocking the drinks trolley with my body and swiftly poured the entire contents of my flask into his glass before adding a good couple of inches of dark, peaty scotch. In the dim light of the study—the only light being a small lamp on the desk—the drink didn't look any different. "I think that we all should continue from today in a manner that we mean to go on, don't you agree? It's a new beginning. For everyone, in a way. You and Margaret are able to put the past behind you at long last and I'm afraid Charles will just have to learn to live with it. It will be a new start for him."

I turned around with the tray in my hands, a wide smile on my face. I brought bottle and glasses over to the table and raised my glass to him. "Congratulations, Mr Holland. I hope you'll always be as happy as you are right now." I gulped my drink down in one. Holland earned a widow's mite of respect as he hesitated, looked at me in the *most* suspicious way, before pouring his own drink down his throat. I beamed at him. "That's the way," I said, refilling his glass. "What shall we drink to now?"

He thought a moment and said "To absent friends." I echoed the sentiment and drank with him. Then I sat down in the chair opposite him.

"What was your brother like?" I asked.

"What?" he said, sharply. "Oh, I don't know. He was a good man, all in all. We had our differences—what brothers don't?—and we were as close as any brothers are, I suppose." He poured us both another drink.

"I'm sorry. I didn't mean to intrude. Tasteless. You know. Today being today, and everything."

He held his glass against his chest for a moment, his face flushed and his eyes seemed to focus on a spot above my head. "I didn't mean to snap your head off. I suppose I've been defensive about him—and my feelings for Margaret—for such a long time—"

"It's all right," I said, feigning embarrassment. "Once I heard your intention to marry I knew I was in for it on all sides. I just thought it was better to stay." I gave him the campest of smiles. "For his sake." I was delighted to see an expression of disgust pass over his face. The brothers weren't that different. Both were revolted by me, and what I was in Charles' life. It brought a kind of balance to the whole thing in a way, an action bringing an opposite reaction or however that goes.

He looked deep into his glass, and began to talk, almost to himself—in fact as he went on it became clear that if he was speaking to me, he'd forgotten who and what I was because he unburdened himself in ways I would never have guessed of him. He spoke of the way he missed his brother, the guilt he'd felt all these years waiting for Margaret, waiting for the seven years to pass—the way the ambivalence nearly tore him apart. One half of him longing to marry Margaret, one half of him hoping against hope that his brother was alive and then dreading that because he knew he'd lose everything he'd been waiting for.

I felt sorry for him. As he rambled away his voice slurred, but his eyes became wild and agitated and I knew the drug was working its way through his system. His words became jumbled, he used the wrong words for words that he seemed to be sure of, and in less than quarter of an hour he was making as little sense as Lawrence. When he finally went still, slumping back into his seat as if peacefully asleep I waited, breathless, half thinking he would wake, or start behaving like Lawrence but he was endlessly still.

I stood, moved over and took his hand, held his wrist like you see all efficient nurses and doctors do. Despite it seeming simple, I soon found that I had no idea on how to take a pulse. This galled me and I promised myself to practice when I had the opportunity. I realised that it could be that he *had* no pulse, so I checked his nose for any signs of breath and there came only the briefest gust, his breast hardly moving. As I watched, even that small movement ceased after ten or so minute breaths and for all that I could observe, he had indeed stopped breathing. Entirely ignorant as to whether a pulse or a breath stopped first it seemed that the deed was finally, and hopefully irrevocably, done.

The wave of euphoria that swept over me, standing over this shell of a man was like a tidal wave that threatened to knock me off my feet. The utter sheer power to bring someone down with no more effort than it took to flick a fly from one's arm. How simple it was. How beautifully simple.

I found myself out of breath with the revelation, and I had to snap myself out of it, forcing myself away from the desk. It was the work of a moment to empty and to wipe my fingerprints from both glasses and then to carefully put Claude's back on his, which is more fiddly than it sounds, believe me. I left them on the decanter. I could easily explain my fingerprints on there, but no fingerprints at all would look suspicious. I had read some books other than law books, after all. It was likely there were many other prints there too—Stephens and Charles must have handled it at some point, and as the decanter had been more than half empty it was unlikely to have been polished.

Not with everything else that had been going on.

Luck was with me as I left the room, and I could hear "Auld Lang Syne" playing, so everyone was probably grabbing the last dance. I found myself wearing a positive rictus of a smirk and had to school my features to mere merriment. Probably I should have been penitent, but I really couldn't find it within myself. All I felt was smug.

Back at the party I went straight to Margaret's side, wondering what she'd say if I announced her bridegroom was lying dead just along the hall and her first husband was in the garden. Instead of which I smiled. "I had to leave Charles in the garden, I'm afraid, he was rather unwell. The night air will sober him up a little. I'll deal with Lawrence now."

"Have you seen Claude?" she asked. "He went for some fresh air about half an hour ago."

"I did see him, he was coming back from the Gallery, I think."

"All right." I wasn't sure she even heard me as she was surrounded by friends offering thanks, goodbyes and congratulations; she simply waved at me, her gaze a little glassy as she too had had one drink too many. So had Claude, of course.

Chapter Nineteen

The trouble with a death is that there has to be a fuss afterwards. It's terribly tiresome. After my father died there were people in the house for days, upsetting the cook and the parlour maid so much that meals were irregular for a week at least. If a dog dies, either by poisoning or by natural means, we don't immediately call the police, do we? Why then is a death of a human being automatically treated as suspicious?

Claude could easily have had a heart attack. In fact you'd think that's the first thing people would have thought, due to the strain everyone had been under and he wasn't exactly young, but from the first clichéd scream of the servant girl the fact that he had been killed seemed to be the first conclusion that anyone jumped to. People are so mistrustful. I blame the moving pictures. I had managed to hurry my steps, and my plan—such as it was—was running on time; I had put Lawrence into bed and he had gone willingly and quietly, which was a relief. I admit to having simply pulled his outside clothes off, leaving him in drawers and vest, for I didn't want to waste time finding pyjamas and struggling with a grown man who was stronger and heavier than I. I simply don't have that kind of experience, not of putting pyjamas on a man at least.

Then I'd run down the stairs and made a swift exit out into the garden to meet up with the Charleses: Junior and Senior. "Sorry to keep you, sir." I sat next to the younger model and peered at him; he peered back, blearily.

"Lawrence gave me a little trouble, seems he didn't want to be put to bed. How are you?" I asked my drunken friend. "You look appalling."

"I am appalling," he said in a voice that sounded like his throat was made of sandpaper, which it probably felt like.

"I know that," I said. "Can you stand? I think bed's the best place for you, too."

"Dear Harry," he said. "You always know the best things for me. Take me to bed." He declaimed this like the worst kind of actor, flinging his arms wide.

"Shut up," I said, hopefully looking annoyed, although I was on the brink of laughter. "Your father doesn't need to be reminded what a delinquent you've turned into."

"I wash always a dellinquintante," he said with a smile.

"I'll say goodnight," his father said. He paused a moment after turning away, as if struggling to find the right words. I could imagine his chagrin. He could hardly say "He's in the best hands," so he settled for patting his son on the shoulder and was rewarded with an imbecilic grin.

"Goodnight, sir," I said. "And thank you, for earlier. I hope we meet again."

His father nodded at me, patted his son again as if he were some kind of nervous mare or a parcel that might explode, and turned away, walking into the dark.

It took me a little while to manhandle my second charge into bed, and when I finally got him there I fed him a large whisky, hoping that it would knock him out for the night and prevent him from wandering the corridors as he had occasionally done in college. If alibis had to be formed, it was better that I was forming them.

The scotch had an immediate effect. He slumped back onto his pillow and was snoring in about four minutes, his mouth open and drooling lightly. I hazarded that he was out for the count and went to my room.

First I washed the flask out as thoroughly as I could, hot and cold water, concentrating on all the nooks and crannies. Then I dried it, and put a load of fingerprints back all over it, half filled it with scotch and put it into my drawer. Then I pulled off my tie, removed my jacket and sat on a chair, letting the excitement flow through me as I waited for the alarm to be raised. I knew it couldn't take that long. Someone would go hunting for Claude. I was surprised Margaret hadn't sent someone to look for him already.

When it came it was as shrill as a banshee; a female voice wailing from downstairs somewhere, expected but still chilling and exciting when you hear someone in such distress. I gave it a good twenty seconds or so, letting the scream fade and counting the moments before I lifted myself out of the chair, pulled on my dressing gown, stepped into slippers and made sure my hair was good and tousled before trotting out into the hall and down the stairs.

In the hall, Stevie came running in through the garden door and ran right into me. "Oh, God, Harry. Thank God it's you. I think he's dead."

I was glad to hear it, but looked solicitous and as shocked as I could.

"I woke up and needed some air," she went on. "I found him on the lawn. I poked him and tapped him on the back, but he's not breathing."

"On the lawn?" I said, surprised. How on earth had Claude managed to stagger out onto the lawn?

"Of course it's probably just his age. If the house's history is true, he has to be getting on for a hundred—"

"Wait a moment. You aren't.... What *are* you talking about?"

"Polonius. I just *said*. He's collapsed on the lawn and he's not breathing. I was out there when I heard someone screaming from inside the house. What's going on?"

"Haven't the foggiest, my dear. I've only just come downstairs myself. Rotten luck about Polonius though." I had a feeling that I had been responsible for that death, too, and it was the only one I felt bad about.

"Where's Charles?" She looked around. "Where's Lawrence? Where *is* everybody? Who the hell was screaming?"

I led the way along the hall and paused a moment outside the drawing room. "Lawrence is safe in bed. So is Charles. As for what else…I'm not sure. In here, perhaps. I think most people have gone."

The drawing room was less full than I had expected. Margaret was not in attendance but Clarissa was, seated on an upright chair and pale as milk, her moon-face slack and looking a good ten years older than she had an hour before, when I had last seen her, laughing and dancing. She was girded on two sides by dour-faced men, people I'd been introduced to but had forgotten their names the moment I'd stepped away. I think they were relatives of hers and Claude's and from their faces, set naturally in scowls rather than showing any lines that might denote laughter, I suspected that indeed was the case.

"You've got to calm yourself," one of them was saying. "You can't do anything. I know what it's like. When June was hit by that damned motor I wanted to pick her up and run the ten miles to the hospital. The worst of it is doing nothing."

"What's happened?" Stevie said, rushing to Clarissa and kneeling in front of her. "Where's Margaret. Oh, God," she said, repeating herself. "Where *is* everyone?" When several people exchanged glances she started to panic. "Why won't someone tell me?"

The dour man who had not spoken put his hand on her shoulder. "I'm afraid…" He looked up at his mirroring friend. "I'm afraid it's not good news. Claude was found in the library. It appears…. Well. He's dead."

The relief that flooded through me at that point was like a warm tide of water that started somewhere around my temples and flowed through every part of me. As though I could feel the very blood moving around my body, hot and calming. I'd done it. It took real effort to start myself from actually laughing out loud and I had to raise my fist to my mouth. A nice touch, I thought. It looked as though I was as shocked as Stevie. She looked around wildly. "Claude? That makes no sense—at least…" She had the sense to shut up then.

"Would anything make any sense?" I said, taking her arm. "Of course not. Come and sit down." I looked around, aiming my question at anyone who might be listening. "Has anyone called the doctor?"

"Didn't you hear me?" one of the men said, his voice harsh. "He's dead. No doctor can bring him back. Stephens has phoned the police, I believe."

Controlling my impulse to smack him one on the nose, I knelt before Stevie. "You'll be all right? I need to speak to your father."

She nodded.

"Want a cigarette?"

She nodded again. I got one from the cabinet, lit it for her and she took it in trembling fingers. She inhaled once, then twice and looked up at me, her expression hardening once more. "I'm sorry. I'll be all right now."

"I know you will. I understand. I'll tell you why one of these days. Keep control in here?"

She nodded a third time. "I won't fall apart again."

"Good girl," I said, and made my way outside and down the servants' stairs. Stephens was giving orders to the staff and I waited while he finished up.

"Once that's done, off to bed with you all." A housemaid began to wail that she'd never be able to sleep, not with murders being done all over the place and Stephens snapped at her, forcing her silent once more. "Ethel! It will be a long day tomorrow so I'll need things to run as normal. Mrs Holland is not to be bothered with anything."

The little crowd disappeared off to do whatever parlouring and footmanning they did last thing at night and Stephens turned to me. "Mrs Holland is in the morning room, sir."

"On her own?"

"She's a strong woman," he said. "When she needs to be. And she's needed to be at several times in her life. Is Mr Charles…"

It took me a second to process who he meant. "He's de—He's rather indisposed, I'm afraid. A surfeit of dancing and champagne. I couldn't wake him with a trumpet, take it from me."

"I took the liberty of telephoning the police. There was a fair amount of confusion after Mr Holland was found."

"Of course," I said. "You did the right thing. Could you telephone to the doctor too? Or should we wait for the police before we do that?"

"Already done, sir," he said with that butlery assurance he had. "He is actually out at another call, but I left a message. I didn't think it merited anything more urgent, under the circumstances. I hope I did right."

"Of course. If you can encourage the last of the hangers-on to leave, that would be a boon, too. Even relatives. The fewer people we have cluttering up the place, the better."

"I'll see what I can do, sir."

MARGARET HAD HER BACK TO THE door, and she didn't turn when I entered. "Is that you, Charles?" she asked. It was a little bit unnerving.

"Harry," I said. "Charles is in bed, I'm afraid. Margaret, there'll be no rousing him tonight. I'm so s—"

"Thank God," she said, interrupting me from saying something that might get me struck down by lightning. She was as tense as a bowstring, anyone could see that, but it was rather a transformation, too. I'd considered her weak and vulnerable, but she had hidden strengths. Just as well, really. "Thank God he'll be spared tonight, at least." She turned around, her hand still clasping one of the curtains which swung with her. "You have known him long enough. You will remember what he was like after his father died."

I nodded, hardly trusting myself to say anything helpful.

"I know you will. We've only known you in person just a little time, but I know you will look after him. He's never been fond of Claude, I know. But any death affects him terribly, I've seen it happen over and over. I was grateful that he didn't take the death of that Indian boy worse than he did. I'm worried, every time. That it might set him back, you see. He was in such a bad way—

manic, the doctor called it, when Charles—his father—went missing. Saying the most impossible things. I just don't know if I could bear to go through that again."

It was then I knew I was right. This selfish household, this selfish woman who was more concerned about whether *she* could go through it, rather than the effect it might have on Charles. Claude, worrying about what the neighbours might say if they'd done the decent thing for Lawrence—I should have poisoned the sorry lot of them. I wondered very, very briefly how that might have been achieved.

"I'll make sure," I said. "Should I wait up for the police?"

"I think it's best," she said. "I don't think any of us should be seen to be trying to hide anything. Of course they will be bound to want to interview everyone at some point."

"Believe me, there'll be no waking him, so that's rather moot. I can vouch for him being blotto. I can get Stephens to try and rouse him if you like, in case they don't believe us." She nodded. "Should I send someone to you? Clarissa's in a bit of a state, and Stevie is with her, but I'm sure she'll come."

"No, I'll come. I only came in here to catch my breath. There were so many people around. Thank you, Harry." Centuries of English breeding shored up the barricades of her resolve. It was not done to simply collapse, no matter whether the natives were bashing the door down or your husband of a few days had just died.

I nodded, and we left together. I trotted upstairs and checked on Charles. He was, as predicted, dead to the world and snoring with abandon. As if to prove a point to myself, and in case a nosy policeman were to doubt my word—imagine!—I gave his shoulder a shake which was, as expected, entirely fruitless.

It wasn't until I sat down and picked up a book, which I stared at without seeing, that the adrenaline began to wear off little by little and lethargy crept up on me. I was therefore fast asleep when a housemaid called my name, shocking me back into wakefulness.

"Sir, the police are here, and they'd like everyone in the drawing room."

So much for everyone being in plain sight when the rozzers arrived. This was not a good start for H Bircham, Esq.

I grunted. "I'll be down in a few minutes. Please tell Mrs Holland." She went towards the door and I called her back. "Annie, isn't it? Could you try and wake Mr Holland? He won't stir, I'm sure of it, but the police will want to know why he's not downstairs with the rest of us."

She looked mildly startled, but did as I asked, shaking him gently on the shoulder when her voice did not wake him. He continued to snore lightly and I nodded in grim satisfaction. "Good. That'll do."

I took a little longer to tidy and ready myself than necessary, I ran over the facts and the fictions in my head because this was really it, I'd pushed Fate—or Luck or whoever had looked after me thus far—as far as they could be pushed. From now on, I suspected, I would be on my own; and what was worse, I was responsible for Charles in a way I'd never been before.

Once dressed—soberly but not in my evening clothes now—I walked downstairs, letting the butterflies in my insides buoy me up.

Stephens was sitting on a chair in the downstairs hall. He looked grey, poor man. As he ushered me into the drawing room I said loudly, "Margaret, can we let Stephens get some sleep?" He went to interrupt me but I cut him off with a gesture. "I'm sure anything he has to say to the police can wait until the morning."

Stevie darted a glance at Margaret, who nodded. Stevie leapt out of her chair as if scalded and took her father's arm. "Come on," she said. "They can come back for both of us." Her voice was so kind it hardly sounded like her. She led him out of the room and the door closed.

Apart from Margaret, there were only two other people in the room, a uniformed constable, holding his helmet under his arm and standing as ramrod straight as though he had a broom handle inserted where the sun shineth not, and a tall, sandy-haired man in a dark grey dog-tooth suit.

"Inspector Tanner's the name." He nodded. "Good evening, sir," the man in plain clothes said, so obviously a policeman from his too short hair to his shiny—horrors!—brown boots. "You must be"—he glanced down at a notepad in his hand—"Harry Bircham? Is that short for Harold?"

"I am, and it certainly is not." I took a seat on the chair opposite to where Margaret sat. There was no sign of Clarissa and I wasn't surprised.

"I'm sure you realise that we have to make enquiries, sir. Although I do think we can cut them short for tonight once the deceased has been taken out of the house. I'm taking short statements tonight, just where people were at what time and I'll leave a constable here overnight—"

"Is that necessary?" Margaret said. "I'm sure no one here is likely to abscond, we have nothing to hide."

Tanner looked suitably cynical at that, but the expression was so fleeting, Margaret, from her position was unlikely to have caught it. "It's policy, madam," he said. "We'll need to speak to everyone tomorrow, and I'll need a list of everyone at the party. It was a shame that you allowed people to leave."

Margaret's core of strength showed quite clearly as she squared her shoulders. "It was not a case of allowing people to leave, Inspector, it was a party. Most people had left before...before..." She seemed to run out of strength for a second, then rallied. "Before my husband's body was discovered. After Lawrence's mishap, we assumed that he'd—"

"Lawrence?" The inspector looked sharply at the constable who answered immediately, belying the fact that he was as dim as the proverbial Toc H lamp. You know I've always wondered what a Toc H lamp *is*. I really must find out. "Son of the butler here," the constable said without referring to his notebook. One could only assume he was a local lad. "Was taken ill at a party a couple of weeks back, collapsed at dinner and hasn't—as far as I'm aware—recovered his wits since."

"Hmm," the inspector said. We all hung on the silence thereafter hoping the "hmm" would be explained, but we were unlucky. Instead he turned to me. "Just briefly, Mr Bircham, because I think everyone's had enough, would you supply me with your full name and address, and advise me of where you were last night from ten o clock onwards?"

After I'd supplied the necessary facts, I made a show of thinking, it wouldn't do to let him think I had it rehearsed. "Well, let me see. I was in here for most of the evening, helping with drinks and generally mingling. Once or twice I wandered along to the Gallery to watch the dancing and I danced with a couple of girls there. Miss Wrigglesworth and Stevie of course, and a blond in a green dress."

"You don't recall her name."

"I'm sorry, I only remember Miss Wrigglesworth because of the joke she made."

The inspector looked blank, coupled with an air of disapproval. I fancied he'd seen through my machismo.

I sighed. "She said, upon being asked to dance: 'You're taking a risk, Mr Bircham, for I wriggle for all I'm worth.'" Tanner's face grew stonier, were that possible. "I dare say it was funnier after a bottle or two of champagne."

"Quite likely," he said, and his voice would have outweighed lead. "I wouldn't know. Then what?"

"She didn't say anything else much; the band was rather noisy as it happens."

"Not the Wrigglesworth girl," he said, so sharply as to cut steel. How metallic he was! "What did you do next?"

"Oh, well, I vacillated back between there and here, then Margaret asked me to see to Lawrence, put him to bed, you know. But as I was on my way there I saw Holland, that's Charles Holland, obviously, had had rather too much to drink—a skinful and a half at least—sorry, Margaret. I felt it wasn't in his best interests to stay at the party—"

"And why was that, sir?" If a tone could describe as crouching, ready to pounce, his was. Luckily, I'd heard prosecution counsels with the same trick. No brown-booted lackey was going to catch me out so easily.

"Because he has a tendency to keep going and going when he's drunk and then throwing up spectacularly before passing out. I thought it was better to have him away from ladies in pretty frocks if that was likely to occur. Which as it happens, it did, but safely in the garden. The evidence, no doubt, is still out by the rustic bench. Unless that's what killed Polonius. Oh, I do hope not."

I knew pretty well what had killed Polonius and I wasn't going to talk about that! "He will eat anything, I've been told."

"I'm sorry?" Tanner looked angry for a moment and glared at his constable. "The deceased's name was Claude wasn't it?"

"Yes, sir," the constable said. "Claude Anthony Edward Holland. No Polonius there, as far as I'm aware."

"My son's friend means the tortoise," Margaret said. "I had no idea the poor thing had died."

"I'm afraid so," I said. "Stevie found him just before the alarm went up about Claude."

A sigh, which was more of a huff, and would not have been out of place emanating from a bull's flared nostrils, sounded from the inspector. I suspected I was annoying him. Imagine that. "What time," he said, each word cut in half by gritted teeth, "was this?"

"Which this? When Stevie found Polonius or when—"

"When you took Charles Holland out into the garden."

"I don't know. What time did Auld Lang Syne play?"

"I'd asked them to play it at one-thirty," Margaret said.

"So it was one-thirty?" Tanner asked, with the patience of a saint—if saints look likely to lamp you one.

"Oh no, it was long before that. A good three-quarters of an hour. I don't wear a watch with evening clothes because I don't have anything grand enough, and anyway, who needs to keep time, unless one has an assignation—which of course I didn't. But it was a good while before the end of the party. Then I came back for Lawrence, I spoke to Margaret briefly and took Lawrence away. I say, Inspector, you don't suspect foul play—who on earth would have wanted to do anything to Claude Holland—on his wedding day of all days?" I felt like Peter in Gethsemane.

"These are merely routine questions, Mr Bircham," the inspector said.

Another policeman stuck his head around the door. "We're done, sir."

"And I won't bother you any further this evening, Mrs Holland, or rather this morning as it is. Please can you ensure *all* of your household are here tomorrow as I'll want to speak to everyone. The servants, Miss Holland and your son."

"Normally we'd attend church, most of us, but of course tomorrow will be out of the question. Yes, we'll all be here. I'll speak to the staff, any half-days can be rearranged."

"Thank you," he said. "I offer my condolences again." He gave a stiff little nod, which spoke volumes about himself and his brown boots. Ambitious working-class roots if I was any judge, despite the self-taught accent. He was absolutely not at home with the landed class. "I'll see myself out," he said just as Margaret was about to speak. "Good night."

The door closed behind him, and just for a second or two, Margaret and I were joined in an inhalation of breath. Under other circumstances we might have laughed about it, but we simply said goodnight to each other.

"Margaret," I said, at the door. "You'll be all right?"

"I still have Charles," she said.

She didn't move away from where she sat, and the vision of her sitting alone in that big room lost on that enormous sofa stays with me still.

Chapter Twenty

don't know about anyone else's actions that Sunday morning but I crawled out of bed at ten, and discovered a cold cup of tea on the bedside table. Forcing it down—because there is little in the culinary world that is more revolting than cold tea—I found it restored me somewhat, giving me enough strength to stumble into Holland's room. He was up, to my great surprise, and nowhere to be seen, the bed rumpled and cool to the touch.

There was a constable lurking in the hall; not right outside my door, but near enough. I knew he was waiting to get in our rooms and start searching. I was tempted to look down my nose at him, ask him what he was playing at and generally "my good man" him into submission, but I didn't. Priorities have to be observed and I was hungry.

By the time I'd made the morning room there was no one in it, but one of the maids had held on for me, which I appreciated greatly and made a mental note to tip her a couple of bob upon leaving. It's this caring attitude that has declined so much since the war. I would have bet good money that the woman had been a nurse during the late unpleasantness, as the Americans would say. I felt touched and wrapped myself around kidneys and bacon in gratitude.

When I'd finished, the paragon of womanhood rather dimmed herself in my eyes by saying: "The police are back again, sir, we're both to go into the drawing room when you've finished. I was asked to wait for you."

Probably to ensure I didn't abscond, I thought to myself. Now I had a good look at her with her meaty arms and strong body, it wouldn't surprise me at all if she was in Tanner's pay and would fell me like a tree were I to make an ungainly dash towards the French windows. I kept my dignity. In the drawing room, the whole family was assembled, together with the constable from the night before who wore a shining morning face which told of a late night and a hasty shaving. The good inspector was missing, and so, I noticed with a sinking heart, was Holland. Clarissa and Margaret sat side-by-side holding hands. An odd couple they made, but wasn't the whole house filled with odd couples now?

"Please wait here," the constable said. "The inspector will ask to see anyone he hasn't yet seen, and we are searching the house."

"What on earth for? Is that actually allowed if there's not been evidence of foul play?"

"I'm sure the inspector will answer any questions you have, later on, sir. If you'd be so kind as to wait."

Divining that this was going to be the only answer I was going to get, I sat on a hard chair near Stevie and Lawrence. No one seemed ready to start any kind of conversation. I was about to break the silence—I cannot abide a room full of people and no one speaking at all—when Stevie caught my eye and with the drawing together of delicate dark eyebrows stunned me into submission so that the words dried in my mouth. Her eyes flicked to where the constable stood at the side of the room. How stupid I'd been; police sometimes have an ability to disappear into the woodwork—and I daresay they use it to their advantage—and I'd been about to spout whatever I was going to say. To be honest I can't even remember what it was, which is probably just as well.

My mother says when that happens, it must have been a lie to start with and she's probably right.

After a while the silence stretched me again and this time I gave in to it.

"Are they going to speak to Lawrence?"

"No," said Stevie. "Apparently the doctor has spoken to the inspector already and he's been told that it's a pointless exercise attempting to get any sense out of Lawrence. He was actually quite chatty when the inspector first arrived, but as usual, despite him speaking in a way that made it sound like he knew himself what he was saying, sadly none of us could unscramble his thoughts." She turned her face away and touched Lawrence gently on the face. He smiled at her and clasped her hand in his. It was probably very moving, if you like that kind of thing. "Perhaps there's some kind of code to it, perhaps I'll learn his language, or perhaps we'll invent our own…" She sighed and I could hear her breathing, as she fought to keep control. "Or perhaps he's going to be like this forever, and actually has no idea of where he is, and who I am. Perhaps anyone would do. Maybe that would be best."

Despite the fact that Lawrence didn't react to this speech, which bore out much of which she said, she didn't seem to notice, and I made suitable demurrals. We lapsed back into silence for another ten minutes or so while I worried. What was taking Holland so long? Why the devil didn't he wait for me this morning so we could have spoken about it? How had he learned the news? How had he reacted? How was he coping? There was so much I wanted to ask, but there was no one, in the room or out of it that I could.

The door opened but it was only Stephens bringing in fresh tea. I don't think anyone except the constable, who looked like he'd rather be holding an enamel mug than wafer-thin Spode, had actually drunk any of it.

Where I had been gasping an hour ago, now I felt a cup of the stuff would choke me. But it's what we do. Hot water, clean towels, soap and tea. The staples of emergencies for as long as England has had its crises.

As Stephens took the tea out, the door opened again and the inspector and Charles came in. Charles looked as dreadful as I had expected him to look; not only did he have the familiar hung-over look I knew all too well, but there was a blankness in his face that I'd only seen a few times before and his fingers were not exactly trembling, but on the hand I could see, the other shoved into a trouser pocket, his fingers were flickering on the corduroy of his trousers as though he were playing the piano. He didn't look at anyone, not his mother nor at me, as he took a seat by the window.

"Ah, Mr Bircham," Tanner said. "You are here at last. Come with me, will you, sir?" I followed him meekly into the morning room where we both sat. "I've had your statement typed out. Could you just read through it and if you agree with what is there, could you sign it?"

I read it swiftly. "It doesn't sound like me." It was horribly sanitised and had none of my voice. I felt rather misrepresented. It did however have all the salient facts that I'd divulged, at least.

"I apologise for that, sir," Tanner said. "My staff aren't famed for decorative prose." He handed me a pen, pointedly, as if I were holding matters up. I signed. "What kind of man would you say Mr Claude Holland was?"

I hesitated. "Will you be adding this to my statement? Because I've already signed it."

"No. I don't think that your opinion is evidence. If it were to become so, then we'd make a new statement. I'm just interested to know what you thought of him."

"He was rather…commanding," I said. I didn't want to let out any hint of my sexual attraction, I wasn't ready for throwing myself on my sword.

"He tended to take for granted that things would be done his way—but I understand he operated a mine or what-not for years so he would have had things just so for years."

"How did that manifest to you?"

"He tried to get me to control Charles. You see, Charles can be a little impulsive. Dashing off without notice, that kind of thing, and Mr Holland seemed not to appreciate that joie-de-vivre."

"And you declined."

"It wasn't a case of declining, Inspector. I have no right to control anyone. If Claude had a problem with his future wife's son, then he needed to handle it himself. I don't appreciate being a double agent. Apart from that, he seemed rather unbending. But Charles wasn't—well, Mr Holland and I, us. We didn't mingle that much."

"No, that's fine. Thank you, Mr Bircham."

I rejoined the others, Tanner following and as I sat by the window, Tanner stood by the door, as if stopping us from legging it and his constable came to join him. "I have statements from everyone," he said. He wore the same clothes as the night before, although more rumpled, denoting a lack of sleep.

"Please could you all remain here, that is to say, kindly don't leave the county until I let you know when that's advisable. I'd rather not have to chase anyone around London—or anywhere else," he said, looking at me for some reason. "And I wouldn't be in a good mood if that's what I had to do. It wouldn't reflect well on anyone who tried it, either. Until we are satisfied about Mr Holland's death, please stay calm, but stay available.

"We have a good many statements yet to take from the villagers and the friends and relatives on the invitation list so I'm afraid you may have to wait for a few days. I can only apologise for any inconvenience that may cause you."

He was reciting now, clearly words he'd said many times in many situations as if he were reading from a card in his head. "I dare say there's things to be organised…well. That's all." He tightened his mouth, briefly. "Thank you for your co-operation. You have the station's number, in case anything occurs to any of you—anything at all—that you haven't thought of up to now."

"How long will you have my husband's body?" Margaret asked. "As you say. Arrangements…"

"I'm afraid I can't say. You'll be unable to make any…arrangements," he looked out of his depth, having to defer to a lady, and to skirt around the hard words, "until the doctor produces a death certificate. That may take a little while, I'm afraid. Sudden deaths cause us to sit up and take notice, but in the light of what happened last week, well…we need to be sure."

"What a perfectly dreadful man," Margaret said as soon as they had gone.

Despite the force of her tone, she was almost whispering, as though he'd left a spy under the table. "How can he even suspect that anyone would… would try to harm Claude—or Lawrence?"

Clarissa raised her head as if it was too heavy for her neck. "Do you think that's what they think?"

"They are police, dear," Margaret said. "There's no logic to what they think. They see a death and immediately they assume that it's foul play of some sort. They must be on commission; the more foul play the better, natural deaths don't count. It's inconceivable. Claude was liked, universally liked. The party proved that. At least he went—" She broke off and sobbed quietly into a handkerchief. I wondered if she was going to say "went happy." He certainly hadn't been, not from the look on his face.

Universally liked. Yes. Until the moment that someone killed him. The silence that followed Margaret's speech made me wonder if the others were thinking the same thing. There was one person that didn't like Claude and had made no secret of the fact. It is a joyful thing to me that the English can push such matters aside and that in even admitting that someone might not have liked the man, they would, in effect, be speaking ill of the dead. But in a way, they were right. If someone did kill him, then it was better that it was someone who didn't dislike him. I acted, yes—but I only disliked him vicariously, he was too full of sex appeal for me to hate him that much. A crush is hardly a motive for murder, if I ever did admit the crush to Tanner. Unless he'd rejected my nancy advances which of course he had not, as I had made none. I wondered idly what he would have done, and I realised I'd lost an opportunity to find out.

"Charles," Margaret said. "Darling," she added when he took no notice, "come and sit here."

He said nothing, continuing to stare out of the window into the rain. She turned in her seat, dropping Clarissa's hand to do so and looked at her son, her face almost a mirror-mask of his, both beautiful, both almost medieval in their tragedy. The trouble was, it was only a reaction with him, not actual emotion, like hers. So his reflection was like one of those warped mirrors in fairgrounds. It seemed it reflected you exactly—until you walked close, when it all went horribly wrong.

"What did they want to know, darling?" she continued.

He was quiet for a long ten seconds or so, and she asked once more before he answered. "Same as they wanted to know for everyone else, I suppose. Where was I, what did I think of the deceased, what was my relationship with the deceased." He stood, his fists clenched. "Relationship? Why would they ask me that? Did they ask you that? Did they ask you, Mother, what your relationship was? What you thought of him? Why would they ask me? Harry? You?"

I shook my head. "They asked me what kind of man I thought he was… and where I was. I hope you told them you didn't exactly know where you were."

"Of course. They just look at you, though, giving nothing, taking everything. It must be a uniform that gives them that talent, but no—he's not got a uniform." He took a deep breath, the short of sharp intake one takes when one wakes or surfaces from a deep dive. "I want some air."

I was worried about his train of thought. "Let's go out for a walk."

"But it's pouring, Harry," Stevie said. "You can't go out in that."

"I hear Hurst is burying Polonius," he said. "Someone should be there."

He gave Stevie a look which couldn't be described as anything but poisonous. I wondered if he thought she had done it, and would he look at me like that?

"I would have thought you would, if anyone."

She dropped her gaze, and one single tear fell onto the satin of her dress, spreading like dark water on the fabric. "I can't. I just can't."

"Of course. Come on, Harry." I followed him out.

He didn't speak, and he didn't go and get his coat either, leaving me with a choice of abandoning him while I went to get mine, or doing without. I did without, remembering sharply Claude's comment about Charles wandering around in the rain. The garden was storm-washed with grey as the sheets of water came down, as heavy a summer storm as any I'd seen, the drops heavy and warm, soaking us in seconds. He led the way around the house and then out towards the tennis courts. On the other side, between the courts and the herbaceous border, two men stood, strangely immobile.

We stopped a short distance away and the older of the two gardeners, who I assumed was Hurst, tipped his head to Charles. We watched as they shovelled earth, alternately, covering the shell of the deceased in black, sticky mud. When there was no more tortoise visible, Charles turned away and we strode back to the house as silently as we'd left it.

As we climbed the stairs up to our rooms, Charles said: "He's been here longer than the family. When I was a child, there's photos somewhere, although I don't remember it, I used to ride him around the garden. I wish I did remember that." We entered my room and I grabbed a couple of towels, threw him one. "Funny how death strikes one. One minute it's brainless trundling around the lawn, or dancing a reel, or driving a car—and then you're gone. What's the point? What do you leave? Other than grief?"

"I don't know," I said. "Some people do things that are remembered."

"Most don't, though. Will you? Will I?"

What I said was "Of course, how could we not?" but what I was thinking was *I bloody well hope not.*

"I did want him dead," he said, sitting at the window seat and rubbing ineffectively at his hair until I took over and worked a bit harder. His voice sounded vibrato as I tousled his hair dry. "And now I look back and think, 'Why?' Why was I so petty, just because I didn't like him much?"

"You knew your father was alive. It's understandable," I said.

"Don't be so infernally reasonable," he snapped. "How can it be *understandable* to want someone dead for such selfish bloody reasons?"

I saw the error too late and tried to cover. "I'm just saying—"

"Well, don't!" He'd slipped into near-hysteria and I hadn't had the presence of mind to forestall it as I would try to, normally. "What if it *is* murder? Don't you *see*?"

"Some villager, some strang—"

"No, because they did it to Lawrence, didn't they? I'm sure of it. It can't have been a villager. It was someone there. At the party, and at the dinner. Someone in the family. Or—" His breathing was ragged, and he curled his legs up on the seat, hugging them close. "Someone…with access…someone who knew his way around."

"No, Charles."

"You've thought it."

"No." That much was absolutely true. "No, no! I haven't. And neither must you. Not for one moment. He wouldn't."

"You don't know him."

"Neither do you, for God's sake!" I knelt down by him, took his hands in mine and rubbed them, banishing the chill. "How on earth would he have managed it? Bribed Stephens? Come in disguised as a waiter? Do you think no one would have spotted him? Clarissa? Margaret?" I knew deep down that here was an easy way out, to let Charles Senior take the blame, but I couldn't do that to the son. Not when his face was begging me to come and look for him in the places where he was lost and desperate. "I can't, and I won't believe that he'd hang around all this time, getting to know you—only to nip in and start poisoning people willy-nilly. Look, I'll give you Claude, who knows how much your father has resented that situation, but Lawrence? I'll never believe that of the man I met yesterday. And you shouldn't. Not ever." He turned his face away, but didn't pull his hands from mine. After a minute or two his voice was calmer and I knew I'd calmed the storm, for now, at least. "You're right. But it doesn't help. Someone did it, and someone did it to Lawrence, and God strike me down for thinking that that's the worse crime of the two."

"Don't say any of this to anyone else, Charles." I busied myself with folding the wet towels.

"I'm hardly likely to. But why shouldn't I? Of course I'm not going to tell the police that I think Lawrence's misfortune is worse than Claude's. God." He stood and ran a hand through his hair. "I must go and talk to Mother. It must be bloody for her, and I've not helped at all."

I listened to his footsteps thud down the corridor before I sat on the window seat where he'd been. The seat was still warm.

Chapter Twenty-One

The news reached the village fairly quickly, as Clarissa had predicted. During a late lunch on the Sunday, as the family were sitting down to a roast dinner that no one wanted and no one was eating (except for me, but I had to appear as if my appetite was impaired, and apart from Lawrence who knew no better), Stevie, who was staring out into the garden, said, "Oh, Lord, no. Just what we don't need."

Margaret didn't seem to hear her, sunk in a reverie of her own, but Clarissa said, "What is it?"

"It's the indomitable Mrs Witherspoon," Stevie said, pushing herself to her feet as if she were eighty years old. "I suppose we should have expected something like this. I'll go and deal with her." As Margaret looked up, Stevie added. "I'm assuming you don't want her poking around?"

"Oh," said Margaret. "Don't you think it might be better if we are open about it all? If we start hiding behind closed doors, then the gossip will be much worse."

"I can't see how it could ever be worse," Stevie said.

"Don't you?" Clarissa said. The expression on her face was one of incredulity and I fancied I had an idea of what she meant. "I agree with Margaret. If we are going to see anyone—obviously we don't want a swarm of people from the village coming in and out—then Mrs Witherspoon is probably the best person to have. For all her...efficiency, she could be a useful ally."

"Ally?" Stevie's face was full of bitterness.

Clarissa nodded, pushing her plate away. "I mean it. Keeping people at bay, passing on information that we want passed on and not just random gossip. Of course there will be gossip, but if you get Ida Witherspoon on our side right now, she'll stand before us like Uriel guarding Eden. She may be funny and nosy and a bit annoying, but she'll help us, and we won't need to ask. Plus, of course, having Hillyard behind us will also be extremely helpful." It was the longest speech I'd heard Clarissa make. Perhaps coming out of the shadow of Claude would be a good thing for her. "Go and tell your father to let her in, Stevie."

As Stevie went out, Margaret said, "We can't expect Hillyard to be on anyone's side, you know."

"No, of course not. But he's fair, and respected. He'll help keep a lid on things. We know the gossips in the village and Hillyard will help stem it as much as he can."

"If there was only some…. You are right, of course, dear." We could hear Mrs Witherspoon's voice in the hall and she burst through the door. "Oh dear, forgive me, Margaret. Stevie said you were eating. Should I wait in another room?"

Margaret stood and embraced Mrs Witherspoon lightly. "Not at all, my dear. None of us is particularly hungry. Come through to the drawing room."

"You poor dear," Mrs Witherspoon said. "What a terrible thing to have happened. Have the police said anything about who they think could have done such a thing?"

"No, they don't say much, do they?" I jumped up and opened the door for them both. "Just ask questions and make non-committal comments on anything asked of them."

They moved out into the hall. Charles showed no sign of moving from the table. Margaret gave him a pleading glance which he didn't even see, and when he still didn't move she led the rest of them out and through to the drawing room. The door closed.

Clarissa was right, once again. After an hour or so secluded with Margaret and Clarissa, Mrs Witherspoon left the house with all the zeal of a Suffragette. We'd stayed in the dining room and we heard her resounding voice reassuring Margaret that she would do what she could to stem any interest in visiting the house, and would deal sternly with gossips. "Of course, dear Hillyard should be promising them hell and damnation, but I think the most we can hope for from that quarter will be a gentle admonishment on how one should think well of others, with perhaps a biblical reading. Luke 6:31, I would hazard. 'And as ye would that men should do to you, do ye also to them likewise.' It's a nice sentiment, though."

Her voice faded as she said her goodbyes.

Charles looked at me. He'd not said much all day. "I wish there was a way you could clear out."

"Well, that's charming," I said, swinging into the seat next to his. "Just when I thought I was being all keystone-ish."

He frowned.

"Supportive, dearest idiot. Supportive. I'm crushed you want rid of me. Tossing my sandals out onto the street."

"You know damned well I didn't mean that," he muttered. "Just stop camping it up for five minutes. I know you think you are Oscar Wilde, but— well, that's rather the problem, isn't it?"

I sighed. "I know. Obviously we don't want the delectable Tanner to find out about us. Don't make a face. I swear on…well…I promise that I haven't been 'camping' it up for Tanner. Not in the slightest." Not entirely true, but it caused his shoulders to soften a little.

WHATEVER SHE DID, OR WHATEVER HILLYARD did, it seemed to work, at least to begin with, and at least in relation to the village. I knew we wouldn't be left alone for long, but for Monday and for most of Tuesday there was a calm. Though it was a calm that everyone knew—I'm sure—wasn't something that could ever last. Calm before the storm, which I'd always thought was a rather daft expression, as how did one know that any calm presaged a storm? You didn't know that it was a calm before a storm until the storm had actually begun. But this was a storm we knew was coming, so we noticed the calm and bit our fingernails throughout waiting for the first rumble of thunder.

Tanner returned on Tuesday afternoon, and set himself up in the morning room. He asked that we all wait together in the drawing room, then asked to speak to Margaret. We sat in silence once again, Stevie pretending to read a book while Lawrence stared into the garden humming a tune that no one recognised. Margaret was away for over an hour, and she had not returned when the constable asked me to come through. I sighed, faking an irritation I didn't feel, and followed the constable out and through to where Tanner sat behind the morning room desk. Papers and files were piled up by his right hand, but he only had a small file in front of him. He looked away from it, catching my eye only briefly, and indicated the chair opposite him. We sat in silence for a while as he flipped through the few papers in the file. I knew a ploy when I saw it.

Our deputy head at Druitt's was a tyrant and a bully (whereas the head himself was a more kindly disciplinarian) and would use all kinds of mental torture on boys called to his office, one of which was to leaf through "evidence" of wrongdoing while the boy sweated out his guilt—or supposed guilt—on an uncomfortable chair. It was probably because Tanner had *not* been to a public school that he employed this method. If he'd encountered our deputy head he'd know how ineffective it was, and even more so, particularly on me.

Tanner was good at it, I'll give him his due. He knew all the things that would unsettle a guilty mind. He raised his eyebrows at something he'd read; he frowned, turned pages back and forth as if either confirming what he'd found or couldn't believe the inconsistencies. I knew that, apart from one or two small omissions that no one could confirm or deny (to my knowledge), my story was full and frank and irrefutable. Except when it wasn't, of course, which might yet cause some friction.

Eventually he looked up. He left the file open. "So, we've been checking up on you, Mr Bircham."

"I imagine that you would be negligent if you did not, Inspector. I do hope you haven't found anything *too* scandalous."

He gave me a blank look, which rather rattled me. That was a tactic our dear deputy head never tried; he was far too deliriously happy when he found misdemeanours upon which to pounce. Tanner was hard to read, despite using methods I'd seen before. "Nothing that surprises me," he said. Well, there was a world of information in *that* statement, if one chose to be paranoid about it. "It seems you haven't been here before, and seeing you have been friends with Mr Charles Holland for"—he consulted the file again, although I would have bet good money it was just for effect—"hmmm...since you were ten?"

"Eleven," I said.

"Eleven. It strikes me as odd that it took him such a long time to introduce you to his family. May I ask why?"

"May I ask if my perceptions of a friend's reasons for not introducing me to his family has anything to do with the death of Claude Holland? That's conjecture."

"Ah, yes. You are studying law, aren't you?"

"Guilty as charged. Don't think any the worse of me, though."

He sighed. "We aren't in court, sir. Conjecture never applies. And all I'm attempting to do is establish answers to questions that sprung up as I've spoken to people."

"You've spoken to Charles, surely he gave his reasons."

"Do you have something to hide?"

"Of course not."

He closed his file. "That is of course what everyone says. Being defensive isn't going to help matters, Mr Bircham. You are making things more difficult for yourself."

I was aware of that, but part of me wanted to have some fun, and part of me was nettled at the question asked. I decided to err on the much more prudent side of valour. "I'm sorry, it's my first encounter with the law on such a first-hand basis. You can't blame a student for testing out the rules."

He looked as though he could blame a student but his cheek twitched as if he were grinding his teeth—how delicious!—before he continued. "Shall we begin again? Why do you think it's taken so long to be invited?"

"Well…I can only surmise, of course. Or repeat what Charles has said— which isn't always the same thing—but I'd say it's because Charles wanted to keep his friends and his family at arm's length from each other."

"Obviously," he said, dryly. "But don't you think it odd?"

The chasm opened up under me. *He's not searching for homosexuals,* I thought, repeating it to myself like a Gregorian chant. But it wasn't something I could trust. Not only could I not be sure that Tanner might not look for evidence of homosexuality—especially if he didn't arrest anyone for murder— but it takes two to tango, and it wasn't only my secret to keep. I'd been sloppy, certain in the innocence, or more likely the blind-eyeness of the Hollands.

"Not particularly. You see, since Charles' father died he's not been at home all that much. He has spent a great many of the vacs with me at my mother's home."

"And you never felt this was rather one-sided? You never felt that— perhaps—you were being hidden away?"

No, you idiot, I thought, *I was proud that he wanted to keep me to himself. Even my mother was too much company.* "I don't think I thought much about it, to be honest. It was just normal. Especially after his father died, you see. I imagined that he'd want to be less at home—and he did."

"Why would he want to be less at home?" Tanner missed nothing.

"I'm sure you've already found out from the gossips in the village, Inspector, but Claude Holland appeared on the scene shortly afterwards, and

Charles wasn't exactly over-fond of his dear uncle. That's...that's not to say he'd ever do anything about it." I felt the ground beneath me sliding away and I let myself slide towards the precipice that I'd been digging for both of us. In a few seconds I would be hanging on by my fingertips and hoping that I'd built enough of a crash mat to fall onto. "You mustn't think that. He stayed away because he simply didn't like Claude."

"And he would have been resentful that his mother was marrying him, then."

"Well, no.... That is to say..." I pinched the bridge of my nose. "A boy's father.... He did worship his father, you see. You can't blame him for feeling that his father's place was being usurped. Almost from the beginning. He didn't take it well. But he didn't grab an axe."

"No. I understand he was put into an asylum."

"It's no secret, and I don't think Mrs Holland would thank you for calling it an asylum. I say, have you spoken to Mrs Holland about this?" I felt sure Margaret would be a lot more upset than she seemed if the subject had been brought up.

He ignored my question. "Now, your room is adjoining Mr Holland's, that is, Charles Holland's?"

"Yes."

"And I suppose you spend a fair amount of time together?"

"Actually less than you'd think. Perhaps it's because we are so pushed together at college—apart from lectures, of course."

"But you do spend time in each other's rooms."

"I think you know the answer to that, Inspector," I said. "You've been talking to the staff."

"Just answer the question, please."

"Yes, Inspector. I have been in and out of Charles' room, and he in and out of mine. Although more in his, to be honest, as it's quite a bit larger. No sense of FHB with him, I'm afraid."

"FHB?"

"Oh, I'm sorry. Family Hold Back. Putting one's guests first, you see. Letting the guest have the first cake, the last cake, the bigger room, that kind of thing."

He screwed his honest forehead up and I could see he hated us all at that point. I could almost see his grubby working class boyhood in a terraced house. "Hmph. Did you know that Claude Holland took morphine?"

I appeared genuinely startled, as I hadn't been expecting the question to be so easy, I'd been trying to work out how to raise it. "As a matter of fact I suspected it."

"Oh, really? How so?"

I swiftly outlined the night of Lawrence being taken ill, and of Claude "finding" the syringes.

"Why didn't you mention this before, Mr Bircham?"

"I wasn't asked about that night. I can't see what relevance it has. It might explain his odd—Oh, unless you think that he and Lawrence were doping up together, and when he lost his dope partner he did a bit too much?"

"In my experience, Mr Bircham, dopers don't have 'dope partners'."

"Well, really, I wouldn't know, of course. But Stevie did say that she thought—"

"Yes, we've spoken to Miss Stephens. You should know that hearsay is, as you say, irrelevant. Did you ever see Charles Holland doing anything odd?"

"Oh dear, Inspector, I'm afraid you are going to have to be a lot more clear than that. Much of what Charles Holland does could be termed as odd. He prefers to saunter around in soft shirts and un-ironed Oxford bags. You should see his rooms, he—"

"I have."

"Oh," I said, shaken. God, they had been a lot more thorough than I had given them credit for.

"Let me put it more clearly, then. Did you see Charles Holland ever mixing up any kind of potion? And would you tell me if you had? Protecting a felon, Mr Bircham, has almost as stiff a penalty as the felony itself, so please be very careful about your answer."

I paused, looking down. Then with every ounce of honesty I could summon I said, "Absolutely not. Hand on heart, on the Bible, on my mother, whatever oath would make you believe me. I have never in my life, not here, not at Oxford, seen Charles Holland mixing anything more suspect than experimental cocktails for the men on our staircase. And by experimental I mean cacao with gin and bitters. But no potions. No poisons. I'm assuming that you've found something in Claude's body, then? Morphine? Something else?"

I should have known better than to think the inspector would give an inch, or even a fraction of one. "Thank you, Mr Bircham. That will do for now. Please don't leave, or if you do, make sure you let the police station here know where you can be contacted. You may be required to give that oath again."

I walked out of the room a lesser man than I had been coming in. I knew what it felt like to have the stuffing knocked out of me and my legs felt as weak as if I'd run cross-country for the college. Outside I climbed the first step to my room and leant against the wall, nausea flooding through me. Had I done too much? Had I done enough? The future was just a grey fog.

Somehow I managed to pull myself up that damned staircase and I fell onto my bed while the world reeled. I heard wheels on gravel and pulled myself up to look out of the window. The police were leaving, just the police.

It was a huge relief, but still, I felt the sword above my head shift in the wind and grate noisily against its moorings.

I HADN'T EVEN REALISED I HAD slept when I was woken by a familiar sound of gravel being churned up. I leapt off the bed, noting that somehow I'd missed lunch, and peered out of the window, out and down. Below and to the left, parked directly outside the front door was Tanner's car, unmistakable and shining black in the sunshine. Just behind it was another car, another unmarked vehicle, but three uniformed police officers clambered out of it.

One stood by Tanner's car and as I watched, Tanner gestured to the other two, who started to walk around the side of the house. They were cutting off the exits and I had almost no time to act, because my beautiful, stupid friend—with his trust in the truth—was going to be snared like a rabbit.

I tore open the door and ran along the corridor, took the stairs in what seemed like two jumps and made the morning room before Tanner had even knocked on the front door.

Inside the morning room, the family stood, frozen in tableau, looking as I had at the police cars and activity outside. I had mere minutes. I pulled Charles out of the room and out into the hall. Stephens was standing just outside, and he walked up the hall and then back as the door bell went. It was the nearest to dithering I'd ever seen him do. He cast a look over his shoulder at us and I ducked into the drawing room, pulling my friend with me.

"Look," I said. "Don't say anything—not anything at all."

"I don't understand." His eyes were wide, and I felt like shaking him. Did he not see what was happening?

"The police are here again," I said slowly, as if speaking to a child I didn't want to frighten. "And it's possible they may ask you to go with them."

"But I told them I had nothing—"

"They are police. They don't take any notice of what you tell them. Just listen. Listen to me. You'll say nothing; say you'll not say anything until your solicitor gets there."

"I don't have one—Harry," he sounded frightened at long last. "Harry, you're not saying I need one? I didn't do it! You know that. Not that I didn't want to—but Lawrence…. I have nothing to hide."

"Really?" I gave him a strong look. "Nothing? How about if they start to make assumptions about you and me, or you and the verger, or you and Lawrence? I am pretty sure that damned detective suspects me, although he's said nothing outright—"

"What will you say if he does?" He'd lost all colour now and I felt so sorry for him, that I had to put him through this.

"Deny everything, of course—what do you think? They have no proof, and hopefully that's not what they'll want to prove. They are after whoever killed Claude and we both know it's not you. If we stay calm, and give them nothing else, there's no reason why they should suspect you, even if they think I'm as queer as a nine-bob note. Proof, my dear Watson, that's what they haven't got. Not between us, and not about you poisoning Claude and Lawrence."

"I didn't. You know I didn't."

"I do—but…"

"Don't throw buts at me, Harry. Not now. What but?"

"Your father. Why can't I—"

"Because you can't."

"Give me one good reason, Charles. Please, one good reason, and I promise I'll keep quiet but God you make it so difficult!"

He gritted his teeth. "Because… Oh damn this—I thought you would have had some clue. Didn't you?"

"My dear idiot, I haven't the foggiest what you are on about. We need to go, we can't be seen to be hiding." I heard voices and then footsteps went past the room. "What? Whatever the hell it is, tell me."

"He deserted." He exhaled as if keeping the words inside him had cost him much in effort, which it probably had. I didn't have time to boggle at him, no matter that I felt like it. "Oh."

There was no time for this, and we needed time, we just didn't have it. Why did he keep things like this from me until it was too late? "Come on," I said. "I won't say anything, *unless I have to.*"

"No, Harry—"

"There's no way you are sacrificing yourself, but it won't come to that. I promise. *I promise.*" I tugged him towards the door. "Now, whatever happens, just keep denying it."

He looked at me hard then. "You're serious, aren't you? You think they suspect me? Why? I was drunk—and in bed."

"There's no time to explain," I said. "Come on, let's go. Just say *nothing* until we can get a solicitor for you. Promise me."

"But—"

"Promise me!" I pulled him close for a brief second, and it was rare that I took such liberties with him, but I was going to be separated from him, and there was no guarantee I'd get him back. It was me against the police, and I had to trust on me—I had no one else. He felt warm but solid against me; as I put my lips to his neck I could feel his pulse, far too fast, beating like terrified wings against my skin. "Promise me."

"I promise." His voice shook, but he'd bucked himself up. "I'll say nothing until a solicitor comes."

"Not any old solicitor—make sure it's one that your mother has sent—or I have. I don't trust the police."

"Oh, God. I trust you, Harry." He pulled away and ran a hand through his hair as if that would magically tame it, then pulled the door open and led the way back into the morning room.

Inspector Tanner didn't seem to hear the door opening, but his constable did. Tanner had his back to the door, and he was silent. As the constable turned to face us, so did the entire room, Tanner included, and I had the leisure to notice the expressions arrayed around us, ranging from fear right through to feigned—or I assume so—calm.

"Charles Anthony Holland," the inspector said, and with those words, Margaret sank onto the chair, pulling Stevie, who happened to be standing next to her, down with her. Her face was as white as her son's. "I am arresting you on suspicion of the murder of Claude Holland and the attempted murder of Lawrence Stephens. You do not have to say anything if you do not wish to do so—"

"No, it's all right," he murmured, almost beyond hearing. "I'll go with you." I longed to touch him, in our familiar "I'm here" signal, but I did not dare. From now on I was dancing on the edge of the volcano and I must not put a foot wrong.

"Let me finish, sir. It *is* a formality, however unpleasant."

"I'm sorry, Inspector," he said, tipping his head up, and looking so damned brave my heart felt it would burst.

"But anything you say will be taken down and may be used against you in a court of law."

"If you'll come along, sir," the constable stepped forward with handcuffs and Margaret gave a sigh of anguish.

"I say, Inspector," I said. "That's hardly necessary, is it?"

"I'm afraid so," he said. No "sir" for me, I noted bitterly. Better I stay quiet than to garner more of his disdain, or worse, suspicion. The world slowed then; and it seemed wrong that it was so warm in the room, so light—the morning sunlight so strong that motes of dust danced in the sunbeams hitting the carpet.

I had to watch as they pinioned his arms behind him, had to watch him wince in discomfort and the oik who mishandled him did not even apologise. The women clustered together, their eyes, already sorrowful, concentrated purely on him as he was led away. I was frozen in place, unable to move towards the women I didn't want to comfort anyway, and unable to follow him leave. All I could do was watch.

Margaret made as if to stand, but Stevie held her firmly in place. "No, Margaret," she said. "Don't make it worse."

"How could it be worse?"

"For him, Margaret."

"They can't think it was him," Margaret said, turning her head frantically from Stevie to Clarissa. Margaret's voice was almost an ululation of sorrow. "I thought they'd understood it was some…madman—Charles would never— could never. Why—" She trailed off and I could see the sense of doubt in her eyes, the confusion. Her love for Charles was so visceral, so primal, it heated my blood in a way that I thought the expression of a woman could never do.

"Harry." She turned to me at last, as if remembering I was there. "Go out and…just be there. He'll think that we…that we believe it."

I nodded and as I went out, I heard Stevie say, "He won't think that, Margaret. He won't. Of course it wasn't him. He may have disagreed with you marrying Claude but—"

Margaret said something else, but I was already out of the hall and their voices faded away. Stephens was just opening the front door for the small retinue, Charles had his coat resting on his shoulders and Tanner led the way outside. I followed and all I could do was watch as they put him into the car and drove away. He seemed set in stone, staring forwards, like a dog, setting its face towards prey. And I was helpless to do more than watch him, like a spectator at the most ordinary of plays.

Little details clung to that moment that have stayed with me, clear and sharp. They remain with me even now: the crunch of the gravel; the smell of the police car, dripping oil onto the driveway; the way the constable's boots shone in the sunshine; the way Charles faced forward and did not turn to lock his eyes with mine, no matter how I longed for him to.

"Please look," I whispered, for no one could hear me. "Please look. I know what I'm doing, Charles. Trust me. Please look." But he seemed to be somewhere else; being brave perhaps, putting on the sort of face that he knew he should put on, that brave, English face, stiff upper tea-drinking face, never letting the lower classes seeing you rattled. The sort of English colonialism we both despised, but probably would both revert to, given enough inducement. Perhaps he thought that his father could see him, hidden somewhere in the shrubbery, or perhaps it simply was no more than the shock hitting him at last, the last few days all crystallising into one huge event he couldn't see past. Whatever it was, I was cheated of one more look as they drove him away, leaving me alone on the gravel. I felt a cold chill on the back of my neck and I imagined Claude Holland standing behind me, or the lumbering ghost of Polonius as he trundled round the garden in search of spirit leaves.

For all my legal study, for all the Latin phrases and definitions I had stored in my head, I realised I knew next to nothing about the processes of the law—or rather, the processes of the police station. I didn't even know where they were taking him, and that sudden feeling of loss, for once in so many years, that feeling of not knowing where he was shook me and the volcano shuddered beneath my feet. It took me a second or two to steady myself, so I watched the dust settle as the car disappeared. When I got back to the morning room, Margaret was on the edge of losing her control. It surprised me that she had taken so long to do so. The contrast between Margaret and Clarissa was startling: a representation of theatre masks, but showing dead emotion and high emotion, rather than the usual and far less interesting images of sadness and laughter.

"Charles was right, he kept saying it was wrong. The wedding. He was right."

"You shouldn't say such things." Clarissa was standing by the window, and the morning light, having passed on, left her face in shadow. It suited her voice well. "It's a terrible thing to blame yourself."

"Who else can I blame?" she wailed, and her hands shook in her lap. "If there's a curse on me, I don't know it."

"Marg—"

"Don't tell me to stop!" she said, finally snapping. "Allow me—in my own home, and in the face of people I know, to behave like a mad woman—God knows I feel like one! Charles, and his brother *and* his son. All taken from me. All because I thought...I thought..." She fell forward, resting her head on her knees, and her voice became muffled. "Take me, don't take my son. I'm to blame. I'm to blame."

It was a horrible thing to have to watch. Stevie chimed in then, and her control was impressive. I could see the violent emotions beneath the surface but she was magnificent as she kept them in check. "Harry," she appealed to me, then turned back to Margaret. "Margaret, Harry will know what to do, won't you, Harry?"

Margaret looked up at me, her face blotchy, her eyes huge and drowned, her face lit with a subtle light. Not hope, but some glimmering that there wasn't dark all around her. Again I was struck by her son's resemblance to her, especially when he reached a nadir of emotion.

I nodded. "Well, not exactly, but he'll need legal representation. They'll offer it to him at the station, but he doesn't want the kind of man they'll have on call, believe you me. You have a solicitor?"

"Oh God," Stevie said. "The local firm? No, we can't..."

"I could find someone. I have contacts—college, you know. But I-I don't really want to ring the operator."

"No. Of course not," Stevie said. "Word won't have got around about this latest development yet."

"Don't be too sure," Clarissa said. "Someone is bound to have seen them driving through the village. It's obviously a police car, and people know they were here before. Even if the police had the decency not to use a more obvious car with ringing bells and the like." And as if it had heard what she said, the phone began to ring in the hall, and I don't think I was the only one to jump.

For a stunned second we were silent, then Stevie threw me a meaningful look, so I went out into the hall and caught Stephens before he picked up the receiver.

"It's all right, sir," he said. "I'll deal with it." His sang-froid was remarkable. I think that in his position, I would have taken my remaining child and headed for the hills.

"Thank you, Stephens."

I lurked for a moment and then I heard him say. "Thank you." Then he was silent for half a minute. "No, I'm afraid that's not possible. No, I don't know. I wouldn't advise that, sir. Goodbye." He wiped the handset with his apron before replacing it, as if the person to whom he'd been speaking had somehow contaminated the apparatus. "The gentleman was another member of the press. This time from London, I understand."

"Good Lord," I said. "Surely the news of the arrest couldn't have got there already."

"I understand not, from what he said. He wanted to interview Mrs Holland about the deaths and asked if the family would be issuing a statement. When I said that I didn't know, he said he would come down anyway. I attempted to dissuade him, but I think once news of Mr Charles' arrest becomes more widely known we are going to have some trouble about reporters attempting to gain access to the family."

"You sound knowledgeable about the gentlemen of the press, Stephens."

"I have a couple of the London papers delivered to the servants' hall, sir, and this will certainly stir the public's interest. I regret to say from the articles I've read on similar tragedies, there is nothing gentlemanly about the press."

"You are probably correct," I said. "Stephens, what firm of solicitors do the family use?"

"There's Gantreed and Son," he said. "Mr Claude instructs them from time to time. They've handled matters about the house and tenancies. Very old and established firm. But Mr Holland, that is Mr Charles Senior, he used to instruct Benton and Smead in London."

"Thank you, Stephens."

"About lunch, sir?"

I realised I had, without knowing it, become the head of the household, and I had myself to blame for it. It was a complication I could do without and the last thing I needed was to have to start worrying about lunch menus and reporters holding siege. This was something to be addressed, but not now.

"Something easy," I said. "I doubt anyone will be hungry, so cold meats? That sort of thing? I'll leave the menus *entirely* in your hands and Cook's, if I may. You can manage that? I don't think any of the family want to concern themselves with it—and I'm sure you'll agree that some things should continue as normal. As much as possible."

He nodded. "Of course, sir. Very good, sir." He recognised the hand of the master, I'm sure.

"And, Stephens?"

"Yes, sir?"

"I haven't had the opportunity to say so, but I'm sorry about Lawrence. I wish it had been otherwise."

"Thank you, sir." His face betrayed not one glimmer of emotion, and he turned and disappeared through the servants' door. The English butler is an amazing thing. I hope I have such a man one day.

Back I went into the morning room. "I will need to borrow the car," I said. "I don't want to have to telephone to Gilbert. Believe me, you don't want them cluttering up the place now."

"Of course," Clarissa said. "I suppose there's keys. I don't know where Claude…"

"It's all right," I said, as her control appeared to be breaking too. She'd been so helpful, and calm it had been easy to forget she'd lost her brother, despite the deep mourning. "Stephens will help me with anything, I'm sure. I'll go the local police station, find out where he is, and then I will telephone to the solicitors in London. If I do it from Minehead, it will be easier— confidentiality-wise, that is."

"See," Clarissa said, addressing Margaret. "We are lucky that Harry's got his head screwed on." Her voice reminded me of an uncle, one who had fought at Balaclava. Or a games master I loathed for his eternal enthusiasm, rain or snow. "He'll get us all whipped into shape. The one thing we don't want to do is to let matters slip to the local exchange."

"I'll take a bag."

"Where will you stay?" Stevie said.

"I'm not sure yet, but I'll send a wire—saying just that—when I do."

"And you'll keep us informed?"

"I don't know what would be better—perhaps a letter…. Look, I can't think about that—but I'll stay in touch. Once the news is out in the village there won't be any point worrying about keeping it secret. It won't keep quiet long, Clarissa's right about that, so the sooner—"

"Yes, go," Stevie said, and I had the feeling she was almost glad to be cutting me off. I felt mildly aggrieved, it was nice to be powerful for a few minutes. "Thank you. Tell him…Well, you know what to…won't you?" She gave me the smallest and saddest of smiles and the small touch of empathy warmed me.

"Perhaps you should think about removing…perhaps to London?"

"Surely that won't be necessary?" Margaret was dabbing at her eyes now and getting herself back into control. "You think it might be that bad?"

"I don't know." I opened the door. "You are probably right. Let's see. Let's see where he's going to be—if we can get bail for him. I'm sure—" In fact I wasn't sure of anything and I needed guidance. I knew where I would start looking for that, at least.

Chapter Twenty-Two

Two days later I was sitting with the solicitor Gordon McKenzie in his chambers in the Inner Temple, and despite my frantic worry for Charles' welfare, I knew being in this strange, quiet haven of London, that I had picked the right profession. Our barrister—the learned Sutton-Winson—was a delicious mix of outrageous theatrics and deadly concentration.

If one couldn't go onto the stage—and as much as one might want to, it wouldn't keep myself, Charles and my mother in cushions—then it seemed, from Sutton-Winson, the Bar was the next best thing. He was at times so theatrical that I could not but wonder about his…leanings. He did have a picture of a dark-haired woman in a Queen Alexandra's Nurses uniform on his desk, but that could be camouflage, I'd seen that trick before. I suppose I shouldn't suspect everyone, but then why shouldn't I? They all suspect me.

"I intend," the barrister addressed McKenzie rather than me, quite correctly, "to state that Mr Holland is in no way a risk to the public and to himself, that he's willing to submit his passport, and that—other than youthful adventures which I'm sure even any Justice can remember doing themselves—he has never been under the scrutiny of the law."

McKenzie turned to me. "That's right?"

"Absolutely," I said, not altogether truthfully and youthful discretions aside, "we can get any amount of character witnesses from college—"

Sutton-Winson waved me away as if I were no more than a gnat. "Pooh. Not worth the time they take," he said. "Any of us can find some old fossil to say what a decent chap they are, and how they'd never been in trouble before."

I wasn't sure I could.

"He's studying law," McKenzie said, and the two men exchanged a look which made me feel about six.

"Really." Sutton-Winson went back to his notes.

"Do you think there's any chance of him being released on bail?" McKenzie asked.

"Frankly? No. It makes no difference if they think he bashed someone over the head, or strangled them, or poisoned them. Suspected murderers are rarely bailed. They aren't likely to let him loose on the public. They've done it a time or two and regretted it when the suspicion turns to fact. Public opinion, and all that." He saw me about to speak, "It might matter to me, but it doesn't matter to them that he didn't do it, and having had a long talk with the young man, I'm convinced of his innocence, or we would not be having this conversation at all. But they obviously think there's a case to answer. He's been charged and the law must grind on. Yes, and grind it will. Just how much is left of young Holland once the mill has moved on and over him remains to be seen.

"My main arguments at the committal will be that there is no case to answer, and their evidence is sketchy at best. I doubt the judge will listen to me, because of the risk factor of the prosecution being right."

"What about every man is innocent?" I regretted it almost instantly as both Sutton-Winson and McKenzie gave me such pitying looks I could have sunk through the floor. It seemed that the lofty morality-filled debates in college, and the reality of the criminal justice system were not exactly simpatico.

I'D BEEN RECOMMENDED TO MCKENZIE BY my college tutor, who was pretty bucked with me being involved in the matter, although concerned for the reputation of the college. "No way we can keep the college out of the news, I suppose," he said. "No, I suppose not. Lucky that young Holland isn't reading Law. Wouldn't look good at all. Not at all."

"Oh come on, Professor, it's not as if we are given books of poisons to study, as a lesson on how to get acquitted."

"No, but the public, my boy." He peered over his spectacles at me. "The public thinks all sorts of peculiar things. If I only had the time to tell you all the stories I've heard from juries over the years. Now, let me see." He leant back in his chair and studied the ceiling. "You'll want the best. He *can* afford the best, I assume?"

I made a face. Money—it was odd that the legal profession found no difficulty in discussing it when so many other professionals considered it taboo.

"I quite understand," he said. "Well, there are a couple of options you can try. But if I were you, I'd go for a younger man. Elsworth is the man of the hour, of course, and if he's heard about it already which I'll wager he has, he's expecting his phone to ring at any moment, but he's a little too hide-bound these days. I went to his last three murders, and found his reasoning in the matter of Crown vs Hyt—"

"So if not Elsworth, sir, then who? I have to say he was who I had in mind."

"Not for this. No. Quite the wrong approach. Now, let me think." He screwed up his face and his eyebrows—alarming grey and black bushes which threatened to obscure his eyes—leapt up and down like rampant beetles. "Either Grey Sutton-Winson, that's Sutton-Winson Minor of course, although he was a good while before your time, of course. His brother went into shipping or something just as pedestrian. Or was it India? No matter. Or you could try Guy Bedlington. Out of the two, I'd recommend Sutton-Winson, if you can get him. He's got more poisoners off than you would expect. Mainly women, though, of course. Strange that the uncle was poisoned. Wouldn't have thought—"

"Sir, Holland didn't do it."

"Of course. Of course." He sat back up and pulled his pile of books toward him. "What does your solicitor advise? Who is the family solicitor?"

"They are going on my recommendation. Since Claude and Charles.... Well, I thought it best to use a London one. Just in case. Metfield, Spriggs, McKenzie—"

"—And Gowan. Yes, yes. Perfectly sound. Although young Gowan, now. There were times I thought he'd end up in the dock himself, the trouble he seemed to get into. Well, I won't hold you up. You'll have a busy few days."

He stood and reached across to shake my hand. "I will stay apprised of the matter. I hope that it doesn't come to it, but if so, I dare say I'll see you in the Old Bailey."

I had hoped it wouldn't even come to that, but it seemed they were eager to charge Charles, and charge him they did, a few hours short of having to let him go. McKenzie had zipped down to Somerset but returned the next day with the news that they were bringing Charles to London for the committal hearing and before I knew it he had been moved to Bow Street.

I had rented a bed-sit in the Paddington area which was handy for the station, and well within my budget, although rather sordid and although the landlady walked like a drunken sailor she kept the sordidity spotless. I sent letters daily to his mother, sometimes several times a day, keeping her up to date, not wanting to use the telegraph or the telephone unless it was something relatively innocuous. I had myself to think of too, Stevie told me the press were already making inroads on the house, and I didn't want them finding me, or linking me to anything regarding the case until there was absolutely no hope of being anonymous.

My mother had been mildly alarmed, and a letter sent to Hellsingers reached me within a day or two of me moving in to Penfold Street. She expressed concern, and although she didn't say anything against Charles, the implication was clear. She had never been his biggest devotee, finding him too quiet and shut off. After all, she was used to a more garrulous type. I telegraphed her back with my address, and in as few words as possible attempted to pour oil over her fears. I don't know why that's considered to be a good thing, pouring oil on something; I'd have said it would make matters a good deal worse.

So Charles was charged, and with alarming speed, and his hearing—with him of course pleading Not Guilty—was held with just McKenzie, Sutton-Winson, the prosecuting Counsel and Charles. Oh, *and* the damnable press, *and* a few vultures of the great unwashed. Just not myself. I was not allowed into the courtroom, but was kept off to one side, so not as to run into the papers. Oh, it was an open hearing, but Sutton-Winson advised against me being present. "In case you have to be called," he said. I paced outside, smoking cigarette after cigarette, just hoping against hope that those wooden doors would swing open at exactly the right time and I would see Charles' face—and more importantly he would see mine. I was not that lucky, but I'd impressed upon McKenzie more than once he was to make sure Charles knew I was there. I really believed—with that tiny shred of hope that we all cling to when everything else is dark, and despite that it was me who had helped put him where he was—that he might be bailed.

As they came out of court, it took only a glance at McKenzie's face to confirm that bail had not been granted. Sutton-Winson's face was as it ever was, and in fact he seemed on pretty good terms with opposing Counsel. They came out of court together, smiling as if they'd just made an appointment for golf, which they very well may have done. I knew—I *knew*—that Counsel were this dispassionate; I'd haunted courtrooms from time to time, and a couple of my relations were at the Bar, which had given me the direction in the first place, but now that it was personal, I wanted Sutton-Winson to cut opposing Counsel like an avenging fury, and to work his fingers to the bone until Charles was free. To hate the prosecution as much as I did. The papers were out en masse outside the court, and the journalists with their cameras and vile little notebooks impeded our progress until Sutton-Winson stopped to say a few words. "Mr Holland is not guilty of the charges levied against him, and has stated his innocence clearly and confidently in court. He trusts to the justice system to prove that the charges are entirely unfounded. Thank you." Sutton-Winson's large car waited for us at the kerb. Sutton-Winson got into the front, next to the driver, McKenzie and I clambered into the back. My pulse was still racing, and I felt the loss of Charles more acutely than before, knowing he was so close to me and yet held back by forces I myself had put in motion.

I had to believe I was doing the right thing. *Hold on,* I thought fiercely, a little to me as well as to him.

"That's just the start of it," Sutton-Winson said to me, over his shoulder. "You'll have to decide whether you want to speak to them, because they are going to keep asking. I can draft you something innocuous to say—something along the lines of 'the family's representative, blah blah.' It won't stop them printing any kind of falsehoods, of course. You'll be lucky if they can manage to spell your name and get your age right."

"Thank you. How is he?"

"He's bearing up. He said specifically that you are not to worry, and I told him that was a forlorn hope on his part, and that made him smile. He said you worried about too much. He's in a fair bit of shock at failing to make bail, even though I have been as honest with him as I was to you—the next period is not going to be easy for him, and I'd advise that you get his family up here as soon as they can come. He's going to need support, if I know anything about reactions. He said he didn't want his mother put through it—"

"I'll get them to come. She's going to have to face it one way or the other."

McKenzie spoke for the first time since leaving the court. "The trial's in two weeks, so get them to hurry."

There was an edge to his tone I didn't like, but I didn't query further. I looked out of the window at the bleak, grey city and wished it were all over. The next two weeks were busy enough. I wrote letters, I made phone calls, I visited Richardson and Gilbert, and travelled down more than once

to Hellsingers to convey matters that I didn't want to pass on by letter or—
heaven forbid—telephone. The press, local and national, had found the family
and were at the entrance to the grounds every day. It necessitated a village
bobby on permanent guard there to prevent anyone entering the driveway.
Even with such precautions, Stevie told me that it was a regular occurrence
that someone slipped by, through the woods, usually, and would be found
knocking on a side door or, one time, having tea with the cook downstairs.

I visited Lawrence while down there, but the poor, handsome boy was
gone forever. In his place was a slack-jawed dependent child, sometimes lucid,
but more often not. He was always looking for something, although, Stevie
said, no one knew exactly what it was, and no matter how often they asked
Lawrence about it, he only knew it was lost, and not what it was. Stevie said
she thought it might be Polonius, and she'd cry when she talked of the tortoise.
I think it was a release—easier to let the emotions go for the tortoise than for
the family that was fracturing before her eyes.

I felt sorrier for Stevie than I did for Lawrence, because it seemed that she
was determined to waste her life looking after him instead of putting him into
an asylum which is where he belonged. Stephens—well, you never really knew
what Stephens thought. He kept that house together when I thought it wasn't
possible to do, that it would tear itself apart from the weight of the tragedy.

Margaret came up to London a few days before the trial and rented a suite
of rooms in a discreet house in a quiet street in Aldwych. I left the horrible
bedsit in Paddington and joined her and Clarissa there. We knew that the press
would find it eventually, but for a day or two we had an idyll of borrowed
peace. Alone, without her son to shore up her pride and Claude to protect her,
Margaret seemed younger, somehow, and so fragile—like a candle wick made
of spidersilk—which would disappear before the flame even touched it. She
had lost that core of steel she had shown in standing up to Claude. Perhaps
the odds she had to face now were just too much, perhaps she had known how
weak Claude was—weaker than her, and easy to cow. Whatever it was, I had
little respect for her now. Once she had captivated me as a female version of
Charles; now she was a burden, another responsibility and something I left
almost entirely to Clarissa.

Sutton-Winson came to the house, walking swiftly from the corner where
he'd no doubt dropped his car. He came to tutor Margaret and me in our
responses, to warn us what the prosecution might say, might try to imply.
"They *will* attempt to establish motive, as that's the only real thing that they
probably can. I'm afraid that there is a little too much evidence of your son's

dislike of Mr Holland, and I'm very much afraid that they will drag his... previous mental problems into the light of day. One of the witnesses for the prosecution is a former doctor at the clinic where he was...a patient before."

"It was such a long time ago," she said. "Surely they must realise that it was an aberration?"

"But it wasn't a solitary instance, Mrs Holland," Sutton-Winson said. "Apparently there's some evidence that Charles was sinking back into that fantasy, that he was seeing his father again."

She stared at the barrister with a glassy expression. Her mouth didn't seem to want to form any of the words that were clearly behind her eyes.

"I need to warn you in advance about this, and anything else that might come up—no matter how unpleasant," he said, "or I am not doing my job. There well may be questions that I haven't anticipated—although that is a rarity, say it myself... I hope I've covered everything I can think of—but there's always something thrown in that one isn't expecting, no matter how much the other side reveals. By calling these people as witnesses they are showing the path they mean to take, and it might be useful for us. At the end, if things don't go well."

"I'm sorry." Her vowels were as clipped as I'd ever heard them, as if she was one small tug away from breaking. "You must find me dreadfully stupid, but I don't understand what you mean."

"I think," I said, taking advantage of Sutton-Winson's small hesitation as he considered the best way to break it to her, "that should Charles be found guilty, if the prosecution are going to use his mental state as part of the motive—then he may escape the noose."

"Exactly so," Sutton-Winson said. "But we mustn't think that we are going to fail in the first place. Your son is innocent, Mrs Holland. I'm convinced of that, and all we need to do is to find some way to convince the jury that it's possible—just possible—that someone else may have done it."

It sounds silly, and you'll hardly believe me when I tell you that I hadn't even factored this into my calculations, but I was for the first time aware that I myself might be in some considerable danger. Silly me.

Chapter Twenty-Three

So it was time, well past time, to speak up. I was not going to step into the shoes of the accused, even at the risk of Charles's safety.

"I don't think we need to go that far," I said.

Sutton-Winson fixed me with his steeliest stare, the one I imagined he used for stern-looking juries, the ones who sat there with their arms folded as if to say "go on then, you big toff, convince us."

"Mr Bircham, I think you can rely on me as to how far we go. I'm rather more expert at it than you."

"That's not what I mean. Or rather," I found myself forcing myself to calm and took a deep breath before I fell further into the unknown fears, "it's just—look, this is something that I didn't want to have to raise, but if it's going to stop the whole thing I feel that I should break a promise made."

"What the devil are you blithering on about?" Sutton-Winson said, losing a little of his sang-froid. "If you've something to tell me now, after all this time."

"I told you, sir. It was a promise." I turned to Margaret. "You might not want to hear this."

"Surely a promise is trumped by a capital case?" Sutton-Winson growled.

"It depends," I said. Margaret hadn't moved. "Margaret?"

"Please speak, Harry. If you think it will help. Whatever it is. Whatever it is." She reached out and held my arm.

Sutton-Winson was positively vibrating with suppressed impatience.

"Charles Holland Senior is alive," I said. Margaret's hand stayed where it was, but her fingers clasped me, her fingers positively digging into the cloth. "I promised Charles, that is, Charles the younger, that I would say nothing. Even now. But there's your alibi. If we can find him."

"Is the boy mad?" Sutton-Winson thundered. "He kept quiet all this time?"

I put my hand over Margaret's. "I think he felt that—as he wasn't guilty—he had nothing much to worry about. He trusted the system."

"Then he *is* mad," Sutton-Winson muttered. "Forget I said that. You'd better tell me everything, and God help you, Bircham, if you are lying to me again. You are going to cause enough problems as it is, changing your statement like this."

"But if someone backs it up? I had good reasons to lie."

"We'll see. I'm afraid English justice isn't interested in 'I made a promise to my friend.' It expects you to tell the truth, however laughable that concept is. Where is the senior Holland?"

"I don't know."

I thought Sutton-Winson was going to have an apoplexy. His eyes bulged. "You don't…know?"

"Not exactly. He said he was leaving the country."

"Harry," Margaret interrupted. "How long has Charles known his father was alive?"

I almost hated to do it to her, but in a way, she deserved it. She had put him in an institution. She hadn't even been aware of the damage that had done to him. "Since the first time," I said in leaden tones—just to hammer the point home, you understand, I'm not normally so dramatic. "I think perhaps we should have believed him."

"Give me strength," Sutton-Winson said. He pressed a button and called his secretary into the room, then pulled a file from a shelf and opened it. "This is your original statement to the police. Tell me the truth now. All of the truth, not those pieces you think I might need to know."

The next half hour was filled with me running through my newly amended statement. I had collected Charles from the dancing, as previously described, but we hadn't both gone into the study. He'd wanted to throw up and I'd shuffled him into the garden where we'd encountered the elder Charles Holland. I'd promised to see to Lawrence and left them alone.

I put Lawrence to bed, collected Charles, then went up to bed myself where I'd given him a glass of whisky. No, I had no idea how that glass had got down to the study. No, I didn't notice it being there in the morning, but one doesn't look for things like that, does one? Perhaps a maid had taken it down there. No, I don't think it was deliberate, but everyone was rushing around—it would have been easy for something like that to have happened. I gave him the whisky well after one o'clock. How did I know that? Because by the time I got back to the party, Auld Lang Syne was playing and that was about half past one. He'd had his whisky about ten minutes before that. Enough time for me to watch him drink it, turn down the lights and leave. That must have been after one-thirty and it wasn't until I came out of Charles' room that I'd heard the screaming, so it couldn't have been him, unless Mr Holland had let him out of his sight earlier on.

Over and over, Sutton-Winson questioned me, and I kept on with the answers, the same answers until he finally stopped. He was a little disheveled, which I rather liked. "Well, you sound convincing to me," he said. "Unpolished and earnest."

I resisted batting my eyelashes at him, but it was difficult. Unpolished? *Moi?*

"Now all we have to do is find a man who has been declared dead."

"Is that going to be difficult?" Margaret asked. She'd said nothing through the questioning, but obviously had been taking it all in. Her capacity for taking shock after shock impressed me. "If there's anything I can do—"

"It's difficult, but I have contacts who have contacts. If he hasn't already gone abroad, it will be easier. I doubt he has. But it won't be cheap."

"Of course." She blushed, the vulgarity of money embarrassing her. English women are odd.

"He said he was going straight away," I said.

"Yes, but that was before his only son was arrested for the murder of his brother. A man who can go abroad after that hasn't a human bone in his body. I'll need a photograph, the latest one available."

"Of course," Margaret said. "I'll telegraph to Stevie today."

"Will it work?" I said. I mentally crossed my fingers.

"I can't promise anything. You *may* have made matters worse." He ran a hand through his hair. "Now get out of my sight," he said. "You might find yourself on a charge, you know. Giving false evidence." I goggled at him and he had the audacity to smile. "Don't worry. They won't hang you for it, and I know a good barrister."

Chapter Twenty-Four

There you have it, then. The story of how I rescued him from his family, and from a fate he didn't deserve, or want, or need. I look back at it, and I wonder if I should, if I could have done things any differently?

Should I have swallowed my hubris and not thought myself as clever as I was? If I hadn't have played on the Mad Dane theme quite so much—although it was impossible not to, I'm sure anyone would agree, given the material one was given—it might have been…less conspicuous, perhaps. Caused less notice, which probably would have been good in the long run.

The press, the damned press. I blame them for so much. The last thing he wanted, I am sure, was the level of public attention we both achieved once Charles Holland Senior's trial was over. Maybe one day the public will be more sensitive about these things, stop hounding those who are unfortunate enough to be associated with criminals. It's hardly Charles' fault that the two men he cares about so much are criminals. It's just a shame that only one of us really is. But what has it gained me? I hear you ask. Can Harry Bircham sleep at night? Do the rotting faces come to me in dreams, or am I plagued by visions of my actions? Well, I have to say that as for sleep, I've never had much of a problem in that respect. What I did, I did, and I left it to chance, or karma, or fate or whatever the terms are. My father might not have helped himself to that particular mushroom, the girth might not have snapped when it did—Stevie could have taken the glass, Claude—well, perhaps Claude was the one I made certain couldn't have escaped his fate, after all.

But whether it was all worth it, ah, that's the rub and a half, as they say. We are where I hoped we be—geographically at least. We have the nicest and most bijou residence any couple of confirmed bachelors could expect, complete with a garden and an area, railing and all. The canal lies just across the road, and Mother bought us a boat in which we emulate the devoted Ratty and Moley. With his father's money, he bought this place, but wouldn't take a penny from me towards it. I can't say I wasn't disappointed, I had some romantic notion of sharing the ownership, but he wouldn't hear of it, seeing that I'm not earning. I haven't yet managed to find a Chambers to take me on, perhaps the notoriety is still a bit raw, but I'm sure it's only a matter of time. We live simply enough. It's not the traditional splendour of a morning room laid out with breakfast. It's just toast and tea, and sometimes sausages, if we are lucky, but I face him over the breakfast table and I know that dreams come true. You just have to nudge them along sometimes, that's all.

AND WHEN YOU HAVE WHAT YOU want…

I came home today to find Charles sitting in the dark, watching the road outside as the rain poured unevenly down the huge windows. He's been increasingly taciturn over the last few weeks, ever since his last visit to the solicitors—something to do with the Will, or that's what he told me.

I opened the door and he didn't hear me—I think. The house lights were off, and his face looked half-green, half grey in the illumination from the lantern outside.

"If you saw me coming, you might have opened the door. I was struggling with brolly and keys for a good twenty seconds."

"I didn't." The remoteness in his voice seemed to stretch the room, making him even further away than he'd been recently.

"I don't know *how* you missed me." I shrugged my mackintosh off and took it into the bathroom to drip. Raising my voice so he could hear me I chatted glibly about my day. Inconsequential rubbish, the sort of thing I'd been saying to him day after day—signifying nothing. He didn't reply, and as I washed my hands, watching the soap on my skin with a feeling akin to hate, my spirits sank for I knew he'd not been listening, or not been replying for some little while now and I had been pushing the knowledge of that fact away from me. I continued to talk, wiping my hands on a towel, letting my words run slower and slower as I walked back into the lounge and found him there, still there, still looking out onto the rainy street with no expression on his face.

I moved behind him, and in another time—was it only last week? Yesterday? I might have taken him in my arms, put my head on his shoulder and let his warmth take the dull ache of the day away from me. I'd look forward to that cramped kitchen, sharing jokes as we boiled up potatoes, and drinking horrible wine with whatever we cooked. This—until the last little while—had been the tenor of our evenings. But something has broken into our fortress and I have a good idea what it was.

I think—no, damn it. I am certain that gallant Charles *knows*. Or at the very least he has grave suspicions. I can see it in his eyes, and I see it in every motion that he makes when we are together. That casual grace, that careless kindness—or subtle cruelty—has slipped away from him as completely as a second skin and there's not a trace of it left. When he's in the same room as me, or even suspects I might be watching, he's wary, and, if not stiff exactly— he's resistant, a magnet pushed towards the same pole. Fanciful, I know, but I thought I knew every action of his, every mood. This constant awareness of me has never been one of them. He watches me, and I'm not used to such attention.

He no longer trusts me. When he talks, which is rare, he never speaks of his family even if I mention them first. He's thoughtful, and that fact alone worries me more than I can say. For if he's having to think things over, perhaps he thinks that there's something that needs addressing.

I'll wait. I can't act without being sure. One day he'll accuse me, or let it go, thinking that he must be wrong. But what if he does accuse me—or worse, what if he just takes a stroll one day and instead of passing Paddington Green police station, he goes in. What if he calls a detective; tells what he knows. "I know it wasn't me," he'll say. "The court agrees that far—but it seems to me…"

I'm sure he won't. Not Charles. Not after everything I've done to make sure that we are here—now. Everything I've done—everything—well, all right, perhaps *not* Lawrence, but it was a necessity—was to free him from Claude, free him from his family. So we could be together. It should be enough. I am quite sure, quite sure. He won't.

But then…. What if he would? Do I have to then call on Fate again?

About the Author

Frastes is the pen name of a female author from the United Kingdom, known for writing acclaimed gay-themed historical and romantic fiction. Her short fiction has been featured in such anthologies as *Best Gay Stories*, *Where the Boys Are*, and *Blasphemy*. She has written several novels—*Standish*, *Mere Mortals*, and *Transgressions*, which was a finalist for the Lambda Literary Award.

www.ingramcontent.com/pod-product-compliance
Lightning Source LLC
Chambersburg PA
CBHW030816020726
47499CB00006B/1943